CW01455436

Bad Blood
Copyright © Barry Hunt 2016

A catalogue record for this book is available from the British Library

ISBN 978-178456-347-9

First published 2016 by
FASTPRINT PUBLISHING
Peterborough, England.

iii

Also by Barry Hunt

The Code-breaker
The Maddalena Project
Julius and the Titanic
Julius and the Mona Lisa
Julius and the Black Hand

The above books are available online as e-books or can be ordered as paperback from FastPrint Publishing at www.fast-print.net/store.php

Prologue

Had he known he had less than fifteen minutes left to live, Michael Pemberton might have thought twice about swearing so viciously. Nobody wants to meet their maker with the taint of a curse still fresh on their lips. However, since he had no idea what lay ahead, he gave vent to his frustration in the worst language he could think of. Earlier that evening when he had arrived, the car-park was busy and the first available space to leave his car had been on the fifth floor. The lift was working then but now, three hours later, it had ceased to operate. At sixty-two years old and a heavy smoker for most of his life, Pemberton viewed the climb with a little trepidation. It wasn't just that he was unfit, he was sure by now some landings on the higher levels would be populated by a few of London's homeless wanting to bed down for the night. He clutched his briefcase close to his chest, pushed open the doors leading to the staircase and was immediately hit by a pungent smell of stale urine and vomit. Glancing at his watch, he saw it was half-past eleven and cursed again as he entered the stairwell.

Although it was late and he had a long drive ahead of him, he was in no hurry; in fact, he had even stopped off for a drink on his way to the carpark. Twice divorced and childless, there was no one waiting for him at home; he could take his time. Pemberton didn't often come into the city these days. When he was younger he had regularly visited the clubs around Soho. That had been when all-night parties had not left their mark on him the following day and, he remembered with a tinge of regret for the past, when some women had found him attractive. The passing years had not treated him well: he was now overweight, short-sighted and his thin hair was scraped across a bald crown. Despite being a doctor and one of the country's leading microbiologists, he had never done anything to keep himself fit. Fortunately, his mind still remained as sharp and brilliant as when he had gained a scholarship to Oxford University at the precocious age of fourteen.

Pemberton had been one of those child prodigies the red-top newspapers liked to appear to celebrate, posting a geeky photograph alongside a report that managed to make him sound like a freak of nature. Had he ever given it any serious thought, Pemberton would probably have thought it was a compliment. He had recognised that he was different from his contemporaries since he was seven years old and taken pride in the fact. As an only child he had preferred the company of adults and didn't mind not having any friends his own age. Books had filled the gaps in his childhood and compensated for the inevitable bullying at school before his parents took him away for private tutoring. In fact, his whole life experience had merely confirmed his view that other people belonged to an altogether different and unpleasant species.

He reached the fourth floor and paused a moment to catch his breath. He looked up at the top of the next flight of steps and experienced a flash of anxiety as he saw a figure sprawled across the landing of the next level. The man was snail-backed against the wall and covered with a pile of flattened out cardboard boxes. Pemberton realised he had no option but to walk past the man and began to mount the stairs. He had his own ideas about such people. They were safe enough on crowded streets in the daytime where he could ignore them, but alone, at night and in a deserted carpark, he felt nervous and moved hesitantly. The man stirred and Pemberton realised he had been seen.

"Spare the price of a cup of coffee, mate," said the man as Pemberton reached the landing.

"Sorry, I'm in a hurry," he said, gripping his briefcase tightly to him.

"Just a coffee, mate," the man persisted. "A pound would do it."

"Sorry."

2

Pemberton avoided looking at the man and reached into his pocket to grab hold of his car keys. In his haste he stumbled against the man's legs stretched across the landing.

The man flinched and looked up angrily.

"Watch it, mate!" he said. "No need for that."

"Sorry."

Pemberton had reached the doors and pushed them open quickly, almost sprinting through to the level where he was parked. His heart was beating fast and he was breathing heavily. The area was almost empty now; just a few vehicles remained in the spaces between the concrete pillars. In the dim glow of neon lights he could see his own car half-way along the level on the outside row overlooking the street below. He swiftly made his way toward it, glancing once over his shoulder to make sure the tramp was not following him. As he reached the car, he clicked the key-fob to turn off the alarm and the indicator lights flashed orange. He slid the key into the lock.

"Michael? Michael Pemberton?"

The voice was low but the unexpectedness startled Pemberton and he dropped his briefcase to the ground as he spun round to face the man who had spoken.

"I'm sorry, did I surprise you?" the man said.

"Who – who are you?" Pemberton stuttered, his heart still racing.

"I'm a friend of Andrew's," the man said quietly.

"What – what do you want?" Pemberton asked, not reassured by the man's answer.

"Something's come up. We need to talk."

The man was keeping his distance and did not appear to be threatening. If anything, he seemed nervous. Pemberton began to calm down a little.

"You scared the hell out of me," he said. "Where did you spring from, anyway?"

"I've been waiting," the man said, nodding in the direction of a car parked in the shadows on the other side of a row of columns. "Like I said, we need to talk."

3

"What's happened?" Pemberton asked, uncertain of what was going on.

The man said nothing but sauntered across to the parapet that overlooked the street below. He peered over the edge and then turned round to face Pemberton again, resting his back against the low stone wall. Pemberton had still not fully recovered from the shock at the unexpected meeting. He bent down and picked up the briefcase, keeping his eyes fixed on the stranger. He opened the car door and threw his case onto the passenger seat.

"Well?" he asked.

"Before I begin, there are a couple of things I think you should know first," the man said. He reached into his pocket and produced an envelope which he held out to Pemberton.

"What's that?"

"Something I think you should see," said the stranger.

Pemberton warily approached the man and cautiously took the envelope from the outstretched hand.

"Open it," said the man.

The envelope wasn't sealed. Pemberton pulled up the flap and drew out a single, folded sheet of A4 paper. He straightened it out and leaned back against the parapet so the light from the street could fall upon the paper. It was a printed letter consisting of a single paragraph.

'*To whom it may concern,*

It will come as no surprise to those who know me that I have decided to take my own life. For the last couple of months I ...'

Pemberton stopped reading and quickly glanced at the man before returning to the letter. His eyes jumped straight to bottom of the paragraph where it had been signed and he looked up again in shock. The signature was his own. He blanched.

"What's all this about?" he asked with a sense of rising panic.

"As I said, something's come up. There's a couple of things I think you ought to know."

The man took a step toward him.

"Keep away!" Pemberton cried in alarm as he was backed against the parapet. "I'm going to call the police."

He reached into a pocket to get his phone.

"Don't do that!" the man warned quickly.

But Pemberton had already turned aside with the phone in his hand.

"Get away from me!" he shouted.

"Give me the phone," the man demanded menacingly and took another step forward with his hand outstretched.

But Pemberton was thoroughly scared. He looked for a way out and realised he was trapped against the parapet overlooking the street and five floors up. The man was now standing right next to him. Pemberton held the phone out of reach but, before he could say anything else, the man unexpectedly bent down and hooked one arm behind Pemberton's knees and the other round his back. As the man pulled himself upright, Pemberton was suddenly jerked off the ground onto the parapet. For a moment he was balanced precariously on the ledge, still clutching the paper in one hand and the phone in the other, his eyes wide with surprise and terror. He opened his mouth to cry out when, without a word, the man used both hands to push him roughly over the edge.

Pemberton fell, clawing in desperation at the air. He bounced off the parapet of the next floor down and the phone flew from his grasp before he cartwheeled once and hit the pavement far below with a sickening thud.

Chapter One

"Suicide?"

"That's what I heard. Someone said it could have been an accident but how likely is that?"

The lab technician was speaking in the hushed, reverential tones he thought the moment demanded but Martin Greaves was not impressed and stroked his chin thoughtfully.

"Well, I can't say as I'm actually surprised," he said. "I know one shouldn't speak ill of the dead but we all knew Michael was a bit unstable. Brilliant, of course, but, well," he hesitated before finishing, "there was always something a little odd about him."

Martin Greaves had worked alongside Michael Pemberton in the Institute on the outskirts of Brighton for over ten years and the lab technician who had just brought him the news thought he could have shown a little more sympathy; in fact, any emotion might have been more appropriate. But Martin was right; Pemberton had been odd. Nobody in the lab had really got to know him. Most of them thought he was a surly individual and had learned to avoid him if they could. They respected him and admired his work but from the start Pemberton had resisted all overtures of friendship and his abrupt manner had kept people at a distance. His death was a tragedy, of course, but the only loss really felt by his colleagues would be for the projects he had been working on and which, without Pemberton's input, might now at worst remain unfinished and, at best, take a lot longer.

"I suppose I'd better go and see The Prof," Martin sighed. "I expect we'll have to make some sort of statement for the press once they get hold of it."

He picked up a folder from his desk and, leaving the technician in the lab, strode purposefully down the corridor to the lifts. Martin Greaves was fifty-six years old and the Assistant Director of Bioprix Institute for Research and Development, or

BIRD as it was more commonly known amongst those who worked there. The majority of the organisation's work was mainly sub-contracted to it by the large pharmaceutical companies but what few people, including most of Bioprix's staff, did not know was that one section was entirely devoted to experimental projects funded by the government. This was where Pemberton had worked and, as Martin made his way to the Director's office on the fourth floor, he was already wondering how they were going to fill the gap left by Pemberton's death.

Knocking once on the door as he opened it, Martin went straight into the Director's office. It was a small room, designed to be entirely functional with nothing about it to indicate the eminent status of the tall man hunched over the desk in front of the window. Professor Ken Robinson, known to everyone who worked in the building simply as 'The Prof', was sorting through a sheaf of papers. He was, at sixty years old, a little portly but still surprisingly agile. A shock of wiry white hair was brushed untidily back from his high forehead and a pair of half-moon glasses dangled loosely from a string around his neck. He looked up and the expression on Martin's face told him why he was there.

"Martin," he said with a slight frown, "you've already heard then? I was about to call you. Terrible news, isn't it?"

Martin nodded silently and dropped into the chair by the side of the desk.

"Could it have been an accident?" The Prof asked, raising an eyebrow.

"I suppose it could have been," Martin replied, "but nobody here seems to think so."

"No," said The Prof, "me neither."

Martin nodded in agreement.

"What do you think made him do it?" The Prof continued, returning to look through the papers. "You don't think we were driving him too hard, do you?"

"No," said Martin. "He loved the work. If anything, that probably kept him going. I think it must have been something else."

"Did he ever say anything to you?"

"No. You know what he was like."

"Well," said The Prof, putting down the papers he was holding, "it's left us in one hell of a mess. I've already had the Ministry on the line. They're sending down one of their men."

"What for?"

The Prof pushed the papers to one side and shrugged his shoulders.

"I don't know," he said, now giving Martin his full attention. "Don't they always do that when something like this happens? I suppose they'll want to talk to some of the team, though heaven knows what they expect to find. You'd better warn them."

"Will do," said Martin. "What about the press?"

"What about them?"

"Shouldn't we have something ready to tell them? Michael was quite well-known. I expect they'll want some sort of statement once the news gets out."

The Prof looked helplessly at the piles of paper on his desk.

"Don't worry," Martin continued, "I'll see to it if you like."

"If you could," said The Prof with a grateful smile. "You knew him as well as anyone, probably better than most, in fact. Anyway, I'm going to be tied up trying to sort out exactly where he was in the project. These are his notes I'm looking at now but they're all over the place. I don't understand it, they're a complete mess; I can't make head nor tail of them at the moment. You know, I think he still wasn't writing everything down."

"Do you want any help?"

"No, it's alright," said The Prof quickly and then gave a rueful smile. "Thanks Martin, but I think it's something I should do myself."

Martin was relieved. He knew how Pemberton had worked and the thought of going through the man's scribbles and shorthand memos was daunting. The usual code of practice was to make clear notes of every stage involved in an experiment or test as it was performed. It ensured there was an exact record of everything that had been done along with the results. It was not only good scientific practice but also should have avoided the possibility of the lab finding itself in its present position. But Pemberton had been a rule to himself and, because of the sort of man he was and because he got excellent results, nobody had really tried to make him comply with the normal rules. Martin had talked to him about it on several occasions but Pemberton had simply pointed to his head and said the whole thing was in there; he didn't have time to stop and write bits down as he went along. It would all get written up once he had finished.

Martin stood up. He could see The Prof wanted to get on with his work and anyway, there was nothing more to say. He left the office and made his way back to the lifts as the The Prof returned to the papers strewn across his desk. Neither of them knew nor could even suspect that the notes The Prof was struggling to decipher were meaningless; the true record and results of what Pemberton had been working on were now somewhere else.

★

The following morning, Charlie Watts pressed a button on the washing-machine and took a step back to check the water was going into the tub. Although it had been over three years since his wife had died, he still didn't trust himself to do the right thing as far as domestic appliances were concerned and had thumbed through the manual to make sure he had followed the instructions correctly. After a few minutes, satisfied the machine was operating properly, he picked up his cup of coffee and sat down at the kitchen table. There were two hours to wait before Daniel arrived and Charlie glanced at the clock impatiently.

Charlie was not his real name; someone had christened him that the first day he joined the force in the late 70's and it had stuck. All new recruits in the police were given a nickname when they started but nowadays everyone called him Charlie, even the local newsagent, and, in fact, it was how he had thought of himself for many years. Having risen through the ranks to become a Detective Chief Inspector, Charlie had taken early retirement from the police the year before. It had been a hasty decision, brought about by his disillusion with the way his last case had been resolved. But it had not taken long before he realised retirement didn't suit him. It was Daniel who had rescued him from regret by recruiting his help in working on a problem facing MI6 a few months later. They had met for the first time on Charlie's final case with the force and working together again had cemented their friendship. After the success of their last operation, Daniel had asked if he might call on Charlie's help again in the future. Charlie had eagerly agreed and thought Daniel's visit that morning must be connected with his decision. Daniel had not mentioned anything when he had phoned the night before to ask if he could call in the following day, but Charlie was sure this was not going to be entirely a social call.

Almost exactly two hours later with the washing now hanging on the line in the back-garden, Daniel Rankin arrived at Charlie's house. He had travelled to Bristol by train and taken a taxi from the station. Charlie had seen the car draw up from his lounge window where he had been waiting for the previous twenty minutes and he opened the front door as Daniel was still walking up the path. Daniel Rankin was in his early fifties and had worked for MI6 most of his adult life. He looked young for his age. He was slim with an athletic build but his short brown hair was tinged with white at the sides, giving him a slightly distinguished air. He smiled when he saw Charlie and the two men shook hands warmly before they went inside.

"Well," Charlie said half an hour later after the two of them had caught up with each other's news over coffee, "I expect you're wanting to get down to business."

"Business?" said Daniel with an innocent grin.

"This is all very nice but I'm sure you didn't come all this way just for a friendly chat. What's up?"

"Well," said Daniel, "as a matter of fact there is something you might like to help us with, that is if you're not too busy."

Charlie gave a wry smile.

"I think the housework can wait," he said. "What do you want me to do?"

"Have you heard of someone called Michael Pemberton?"

"No, I don't think so. Who is he?"

Daniel picked up the newspaper he had brought with him and turned several pages before folding it and passing it over to Charlie, pointing to a short article at the bottom of the page as he did so. Charlie reached for his glasses and slipped them on before starting to read.

Famous Scientist found dead

The well-known scientist, Michael Pemberton, 62, was yesterday found dead on the pavement below a multi-storey carpark in Welbeck Street, central London.

Pemberton, who lived and worked at a scientific research institute in Brighton, was discovered in the early hours of Friday morning following an anonymous call to the police. His car was later found in the carpark.

Pemberton sprang to fame when at the age of fourteen he gained a scholarship to Oxford University. Qualifying first as a doctor specialising in tropical diseases, he later went on to lead a number of research teams in Nairobi before joining Bioprix Institute for Research and Development where he has worked for the last ten years. Doctor Martin Greaves, a friend and colleague at Bioprix, said, "Michael was a visionary. His work in the field of microbiological research was unparalleled and he will be greatly missed by all who knew him. His unexpected death is a tragedy which has affected everyone at the Institute."

Inspector Cornwell of the Metropolitan Police has asked the public for their help in the inquiry that has been set up. In a statement released to the press he said, "The body of an elderly man was yesterday recovered from the street below the NCP in

Welbeck Street. It would appear he could have fallen from one of the levels. We would very much like to ask the person who contacted us to do so again and to speak to anyone else who might have seen what happened or was in the area at the time."

Charlie took off his glasses, put the newspaper down and looked expectantly at Daniel.

"Well?" he asked.

"Pemberton was working for us," Daniel said. "I think he could have been murdered."

"That's not what this says," said Charlie, pointing at the newspaper. "The press obviously think it was an accident or suicide."

"The press only know what we've told them."

"What makes you think it was murder?"

Daniel paused and pulled the briefcase he had with him onto his lap. He opened it and drew out a plastic envelope sealed at the top with a broad red tape stamped with the word '*Evidence*'. It contained a single sheet of A4 paper which he passed to Charlie. The paper was creased where it had been scrunched up in the middle but was now carefully flattened out inside the transparent envelope.

"Before I go into that, have a look at this. Pemberton was holding it in his hand when he was found," he said. "We haven't released that fact to the press yet."

Charlie turned the sheet over and saw it was only printed on one side. He put on his glasses again and started to read.

'*To whom it may concern,*

It will come as no surprise to those who know me that I have decided to take my own life. For the last couple of months I have been reviewing my situation and have come to the conclusion that the future holds nothing for me. The inspiration and curiosity which drove my work when I was younger has deserted me. I am no longer interested in the research which has dominated everything I've done in the past and cost me so much. I put everything into science and paid for it with two failed marriages and no friends. As I approach retirement, I realise now it was not worth it. It has taken me a long time to recognise that I face a lonely old age and that is a prospect I do not relish. With no further interest in my work and no one to share the rest of my life, I have decided there is no point in prolonging the despair I am living with. It would be nice to think I will be missed but if that were the case I would not be doing this.'

There was a scribbled signature at the bottom which Charlie recognised as Pemberton's name. He put the envelope on the table and looked at Daniel.

"Interesting," he said, "but this note would appear to confirm it was a suicide. Why do you think he was murdered?"

"First of all," said Daniel, "it just doesn't add up. If you were a top-notch scientist and going to end it all, would you choose to do it by jumping off a multi-storey carpark? Even if you did, why not go right from the top? Why stop at the fifth floor? And that's not all, his phone is missing. It's not at his living quarters in the Institute and the police didn't find it at the scene. Anyway, why go all the way to London to do it, and why hold the note in your hand as you jump? Don't most suicides leave the note somewhere safe where someone can find it?"

"OK," said Charlie, "it does sound a little unusual but he might have had his own reasons. I think I should know a few other things before I offer an opinion. To start with, is this signature on the note genuine?"

Daniel nodded.

"As far as we can tell," he said. "If it's a forgery it's a damned good one."

"And what about the note itself," Charlie asked, "is it true? Did he really want to kill himself? Losing interest in his work doesn't sound like a very good reason to me. Was that all there was to his life?"

Daniel was silent a moment.

"Was he the lonely and depressed man this note suggests?" Charlie prompted.

"By all accounts he was not an easy man to work with," Daniel said at last. "It's probably true he didn't have any friends.

13

Both his wives divorced him on the grounds of his unreasonable behaviour and everyone says he was brilliant but nobody seems to have actually liked him. They appear to have avoided him if they could. I suppose he might have been lonely but there was nothing to suggest he had lost interest in his work. Quite the opposite, in fact. I understand he was on the verge of a major breakthrough."

"Was he depressed?"

"Difficult to say. There's no evidence of it. He tended to keep to himself but he hadn't mentioned anything to the people he worked with and hadn't seen a doctor for years. Although the results haven't come back from the lab yet, I'm fairly sure he wasn't on any medication. There were no pills or anything like that in his flat. We all have bad days but his colleagues said they hadn't noticed anything different about him. Wouldn't they have noticed something?"

"I don't know," said Charlie. "Depression's a strange thing. Most people tend to keep it to themselves; put on an act that everything's alright. If he really was determined to kill himself, he would hardly be likely to broadcast it beforehand."

"You said there were several things you wanted to know. What else?"

"Do you know if anyone had a reason to kill him?" asked Charlie. "Murderers usually have a motive of some sort."

"That's not an easy one to answer," said Daniel "If I knew that, I might not be here but there are a number of possibilities. It could be something personal. If he was such an unpleasant fellow as our enquiries suggest, he could have made some enemies, perhaps amongst his colleagues. There could have been a violent argument."

"Unlikely," said Charlie. "Arguments can sometimes lead to impulsive acts of killing, but the circumstances here suggest this was planned. If someone killed him, they went to a great deal of trouble in advance to make it look like something else."

"I agree. I don't believe this was anything sudden either but there is another possibility which I think could be more likely:

perhaps someone found out the sort of work he was doing and believed he should be stopped."

"OK," said Charlie, looking interested, "that sounds a little more promising. Murder is not unknown in such situations. Anti-abortionists have killed doctors in the past, perhaps not in this country to my knowledge, but animal-rights activists have made threats against people involved in experimental programmes. What sort of work was he doing?"

Daniel did not answer immediately and Charlie noticed the hesitation.

"You don't have to tell me if it's going to be a problem," he said. "But if you want my help then it might be important for me to know."

"You're right," said Daniel, "and that's why I'm here. Pemberton was working on a top secret project for the Ministry of Defence called 'Operation Sundown'. I don't know all the details, but basically it's to do with biological warfare."

"I thought that was banned," said Charlie.

"Technically, yes," said Daniel. "There was some sort of Convention we signed up to about forty years ago along with a lot of other countries. However, it seems there is nothing in the Convention which denies any country the right to conduct biological research for defensive purposes. That's still been going on all over the world."

"And Pemberton was involved in that?"

"Yes. 9/11 was the real wake-up call. Until then terrorist targets had been specific and localised; you know, things like embassies. 9/11 was a declaration of war against a whole country. It changed everything. Suddenly people realised they were in a war where there were no rules. The enemy was well-resourced, highly intelligent if fanatic and, most importantly, well-versed in the techniques of modern warfare. Many people believe it's only a matter of time before they access the materials and research that has already been done and try to use biological weapons against the West. We can't afford to let that happen."

"So the Convention's been scrapped, then?" said Charlie.

15

"Not exactly," Daniel explained. "The Convention is still in place but all over the world countries are preparing themselves for what the terrorists might do. Much of the research has been focussed on detecting the introduction of biological or toxic material into an area. Speed of identification is essential for any effective containment and in California the Lawrence Livermore Labs have developed a technique that can now identify these agents in hours rather than days. The Netherlands has a similar device called the BiosparQ and Israel is working on its own Bio-pen which is supposed to recognise known biological agents in the environment in only twenty minutes."

"Is that what Pemberton was working on?" Charlie asked. "A UK bio-detector of some sort?"

"To start with, yes," said Daniel, "that was the aim of 'Operation Sundown', but then he stumbled across something else. He learnt how to change the DNA of a bacterium or virus in a way that could effectively affect the environment in which it was able to survive. It was a major breakthrough."

"I don't quite understand," said Charlie. "If Pemberton had found something that was going to contain the spread of biological warfare, isn't that a good thing? Why should anyone want to prevent him or are you suggesting some terrorists found out what he was doing and thought it would stop them in their tracks?"

Daniel paused a moment before continuing.

"Most of what I've told you so far is no longer secret. Much of the information is already in the public domain. What very few people know is that Pemberton discovered how to change the DNA of a bacterium to make it temperature specific. He was about to produce genetically modified bacteria which could only survive within a certain defined temperature range."

"I'm still not sure I understand," said Charlie. "What's the point of that? How does it help identify if terrorists have let bacteria loose in this country?"

"It doesn't," said Daniel. "One of the main reasons why biological warfare has rarely been used in the past is because so far we've been unable to limit its spread. Once released, the bacteria can just as easily turn round and infect us as well as the enemy. It's exceptionally difficult to contain. Think of the Black Death; once it started, it spread like wildfire, decimating most of Europe. It couldn't be controlled and had to run its course before eventually dying out on its own."

"Like the Spanish Flu last century," said Charlie.

"Yes. In fact, that's probably a better example. The only way we've been able to contain such diseases until now has been through vaccination, controlling travel and the way we deal with dead bodies. It involves a massive operation and, to tell the truth, a lot of luck. However, if we are able to determine the conditions in which bacteria can survive it opens up a totally different ballgame. It means a disease can be released into an area with a specific temperature range, do its work and then die out once the temperature changes with the season."

Charlie got up from the table and went to fill the kettle. He was thinking about what Daniel had just said. He wanted to be sure he had understood exactly what it meant. He switched the kettle on and turned round to face Daniel.

"You're no longer talking about just detecting bacteria now, are you?" he said. "You're talking about us actually using it as a weapon."

"Exactly," said Daniel. "Now you see why some people might have wanted to stop Pemberton."

"But what about the Convention?" Charlie asked. "You said it meant we couldn't use biological warfare."

"I said it couldn't be used offensively."

"What's the difference?"

Daniel took a deep breath.

"There is an argument," he said slowly, "and one currently finding favour amongst many in the military, that since the terrorists have effectively declared war, a pre-emptive strike using biological weapons is actually a defensive measure and therefore justified within the terms of the Convention. The only reason it hasn't already been deployed is because until now we haven't been able to control it. Pemberton's discovery could change all that."

"So you're saying we really do plan to use it?"

"It's being talked about seriously," said Daniel with a shrug.

"That's obscene!" Charlie exclaimed with feeling. The kettle switched itself off and he went over to the table and picked up their empty mugs.

"More coffee?" he asked.

"Please," said Daniel. "So, what do you think?"

"You could be right," said Charlie, still bitterly indignant at what he had just learnt. "I think that's a good enough reason why someone would want to murder him."

★

The following day, The Prof was waiting in his office feeling nervous. A phone call earlier that afternoon had told him to expect the two men who would be arriving any moment now and he wasn't sure what more the Ministry could want from him. He had thought their previous visit would have told them he had little to offer by way of explanation for Pemberton's death. The only reason he could think of for this second meeting was if they wanted to discuss 'Operation Sundown' itself and that was going to be awkward. Despite spending a large part of the last two days going through the scribbled notes Pemberton had left behind, he had still not been able to work out where the microbiologist had reached on the project. It was more than embarrassing. After all, he was the director and should be in a position to know exactly what was going on in the labs he controlled. He felt responsible; he was responsible. But how could he explain that was not how things had worked? Pemberton had been a maverick; he hadn't followed the rules and The Prof had felt unable to do anything about it. Pemberton's genius had protected him in the job and his aggressive, surly manner had helped him escape discipline; nobody, The Prof least of all, had wanted a confrontation by pointing out he should be submitting a daily report.

The Prof, like Martin Greaves and a few others, knew what Pemberton had achieved but the notes that should have detailed how he got there appeared not to exist. Simply knowing the result was useless without the information explaining how to replicate it. The Prof unkindly thought how typical it was of the man to leave him in this situation. And now he was going to have to admit that 'Operation Sundown' had ground to a halt. He was sure it would be possible - eventually - for others to reach the same point as Pemberton but without his brilliance it would take time. And the Ministry was impatient, especially now they already knew about the breakthrough.

The Prof had been intimidated by Daniel Rankin's visit to the Institute two days before. It was the first time the two of them had met and, although the official had been polite enough with his questions, The Prof got the impression he had left unsatisfied with the answers he had received. At the time, The Prof had thought Rankin could have been more understanding considering the circumstances; what was he going to think now when he discovered the actual state of 'Operation Sundown'? The Prof's dealings with the Ministry of Defence before this had always been with more sympathetic officials, people who were slightly in awe of him and who clearly respected his position. None of them had been scientists and he had always been able to cut an impressive figure as he explained in layman's terms what his team was working on. He had the feeling this meeting was going to be different.

The phone on his desk rang and he quickly picked it up.

"Your visitors are here," his secretary's voice announced.

"Show them straight up, please, Barbara," he said and replaced the receiver.

He stood and walked over to the door. He was wearing a white lab coat, not because he had been working on anything practical that day but because he felt it gave him some sort of status. Just as he was sure they would be wearing the dark suits of their bureaucratic job, he wanted to distinguish himself as a professional in his own field. He opened the door and looked along the empty corridor.

He heard their voices before he saw them. Barbara was chattering cheerfully as she led them from the lift to his office. He recognised Daniel immediately they turned the corner but had never met the other man who was walking behind him. He stretched out his hand as they reached the door.

"Come in, Mr Rankin, please," he said, shaking Daniel's hand. "I wasn't expecting to see you again so soon."

Daniel introduced Charlie and they went into the office. The Prof waved toward the two chairs he had placed in front of his desk and sat himself down behind it.

"Have you been able to find out anything more regarding the … er … tragic circumstances surrounding Michael's death?" he asked hesitantly.

"Not exactly," Daniel replied, "we're still investigating."

"Well," The Prof smiled apologetically, "I'm not sure there's anything I can add to what I told you last time."

"Actually, we wanted to talk to you about 'Operation Sundown'," Daniel said.

The Prof felt his heart sink.

"I'm afraid that is classified," he said. "I will need to see some clearance."

Daniel reached into the inside pocket of his jacket and produced a folded sheet of paper which he passed over. He leant back in the chair whilst The Prof read the letter.

"Well," The Prof was unable to keep a hint of nervousness from his voice as he handed the sheet back, "that seems to be in order. How can I help?"

"There are a number of points," said Daniel, "but let's start with your security arrangements."

"Security?" The Prof asked, a little surprised.

"Yes. This is a very sensitive project. I should like to know what special security measures you have in place."

The Prof hesitated. He had not expected this and for a moment was at a loss what to say.

"We have followed the Ministry's guidelines to the letter," he began. "The Sundown team work in isolation from the rest of the Institute. Everyone else thinks they're working on developing an antibiotic for superbugs, things like MRSA. In fact, there is a programme for just that to serve as a cover and they are actually making some progress too, but the real work is known only to a few who have all received clearance from the Ministry."

"I know that already," said Daniel. "What I meant was what happens to the documentation? I presume experiments are recorded somewhere; how is the information stored and protected? For example, what would Pemberton have done?"

"Daily reports should have been entered in an encrypted program ..."

"*Should* have been?" interrupted Charlie, speaking for the first time. He had sensed Professor Robinson's wariness and immediately picked up on the way the scientist had begun to phrase his reply.

The Prof looked at him and realised what he had just said. It was time to come clean.

"Well, it's not always easy, you know," he tried to explain. "Not everyone on the team is used to working in this way. Some people take time to adjust to a different routine and one or two of them found it difficult to change old habits. You need to understand, it's the science which interests them; as long as they are still working on the experiments some of them don't always write up their reports as often as they should."

"Was Pemberton one of those?" Daniel asked.

"Michael was – how shall I put this? – not always appreciative of the need to record everything at the end of the day."

"So he didn't always make a daily report?"

"No."

"But he did make some record of what he was doing as he went along?"

"He should have done but, well, to be absolutely honest, I'm afraid it's beginning to look like he didn't. We did speak to him about it but Martin, my Assistant Director, tells me he kept a lot of his research in his head."

The Prof was now avoiding looking at the two men opposite. He pulled a folder toward him and opened it, lifting some of the papers it contained and letting them fall back onto his desk.

"These are all the notes he left," he continued. "We found them in the safe but they are incomplete and not entirely intelligible as they stand. Martin went through Michael's apartment but found nothing more there. I've been going through these papers for the last two days but I'm afraid it looks as if the results of the work Michael was doing just before he died went with him when he jumped."

"Were they important?" asked Charlie.

"Crucial," admitted The Prof and his embarrassment was now clear.

Nobody spoke. The Prof appeared to be waiting for some sort of reprimand but neither Daniel nor Charlie were interested in the present state of 'Operation Sundown'. They had come to the Institute to find out whether it was possible there had been a leak. If Pemberton had been murdered to stop him working on the project then someone from outside must have discovered what he was doing. If they had not found out from accessing the available data then they could only have learnt of it from someone in the team - or possibly even Pemberton himself. Daniel glanced across at Charlie and the look they exchanged told him they had both come to the same conclusion.

"I think I will need to speak to the team again," Daniel said at last.

"Of course," said The Prof and looked quickly at his watch. "However, I'm afraid it's already gone five and they have probably left for the day. I'm sorry, but when you called you didn't say you wanted to see anyone else or I would have asked them to stay on."

"It doesn't matter," said Daniel. "If you can let me have their home addresses I'll call round this evening. It seems silly to come down again tomorrow now I'm already here."

The Prof was both thankful and a little surprised that Daniel did not want to ask any more questions about the state of 'Operation Sundown'. He picked up the phone and asked his secretary to prepare the information Daniel wanted. He smiled as he replaced the receiver.

"Barbara will get the addresses ready," he said. "You can collect them on your way out." He paused before continuing, "Was there anything else or is that it?"

"That's it, for the moment," said Daniel, getting to his feet. "Thank you for your time. I expect we'll probably have to meet again soon. There are still a few points that might need clearing up. I'll let you know."

The Prof stood up and accompanied them to the door. Just as they were about to leave, Charlie turned round.

"Actually, there is just one more thing," he said. "Was Pemberton particularly friendly with anyone on the team?"

The Prof thought for a moment.

"Not really," he said. "Martin Greaves probably worked the closest to him but I wouldn't say they were friends. Michael was a bit of a loner, he didn't make friends easily."

"OK, well thanks for that," Daniel said. "We'll be in touch."

He closed the door behind him as they left the office and The Prof sat down behind his desk, looking despairingly at the papers still spilling from the open folder in front of him. The meeting had not been as bad as he feared but he had the feeling that the two men from the Ministry would be back. Perhaps he ought to warn the others they could expect a visit that evening. He reached across the desk for his phone.

As soon as they were back in the car, Daniel glanced down the short list of names and addresses they had collected from Professor Robinson's secretary and passed it over to Charlie.

"Not many," he said. "We should be able to see them all and be back in London well before midnight."

"Let's hope everyone's in," said Charlie. "You've already spoken to them once, haven't you?"

"All but one," Daniel replied. "Emma Nelson was out of the country when I came down a few days ago."

"Is she back?"

"I don't know. Let's start with her and find out."

"Shouldn't we call first?"

"No. Let's surprise her."

Daniel tapped the post code in the satnav and turned the ignition. The Ford Focus engine purred quietly as he pulled out of the parking space and drove quickly away from the Institute's carpark.

★

Emma Nelson was a single, rather attractive forty-three year old American. She had studied Biochemistry at Yale and then moved to England to read for her PhD at Oxford. After working with a number of the larger pharmaceutical companies in England, she had joined Bioprix eight years before. Although she had been involved in several serious relationships, she had never married. This was not for want of offers but because she had never wanted a commitment that might interfere with her work. Her specialty had been tropical diseases and meant she was often abroad; a husband and children would have complicated her life. Moreover, she was not so naïve as to think, even in these enlightened times, that a family would not have halted her career. Female researchers were common enough in the practical labs but not at the level she had reached. She was almost at the top of the ladder and she had always been ambitious.

She was in the kitchen preparing a light supper when the doorbell rang. Quickly drying her hands on a towel, she walked along the hall to receive her visitors.

"Ms Nelson?" said Daniel as she opened the door.

"Doctor Nelson," she corrected, staring at him with her cornflower blue eyes.

"I'm sorry, Dr Nelson," said Daniel, "I am Mr Rankin and this is Mr Watts. The Ministry sent us down to follow up what happened to Michael Pemberton. We have just come from Professor Robinson at the Institute and were hoping you might be able to spare us a couple of minutes to talk about Michael."

"Come in," she said, pulling the door open and standing to one side, "I was expecting you. The Prof called about ten minutes ago to say you might be coming round."

"The Prof?" asked Charlie as he passed into the hall.

"Ken, Professor Robinson," she explained. "Everyone calls him 'The Prof.'"

She closed the door and led them into the large, modern kitchen at the back of the house. She pointed to four wooden chairs at a long bleached-oak table and went over to the granite work-surface to switch on the kettle.

"Tea or coffee?" she asked.

"Coffee would be nice, thank you," said Daniel, sitting on one of the wooden chairs. He looked around and saw the preparations of a meal underway. "I'm sorry, we seem to have come at an inconvenient time."

"That's alright," Emma said as she spooned instant coffee granules into three mugs, "it's only a salad. It can wait. Now, how can I help?"

"I came down last Saturday," Daniel began. "I spoke to the rest of the team but you were away."

"That's right," said Emma. "I was at a conference in Stockholm. I came back yesterday."

"We wanted to find out more about Michael Pemberton," Daniel continued. "We would like to try and understand why he did what he did. You and he must have worked closely together. What was he like?"

The kettle finished boiling. Emma turned away to pick it up and began to pour steaming water into the bone-china mugs.

"If you've already talked to the others then you must know," she said, still with her back to Daniel. "We all thought he was an unpleasant son of a bitch."

Charlie was a little startled by her directness. The soft drawl of the American accent she had never quite been able to lose told him she was from the States and he supposed that accounted for it. An English person would have been more tactful when speaking of the dead; not dishonest, perhaps, but more subtle.

"Does that mean you didn't get on?" he asked.

"Professionally I thought he was brilliant, everyone did," Emma said, bringing the coffees over and setting them down on the table." But personally he was a pig."

She sat down opposite them and lifted her mug, cradling it in her hands.

"Now don't get me wrong," she continued, "I'm sorry he killed himself, of course I am, but he was not a nice person. To tell the truth, he gave me the creeps."

"In what way?" Daniel asked.

"You know, the usual thing," Emma replied. "Standing too close, leaning over me when I was working, putting his hand on my shoulder. That sort of thing. There were quite a lot of inappropriate remarks as well. Nothing I said put him off. He made it obvious he would have liked more than just a professional relationship."

"I'm sorry for asking this," said Daniel, "but since you've brought it up, I do need to be absolutely clear. Might you, perhaps unwittingly, have given any signs which encouraged him to think there could have been something?"

Emma gave him a withering look.

"What do you think?" she said.

"I think you're a woman who is obviously capable of looking after herself and warding off unwanted attention. I'm just a little surprised he was as persistent as you say."

Emma shrugged and took a sip of coffee.

"That's what he was like. He was what you British call a dirty old man."

"Did you ever make a complaint?" asked Charlie.

"You must be joking! Look, I'm in a profession where women are outnumbered five to one by men who have made it beyond a certain point in the universities. In my own field, the percentage is even less. I learnt long ago that if a woman wants a career in biochemistry she doesn't rock the boat. Anyway, Michael might not have been the actual team leader, but he was the one leading the way. He was indispensable to the project, I'm not."

"So what's going to happen to the project now?" Daniel asked.

"We carry on, of course," Emma replied with a trace of surprise at the question.

"Without Pemberton?"

"It will be more difficult, take longer perhaps, but we have his notes to work from."

Daniel glanced at Charlie before speaking again.

"When I spoke to Professor Robinson, he said Pemberton was a little slapdash when it came to keeping his notes up to date."

"That was just the daily reports," said Emma dismissively. "Michael always said he could never see the point of those, but he kept his own notes. He was a scientist; keeping a detailed record of what you're working on becomes second nature. I know for a fact that Michael kept a personal notebook in which he wrote everything down by hand."

"Can anyone else in the team confirm that?"

"I don't know," Emma said, a little surprised that Daniel needed to verify what she had said. "You'd have to ask them. I suppose they might. We all keep our own records though Michael tended to be rather secretive about it. Some scientists are like that with their work, but he did show it to me once. There were pages and pages covered in his handwriting. I think he was trying to impress me."

"Could he have shown his notes to anyone else?"

"Possibly not, thinking about it," Emma said and paused a moment. "I'm the only woman on the team," she added as if that explained it.

Daniel sat back in the chair and took a gulp of coffee. He was thinking fast.

"What happened to this notebook?" he asked casually, setting his mug back down on the table.

"I suppose it's with The Prof," Emma said. "We have to lock up all our notes each night when we finish in the lab. Security. The Prof would want to know exactly where Michael had reached before he died. Hopefully the notes should enable us to carry on where he left off. Everything should be in the book."

Daniel realised Dr Nelson was going to learn the truth sooner or later and decided he would like to see her reaction when she found out.

"Actually," he said slowly, "The Prof doesn't have it. When we spoke to him earlier this evening he told us he had recovered all the notes Pemberton had left but they were incomplete and muddled. He showed us everything he had and it was just loose papers; there was no notebook. He sort of suggested that trying to continue Pemberton's work was going to be very difficult now."

"That can't be possible!" Emma sounded more shocked than surprised.

"You didn't know?" asked Daniel.

"No. I got back late last night and haven't been into work today. We need those notes."

"Well, I'm afraid Professor Robinson doesn't seem to have them. What do you think could have happened?"

"I – I don't know," Emma stuttered. "Are you sure he hasn't got them?"

"It would appear not."

Emma got up from the table and began to pace up and down.

"This is serious," she said, more to herself than to Daniel and Charlie. "I need to speak to The Prof."

She stopped her pacing and turned to face Daniel.

"Look, do you mind? I think I should see The Prof right away. I'm sorry, perhaps we could finish this another time."

"Of course," said Daniel, standing up. "We should have made an appointment."

He reached into his wallet and pulled out a card which he placed on the table.

"This is my number. Give me a call when it's convenient."

Emma led the way to the front door. As they left, she put out a hand to stop him.

"I'm sorry to chuck you out like this," she said, "but it's really important I go to the Institute right now. If Michael's notes are missing then it could mean ..." she hesitated, "could mean the project will be put back months, even years."

Daniel had the impression she had been about to say something else. He waited a moment to see if she was going to add anything but Emma simply gave him an apologetic smile.

"I understand," he said. "You've got my number, give me a call."

He followed Charlie down the path and she closed the door.

"That was all very interesting," said Daniel as they reached the car. "Any thoughts?"

"On Dr Nelson or the fact there is a missing notebook?"

"Well, both I suppose."

Charlie stopped to think for a moment before answering.

"Now we know there was a notebook," he said, "it opens up new possibilities to explain why Pemberton could have been murdered. If, as we first thought, he was killed in an attempt to stop the project, then it would have failed unless whoever did it also destroyed the notebook. If that was found then, from what the good doctor just said, the Institute could simply continue their work with someone else at the head. That would help to explain its disappearance."

They got into the car and put on their seatbelts. Once he was comfortable, Charlie continued.

"However, I think we should also consider the possibility that he was killed by someone who wanted to get their own hands on the notebook. They might want to continue his work for themselves."

"That's a worst case scenario," said Daniel grimly as he started the engine, "and, unfortunately, much more likely. It's exactly what I'm beginning to think."

"In either case," said Charlie, "we need to ask ourselves why Pemberton should have taken the notebook with him when he went to London, assuming he did, of course."

"If it was that important, perhaps he just didn't want to leave it out of his sight," suggested Daniel.

"Or he was going to show it to someone, or pass it on. How sure of him were you?"

"Everyone on their team was screened and cleared to work on the project at the start," said Daniel, "but it's impossible to keep tabs on everyone all the time. We carry out spot checks occasionally but unless we have reason to think something is suspicious we just haven't the manpower to keep a constant watch. At some point it comes down to a simple matter of trust."

"So, since he was checked out he could have been turned. Is that the right expression?"

"That's the expression," said Daniel with an indulgent smile, looking down the list of addresses the Prof's secretary had given them. He tapped a fresh postcode into the satnav, indicated right and pulled the car into the stream of traffic that was moving along the road.

"Where are we going now?" asked Charlie.

"I thought we should see Martin Greaves, the Assistant Director. The Professor said he had probably been the closest to Pemberton and, when I spoke to him before, I got the impression he was a little more clued up than the Professor."

"Are you going to tell him about the notebook?" Charlie asked.

"If he doesn't already know, he's going to find out soon enough. It would be interesting to see how he reacts to the news. I feel like stirring things up a little."

Charlie nodded. It felt good to be back in an investigation; it made him feel more alive. And he and Daniel made a good team. Throughout his career in the force he had tended to work alone and had preferred it that way. Policing methods had changed over the years; they had become more rationalised. Advances in forensics had shifted the emphasis more towards the examination of evidence, but Charlie had always had a nose for finding out the truth. He was old-school and had relied on an instinct that had been honed through years of experience. He couldn't explain it and other officers who worked with him had at first been a little sceptical of his methods. However, they had soon come to respect him when, more often than not, he was proved to be right. Daniel had recognised Charlie's ability from the first and, whilst his own skills lay in interpreting evidence and reasoning his way toward a result, he valued his friend's instinctive judgement and trusted it.

Charlie's instinct was now telling him that Pemberton was not a traitor. Although he had queried whether Pemberton could have been turned, he believed that people who are going to betray their country would at least try to get others to like and trust them in order to cover up what they were really doing. Pemberton had done the exact opposite. He had apparently been actively disliked by his colleagues and done nothing to change their opinion of him. It seemed he didn't care what anyone thought, with the possible exception of Dr Nelson. Charlie was starting to think that as far as Pemberton was concerned, the work itself was the important thing in his life and, if he was right, he was sure the scientist would have done anything to make sure he could continue with it. Charlie decided that was a line of enquiry he would like to pursue further.

"What did you make of Dr Nelson?" Daniel asked after they had been driving in silence for a couple of minutes.

Something about the casual way he said it made Charlie think Daniel was looking for more than just a professional opinion on the interview. He was not quite sure what sort of reply was expected and it made him pause a few moments before answering.

"Well?" Daniel prompted.

"She's not afraid to speak her mind, is she?" said Charlie at last. "I suppose it comes from being an American."

★

Professor Robinson was waiting in his office at the Institute when Emma arrived. She had called him as soon as Daniel and Charlie had left and he had agreed to stay on to meet with her. He realised it was no longer possible to contain the fact that Operation Sundown had now ground to a halt and decided it was better to see the members of the team individually rather than give them the news when they were all assembled together. It was his responsibility and he would rather talk to them singly than face the combined barrage of criticism he knew was likely to come when they learned he had allowed this to happen. He had already discussed with Martin Greaves what they should do and the visit from the Ministry officials earlier that evening had gone better than he had thought, but he knew facing Emma Nelson was going to be a different matter.

Emma opened the door as she knocked and The Prof stood up to greet her.

"Is it true?" she demanded before he had a chance to say anything. "Those men from the Ministry said you didn't have Michael's notes."

"Hello Emma," The Prof said, trying to smile pleasantly. "Come in and sit down."

Emma remained standing as she confronted The Prof.

"Well?"

"No," The Prof replied, avoiding her gaze as he sat down. "I have his notes but they are muddled and incomplete. I have been working on them for the last few days but I'm afraid it looks as if we're going to have to try and replicate a lot of what Michael was doing."

"I meant his notebook," said Emma, sitting down on the chair opposite the desk. "Everything he was working on should be in there."

The Prof looked puzzled.

"There was no notebook," he said. "I've got everything we found in his rooms and the lab. This is all there is."

He held up the folder he had previously shown to Daniel and Charlie.

"There is a notebook," said Emma. "I saw it. He showed it to me. You can't have looked properly."

"I can assure you, we were very thorough," The Prof said patiently despite being annoyed at her accusation. "Martin has checked his apartment as well and there is nothing more."

Emma pursed her lips. Something was very wrong.

"There *is* a notebook," she repeated. "He must have hidden it."

"Why would he do that?"

Emma thought she might know the answer to that but didn't want to share her suspicions with The Prof. At least, not until she could be more certain.

"Can I see what you've got?" she asked.

"Yes, of course," said The Prof, passing over the folder, "but I can assure you there's nothing useful there on his latest work with the DNA. I've gone through it all several times now but nowhere does he identify the transgene he was using."

Emma wasn't listening. She scanned the papers in the folder, recognising bits which overlapped with her own research, but was unable to find the crucial bit of information which had led to Pemberton's breakthrough.

"It's unfortunate Michael didn't write everything down as he should," The Prof continued after a moment. "Martin says he tried to get him to do it but, well, Michael was a law unto himself, wasn't he? Martin told me he preferred to keep it all in his head until he was completely finished."

"That's not true," said Emma, closing the folder abruptly and putting it down on the desk in front of her. "I know he was a bastard to work with, but he was thorough. I know he must have recorded everything he did. I told you, he showed me his notebook with everything in it."

"Did he tell you the genome he was using? Did you see what it was?"

"No," Emma admitted. "He only flicked through the pages in front of me. He was just showing off; I thought he was being a bit of a prat and, to be honest, I told him to go away and grow up."

"Weren't you curious?"

"Well yes, a bit, but …" She hesitated for a moment before the need to explain overcame her reluctance to admit how Pemberton had made a nuisance of himself. "Look, at the time I thought he was just coming on to me and I didn't want to encourage him. He'd done things like that before. This time he said the notebook was going to make him world famous. He actually used the same quote as Oppenheimer, you know, the one from the Bhagavad Gita, 'Now I am become death, the destroyer of worlds'. To tell the truth, I thought it was all a bit pathetic at the time."

She paused, remembering the scene. She had been alone in her lab working at the electron microscope and hadn't seen him come in. The first she had been aware of Pemberton was when he laid his hand on her shoulder. He had looked very smug and said he wanted her to be the first to know what he had done. She had been surprised; Michael rarely shared information with the rest of the team, preferring to confide in Martin only when he had something really important to report. She had thought this was just another attempt to impress her and had dismissed him curtly, saying she was busy. It was only later that she learnt from Martin what Pemberton had actually achieved. Now she felt a pang of regret for not letting him talk. However, it was done and there was nothing she could do about it.

"Doesn't Martin have the information?" she asked abruptly. "Surely it's part of his job to know these things."

The Prof shifted uncomfortably in his chair and looked away. He had known their conversation was going to reach this point. Emma was absolutely right; it *was* Martin's job and it was his own job to make sure that Martin was doing it. At least Emma should be able to understand. She had been on the team with Pemberton and knew how touchy he could be, how awkward he was to work with.

"Martin knew the first results Michael had achieved," he said, sounding a little defensive, "well, we all knew that; I think Martin told everyone in the team about the breakthrough. But you know what Michael was like; he didn't confide anything about the method. Martin asked, of course, but Michael said he wanted to do some more tests before he submitted his final report and Martin didn't like to press him."

Emma was silent. She was angry at the incompetence but not surprised. However, it was all very well to be critical with the benefit of hindsight and The Prof was right; everyone had avoided having a confrontation with Pemberton, including herself. There was nothing to be gained by pointing the finger.

"In that case," she said, becoming business-like, "I think you should be looking for his notebook."

The Prof removed his glasses and gently rubbed the bridge of his nose. He looked tired. He was not convinced that even if they found a notebook it would contain any useful information. Pemberton had told Martin he didn't want to write things down until he had finished, and Emma herself had admitted she hadn't seen it properly. Moreover, she was probably right in one respect; Michael had probably just been waving something in front of her to show off. However, The Prof was not prepared at that moment to enter into an argument.

"I will look for it, of course," he said. "Have you any idea where it might be or what he could have done with it?"

Emma shrugged. This was not the time to voice her suspicions.

★

Martin Greaves had been married to his wife, Anne, for thirty-two years. She was a petite woman and had gained a couple of stone since meeting Martin at university where she had been reading music. She had now reached the stage where her friends kindly described her as homely though, in fact, she had always been rather plain. She and Martin had liked each other the first time they met at a concert where she was playing. As they got to know each other, they had not exactly fallen in love but, both being practical people, realised they could meet each other's needs and got married as soon as they left university. He wanted someone to look after him whilst pursuing his career and, despite being a highly capable and intelligent woman, Anne had simply wanted a comfortable existence, raising a family without having to earn her own living. However, now their two children had grown up and were busy making their own way in the world, life for Anne had settled into a dull routine that she had not anticipated all those years ago.

She was in the kitchen preparing their evening meal when the doorbell rang to announce Daniel and Charlie's arrival. Martin was upstairs in the small room he used as his study and called down for her to let them in.

"They're your visitors!" she shouted back, but hearing no reply she irritably turned off the stove and went to open the door.

"Good evening," said Daniel as soon as he saw her. "I'm Mr Rankin and this is Mr Watts. We are here on behalf of the Ministry of Defence and were hoping to speak to Mr Greaves if it's convenient."

"We were about to eat," Anne replied ungraciously, "but I suppose you'd better come in."

"I'm sorry if we're interrupting," said Daniel apologetically. "We can come back later if you'd prefer."

"No," said Anne, pulling the door open. "Best to get it over and done with now you're here. We were expecting you. Professor Robinson called to let us know you were on your way."

She showed them into the front room and shifted an untidy pile of magazines and newspapers off the settee onto the coffee table so they had somewhere to sit.

"Martin will be down in a moment," she said. "I suppose this is about Michael Pemberton."

"Yes," said Daniel, sitting in the cleared space on the settee. Charlie sat next to him.

"Tragic news," said Anne, though she sounded as if she couldn't care less.

"Yes," Daniel agreed. "Did you know him well?"

36

"Not really. We met a few times at the Institute. You know, Christmas parties and things like that. I can't say as I knew him, though my husband talked about him."

At that moment, Martin arrived.

"Hello again," he said with a smile as he walked into the room. "The Prof called to say you'd be coming round."

"I'm sorry to interrupt your evening," said Daniel, standing up. "This is Charlie Watts. The Ministry asked us to make another visit."

Charlie and Martin shook hands and they all sat down, Martin taking the comfortable armchair by the fireside and Anne sitting opposite him.

"Well, what's this all about?" Martin asked, crossing his legs. "I thought we'd covered everything last time."

"Just a few things that need tidying up," said Daniel pleasantly. He looked across at Anne. "Please, don't let us hold you up. I'm sure you've got things to be getting on with."

Martin glanced at Anne and nodded. She stood up.

"We shouldn't be long," said Daniel.

Anne said nothing and left the room.

"Well," said Martin as the door closed behind his wife, "I suppose that means you want to discuss Operation Sundown."

"Yes."

"Since you've just come from The Prof," Martin continued, "I assume you must already know where we stand at the moment. It's all a bit of a mess, I'm afraid, but I'm sure we'll be able to get back on track soon."

Daniel said nothing. Martin shifted uncomfortably in his chair and uncrossed his legs. He was thinking this visit was probably the precursor to a disciplinary inquiry. He leaned forward to emphasise what he was going to say.

"It's not The Prof's fault, if anyone's to blame it's Michael."

"We haven't come here to blame anyone," said Daniel, "but since you've raised the point, I thought it was your responsibility to make sure Pemberton kept his notes up to date."

Martin blushed. His suspicions were turning out to be correct.

"Well, yes, technically I suppose you could be right, but it hasn't been that easy, you know. Michael tended to do his own thing. I did remind him several times that he should be making a daily report."

"That was on the computer?" said Daniel.

"Yes. Everyone on the team was supposed to do it. Michael just didn't seem to think it was that important."

"Actually," said Daniel, "I'm more interested in his notebook."

Martin looked surprised.

"His notebook?"

"Yes. We know he didn't file a daily report, but now we believe he may have kept all his findings in a personal notebook which he wrote by hand."

"I don't know anything about a notebook," Martin said. "Some people might use them, I suppose, but nowadays most of us record everything on computer. It's more efficient. What makes you think he had a notebook anyway?"

"Dr Nelson saw it," said Daniel. "Pemberton actually showed it to her once. She said she thought he had written up all his findings in it."

"If that's true," said Martin, beginning to get excited, "then it's a life-saver. It could save us months of work!"

"Unfortunately, it's missing," said Daniel.

"Missing?" Martin repeated as if he didn't understand the word.

"Well," said Daniel, "Professor Robinson doesn't have it. It wasn't in the safe at the lab and he said you had gone through Pemberton's apartment at the Institute. I was rather hoping you might have some idea what could have happened to it."

"No, I don't. I didn't even know a notebook existed until now. Are you sure there is one?"

Daniel ignored the question.

"You never saw it then?" he asked.

"No. I just told you, I knew nothing about it."

"Why do you think that was?"

"What do you mean?"

"Just that it seems odd Pemberton should keep it so secret, particularly from you. After all, you were in charge of the team and he'd just made an important discovery. Wouldn't it have been normal for him to tell you what he was doing? At the very least he should have let you know he was recording everything he did, especially after you told him he ought to be filing a daily report."

"Well he didn't."

Daniel's persistence was starting to make Martin feel nervous.

"The information in that notebook could now be very valuable," Daniel continued. "A lot of people would be extremely interested in its contents, don't you think?"

The question hung in the air whilst they all remained silent. Martin recognised there was something more behind Daniel's words and suddenly realised where the conversation could be leading.

"Are you suggesting …"

"I'm not suggesting anything at the moment," interrupted Daniel. "I'm just asking a few questions."

"Why have you come?" Martin demanded abruptly. He understood exactly what was being implied and was now irritated at the way Daniel was pushing the point.

"Actually," said Charlie, deciding now was the right moment for him to intervene, "we wanted to know more about Pemberton. Professor Robinson said you probably knew him the best and could help us out. This is a very sensitive project you're working on, all the more so since his breakthrough. Now there seems to be a missing notebook. I'm sure you must understand why we're concerned."

"If you think that I or, come to that, anyone else on the team could have taken it then you're very much mistaken." Martin was making no effort now to hide his annoyance. "We were all cleared to work on the project or don't you trust your own people to do their job properly?"

"People can be fooled," said Daniel calmly, "just as they can give in to temptation under the right circumstances."

"We're scientists, not criminals or terrorists," Martin protested angrily. "I don't know what circumstances you might be referring to, but for us it's the work itself that is important. We're not in it for the money but the pursuit of knowledge. We're trying to do some good in the world."

He paused, realising he was beginning to sound pompous.

"I'm sure that's all very true," Charlie agreed quietly, "but you of all people must be aware that sometimes knowledge itself can be dangerous. Even scientists must have a moral conscience. This project, for example, Operation Sundown, it has the potential to cause a great deal of harm in the wrong hands. Isn't it just possible that someone, perhaps even Pemberton himself, thought it had gone too far, believed it should be stopped?"

The thought had never occurred to Martin and he considered it for a moment.

"You can't stop ideas," he said. "And once a discovery's made, it's out there; you can't just put it back in the box and pretend it didn't happen. My job, our job is to make these discoveries; what people do with them afterwards is not up to us. We can't afford to let ourselves be distracted by how others might use them in the future. That's your job, thank God."

"So Pemberton's death won't stop anything?" Charlie asked.

"I can't deny it won't hold us up," said Martin, "but now we know it can be done we just have to work out how he did it."

"And the notebook?"

"Well obviously that would speed everything up. If it contained all his experiments and findings we could just pick up where he left off but, at the end of the day, we should still be able to replicate his work eventually. It's just going to take a lot longer without him."

He paused and looked at Charlie before continuing.

"You suggested a moment ago that you thought Michael himself might have felt the work should be stopped. Do you really believe that?"

"It's a possibility, isn't it?" said Charlie. "You know better than most what the effect of his work could be. He could have had a crisis of conscience."

"And you think that's why he might have killed himself?"

Martin was unaware of the contents of the letter that had been found gripped in Pemberton's dead hand when he was found. In fact, the news that a letter had been discovered had not even been released.

"We have to consider every possibility," said Charlie. "If it were true it would explain why the notebook is missing. He could have destroyed it himself."

"I don't believe that for a moment," Martin said dismissively. "Michael would never destroy his findings. That wasn't the way his mind worked."

"Really?" Daniel asked. "How did his mind work?"

Martin snorted derisively.

"If you want to know what Michael was really like, you only need to understand one thing about him - his ego. That dominated everything else. He had a brilliant mind and he knew it, but he was going to make damned sure everyone else knew it as well. He couldn't care less how others used his work provided he got the credit and they spelt his name right."

Charlie detected the note of bitterness in Martin's voice.

"If he was the one to make the discovery, that's only fair, isn't it?" he asked mildly.

"That's not how we do things," Martin explained impatiently. "Biochemistry is a collaborative process. Of course, one person might end up making the right breakthrough but that's only because everyone else has worked on it beforehand, eliminating all the wrong possibilities to point the way forward. Michael was never a team player; he didn't see it like that. He didn't mind taking our findings and using them but when it came to sharing his own work he shut up tight like a clam. To tell you the truth, I believe that's why he didn't want to file the daily reports like the rest of us. He said it was all in his head and he didn't want to waste his time recording things, but I think he was just afraid one of us might use his work to get there ahead of him."

"So why kill himself?" Charlie asked.

Martin realised he had spoken hastily and shrugged his shoulders.

"I don't know," he said slowly, starting to regret what he had said. "Why does anyone do that? Perhaps it was something personal. He didn't have any friends, nobody liked him. Even his wives couldn't put up with him after a while. He must have been a lonely old man."

The door opened and Anne came into the room.

"Are you going to be much longer?" she said, looking at Daniel. "Supper's ready and I don't want it to spoil."

Daniel glanced at Charlie and stood up.

"No," he said. "I think we've just about finished. Thank you for your time."

"Is that it?" Martin asked in surprise, getting to his feet.

"For the time being," said Daniel. "I'll let you know if we need to meet again."

Martin was now starting to feel a little embarrassed for having spoken his mind so openly. He knew he had sounded petty and it suddenly occurred to him that he had somehow been manipulated into revealing what he really thought. Recognising how he must have come across, he wanted a chance to redress the balance.

"You know," he said as he escorted Daniel and Charlie to the front door, "despite what you might be thinking, I did admire Michael. He had the sort of mind that you come across perhaps just once in a generation. He might have been a difficult so-and-so to work with but his death is nonetheless a tragedy. I believe he still had a great deal left to offer and his loss will be keenly felt."

"I'm sure," said Daniel. "Enjoy your supper."

Chapter Two

The following day was a Tuesday and, despite it being late September, the air was humid in London as an unexpected heatwave swept over the city. In his small bedsit near Paddington Station, Rick Townsend closed the leather flap over Pemberton's briefcase and slipped the metal clasp into the lock. He didn't have the key, that had gone over the edge of the carpark with Pemberton but it didn't matter: the contents were now safely locked away in his own security box at the bank. He would get rid of the briefcase soon but there was no rush. He wiped the surface down carefully with a cloth and wrapped it in a black bin-bag. Later it would go out with the rest of the rubbish from the house and Townsend was confident it would never be found. He stretched carefully and went over to his bed to lie down. The stress of the last few days was taking its effect on his body and he wanted to be fully rested before his visitor arrived later that afternoon.

Townsend was forty-five years old and for twenty of those years had suffered from systemic lupus. Twenty years ago the condition had not been so well understood and the correct diagnosis had taken a long time, time in which the disease had been able to progress through his immune system. He had gone to work one morning feeling slightly unwell. By midday he thought he was coming down with flu and had gone home. He returned to work three days later hoping to shake it off but had collapsed at his desk in the insurance company where he was an accountant. He was taken to hospital and never returned to his desk again.

The following years had been a living hell. Numerous doctors had given their various opinions on what was wrong with him. Whilst some had been sympathetic and understanding, most had tried to persuade him his illness was psychosomatic and he

43

was suffering from some sort of mental depression; none of them had offered the hope of a cure. Unable to hold down a proper job, he had wasted virtually all the money he had inherited from his family on a fruitless search amongst alternative therapists and private medicine for a remedy until eventually a proper diagnosis was made.

Six years ago, a consultant had carefully explained what was wrong: his body was fighting itself and his immune system had now suffered irreparable damage. It was the first Rick had heard of lupus and he learned the condition was at present incurable. However, he was told with proper medication and a strictly controlled lifestyle he should be able to function, albeit in a limited fashion, almost as well as anyone else for many years. Whilst it had been a relief in some ways to know what was actually wrong, it was still a devastating blow. Rick had become bitter at the unfairness of life but he was not the sort of man to settle for half-measures and so continued to look for some sort of cure. With his financial resources now at an all-time low, he had eventually turned to crime to fund his search.

As an intelligent man with an active mind and without a job, he had had the time to educate himself to an advanced level in computer technology. He had been unexpectedly good at it, discovering a talent he hadn't known he had. Using this ability, he had developed a particular skill in cyber-theft, specialising in hundreds of small direct-debit transfers from the bank accounts of his victims to his own numbered account in Switzerland. He knew most people rarely checked their statements in detail, especially direct-debit deductions which were identified only by numbers. As long as he kept the amounts small, nobody would notice and the money continued to flow in. If anyone should become suspicious, they would never be able to trace the money back to him and, if they stopped the payments, he would simply find someone else to replace them. He had found it surprisingly easy and successful until one day one of his victims had knocked on his door.

The man had introduced himself as Andrew Farquharson and Rick had recognised the name at once. To his surprise, Farquharson had not been angry; in fact, quite the contrary. He had come, he explained, not to seek revenge or justice but to make an offer. He had been impressed by Rick's ability with a computer and had needs of his own for which he did not possess the necessary skills. He suggested a deal. In return for not bringing charges and informing the police about Rick's criminal activities, he asked Rick to hack into various computers and extract the information they held. Rick would be given a substantial payment each time he delivered and no questions were to be asked. That was how it had begun.

It did not take long before Rick realised he was dealing with top secret information, most of it government sourced. He didn't understand much of the content, just enough to know he was involved in some sort of high-level scientific espionage and in too deep to withdraw safely. It wasn't that he had any moral objections to what he was doing but he was scared; he knew the consequences if he was discovered now would be far greater than if he had been caught just for the money he had stolen. Moreover, as he got to know Andrew Farquharson better, he found him more intimidating. He came to realise Farquharson was not just amoral but completely ruthless and Rick was scared he would probably become violent if he refused to continue working for him. That was more frightening to his mind than anything the law could do. In fact, the risk of hacking into the computers had considerably diminished; technology had advanced remarkably over the four years since he had started, and he had now become extremely adept at extracting the information Farquharson wanted without leaving any trace that the data had been accessed. Their arrangement had continued in this fashion until a few months ago and then things had changed.

About the same time as Rick discovered a new treatment for lupus was available at an expensive private clinic in Denmark, Farquharson had told him some particular information he was providing was incomplete. It should all have been in the computer files but for some reason it was not. Whoever was meant to be storing it was obviously holding things back. Farquharson had seemed particularly interested in this missing information; he had told Rick it was essential to get it and had promised him a generous bonus if he agreed to obtain it some other way. Rick desperately need money for the Danish clinic and, anyway, was too frightened of the consequences should he refuse. A deal was struck. It was only a few days later, after Farquharson had explained the details, that Rick learned he had actually signed himself up to murder.

Hacking into computers and stealing information was one thing; killing was something else. It wasn't exactly a matter of conscience for Rick. Over the years, his moral compass had become so skewed by the unfair way life had treated him that the idea of murder didn't particularly trouble him. But the actual physical act of killing someone did. His cyber-crime allowed him to keep a distance from his victims; this was something so close up and personal that he doubted he could do it. He decided to tell Farquharson he couldn't go through with it and that was when it was made clear what would happen to him if he didn't live up to his end of their bargain. Rick had then agreed, of course, but realised it was time for his partnership with Farquharson to come to an end and started to develop a different plan of his own.

There was a light knock at the door and Rick sat up quickly on his bed, looking at his watch as he did so. Farquharson was early. Rick felt his heart begin to beat faster and took a few deep breaths to try and calm himself down. He couldn't afford to show he was nervous; he had to control how this meeting was going to go. He got up and opened the door.

"What happened?" Farquharson demanded abruptly as he pushed past Rick and marched into the bedsit. "Why didn't you follow instructions?"

"Sit down," said Rick, closing the door. "We need to talk."

"Have you got the information?"

"Yes," Rick replied, "but there's a few things we have to discuss first."

"I haven't the time," said Farquharson, "I've got another appointment. We'll sort out what went wrong later. Just give me the papers."

"Make some time," said Rick brusquely, trying to sound more confident than he felt. "That's what we need to talk about."

Farquharson looked at Rick. Something was different about him. He still had the usual nervy edginess he always had when they met but this time there was something else, something he couldn't quite put his finger on. He opened his mouth to speak and then changed his mind. He sat down at the table next to the window, putting his briefcase on the floor beside him.

"Well?" he said. "What is it?"

Rick sat opposite and clasped his hands together apprehensively as he leant forward over the table.

"I have the papers, but they're not here."

"Where are they?"

"Safe."

Farquharson was no fool and immediately grasped what was happening. He leant back in the chair and regarded Rick with an expression of contempt.

"What game are you playing at now?" he asked curtly. "I haven't the time for this. Just get the papers and we'll say no more about it."

"No. I- I want to renegotiate."

Farquharson now recognised what he had not been able to identify before; it was an air of desperation. He immediately realised he needed to be careful if he was to get the notes and paused before speaking again. He wanted a little more time to gauge this new situation.

"Tell me what happened. Why was Pemberton found on the street instead of in the car as we agreed?"

"He saw me before he got in and panicked. I had to improvise."

Townsend had no intention of explaining he had been going to give Pemberton a chance to live in exchange for the briefcase and his notes. He had planned to show him the note and the syringe filled with poison Farquharson had given him to let the scientist know where the real danger was coming from. He would have told him everything but the fool had freaked out. If Pemberton hadn't tried to call the police, he might still be alive and in a position to deal with the threat from Farquharson himself. It was really his own fault that he was dead.

"Does it matter what happened?" Rick continued. "He's dead like you wanted."

"It matters," said Farquharson quietly. "You see, it's not enough that he's dead, it was supposed to look like he committed suicide. It's important there should be no investigation. That was the point of the injection and the letter."

"So, he jumped instead. What's the difference?"

"The difference is the letter," Farquharson explained. "There was no mention of it in the papers."

"Well, I gave it to him before he fell," Rick blurted out and then realised he had said too much and blushed in confusion.

"Really?" said Farquharson. "Why did you do that?"

"I – I just pressed it into his hand as I pushed him over the edge."

Farquharson now knew Townsend was lying. Something had happened in the carpark to ruin his carefully laid plan but he also knew he was not going to get the truth from Rick. Anyway, did it really matter now so long as he had managed to get the briefcase?

"And you definitely got all the notes?"

"Yes, but if you want them we're going to have to make a new deal."

Rick was staring at him intently and Farquharson could sense the nervousness behind the eyes.

"I'm listening," he said. "Go on. What do you want?"

"I've had enough," Rick began, "I want out. There's a new cure for my condition but it's very expensive and means I'll have to go abroad. I've done more than enough for you in the past, now there's a chance for me to lead a normal life away from all this and I want to take it; make a fresh start. You can have the notes, but in return I want enough money for the treatment and to give myself a new identity. Once I've gone I won't be coming back and I don't want you trying to find me."

"How much?"

"Fifty thousand," said Rick.

"I see," said Farquharson calmly, "and what makes you think I would agree to such a sum?"

"The notes," Rick said. "I know they must be more valuable than that. They're not the same as the other stuff I've passed on. They're important and you need them more than you're letting on or you wouldn't have asked me to kill Pemberton to get them. They're no use to me so you can have them but in return that's it – it's over, no more information and I get to start a new life. It's not that much money to a man like you. Overall, I think it's a good offer."

Now it was all in the open, Rick began to relax slightly. He didn't think he was being greedy. He had given it a lot of thought, worked out carefully how much he was likely to need and then rounded it up to what he thought Farquharson would pay. Fifty thousand was a lot of money to someone like himself but he knew Farquharson was rich and was not going to lose out. There were big spenders in the market-place for information and the extra cost would simply be passed on. He was sure Farquharson would still be able to make a good profit. Everyone could be a winner if he agreed. If he had any sense he should jump at it.

But Farquharson was not looking happy. He was staring at the ceiling and appeared to be considering the offer as if undecided.

"I shall need some time to think this over," he said.

"How long?"

"Not long. I'll get back to you soon."

Farquharson stood up. He stooped to pick up his briefcase and took a few steps toward the door before turning round to look at Rick who was still sitting at the table.

"Just one more question," he said.

"Yes?"

"If I'm not going to get any more information from you in the future, if this is to be the end of our little arrangement, what makes you think I won't simply cut my losses and turn you in?"

"You can if you like," said Rick, "but you want those notes. And remember, you're as much involved in Pemberton's death as I am. This buys my silence forever."

"But there's no proof against me," said Farquharson. "It would just be your word against mine."

"Except for the syringe," replied Rick. "I still have it and it's got your fingerprints all over it. I think you might find that a little difficult to explain away. You can get it back with the notes once I get my money."

Farquharson said nothing but stared at Rick a moment longer before turning his back and leaving.

★

Charlie leaned gingerly on the parapet of the carpark and looked tentatively over the edge to the pavement five floors below. He had never had a head for heights and, as he had grown older, the condition had become worse. He felt his sphincter tighten and a slight fluttering in his stomach as the giddiness began and he quickly drew back and looked at Daniel.

"That's a long way down," he said, taking a step away.

"He hit the parapet just below first," said Daniel. "We found blood on the brickwork."

Charlie looked around. The space where Pemberton had parked his car had been taped off and the car taken away but the rest of the level was busy; every other spot had been taken and a few cars were slowly cruising round looking for a space before moving to the floor above. It was mid-afternoon and Charlie realised if he wanted to see what the carpark had been like when Pemberton fell, he would need to come back later that night.

"Is it always this busy?" he asked.

"Most of the time," said Daniel, "but I understand that late at night it can get quite deserted. We've been trying to establish whether any other cars were around when Pemberton went over the edge but, so far, without any success."

"What about CCTV?" asked Charlie, glancing at one of the cameras positioned against a concrete pillar.

"Vandalised," Daniel replied with a shrug. "The place is targeted by car thieves and there comes a point when the management just gives up repairing them. They leave them up as a bit of a deterrent but they haven't been operating for months."

"Pity," said Charlie.

He had asked if they could look at the carpark that afternoon in the hope of getting some inspiration from the scene. He knew that it had already been gone over by the police and had read their report but he still wanted to see the actual place for himself. It was how he had worked in the past. He hadn't known what he expected to find but the police had been treating the matter as a suicide and it was easy to miss something if you weren't looking for it. He turned away and tried to imagine what it must have been like when Pemberton came back for his car. Had he arranged to meet the man who killed him or was he taken by surprise?

"Have the police found his phone yet?" he asked.

"Nothing's turned up so far," said Daniel.

"What time did Pemberton arrive?"

"The ticket we found in his wallet showed he got here at eight fifteen," said Daniel.

"And the time of death?"

"The police got the call just before midnight and the coroner said he could have died up to an hour before that. It's not a busy street at that time of night, so he could have been lying there for a while before he was found."

"So it looks like he was doing something else for a couple of hours before he died.

"Yes," said Daniel. "But so far we haven't been able to find out where he went."

"What about the caller?"

"Nothing on him, I'm afraid. The call was made from a callbox on the corner at the end of the street and he didn't give a name."

"Can I hear the tape?"

"I'll arrange it," said Daniel, "though I don't think it will help. The voice doesn't sound like our killer, more like someone uneducated, frightened."

Charlie grunted. He was a little disappointed; he had hoped there would be something at the scene which might help to tell him more about Pemberton's killer. However careful you were, it was almost impossible not to leave some trace of yourself behind. But this was one of the worst places to look. Concrete was an unforgiving material; the whole area was open to the elements and thousands of people must have passed through the level both before and since Pemberton had died. However, now he had examined the scene, his instinct was starting to tell him something.

"Whoever killed Pemberton," he began, "I don't think they planned to do it here."

Daniel said nothing. He was waiting for Charlie to finish his thought process.

"It's completely the wrong place," Charlie continued. "There's no way he could be sure he wasn't seen or interrupted. Pemberton came to London for a reason, probably to meet someone."

"Could Pemberton have brought whoever he met back here with him and then something happened?"

"It's a possibility," said Charlie. "We know whoever killed him must have planned it carefully in advance. But I'm beginning to think something went wrong with his plan. Perhaps Pemberton realised he was in danger and the killer had to act quickly. I don't think the plan was for him to go off the car-park."

Charlie glanced at the parapet again and gave an involuntary shudder. He paced for a few more minutes around the spot where Pemberton's car had been parked before eventually giving up with a despondent shrug of his shoulders.

"I think we've seen as much as we can for the time being," he said. "I would like to come back later tonight, though, have another look at the place as it was at the time Pemberton was killed."

"No problem," said Daniel.

He began to make his way to the staircase and Charlie followed him, still lost in his own thoughts. As they turned into the stairway, Charlie saw a pile of flattened cardboard boxes stacked neatly against the wall and stopped.

"See that," he said, pointing at the pile. "Someone's been sleeping here at night."

Daniel went over and pulled out some of the pieces, looking to see if there was anything other than the cardboard.

"We might have a witness," he said.

"Possibly," said Charlie, neatly replacing the pieces Daniel had just moved. "We'll check it out when we come back tonight. Street people can be surprisingly territorial and claim particular spots as their own once they've found a good one. The odds are it's the same person who's been using this place each night. I wouldn't be at all surprised if he's here when we come back later. It could be our mystery caller."

Charlie began to brighten up. As sometimes happened with the way he worked, his instinct was telling him something which his mind couldn't properly rationalise. And this case was presenting him with some of the most difficult contradictions he had encountered in his long career. Whilst many in his position would have decided to follow the path of reason and evidence at this point, Charlie had learnt to trust his instincts and was starting to enjoy the challenge.

He was now as sure as he could be that Pemberton had been murdered and that whoever killed him had not intended it to happen in the way it did. That much was logical from the circumstances, but it did not explain the missing phone nor why Pemberton was clasping the note when he fell. If he was right, then that note meant someone had been intending to kill Pemberton and wanted to make it look like a suicide, but Charlie still had the feeling that whoever had done it didn't actually want Pemberton to die.

"Let's get a coffee," he said. "I'd like to go through everything we've found out so far and try to make some sense of it if we can."

Daniel nodded and led the way back down the staircase.

★

Andrew Farquharson was still raging inside when he hailed a taxi to take him to his next appointment in central London. He was not used to being crossed and his meeting with Rick Townsend had been more than a little frustrating. He liked to be the one in control and, with one possible exception, that was how it had been throughout his life. He was now forty-two years old and had already achieved most of what he had set out to do when he left university. A combination of determination and ruthlessness mixed with a modicum of natural talent and an ability to ingratiate himself with others had seen him rise quickly through the ranks of his peers until now he was the editor of '*Looking Forward*', the most prestigious science journal in the UK. He had travelled the world, lived in an expensive detached house in Chelsea and never wanted for female company, the younger the better. He had expensive tastes and indulged them. His position meant he was courted by the notables of the scientific world and that in turn had led to him being sought out by others who had their own, different reasons for wanting to know him.

In the world he inhabited it was second nature to believe that knowledge ought to be shared. Many of his science friends were involved with secret projects and, as the editor of a renowned scientific journal, Farquharson was a respected and trusted member of their circle. It was both inevitable and understandable his friends should want to talk about what they were doing. In the secure, relaxed atmosphere of dinner-parties and private lunches, the elite of the scientific community conversed with him about their work, showing less restraint than perhaps they should have done.

The taxi moved slowly through the traffic that was building up as the rush hour began, and Farquharson started to consider his options. He still wasn't entirely sure whether Townsend had threatened him with exposure. If that should turn out to be the case then he knew how to deal with it. Life had become too comfortable for him to consider changing what he had become. Farquharson had no illusions about himself now, though things had once been very different.

His role in scientific espionage had begun inconspicuously; it hadn't even occurred to him that the gifts and flattery he was getting from Simon Warbeck could be putting him under some sort of obligation. When Simon had casually begun asking him questions about the government research certain scientists were conducting, he couldn't resist the temptation to show off his insider knowledge. He knew the information he was giving was supposed to be secret but Simon was his friend; he trusted him and it had pleased him to show off his intimacy with various important scientists by revealing some of what he had learnt of their work. Over time, the gifts had gradually become more extravagant and the questions a little more probing until one day it finally dawned on him that what he was telling Simon could be dangerous in the wrong hands. By then it was too late.

When he had lightly tried on one occasion over drinks to suggest his lips should remain sealed, the friendly atmosphere had immediately changed. Simon had suddenly became serious and reminded him exactly how generously he had been treated; sharing some of the information he had learnt was a small favour by comparison. After that, the subsequent gifts had become more generous still and the next time Simon had asked him to share some material on the work his scientific friends were doing, the inquiry had been less subtle. Farquharson realised then that his friend was under the impression it had already been paid for. Unwilling to sever his connection with Simon and the lifestyle he was increasingly funding, and even though he had now worked out Simon was probably working for some foreign government, Farquharson continued to supply him with the information asked for. He knew he had already crossed a line and was enjoying the benefits too much to risk losing it all. Farquharson had fallen into the world of scientific espionage so gradually that in retrospect there had never been a specific point when he could acknowledge this was what had happened. However, there was no going back now even had he wanted to.

He sat back in the taxi and looked out of the window at the tall buildings towering over the shoppers below as they drove slowly along Regent Street. Despite the air-conditioning in the taxi, Farquharson broke into a sweat as he considered his situation. It had never occurred to him before that he could find himself in his present position and he realised that he had totally underestimated Rick Townsend. Farquharson didn't like being held to ransom by anyone, least of all an insect like Townsend, but he still needed him. He now appreciated just how dependent on Rick he had become for his supply of information. If Rick were to leave then it could be years before he found another source as good and, without the additional funding Simon supplied, life would be very different. He could easily pay the fifty thousand Rick was asking, but he couldn't afford to let him go. That was the sticking point and the reason why he had wanted time to think. He needed to work out a strategy, to make a counter offer that would somehow keep Rick as his creature.

Rick was now his only source of information. Inevitably, some of the people in the scientific community had eventually begun to feel uncomfortable when, following Simon's instructions, Farquharson had asked for more details about the secret projects they were working on. Nothing had actually been said, there were no accusations, but his contacts became less communicative about what they were doing. It was about this same time that he discovered his bank account was being raided on a regular basis. It was not large sums, but Farquharson had been outraged that anyone should have the audacity to try and get one over on him. Instead of handing the matter over to the police whom he didn't trust and thought would be incompetent anyway, he had decided to deal with the matter in his own fashion.

It had not been easy to discover the identity of the thief. It soon became clear that whoever was behind the electronic transfer of money from his account was highly skilled in the technology required and had been able to cover their tracks efficiently. However, Farquharson knew some of the leading technologists in the field of computers and, by calling in a few favours, he had eventually tracked down Rick Townsend. Farquharson made a few discreet enquiries into the man's background and it then occurred to him that instead of taking the revenge which had been his first thought, he could turn the situation to his own advantage. As sometimes happens, they had met at a time when each was becoming desperate: Townsend needed money and Farquharson needed the information Simon was demanding.

He had paid Rick Townsend a visit and they had come to an arrangement. As editor of a major science journal, there was nothing suspicious about Farquharson e-mailing a wide range of scientists and, using Rick's technological expertise, covertly introducing an undetectable Trojan horse into their computers when they were opened. It was a simple matter then for Rick to use this to break through even the most advanced security measures that had been installed and get at the material stored in their files. For a relatively modest sum he passed the information over to Farquharson who, in turn, passed it on to Simon Warbeck whom he knew would reward him very handsomely. There was no longer any need to ask questions of his contacts in the scientific community; he now knew exactly what they were doing and how their work was progressing. Except for Michael Pemberton. For some reason, Pemberton was not recording his data on the computer.

The taxi came to a halt at some lights and Farquharson made an uncharacteristically impulsive decision. He leant forward and tapped on the glass partition that separated him from the driver.

"I've changed my mind," he said. "I think I'll go straight back to the office."

He gave an address in Soho and sat back in his seat. He was not going to the meeting with Simon; there was no point without the notes. More importantly, he had now made up his mind not to tell Simon about that afternoon's events. He thought he knew what Simon would do and wanted to deal with things in his own way. Thinking of what had happened to Pemberton had been the deciding factor. He had not wanted any part in that and had argued against it from the first when Simon put the idea forward. He did not want to become involved in another similar venture.

When Townsend had hacked into Martin Greave's computer at the Bioprix Institute the year before, the material on bacterial detection it contained had been interesting but, when Farquharson had passed it on, Simon had seemed indifferent. At the time, many countries around the world were involved with similar projects concerned with trying to identify the onset of bacterial warfare; there was nothing new about this particular one. That had changed four months ago when Greaves filed a report recording that Pemberton had discovered how to modify a bacterium's DNA so that it could only exist within a specific temperature range. Simon had shown some interest and asked Farquharson to find out more. However, although Townsend had managed to explore the files of all the Bioprix team's computers, including Pemberton's, there was nothing further to be found on the subject.

Townsend was apologetic but there was nothing he could do about it if the data wasn't there. He suspected Pemberton was either not entering the information or using a different computer to which he had no access, but Farquharson had met Pemberton several times before and knew of his reputation and how he worked. He knew the data had to be recorded somewhere and believed Pemberton was doing it by hand. Since Townsend was unable to help him, he decided to take direct action himself. He arranged to meet Pemberton to discuss an unrelated publishing project he said he had in mind and, as the two of them talked, he casually mentioned that he had heard rumours of a breakthrough.

Pemberton had immediately become furious. He didn't even ask how Farquharson had found out; he believed the only possible explanation was that someone else at the Institute was trying to take the credit for his discovery away from him by leaking the information. He had been outraged and Farquharson had pretended to be sympathetic. It had then been simple to use Pemberton's paranoia to suggest he agree to an exclusive publishing deal in which he would be acknowledged as the author of the work. His discovery was his own individual work; he should get the credit for it and he was entitled to do whatever he liked with it. Pemberton had wanted time to think about it and said he would get back in touch. He had done so just over a fortnight ago when he agreed to an interview in which he would discuss his research.

That was when things had taken an unexpected turn. Simon Warbeck had told him that, unlike the other pieces of information Townsend had obtained, once he had the information it was now essential this particular research should never become available to anyone else. As long as Pemberton remained alive that could not be guaranteed. There was only one solution: Pemberton had to go. Farquharson gave an involuntary shudder as he recalled the conversation. Simon had worked out a plan and later provided Farquharson with the suicide note, the syringe and a phial of the fast-acting poison. All he had to do was arrange a meeting in London with Pemberton, confirm that he had the information with him and get Townsend to do the rest. It had sounded simple as Simon explained it but Farquharson had suspected even then there would probably be problems with Townsend.

The taxi drew up next to the side doorway of a narrow building. The ground floor had been converted into a chic restaurant serving Moroccan food but the floors above were leased as offices to a number of private organisations who used them as a base, including 'Looking Forward', the journal of

59

which Farquharson was chief-editor. He paid the fare and got out. As he watched the taxi pull away from the kerb and join the stream of traffic, he began to think of what he was going to tell Simon.

★

Even though it was not yet five o' clock, Emma Nelson was getting ready to leave the Institute. She had packed up earlier than usual that Tuesday. Her first full day back after the trip to Sweden had been frustrating; Pemberton's death continued to be the main topic of conversation throughout the building and it was distracting. People still gossiped about what had happened, why he might have done it and the effect it would have, but only those actually in the team working on the project with him had understood the full impact his demise was going to leave. Nobody else in the Institute knew the real nature of their work so could not appreciate exactly how devastating the loss was.

Emma had lunched with the rest of the team in the large cafeteria at the top of the building. Despite four days having passed since they had learnt of Pemberton's death, the mood was still sombre. Since Emma had been away when the news broke, this was the first opportunity for them all to meet together and discuss the situation. Martin Greaves had spoken with The Prof that morning to discuss the possible existence of a notebook. Like The Prof, he had not been convinced that even if there was such a thing it would contain the material they wanted. Nonetheless, he had asked Emma about it over lunch and she had been obliged to recount again what she had told The Prof the previous evening. This was the first the others had heard of the notebook and it had been mildly embarrassing. She had never mentioned Pemberton's harassment to anyone before and couldn't help feeling that some of the team might think she had given him some encouragement. She needn't have worried; they were more concerned with the notebook than Pemberton's interest in her.

"Did he ever show it to you again?" asked Edward, a fresh-faced young man who was the newest member of the team.

"No," Emma replied, "and I didn't ask him. It was just that once."

"What makes you so sure it had all his notes in it?" Martin asked. "He told me he didn't want to write everything up until he had finished."

"It was something he said about it making him world famous. He told me it was going to open doors for a much better future."

Emma realised how weak that sounded but she was sure the proud, smug way Pemberton had flicked through the pages in front of her was something he would not have done unless the notes had been complete. The problem was she knew she couldn't say that without appearing slightly ridiculous.

"And you don't think he might have just been showing off?" Martin added, unable to keep a sceptical note out of his voice.

"Of course he was!" Emma answered curtly. "But that doesn't mean it didn't contain all his notes. Look, I've told you everything I know. I think he had completed his research and in my own mind I'm sure he wrote everything down in that book. We ought to be looking for it."

"Well?" asked Edward, looking expectantly at Martin.

Martin took his time before replying.

"I'm not entirely convinced how useful it would be even if we found it," he said at last. "You said yourself you didn't get a proper look and we can't be certain he wrote everything down. As I said, he told me he hadn't. Anyway, it's not in the lab, The Prof and I gave it a thorough search, and I've been through his living quarters. There's nothing there either."

A silence fell around the table.

"Perhaps you should look again," said Emma.

Martin was irritated by Emma's persistence. He recognised the implied criticism of himself in what she had said and now spoke with uncharacteristic sharpness.

"Perhaps you would like to look yourself."

"Perhaps I should," Emma retorted quickly, glaring at him. She didn't like being doubted and was still annoyed at what she considered to be his incompetence.

"I think we're all a bit fraught at the moment," interrupted Adam, another member of the team around the lunch table. Along with the others, he had sensed the sudden tension between his two colleagues. "It's been an upsetting couple of days for everyone and I think we're all feeling a little frustrated at what's happened. Why don't you tell us about your trip, Emma? How was the conference?"

But Emma was not to be put off so easily.

"You know, I'm beginning to think you don't believe me," she said. "I'm not making this up, there is a notebook. I saw it."

"Don't be silly, Emma," said Adam. "Of course we believe you but if Martin says he can't find it there's not much we can do. Perhaps it isn't at the Institute. Michael could have kept it somewhere else."

Emma was silent. She was sure Pemberton would not have let the notebook stray from his sight. He was far too possessive of his research and verging on the paranoid about others getting their hands on what he was doing. If the notebook really was not at the Institute then it was beginning to look as if her initial suspicions might be confirmed but she was not going to mention the incident that had led her to think Pemberton was about to betray them.

She had come across the letter entirely by chance. On the day she was due to leave for the conference in Sweden she had been tidying up her desk when Barbara had brought in that morning's correspondence. It had consisted of the usual invitations to speak, promotions from other pharmaceutical companies and some personal letters from fellow biochemists. She had put the bundle to one side to deal with later and it wasn't until she was about to leave that she decided to sift through it quickly. The opened letter had somehow been caught up by a paper-clip attached to a promotional leaflet at the bottom of the pile and was addressed to Michael Pemberton. She had immediately recognised the logo heading of '*Looking Forward*', one of the country's leading science journals, and her natural curiosity prompted her to read it.

The letter was from Andrew Farquharson, the editor, confirming his meeting with Pemberton for the following Friday evening. It was the final paragraph that had suddenly grabbed her attention:

'*I am sure once we have agreed the terms, the arrangement we previously discussed will be of mutual benefit. An exclusive publication will help to confirm our journal's position as a leader in its field and your already considerable reputation as one of the country's major biochemists will undoubtedly be enhanced.*'

Emma had been surprised. She had not known Pemberton was about to publish anything. Normally, such arrangements had to be approved by The Prof and there was no way he would have permitted making public any of the research they had been involved with. The only fresh discovery she knew of was the one concerned with genetic modification of the bacterium, and even Pemberton was not so naïve as to think he would be allowed to publish that. It had crossed her mind that Pemberton could have resurrected some previous research of his own and developed it ready for publication. That would be typical of the man and just as typical for him not to tell any of his colleagues.

Deciding she would ask The Prof about it on her return from Sweden, she gave the letter back to Barbara as she left the building and explained it had come her way by mistake. She had not thought about it again until her meeting with Daniel Rankin. On learning the notebook was missing, her first thought had been that The Prof had not looked for it properly. But then she remembered the letter and a much more sinister explanation had occurred to her. When she had left to see The Prof that evening, her intention had been to tell him about the letter but the drive to the Institute had given her time to think it over. She was about to make a very serious accusation and had absolutely no proof to support it. The letter, even if she was able to produce it, proved nothing. Farquharson could have been referring to anything; it could have been nothing more than an interview about Pemberton's life's work. To say anything that might destroy a leading scientist's reputation only a few days after his death without anything to back it up could only reflect badly on herself. No one would want to work with her in the future; this could ruin her own career. Anyway, did she really believe that Pemberton was capable of publishing his discovery? He might have been a bit of a bastard, but was he really that stupid? She decided to say nothing about her own suspicions yet and concentrate on finding the notebook. Pemberton would never have let anyone make a copy so if it was found that would probably mean she was wrong and he hadn't passed on any information. The only problem was that no one seemed to be taking her seriously or making any real effort to track it down.

After lunch she had returned to her lab but was still feeling too annoyed to concentrate properly on her work. She eventually gave up and decided to go home early. She was just getting ready to leave when there was a gentle knock on the door. It was Martin Greaves.

"I've come to apologise," he said sheepishly, poking his head around the door. "I think I might have been a bit short with you over lunch."

"Come in," said Emma. "I'm not busy, in fact, I was just thinking about packing up early and going home."

Martin came in and sat on one of the stools alongside the worktop.

"Finding it difficult to concentrate, eh?" he said. "I think we all are a bit. This business has got to everyone."

"Why do you think he did it?" Emma asked.

"Everyone keeps asking me that," said Martin with a grimace. "I'm not sure why they think I should know. Michael kept a lot to himself. How could I tell what was going on inside his head?"

Emma refrained from pointing out that Martin had worked with him the closest and, as team leader, it was part of his job to know what Michael was thinking. Instead, she smiled sympathetically before speaking.

"Did you know he was about to do some sort of publishing deal with *Looking Forward*?"

"Was he?"

Martin was genuinely surprised and momentarily alarmed.

"I think so," Emma said hesitantly.

"Well, that's the first I've heard of it. How do you know?"

"I – I can't remember now," she said, reluctant to admit she had read someone else's private correspondence. "I think probably Michael might have mentioned something about it in passing."

Martin appeared to relax a little. Emma's vague explanation seemed to have satisfied him.

"Does The Prof know?" he asked casually. "He hasn't said anything about it to me."

"I haven't asked. Do you think I should tell him?"

Martin thought for a moment.

"No, that's alright, I'll mention it when I see him next," he said. "It's probably nothing important."

Emma was disappointed. She didn't know exactly what she had expected but had hoped for a more positive response, something that would spur Martin into action. As it was, she had the feeling she was being humoured again. She wasn't even sure whether Martin had believed her and regretted not being more honest about finding the letter. At least that was proof something was going on but it was too late to say anything now. Feeling as annoyed with herself as she was with Martin, she picked up her bag and slung the long strap over her shoulder, glancing at her watch as she did so.

"Well," she said, wanting to leave quickly, "I think I'll be making my way home. It's almost five o'clock and I'm feeling a bit tired. I think that conference took a little more out of me than I thought."

"Yes, of course," said Martin, standing up. "I'm looking forward to hearing about it." He hesitated a moment. "Once again, I'm sorry if I was a bit off today. It's just that with Michael's death I've got so much on. What with The Prof running around like a headless chicken and now the Ministry on my back, I'm feeling a little pressured. Sorry if I was a little abrupt. I didn't mean to be."

"That's alright," said Emma. "We're cool."

She smiled and left Martin still standing by the workbench. As she walked along the corridor, she was thinking about what he had just said. Until that moment she had forgotten there was another group of people who would be interested in finding the notebook. The Ministry would want to know exactly what it contained. She made up her mind. As soon as she got home she would contact Mr Rankin, the man from the Ministry. The Institute had been nothing short of condescending but there was something about Daniel Rankin that made her feel he would take her seriously.

★

Simon Warbeck angrily stabbed the off-button with a nail-bitten finger and threw the cell-phone into a chair. He hadn't believed for one minute the elaborate story Farquharson had just told him. It wasn't only that Farquharson was a bad liar, Simon had thought something like this might happen from the moment he had learned Townsend was involved. He should have taken over running the hacker for himself a long time ago. He would have made sure this sort of situation could never arise. Simon had a deep understanding of human nature and knew precisely how to exact loyalty from those he could use. Farquharson's vanity and taste for young girls had made him an easy target but Simon had played no part in recruiting Rick Townsend; he had not even found out Farquharson was using him until it was too late. He had not trusted Townsend. The enquiries he made revealed nothing he could exploit except the man's need for money and Simon had never believed in trusting those who kept faith only when they were being paid. They were always on the lookout for a better offer.

Now he had another problem that required his attention. He had made promises of his own and because Farquharson had messed up he was not going to be able to fulfil them. He picked up his phone again and quickly entered a number he had memorised a long time ago. The call was answered almost immediately.

"Hello," he said, "it's Simon from Personal Packaging Services."

"Yes?"

"I'm afraid there's been a slight snag. We're going to have to reschedule."

There was a pause on the other end before the man replied.

"Anything serious?"

The man's voice was deep and cultured with the slightest trace of an accent betraying his origins from somewhere in the Middle East.

"No," said Simon, "nothing I can't sort out but there's going to be a slight delay in delivering your package. I'm terribly sorry about this."

"What sort of delay?"

"It's nothing to worry about," said Simon. "There's been a small hiccup at our end but I'm working on it. I'll let you know as soon as I have more news if that's all right."

There was another pause, longer this time.

"Is the package safe?" asked the man at last.

"Yes. It's just a transportation problem."

"This is disappointing," said the man. "I thought I made it clear just how important this is."

"Yes," said Simon quickly, "I understand completely. Unfortunately, one of our couriers was unexpectedly taken ill but I'm going to handle the matter personally from now on. I can assure you everything is in hand. The delivery will be made, it's just going to take a little longer."

There was silence at the other end of the phone and Simon could imagine what the other man was thinking.

"Because of the inconvenience," he continued nervously, "we're prepared to reduce the price by five per cent."

"Very well," said the man. "When can I expect delivery?"

"I'm sorry, I can't give an exact time right now, but I'll get back in touch as soon as I know for sure."

The line went dead as the man hung up and Simon took a deep breath which he let out slowly. He knew he was in trouble. Farquharson was the one he felt was to blame but he would deal with him later. His priority now had to be Rick Townsend.

Simon liked to have a hold over those he used and experience had taught him fear was the most effective means. Simon knew most people had a dark secret somewhere in their lives and he knew fear of that being revealed was always the best means of securing their loyalty. Exposure was the thing they dreaded most. Farquharson's taste for underage girls had been his weak point. However, Townsend had very little to lose and there appeared to be no dirty secrets in his background. He was a loner; his lifestyle was modest and virtually all the money Farquharson paid him was spent on various treatments for his condition. Simon had waited a long time to find a way of binding Townsend closer to him and when it became necessary to get rid of Pemberton that had seemed the ideal opportunity. Involving Townsend in Pemberton's death would compromise him for ever. Whatever other offers he might receive in the future, Townsend would never be able to stop working for him without the fear of being exposed as a murderer. And Simon had the evidence.

He and Townsend had never met. There had been no need and Simon had preferred it that way. Once he had devised the plan for eliminating Pemberton, he had included a small part for himself. Positioning himself on the stairwell outside the level of the carpark where Pemberton had left his car, he had disabled the lift and then waited for Pemberton to return from his meeting with Farquharson. Disguised as a vagrant bedding down for the night, if anybody came up the stairs they wouldn't give him a second glance. He had waited until Pemberton had gone through the doors onto the level and then quietly followed him, keeping well back and concealing himself behind one of the concrete pillars so he could not be seen. From that vantage point he had witnessed everything. At first he was alarmed that things were not going according to his plan. Townsend had not waited for Pemberton to get into the car but had accosted him as he was unlocking the door. Simon had seen the two men talking but was too far away to hear what was being said. He saw Townsend pass Pemberton the letter and, for a moment, thought the man had got cold feet. Perhaps he had misjudged Townsend; perhaps the man wasn't as desperate as he had thought. Then the two men had argued and Simon witnessed Townsend hoist Pemberton onto the ledge and roll him over. Although it hadn't gone exactly as he had wanted, that didn't matter. Pemberton was dead, Townsend had killed him and Simon had the whole thing on a video card.

When Farquharson had called that afternoon, he had said Townsend was having another bad spell from his lupus, one that had completely incapacitated him and some friends had come round to look after him. There had been no way he could meet Townsend privately so the notes could be passed over and, regrettably, there would be a delay of a few days until Townsend had sufficiently recovered. Simon hadn't believed a word of it but said nothing to show he knew Farquharson was lying. Simon could guess exactly what had happened. Townsend had got greedy.

Simon hadn't expected to use the evidence on the video card so soon, but he realised Townsend needed to be brought into line. It was time the two of them met.

★

Daniel was unable to repress a self-satisfied smile as he switched off his phone and looked across at Charlie. They were in Daniel's Hammersmith apartment where Charlie was staying whilst he was in London and were preparing dinner when Emma Nelson had called.

"I rather thought you were hoping she was going to get back to you," said Charlie, picking up a tomato and slicing it carefully on the chopping board.

Daniel blushed slightly.

"What gave me away?" he asked, still smiling. "Was it the fact we've arranged to meet tomorrow for lunch or that famous instinct of yours?"

"Actually," said Charlie, grinning back, "I first suspected something of the sort in the car when you asked for my opinion of her. I thought then you seemed to be showing a little more than just a professional interest."

"Well, you've got to admit she is an attractive woman."

"Yes, she is," Charlie agreed as he picked up another tomato and stood poised for a moment with the knife in the air. He was a little unsure whether it was his place to ask the question that was on his mind. Deciding to go for it, he continued, "but, well forgive me for asking this, but is it quite the done thing to see her socially? I mean, she is still part of an ongoing enquiry."

"She was out of the country when Pemberton died," said Daniel. "Anyway, this isn't social, not really. She said she has some more information she wants to discuss and would prefer it if we didn't meet at the Institute."

"And you suggested lunch," Charlie pointed out.

"I don't think there's any harm in mixing business with a little bit of pleasure," said Daniel. "This job has few enough perks as it is."

"Well, I expect you know what you're doing," said Charlie, not entirely convinced as he returned to slicing tomatoes. He decided he should change the subject. "What time were you wanting to leave tonight?"

They had agreed to return to the carpark that night where they wanted to find the person who had been sleeping on the stairwell. Charlie thought that the vagrant must have seen Pemberton arrive to collect his car and was hoping that he might also have seen whoever else had been there. They might even get a description if they were lucky.

"I thought we should plan to arrive about ten-thirty," said Daniel. "The closer we are to the actual time Pemberton was there, the more likely we are to meet anyone who could have been around when he was killed. We can stay as long as it takes if you don't mind a late night."

"No problem," said Charlie. "I'm used to them."

As it was, the traffic was light that night and they arrived early. Daniel drove straight to the fifth level to park and the two of them made their way to the stairwell. Sometime over the weekend, it had been hosed down and a faint smell of disinfectant hit them as they pushed open the double doors. The landing was deserted. The cardboard was still stacked against the wall just as Daniel had left it that afternoon and there was no sign of anyone having been there. Charlie couldn't help feeling a little disappointed.

"It's still early," said Daniel. "Let's have a look around."

He started down the stairs and Charlie followed. The stairwell was not well lit. Several of the neon lights on the way down were not working and one or two of them were flickering sporadically. It was eerily silent and it wasn't until they reached the second floor that they saw a huddled figure sprawled on several layers of cardboard with his back against the wall. The man looked up as he heard them and stretched out an open hand.

"Spare a pound fer a cup of tea, mate?" he asked.

He was wearing a pair of dirty jeans and a stained padded anorak, the hood pulled up loosely over his head. Under the hood they could see he had a woollen bobble-hat that was drawn down to his bushy eyebrows, covering his forehead completely. Several locks of greasy, unkempt hair poked out from under the hat and disappeared into the upturned collar. He looked to be in his late fifties and had a straggly black beard that was streaked with white.

"Sure," said Daniel and reached into his pocket to take out some change. He found a pound coin and dropped it into the man's open palm.

"Ta mate," said the man, hastily secreting the coin in an inside pocket of the anorak. "God bless yer."

"Are you here every night?" Daniel asked.

"Why?" said the man, instantly suspicious.

"Actually, we're looking for someone," said Daniel. "I thought perhaps you might be able to help."

"Who are yer?" the man demanded warily. "Yer not a bleedin' copper, are yer?"

"No, not exactly," said Daniel.

"I got every right to be 'ere," the man said. "I'm not causin' no trouble. Yer can't move me on."

"We weren't going to," said Charlie. "We just wanted to ask a few questions if that's alright."

"The management knows I'm 'ere," the man continued, ignoring Charlie and speaking to Daniel. "They don' min', you can ask 'em if yer want."

"Nobody's going to move you on, or any of the others who spend the night here. There are others, aren't there?" Charlie asked.

"Has that geezer been back then, makin' more bleedin' trouble?" the man said, pulling the anorak hood further down over his face.

"What geezer?"

The man hesitated a moment before speaking.

"No one."

Daniel crouched down so he was level with the man's face and gave a reassuring smile.

"What geezer?" he repeated gently.

The man said nothing and turned his head away so he was facing the corner.

"Was someone causing trouble here?" Daniel asked. "Was it last Friday? Four nights ago?"

The man quickly turned back to face Daniel and stared at him, his eyes suddenly wide with apprehension. Now he was close to the man, Daniel caught the stench of stale sweat and soiled clothes mixed with the smell of alcohol.

"Is 'e come back, then?" the man asked again, obviously worried.

"No," Daniel replied quietly. "There's nobody here but us. What did he do?"

The man turned away again and Daniel stood up and reached into his pocket. He drew out several pound coins and knelt down, offering the money in his outstretched hand. The man turned back nervously and slowly held out his own hand. Daniel dropped the coins into the open palm and the man quickly pushed them into the inside pocket of his anorak.

"What did this geezer do?" Daniel repeated.

"'E 'ad no right," the man said. "'E said 'e was management but 'e's a bleedin' liar. They knows I'm 'ere. They don' min'."

"Did he threaten you?" Daniel asked. "What did he say?"

"'E said I had ter go."

"What was he like, this geezer?"

"'E was one of them suits."

"I mean, what did he look like?"

"I dunno, they all looks the bleedin' same."

"And he said you had to leave?" Daniel paused and the man nodded. "Is that all he did?"

"'E took my bleedin' bed. Tha's what 'e did."

"Your bed?"

"I got a new one now." The man patted the flattened cardboard he was sitting on. "'E said I had ter go, but I got the better of that little bleeder. I got my rights just like anyone else."

"What did you do?" Daniel asked.

The man opened his mouth and appeared to be gasping. It was a moment before Daniel realised he was laughing.

"I ain't got nowhere else ter go, 'ave I, so when 'e left I comes back in. I was jus' waitin' roun' the corner, like, till 'e's gone."

"So you were outside? On the street?"

"And then I jus' comes back in again. 'E never knew bleedin' nowt."

Charlie crouched down beside Daniel.

"And this happened last Friday?" he asked.

"I dunno," the man said, shaking his head. "It was the same night that other geezer copped it."

"You were here when that happened?" Charlie asked.

"Nah, like I says, 'e turfed me out. I saw it though."

"You saw it?" Charlie repeated. He was starting to feel a little excited at the prospect of finding a witness. "What happened?"

The man looked confused for a moment.

"Well, 'e fell, didn't 'e?"

"You saw him fall?"

"Tha's what I said."

"Did you see anyone else?"

"Nah, he was the only one."

Charlie's knees were aching from crouching down and he stood up. He was sure this man could tell them more but getting the information was painfully frustrating. Daniel leant forward slightly.

"Could he have been pushed?" he asked slowly.

"I dunno, does I?" said the man.

"What did you do?" asked Charlie.

The man looked up at him suspiciously.

"I never bleedin' touched him, if tha's what you mean," he said.

Something about the way he said it made Charlie think he was covering something up. He crouched down again.

"Nobody's saying you did," he said. "But I expect you went over to have a look, check to see if he was still alive."

"I called the cops," said the man, avoiding Charlie's eyes.

"That's good," said Charlie. "That was the right thing to do. But I thought you said you came straight back in after the other man left."

The vagrant looked confused for a moment.

"I meant after the cops had gone," he said.

"So the other man had gone before the police arrived? The one who tried to move you on?"

The man nodded hesitantly.

"And you were still outside with the man who fell until the police came?"

"Why are you askin' all these bleedin' questions?" the man said nervously. "I ain't done nothin' wrong."

"I'm sure you haven't," said Charlie calmly. "It's just that we knew the dead man, you see, and we really want to know exactly what happened. That's why we're here now."

"I told you all I bleedin' knows. I don' know nothin' more."

Charlie ignored the protest and continued in the same calm voice.

"He had some things with him that night, things we would like to get back if we could but they're missing."

The man's hand went involuntarily to the pocket of his anorak. Charlie noted the movement.

"There's actually a reward for them," he continued. "There was a notebook and his phone. We want -"

"I don't know nothin' 'bout no bleedin' notebook," interrupted the man quickly.

"But you found a phone?" Charlie suggested hopefully.

The man was silent for a long moment.

"You said there's a reward?" he asked at last.

"Twenty pounds."

The man was silent again. He pushed the anorak hood back from his face and reached into the side pocket. When he pulled out his hand it was gripping a cell phone.

"I found this," he said. "It were just lyin' in the street outside." He hesitantly held up the phone for Daniel to see. "Is this what yer lookin' for?"

"It could be," said Daniel, reaching for the phone. "May I see?"

The man quickly snatched it away.

"Twenty quid, you said."

Without a word, Charlie stood up, reached into his pocket and withdrew his wallet. Taking out a twenty pound note, he passed the money to Daniel and put his wallet away. Daniel held out the money in one hand and opened the other to receive the

75

phone. The man hesitated a moment and then snatched the note from Daniel as he dropped the phone into Daniel's open palm. Daniel stood up and looked at the phone. There was a large crack across the screen. He tried to switch it on but nothing happened. He tried again.

"It ain't workin'," the man said, stuffing the note hurriedly into the inside pocket of his anorak, "it's broke."

"Was it like this when you found it?" Daniel asked.

"You didn't say you wanted it workin'," the man said quickly and pulled the anorak tighter around himself. "We done our deal."

Daniel slid the back of the phone down and checked inside.

"It's alright," he said to Charlie, "the sims is still intact."

Charlie was not sure exactly what difference that made but was reassured by Daniel's confidence. He turned back to the man sprawled on the floor of the stairwell.

"Someone else sleeps here at night," he said. "There's more cardboard on the fifth floor. Do you know who that is? Will he be back again tonight?"

"There's no one 'ere but me," the man said quickly. "This is my patch and the management don' mind. They knows me."

"Are you sure you're the only one here?" Charlie asked.

The man looked at him suspiciously.

"You callin' me a liar?" he said. "What you askin' all these bleedin' questions for, anyway? I told you all I knows. Tha's it. Jus' leave me alone now, will yer. I gotta get me rest."

As if to emphasise the point, the man pulled the anorak hood back down over his face. He leant back against the wall, shoving his hands deep into his pockets and turned away. Daniel looked at Charlie and shook his head.

"I think we might as well go," he said. "We've got the phone and I don't think we're going to find out any more tonight." He turned back to the man. "Thanks, you've been a great help."

The man looked up and nodded. Daniel turned and started up the stairs. Charlie was about to join him when he stopped and crouched down to speak to the man again.

"You've got some money now," he said gently. "You don't have to stay here tonight. You could find a hostel with a proper bed."

"What does I want with a bleedin' proper bed?" said the man gruffly and turned away to face the wall.

Charlie got to his feet and followed Daniel up the stairs.

★

They didn't go straight back to the apartment. Daniel first wanted to check out the cell phone and needed the specialist equipment and help to be found in one of the many departments of MI6. Although most people nowadays recognise the imposing façade of the modern building overlooking the Thames as the headquarters for the Secret Service, much of the hands-on work is actually carried out in a number of discreet buildings dotted throughout London. The one Daniel made for had originally been a merchant's house, built in the early nineteenth century from the profits of the East India Company and now totally refurbished inside and modernised to accommodate the equipment and staff of sixteen technicians who worked on communications. Although Daniel had some expertise in the field, he was no match for the young man who greeted them at the door.

"Evening, Robert," said Daniel as he and Charlie were ushered into a small room off the main hallway. "I've got something I would like you to look at now, if that's alright."

Daniel was senior enough to tell the young man to drop whatever else he was doing and deal with the phone but it was enough that he was there in person for the young man to realise there was an element of urgency behind the request.

"Yes, sir, of course," Robert said. "What is it?"

"Nothing difficult," said Daniel, producing the phone and passing it over. "I need to know the numbers called and received, dates and times along with names. The usual stuff. The phone's not working and I can't get the directory but I think the card itself should be OK."

Robert took the back off the phone and briefly examined the sim card.

"Looks alright," he said. "Let's give it a try. How far back do you need to go?"

"We'll start with the last three months and take it from there," said Daniel.

Robert went over to the bench that ran along the length of one of the walls and picked up a thin black metal box about six inches square. It was connected by two black wires to one of the computers on the work bench. He lifted the hinged lid and inserted the sim card into a wide groove on the inside. Closing the box, he placed it back on the bench and sat down in front of the computer. Daniel walked over to stand behind him and look at the screen.

"Won't be a moment," said Robert, quickly typing on the keyboard and pressing the enter key.

Almost immediately, the screen showed a series of columns and then each column began to fill with numbers. After about fifteen seconds it stopped and the cursor flashed silently at the bottom. Robert pressed a key and behind them a printer sprang into action.

"I've got what there is," said Robert, "but it's not three months, this only goes back about seven weeks." He looked at the screen. "Whoever it is only started using the phone a short time ago. Sorry about that."

"Never mind," said Daniel. "What about the names?"

"Coming up," said Robert, typing at the keyboard again.

The screen cleared and remained blank for a few seconds before a list of names began to appear alongside each telephone number. It was a short list, less than a screen's worth. Robert pressed another key and the machine behind them printed it off. Robert went over to collect the four sheets of paper and quickly shuffled them together before handing them to Daniel.

"Are you done already?" Charlie asked in surprise, not quite able to take in the speed at which everything had been accomplished.

"Unless there's anything else," said Robert.

"No, that's it for the time being," said Daniel, briefly looking through the papers. "Thanks, Robert."

He was impatient to get back to his apartment now and study the print-outs. When they had discussed possible scenarios that afternoon, both Charlie and Daniel had agreed it was probable Pemberton had known his attacker. If they were right, then more than likely that person's name was on the list he was holding. However, the first thing Daniel did when they returned was to pour himself and Charlie a generous glass of malt whisky each. Shortly after giving up smoking, Daniel had been introduced to Laphroaig by a colleague and had treated himself to the mellow, smoky flavour from the Isle of Islay by way of compensation ever since. Charlie shared his friend's taste for the amber liquid and gratefully took the proffered glass.

"How do you want to do this?" he asked as he settled himself into one of the comfy armchairs by the unlit gas-fire.

"You look through the call sheets, see if there are any long calls, how many times the same number comes up, things like that. See if here are any patterns. It'll give us an idea who was in regular touch. I want to go through the names. I know more about his circle than you do and I can check them against what I already know, see if anything unusual stands out."

He passed three of the sheets to Charlie, keeping the one with the names for himself and settled back into the opposite chair. Less than fifteen seconds had passed before he suddenly sat bolt upright.

"That can't be right!" he exclaimed under his breath.

"What's up?" asked Charlie.

He had barely started making a count of the numbers on his first sheet and Daniel's reaction had startled him. Daniel said nothing but just looked at the paper he was holding. He got up and went to the desk in the corner of the room and switched on his computer. Charlie watched him in silence for a few moments.

"Found something?" he asked.

"Yes," said Daniel as he started typing quickly on the keyboard, "I think I have. I need to be sure though. Just hang on a moment."

Charlie waited patiently for his friend to finish what he was doing. It took several minutes before Daniel finally looked up from the screen and let out a low whistle. He stood up, walked back to the armchair and sat down before speaking.

"I was right," he said. "It's just one call and lasted for less than a minute, but there's a name on this list that shouldn't be there: Husam al din."

"Sounds Arabic," said Charlie.

"It is, it means 'sword of the faith', but it's an alias. His real name is actually Yusuf al Shamar - and he's an agent."

"Wouldn't you know if Pemberton was in touch with one of your agents?"

"He's not one of ours," Daniel replied slowly, "he's one of theirs!"

Chapter Three

Yusuf al Shamar sat on top of a hillside in northern Syria and watched the sun rise over the distant mountain ridge. This was his favourite time of the day; it made him think how Allah cherished and sustained the world. Yusuf thought each dawn held a promise, taking away the darkness and serving as a reminder of the guarantee that Paradise was waiting for the faithful. He watched the light slowly seep across the valley in front of him until the mountains ceased to be silhouettes and were bathed in the golden glow of a fresh new morning. He stood up and smoothed down the long dishdash he was wearing. The loose tunic was more comfortable than the western clothes he usually wore and kept him cool; and it was going to be a hot day.

Yusuf was thirty-two years old. Although handsome and highly intelligent, he had never married; he already had one commitment that over-rode everything else in his life. Besides, he was always travelling and a wife and family would be an additional responsibility he could do without. He wanted no distractions. He turned and walked back down the hillside to the cave where his companions were preparing a meal. They had been hiding out in the hills for a week, meeting various tribal chiefs, making plans and waiting. This was the day he expected to hear from London and then the waiting would be over. It had been a long time coming.

He had been just six years old when both his parents were killed at Al Fallujah, a city about forty miles west of Baghdad. They had been the innocent victims of a disastrous bombing raid by the British RAF who were attempting to destroy several of the city's bridges across the River Euphrates. As part of the Gulf War, Operation Granby's mission was meant to destroy the support of Iraqi forces but this particular raid had gone very wrong. Instead of hitting the bridges, the laser-guided weaponry had failed. On

February 14th 1991, a missile hit a nearby residential area, killing up to one hundred and thirty civilians. As friends and relatives, including Yusuf and his parents, had rushed to the scene to help the injured, the British warplanes had returned to bomb them as well. His mother and father had been blown apart in front of him and Yusuf's mind was suddenly as scarred as his body which had been torn open by shrapnel.

Living on the streets, left alone in the world with his wounds festering, he had eventually been found by the British Red Cross who looked after him and began to treat his injuries. He had been lucky to survive at all. The muscles of his right leg had been badly ripped and he was always going to have a limp, a permanent reminder of that day in Al Fallujah. When the Red Cross returned to Britain, Yusuf went with them to undergo plastic surgery at a London hospital. As the months passed, he formed a strong bond with one of the Muslim surgeons who was treating him and, having no reason now to return to Iraq, when the physical scars had healed he remained in London as the adopted son of the surgeon. He had been a reserved child, attending local schools where his Arab origins, his limp and his resentment of all things British had alienated him from the other pupils, but life on the streets of Al Fallujah had hardened him and he knew how to deal with the bullying. However, it meant his childhood was isolated and he began to find solace in the only place he could: his religion. With his adopted father's blessing, he had attended the Finsbury Park Mosque and there he found the company he craved. They accepted him for who he was. He no longer felt a stranger in a strange land and very quickly started to come under the influence of his new-found friends and one man in particular. That was the beginning of the long journey which had led him to this Syrian hillside on a bright, clear September morning.

As he approached the entrance to the cave, Yusuf saw his two companions crouched down over a small fire on which a pot of something was simmering. They were both younger than him but more experienced in the ways of hiding out in the hills. All three men were dressed as simple local shepherds and a small flock of goats was penned in nearby, pulling at the stubby grass which grew haphazardly on the rocky slopes. Yusuf raised his hand in greeting and walked over to join them.

Habab and Shiraz al-Assad were brothers. Born in Tunisia and in their late teens at the start of the Arab Spring, they had both played an active part in the movement that swept across the Arab world in 2010. Quickly identified by the authorities as political agitators, they fled to Turkey where they met other insurgents who had made a base for themselves in the Nur Mountains south of the country. This group established themselves close to the Belen Pass which allowed them easy access into Syria and, in the political unrest that followed the Arab Spring, they gradually increased in number. It was almost inevitable given the unsettled conditions that, desperate for leadership of some sort and needing a common purpose, this band of mixed refugees should eventually come under the influence of Islamic State and share its ambition to establish a new caliphate in the Middle East. That was how the brothers had first come into contact with Yusuf.

"What's in the pot?" asked Yusuf as he settled himself down on a small boulder, stretching his right leg in front of him. He thought he knew the answer.

"Stew," replied Habab with an apologetic grin. "It's the last of it."

"Good," said Yusuf, though he had hoped it was something different. They had been eating goat stew for the last three days.

"You said we would be leaving this morning," explained Shiraz. "We can't take it with us and there's no point in wasting good food."

Yusuf nodded. There was not long to wait. His friends had said they would be there at first light and then, after the drive into Aleppo, he would be able to eat properly again. He was hoping they would bring the news that meant he could return to England and put in place the operation he had been planning for the last six months. Everything should be ready by now; all he had needed was the last piece of the jigsaw to fall into place and the revenge he had nurtured since he was six years old would finally come to fruition.

They were just finishing the stew, mopping up the juices with flat bread, when they saw the dust blown up by two jeeps in the distance. It took another twenty minutes for the vehicles to cover the rough terrain and arrive at the bottom of the hill where Yusuf and the two brothers were waiting for them. As soon as the jeeps drew to a halt, two men jumped out and ran over to embrace Yusuf. He returned their greeting and then, still holding one of the men at arm's length, looked anxiously into his eyes.

"Have you heard from London?" he asked.

"Yes," the man said, "I am to tell you that the peacock is dead and the eggs are presumed lost."

He didn't know what the message meant but Yusuf did. However, even though he had understood it, Yusuf didn't want to believe it. He had thought to hear confirmation that everything was in place; this news was completely unexpected and could put all his plans into disarray. He needed to fly back to London as soon as possible. He needed more information.

"How long to get to Aleppo?" he asked.

"About four hours," the man said.

"Have something to eat and drink and then we can set off," said Yusuf.

He turned and walked away, dragging his right leg slightly. He wanted to think and for that he needed to be alone. He silently cursed at the lack of sufficient information. He was impatient to know more, to find out what had happened, but, like all the agents in IS, had long ago concluded the safest way of communication was not only coded but more importantly should always be by word of mouth. Everyone now knew that technology could not only eavesdrop but also locate. In the past, several important figures had been killed or taken because they had used their computers or phones; he was not going to make the same mistake. Irksome though it was, he would have to wait.

★

Rick Townsend was still fast asleep when the doorbell rang. He usually got up late, preferring to work on his computer and watch the free-view channels on television into the early hours rather than go to bed. For a moment he considered staying where he was; if it was important, the visitor would come back later, and if it wasn't then it would be annoying to get up and answer the door for nothing. The bell rang again, this time for longer, and Rick realised the caller was not going to go away. He glanced at the clock on the bedside table and saw it was ten-thirty. He swept the duvet to one side and swung his legs over the edge of the bed. The doorbell rang again.

"Alright," he shouted irritably. "I'm coming. Give me a moment."

His dressing gown was draped over a chair and he picked it up, shrugging his arms into the sleeves as he made his way into the hallway. He stopped at the door and put his eye to the spy-hole. He didn't recognise the man on the other side so, leaving the security chain in place, he opened the door a few inches and looked through the gap.

"Yes," he said, "what is it?"

"Mr Townsend?" said the man, a little surprised to see Rick was still in his pyjamas. "Sorry if I've disturbed you. I'm Simon Warbeck, a colleague of Andrew Farquharson. Perhaps he has mentioned me?"

Rick shook his head.

"No," he said. "He hasn't. What do you want?"

"Could I come in?" asked Simon with a polite smile. "I was hoping we could discuss your last business arrangement with Andrew."

Rick was suddenly apprehensive. He knew Farquharson had been annoyed and it crossed his mind that once the door was opened, this man might not prove as friendly as he seemed to be at that moment. Rick didn't want to let him into the bedsit.

"I'm not dressed," he said. "Can't it wait?"

"I really would like to speak to you now," said Simon. "I'm sure you'll be interested in what I have to say."

Rick paused. If Farquharson had sent this man then he was not going to go away. Rick knew he would have to deal with the situation sooner or later but he was damned if he was going to see the stranger alone in his flat. He wanted some time to work out what to do.

"There's a café just down the road, next to the newsagent," he said. "Give me half an hour and I'll meet you there."

"OK," Simon agreed. "Half an hour and I'll treat you to breakfast."

He turned and walked away. As Rick closed the door, he leant his back against it and let out a long breath. He felt his heart pounding in his chest and realised he was sweating slightly. All his confidence of the day before had suddenly evaporated and he wondered, not for the first time, whether he had been foolish in trying to out-manoeuvre the publisher. There was still time for him to back down; he could contact Farquharson now and agree to their original deal but dismissed the idea almost immediately. This was his chance to break free of the man forever; a chance to get the new treatment; a chance of a new life. And he still had the upper hand: Farquharson couldn't get the notes without him. The thought began to calm him down. Perhaps he was jumping to the wrong conclusions. Perhaps this man had come with the extra money he had demanded. Perhaps it was all going exactly as he had planned. He needed to be sure and, anyway, nothing bad was likely to happen to him in the café. He went back into his bedroom and started to get dressed.

Simon found an empty table at the back of the café and sat down, carefully placing the envelope he had brought with him on the table-top and laying one hand across it. He was feeling relaxed. He had been in similar situations before and knew the sort of thing he could expect. It made no difference to him that they were in a café, in fact, it served his purpose better. Townsend was going to be scared and angry but being in a public place would help to make him more amenable.

Simon didn't have to wait long for Rick to arrive. He gave a friendly wave as soon as he saw him come in and Rick moved quickly through the tables and joined him.

"I haven't ordered," said Simon pleasantly as Rick sat opposite, "I told the waitress I was waiting for someone."

He raised his hand to attract the waitress' attention and she came to the table, pulling out her notebook from an apron pocket.

"I'm not eating," Simon said, "but feel free. This is on me. I'll just have a cappuccino, please."

"The same," said Rick, glancing at the waitress. "I'm not hungry."

The waitress looked disappointed as she wrote down the order and sauntered back to the counter.

There was a moment of silence between the two men before Rick spoke.

"Well?" he said.

"Before we begin," said Simon quietly, "I should like to say how much I admire free enterprise. It's how I got to where I am today, so I can understand that in the market for information you would want the highest price for what you have to sell."

Rick nodded.

"I am assuming, of course, that you have already found another buyer," Simon continued. "May I ask who it is?"

Rick was confused. It had simply not occurred to him that he could pass the notebooks on to someone who would give him a better deal. He had only ever dealt with Farquharson and had never thought of trying to find someone else who might want the information he had been providing. But this was not the moment to admit it.

"That's my business," he said nervously.

"Of course," Simon said. "Forgive me, I was merely curious."

However, he had registered the surprise in Rick's eyes at the question and was relieved. There was no one else; he was sure of it now. That made the meeting less complicated.

"Everything has a price," he continued, "and usually that's what someone is prepared to pay. I must admit, I thought Andrew's offer was fair but obviously I was wrong. So, I am here to suggest a new arrangement."

Rick was immediately cautious. He had not been expecting a counter-offer. However, it looked like the man was here to negotiate not to threaten.

"Let's hear it, then," he said warily.

Simon pushed the envelope across the table toward Rick.

"What's this?" Rick asked.

"Open it."

The envelope was not sealed; Rick lifted the flap and pulled out half a dozen photographs. He looked at the first one and felt a sudden stab of panic. The photograph was grainy and not of good quality but he immediately recognised himself talking to Pemberton in the carpark. He looked at the next one which showed him lifting Pemberton onto the ledge. He put the photographs down without looking at any more of them and stared at Simon. He was suddenly finding it hard to breathe.

"I'm sorry about the quality," Simon said casually as if he was talking about the weather. "They are stills from a video I have in my possession and it's difficult to get good prints. However, I'm sure you'll agree that they are more than adequate. You are easily recognisable, as is Pemberton, of course."

"How – how did you get these?" Rick stuttered breathlessly.

"Like you just said, that's my business. You can keep them if you want, I have more. They make an interesting souvenir of a memorable night, don't they?" Simon smiled. "Perhaps you could get them framed."

Rick said nothing. He clenched and unclenched his fists. He was starting to feel light-headed. Simon swept the photographs back into the envelope and slid it across to Rick. The waitress came over with their cappuccinos and put them on the table.

"Anything else?" she asked.

"No thank you," replied Simon with a smile. "I think that's everything."

The waitress walked away and Rick pushed his cup to one side.

"What do you want?" he asked.

"A new deal," said Simon. "I'm sure you'll agree this changes things."

"Yes."

Rick was barely audible. His mind was in a turmoil.

"Then let's get down to business," Simon continued. "Andrew has been working for me but now he has become expendable. I don't think we need to bother with him again. From now on, I think it better if we cut out the middleman; keep things simple. We should deal directly with each other and the first thing I want are the notes you took from Pemberton. Where are they?"

Now he had Rick where he wanted him, Simon had become no-nonsense and brusque; there was a harsh edge to his voice. Rick was silent. He was staring straight ahead. A cold fear was beginning to flow through his veins.

"Come on," demanded Simon impatiently, "I haven't got all day."

"I – I put them in a safety deposit box at the bank," Rick whispered hoarsely.

"Then we'll need to get them. Is your bank nearby?"

"Yes."

"Good. Finish your drink and we'll go now."

Rick didn't move. He looked up at Simon. He was cowed but not quite beaten yet.

"What's in it for me?" he asked nervously.

"I should have thought that was obvious," Simon said confidently. "You enjoy your freedom, don't you?"

Rick said nothing. He kept staring at Simon, still not quite able to comprehend what was happening. It had all been so quick. Simon seemed to relent a little.

"OK," he said, "I can appreciate you – uh - went to a lot of trouble to get the notes. I'm a fair man. To mark the start of our new business arrangement, I'm prepared to let you have what you originally agreed with Andrew. I think that's a pretty generous offer all things considered."

Rick paused for only a moment before nodding slowly. He knew he was in no position to do anything else. He pushed his chair back and stood up.

"Aren't you going to finish your cappuccino?" Simon asked.

Rick said nothing but turned and made his way out of the café. Smiling to himself, Simon took a five pound note out of his wallet and dropped it onto the table. He stood and picked up the envelope containing the photographs, stuffing it into his pocket. Still smiling, he gave a cheerful wave to the waitress before quickly following Rick through the door onto the street.

★

Daniel decided to park in Churchill Square and make his way by foot to the restaurant near the seafront of Brighton. He was early and so took his time, dawdling to look in some of the shops that lined the streets. The unexpected heatwave of the previous few days had passed and the sky was now overcast. An annoying drizzle fell, too light for an umbrella but thick enough to be uncomfortably damp. Daniel turned up the collar of his raincoat as he snaked his way between the tourists and shoppers who were crowding the pavement. He was looking forward to meeting Emma Nelson again. She had made more of an impression on him than he had been prepared to admit to Charlie. It wasn't just that she was an attractive woman with her blonde hair and cornflower blue eyes, he had been struck by her forthrightness. Charlie had called her blunt but he preferred to think of it as honest and found it appealing. Daniel had no time for people who danced around the edge of expressing an opinion; he liked to know what they were really thinking. And she was highly intelligent, no doubt about that. He understood enough about the science community to know women faced an uphill struggle to get where she was. Ambition and determination could be an attractive mix in a woman if they were in the correct proportion and Emma Nelson seemed to have got it just about right.

He saw the restaurant further along the street and glanced at his watch. He was still early but didn't want to hang about in the drizzle any longer than necessary. Turning his collar down, he pushed open the glass door and went in. Emma was already there. She had been watching the entrance and raised an arm in greeting as soon as she saw him.

"Hello, Dr Nelson," Daniel said as he reached the table. "Good to see you again."

"Emma," she said. "You can't keep calling me Dr Nelson if we're going to have lunch together. Are you Dan or Daniel?"

"Daniel," he replied, feeling a little self-conscious. "Am I late?"

"I managed to get away early," she said, with a friendly smile. "Thank you for coming down."

Daniel returned the smile as he took off his coat and draped it over a chair. She was wearing a pale blue cashmere polo-neck and an opalescent glass pendant hung from a thin leather thong around her neck. It occurred to Daniel this was not work wear and she must have changed before leaving the Institute. He knew it was silly, but it pleased him to think she had made an effort to look good for their meeting.

"It's no problem," he said as he sat opposite. "I had some things to do in the area anyway."

That was not true but he didn't want to give the impression he had gone to any trouble to see her again.

"Well, I hope I haven't brought you down here on a wild goose chase."

"I'm sure you haven't," said Daniel with a reassuring smile. "Why did you ask me down?"

"I'm sorry I had to push you out the house the other day," Emma began, "but when you told me Michael's notebook was missing it was really important that I saw The Prof as soon as possible."

"That's alright, I quite understand."

91

"In fact, that's partly why I wanted to speak to you again."
She paused and frowned.

"This is a little awkward," she continued. "I don't want to seem disloyal to my colleagues at the Institute but I'm not certain they're taking this very seriously. Nobody's making any real effort to look for the notebook. I'm sure they believe it exists but I don't think they believe it contained his notes on Operation Sundown."

She paused again to see how Daniel was reacting.

"What makes you so sure it did?" Daniel asked. "You said you hadn't seen it properly."

"I didn't need to; it was the way Michael showed it to me," Emma continued, leaning forward confidentially, "as if he was trying to get me to ask about it. I know that probably doesn't sound very convincing, you had to be there to see it. But that's not all; it was also what he said at the time. I didn't mention it before, but when he showed me the book he quoted Oppenheimer. When they split the atom and realised what sort of weapons they could create, Oppenheimer said, 'Now I am become death, the destroyer of worlds'. It was obvious Michael was referring to what was in the notebook, but why should he say something like that unless it contained his work on the genome?"

Emma had now become quite animated and Daniel raised his hand to stop her.

"It's OK, I believe you," he said with a grin. "You don't have to persuade me. I'm on your side."

Emma smiled back and relaxed slightly.

"I'm sorry," she said. "It's just that up till now it feels like I've been banging my head against a brick wall. The people at the Institute aren't taking it seriously. They seem to think Michael was just trying to impress me, showing off or playing some sort of a joke. I don't believe they think the notebook is important."

At that moment the waiter arrived at the table to take their order. They quickly made their selection and, as soon as the waiter had moved away, picked up their conversation again.

"There's something else you should know," Emma began. "Michael was about to enter a publishing deal with '*Looking Forward*'. When I told Martin Greaves, he's the Deputy Director, he said the Institute didn't know anything about it. But we're not supposed to publish anything without their permission."

"'*Looking Forward*'?" Daniel said. "What's that?"

"One of the leading science journals. In fact, probably *the* leading science journal in the UK."

"How do you know about this? Did Pemberton tell you?"

"No." Emma hesitated and she looked slightly embarrassed. "I read a letter from the editor addressed to Michael. I wasn't being nosey; it sort of came my way by accident. But in this letter, Andrew Farquharson, the editor, mentioned a deal they had made. I can't exactly remember all the details now, but I think he was meant to meet Michael on the day he died."

Daniel sat up when he heard Farquharson's name. It had been on the list of people who had called Pemberton by phone. He had arranged with Charlie to check it out with the others that afternoon.

"Do you still have this letter?" he asked.

"No. I gave it back to the secretary when I realised it wasn't meant for me. But don't you think it sounds a bit fishy?"

"I don't know, could be. Did the letter say what he was going to publish?"

"No, but it's obvious isn't it?"

Emma stared intently at Daniel.

"You mean Pemberton was going to publish his research on the project?"

"What else could it be?" Emma replied. "Michael wasn't working on anything else. He deliberately kept this deal secret from the Institute and, if he gave the editor his notebook, that would explain why nobody can find it. Isn't it just possible that Michael might have wanted to arrange for his last discovery to be published before he killed himself; you know, like some sort of enduring testament to his genius? I know it probably sounds ridiculous to you, but that's just the sort of thing he would do and it's got me worried. I think someone should check it out."

"And you think I'm the one to do that?" Daniel asked.

"Well, I can't do anything and you're with the Ministry of Defence aren't you? All of this comes under the Official Secrets Act. Don't you have the authority to stop it, ask the right sort of questions or, at least, pass the information on to those who can?"

Daniel had not told anyone at the Institute he worked for MI6. They had simply assumed he was from the MoD and he had never corrected them. It had seemed better at the time to keep his real role under wraps but now he felt he should tell Emma the truth.

"Actually, I'm not with the MoD," he said.

"Then who do you work for?"

"I'm with MI6."

Emma looked surprised.

"Isn't that the Secret Service?" she asked uncertainly. "Spies and things?"

"Yes, sort of."

"So why are you involved?"

It was precisely to avoid answering this type of question that Daniel had not been candid about who he was. However, he wanted to be honest with Emma and it was possible that without knowing it, she might have some more information which could help his investigation. But to find that out he would need to come clean.

"Pemberton's death may not have been quite as straightforward as it first appeared," he said. "There are certain things which don't seem to add up. I was brought in to try and find out exactly what happened."

Emma stared at him. Her surprise was now replaced by a look of confusion. She said nothing for a moment and then took a sip of water from the glass that was on the table. She put it down slowly and leant forward.

"When you say it wasn't straightforward, what do you mean?"

"It's still too early to be sure."

"You don't think it was a suicide. Are you saying you think he might have been murdered?" she asked, almost in a whisper.

"We're still looking into it," Daniel said. "It's important to keep an open mind at this stage; that's just one possibility we have to consider. We want to be certain of our facts before jumping to any conclusions."

Emma leaned back in her chair, lost in thought. She did not exactly seem surprised.

"Well, that might help to explain a couple of things," she said.

"Like what?"

Emma ignored the question. Daniel could see she was going through something in her mind and waited for her to speak. She leaned forward again; her voice was very quiet and he strained to hear it.

"If Michael was killed so someone could get their hands on his notes, I assume that's what you're thinking, then how did they find out about the project in the first place and how did they actually get hold of the notes? That's what you're working on, isn't it?"

She paused and Daniel could see she was waiting for him to agree. He nodded silently. He was actually impressed by the speed with which she had grasped the essentials of his investigation.

"There's only two ways, aren't there?" Emma said. "Only the team and a few people in the MoD knew of his breakthrough, so it was either one of them or Michael himself did it."

She paused again to look at Daniel for confirmation. He nodded.

"I can't believe someone at the Institute would have anything to do with it," she continued, "but it starts to make sense if Michael was up to something on his own, and now I'm beginning to think he might have been."

"What makes you think that?"

Emma hesitated a moment.

"I think he was meeting people in secret."

Daniel opened his mouth to interrupt. He couldn't prevent the sceptical look in his eyes and Emma recognised it immediately.

"No, just hear me out," she added quickly. "About two weeks before he died, I saw Michael in town one night. He didn't see me, it was dark and I was in a hurry to get home so didn't stop. He was with two people, a man and a woman. They were outside the Pavilion and obviously knew each other well, they were all talking in a huddle together. I thought it a bit unusual at the time because as far as any of us knew, Michael didn't know anyone in Brighton. He was a loner; he rarely came into town. Anyway, the next day when we were at work, I mentioned having seen him and he got all cagey and said I must be mistaken. He said he had been in his living quarters at the Institute all night and hadn't gone out. But I know it was him, I'm positive. I put it down to him just being his usual secretive self but now I think about it, why should he lie unless he was up to no good?"

"Did you see who these other people were?"

"I thought there was something familiar about the woman but I couldn't see her properly; she had her back to me. The man wasn't English. I think he was probably from the Middle East but he was wearing Western clothes. Do you think they could be involved in this? They might have been foreign agents."

She was looking anxious and Daniel found it somewhat endearing. However, he didn't want Emma to start getting alarmed.

"I shouldn't worry about it too much," he said with a reassuring smile. "Whenever people find out where I work, suddenly spies and agents are popping up everywhere. Their imagination goes into overdrive. The smallest thing out of the ordinary and anyone becomes a suspect."

He tried to laugh but realised at once he had said the wrong thing. Emma sat back quickly and her blue eyes flashed.

"You think I'm over-reacting?" she said. "That I'm imagining things because you're from MI6?"

"No," said Daniel hastily, realising he had said the wrong thing. "Not at all. I just meant that we need to be careful not to jump to conclusions. There's usually a very good reason to explain why people sometimes behave in a strange way."

"So you agree Michael *was* behaving strangely?"

"Well, yes, to you and me perhaps. But from what I've learned about Pemberton he *was* strange. You just said yourself you thought he was only being his usual secretive self. It could be nothing more than that."

"Except that now he's dead, his notes are missing and you think he could have been murdered for them."

There was suddenly a frosty edge to Emma's voice. There was a long pause.

"Look," Daniel said at last, "I'm sorry for what I just said. I was out of order." He badly wanted to make amends. "I know you're only trying to be helpful and I appreciate it, I really do. From what you say, I admit it could look as if Pemberton was acting suspiciously. I am taking you seriously and I'm sorry if I gave a different impression. When I get back, I promise I'll look into it but you haven't given me much to go on. If you could provide some sort of description of these people that would help."

Emma relaxed. A part of her knew he was right and perhaps she was just jumping to conclusions. She smiled to show there was no offence.

"As I said," she began, "it was dark and I couldn't see the woman properly. She was short, well, a lot shorter than Michael anyway, and a little dumpy. She could have been about size sixteen, I suppose. Now I think about it, I believe she might actually have been with Michael. They could even have been holding hands. They were standing very close to each other at any rate."

"What about the other man?" Daniel asked.

"Foreign looking. Dark-skinned and black hair. He might have been an Arab but, well, if I'm honest now, it's difficult to be sure," Emma admitted. "He did have a beard."

"Anything else about him?"

"He was younger, probably in his early thirties. Good looking, you could say handsome. And he had a slight limp. I remember now as they walked away he dragged his right leg a little. I'm sorry, that's not much to go on, is it?"

"Actually," said Daniel, still eager to make amends, "compared with many of the descriptions we get, it's not that bad. The bit about the limp is useful, it could help to narrow things down."

Emma looked at him to make sure he wasn't being patronising.

"You will look into it, won't you?"

"Yes, of course. I promised, didn't I?"

The waiter arrived bearing their lunch and put the plates on the table. He smiled at them both before leaving. He thought they made a nice couple.

"Now," said Daniel, picking up his knife and fork, "why don't you tell me a little bit about yourself? When did you come to England?"

★

Charlie had never understood why anyone should actually want to live in London. With its theatres and concert halls, he knew it provided some of the best live performances in the country but, as he was the first to admit, he was not a cultured person and honestly believed television was better entertainment. London was dirty, noisy and too crowded. To Charlie it seemed an unfriendly place; nobody smiled. He sensed the vibrant energy of the city but that only served to make him feel more of an outsider; he preferred a slower pace of life.

As he walked down Regent Street towards Soho, he thought the pavements were too wide and the roads too narrow for the constant stream of traffic they carried. After getting off the tube at Oxford Circus, he had decided to make the rest of the way by foot, partly because he thought he needed the exercise and partly because he believed he had the time. Having looked at the street map he carried in his pocket, it had not seemed that far but the scale had been misleading and he now began to contemplate finishing his journey to the offices of *'Looking Forward'* by taxi. He glanced at his watch and realised he was probably going to be a little late for his appointment with Mr Farquharson. However, one look at the slow-moving stream of traffic was enough to convince him a taxi was unlikely to get him there any faster. It was annoying; something else to add the list of things he disliked about London.

Before Daniel had set off for Brighton and his meeting with Emma that morning, they had agreed Charlie should try to arrange a meeting with Farquharson and establish what sort of connection he had with Pemberton. Calling the telephone number had yielded the address of the offices of *'Looking Forward'* and Charlie had made an appointment with the secretary for two-thirty that afternoon. He now had less than ten minutes to get there if he was to be on time. Even allowing half an hour for the interview with Farquharson, he should still be able to make it to the premises of The Eastern Spice Company well before four o' clock. There he hoped to encounter Husam al din or, to give him his proper name, Yusuf al Shamar. The MI6 file on Yusuf had revealed he was working there as an executive officer of the company and Daniel had advised against giving any advance warning of a proposed visit. They both agreed a surprise call to inform him of Pemberton's death was the best tactic. Catching him off-guard and with no time to prepare a story, they would be more likely to get a genuine reaction and Daniel had faith in Charlie's instinct in such circumstances.

As Charlie turned at last into Frith Street, he saw the Moroccan restaurant halfway down on the right. The offices of the journal were on the top floor of the building and Charlie looked at his watch to check the time. He was five minutes late and quickened his pace until he was in front of the door. Against the wall was a door-bell alongside an intercom with a list of names identifying the various tenants. He pressed the button and waited a moment before a crackling voice came from the intercom asking him who he was and to state his business.

"Mr Watts. I have a two-thirty appointment to see Mr Farquharson," Charlie said.

"Just a moment, please."

There was a buzz followed by a click and Charlie pushed the door open. In front of him was a narrow passage leading to a steep staircase at the end. He mounted the stairs quickly and, feeling a little out of breath, came to a small, door-less office on the first floor. There were three chairs arranged along one side of the opposite wall and a woman was sitting behind a desk in front of him, typing quickly on a keyboard. Charlie waited a moment before she looked up.

"I have an appointment with Mr Farquharson," he said. "I'm sorry I'm a little late."

"I'm afraid Mr Farquharson must have been delayed," she replied. "Would you like to take a seat and wait? I'm expecting him back any minute now."

"He's not here?" Charlie asked, a little annoyed at having rushed to be on time.

"He was unexpectedly called away this morning but he knew you were coming. I'm sure he won't be long."

She returned to working at the keyboard and Charlie went over to the chairs and sat down. He was just about to reach for a magazine from the pile on a small table at the side when his phone rang. The secretary looked up with an expression of annoyance.

"Sorry," Charlie apologised, taking out his phone and looking at the screen. It was Daniel. "Do you mind if I take this?"

The secretary gave a curt nod and returned to her work. Charlie pressed the receive button.

"Hello," he said.

"It's Daniel," came the voice. "Have you met Farquharson yet?"

"No," replied Charlie, "he's running late. I'm waiting for him now."

"Good," said Daniel. "I've just met Emma and she told me that Farquharson was going to publish something of Pemberton's. I want you to find out what it was if you can. Apparently it was all a bit hush-hush. The Institute knew nothing about it and Emma thinks it could have been something to do with the project. She said she thought Farquharson might have the notebook."

Charlie was taken by surprise.

"Really?" he said, trying to sound non-committal for the benefit of the secretary.

"That's not all," Daniel continued. "She also said she thought they had arranged to meet on the day he died. She couldn't be sure about the date but we need to find out. Do you think you can do that?"

"Leave it with me," said Charlie. "Anything else?"

"No, that's it for now. There might be another new lead but I'll tell you about it when I get back. Good luck. See you later."

"Thanks for calling," said Charlie and, switching the phone off, put it back in his pocket.

He picked up one of the magazines and sat back in the chair. It was the latest issue of '*Looking Forward*' and he started to turn the pages idly but made no effort to look at it properly; he was thinking about what he had just learnt. Could there be a connection between Farquharson and Yusuf al Shamar? Could they be working together to get hold of the notebook? He considered the notion for a moment and doubted it. There was none of the subdued excitement that usually accompanied his instinctive feelings and he wondered why. After all, it made sense. And then it occurred to him that both their numbers had been on Pemberton's phone directory. Had they been working together it was more than likely only one of them would have appeared. From what Daniel had told him the night before, Yusuf al Shamar was a shadowy figure; if they had been working together then he would have kept in the background. There would have been no need for Pemberton to contact them both.

He was sure that was not how they would have worked it. But if that was the case, then why did Pemberton have Yusuf's number?

Charlie took a deep breath and let it out slowly. He needed more information. Perhaps after he had talked with Farquharson he would have a better idea. At that moment, the intercom on the secretary's desk buzzed. She stopped her typing and pressed a button on the side of a plastic box fixed to the desk. There was a large grid in the top and she leant forward to speak into it.

"Good afternoon, this is '*Looking Forward*'," she said. "Please state your name and business."

"This is the police," came back a crackly voice. "Can you let us in, please?"

The secretary looked puzzled for a moment and then pressed a button on the side of her desk. Charlie heard the sound of footsteps coming up the stairs.

Two uniformed policemen entered the small office and seemed to fill it with their presence. They stood in front of the secretary and the one in front gave her a polite smile.

"We would like a word with any colleagues of Mr Andrew Farquharson," he said. "Can you let them know we're here?"

"I'm afraid Mr Farquharson is the only one in today and he's gone out for the moment. I'm expecting him back any minute now," the secretary said. She glanced at Charlie. "This gentleman has an appointment to see him."

The policeman glanced at Charlie who gave a quick nod. The policeman turned back to the secretary.

"Is there anyone else here connected with '*Looking Forward*', anyone who knows Mr Farquharson?" he asked.

"I'm sorry, perhaps I can help," said the secretary. "I know Andrew. What's this about?"

The two policemen exchanged a look and then the first man spoke again.

"I'm afraid I've got some bad news," he said.

★

Simon Warbeck got back to his apartment feeling a little breathless. Although he had witnessed it for himself, he still couldn't quite believe his bad luck. After Rick Townsend had passed over Pemberton's notebook along with the other sheets of paper he had found in the briefcase, Simon had contacted Andrew Farquharson to arrange an urgent meeting over lunch. He wanted to let the editor know as soon as possible of the new arrangement he was planning: from now on, he was going to take direct control of Rick and manage the supply of information for himself. He knew he was not Andrew's only client. He had a few customers of his own in the science market, but Andrew had been in the field for years and Simon was sure he must have built up a large clientele during that time. Prior to taking over management of Townsend, Simon wanted to know their names. He still had the photographs of Andrew in compromising positions with underage girls and, over lunch, faced with being exposed as a paedophile, Andrew had known he had no option but to provide him with a list of his contacts and how to get in touch with them.

It was still only three o' clock but Simon went straight through to the lounge where he kept a drinks trolley, threw his briefcase to the floor and poured himself a large whisky. He diluted it slightly with tap water and took a large gulp before sitting down in one of the plush armchairs. He looked around the room for a moment and then swore loudly and emphatically. It wasn't so much anger as frustration. Everything had been going so well: he had Pemberton's notes; he was taking over control of Townsend and Andrew was about to give him his secret list of clients. Simon was sure he had thought through every possible contingency but nobody could have planned for what had happened then.

It was as they had parted company outside the restaurant after lunch that the accident occurred. Perhaps Andrew had been distracted, thinking about the change in his circumstances, or perhaps he had simply been careless and wasn't looking. It made no difference. He had stepped into the road just as a bus was pulling in to stop. He had turned quickly to step back onto the pavement but stumbled against the kerb and whilst he tried to regain his balance, the front of the bus had knocked him to the ground and one of its wheels had gone right over him.

Simon had waited, standing far back on the pavement behind the crowd that immediately gathered. The paramedics arrived within minutes and shortly after them an ambulance drew up. Simon had watched whilst a blanket was held up around Andrew as he lay in the road, concealing him from bystanders whilst the medics set to work. It was twenty minutes before the ambulance took Andrew away.

"Is he going to be alright?" Simon asked a policeman who was standing nearby.

"Don't know," the policeman said. "It looks bad."

"Well, at least he's still alive," said another bystander.

"For the moment," said the policeman grimly.

"Where are they taking him?" Simon asked.

"St George's. They'll do their best."

Simon didn't particularly care whether Andrew survived or not but he needed Andrew's list of clients. It was one thing to take control of Rick and receive all the data provided by hacking into the computers, but it was quite another to find the right buyers for that information. Before the accident, Simon still hadn't quite decided whether to keep Andrew on as a go-between for those others or whether to deal with them directly himself. He had been leaning toward using Andrew; it would provide yet another layer of security for himself should that ever become necessary and, besides, the editor had already built up a good working relationship with his customers. There was no reason to spook them by altering that arrangement; they didn't need to know there had been a change in management. However, it now looked as if he would be dealing directly with Andrew's other clients after all. But to do that he still needed their names and contact numbers. Andrew had told him they were written down in a private address book at his home and had been going to fetch it that afternoon to pass over. But all that had changed with the accident.

Simon took another gulp of the thinly diluted whiskey and glanced at his brief-case lying on the floor where he had thrown it when he came in. At least he still had Pemberton's notes. His own buyer would be getting impatient for them by now and he wanted to go through everything in the briefcase before they met. Although he had only been asked for information on the virus, there might be other information amongst the notes that he could sell to others. He wasn't going to have much time. He needed to get the original deal finished as soon as possible. Getting the client list from Andrew's house would have to wait till later. He drained his glass and put it back on the drinks trolley. Taking his phone from his pocket, he picked up the brief-case and started to make the call. It was back to business as usual. At least for the time being.

★

"Unless we are to believe London Transport has somehow been infiltrated by terrorists, I suppose we have to accept this was a genuine accident," said Daniel with a grim smile.

He and Charlie were sitting in his apartment. They had agreed to have a take-away that evening as neither of them felt like cooking and they were having a drink whilst waiting for their Tikka Masala to arrive. They had spent the last half an hour sharing the information each other had found out that day. As soon as Charlie had learnt what had happened to Farquharson, he had identified himself to the two policemen as someone working for the government. A quick phone call to Daniel had confirmed his identity and he had gone back to the station with them in order to learn more about what had happened. Charlie had always been suspicious of coincidence and his first thought was that Farquharson could have been the victim of some planned attack but, as the facts began to emerge, it soon became obvious that the editor had just been unlucky.

The good news was that Farquharson was not dead; the bad news was that he was now in an induced coma and seriously ill. The bus had crushed his pelvis and both legs were also badly broken. The real danger came from internal bleeding and he had already had an operation to seal off a leaking artery. Before leaving the police station to get back to Hammersmith, the last news Charlie received was that as far as the doctors could tell, the operation had been successful, but the prognosis was not good. At any rate, even if he survived, it was going to be some time before Farquharson was in a fit state to answer any questions.

"What do we do now?" Charlie asked.

"Well," Daniel began, "we can get a warrant to search his home and office. Emma seemed to believe he might have the notebook and I think we should check it out. If we found it, at least the Institute would be happy. They could get on with 'Operation Sundown'."

"To tell the truth," said Charlie, "I'm not that bothered about helping the Institute. In fact, part of me is actually hoping they can't continue their research. I still don't accept what they're trying to do is right. There's something immoral about it and I hope 'Operation Sundown' crashes round their ears. But I am interested in finding out exactly what happened to Pemberton. The more we've looked into it, the more suspicious it gets, and now I want to know the truth. Whatever the man was like, if someone murdered him they should still be made to pay."

Daniel smiled. One of the things he most admired about Charlie was his friend's uncompromising belief in justice; his determination to see that if someone has done something wrong then they should be held to account for it. It was the failure on the part of the authorities to do just that which had led to Charlie's early resignation from the force in Bristol. Daniel himself was much more flexible about such matters: he liked to think he lived in the real world where compromise was a fact of life. But that had never stopped him from having the highest respect for men of principle like Charlie.

"I think we're both agreed now that he *was* murdered," he said, "and I think we can also agree that man the vagrant told us about had something to do with it. Someone's gone to a lot of trouble and that means it's not likely to be personal but because of something to do with his work. There's some sort of conspiracy going on and if we found that Farquharson was in possession of the notebook then that would be a good indicator he was involved in some way."

Charlie didn't say anything. He couldn't immediately fault Daniel's reasoning but there was something about it which just didn't feel quite right. He took a sip from his gin and tonic and nursed the glass in both hands whilst he tried to get his thoughts in order.

"Don't you agree?" asked Daniel after a moment.

"It could appear to look that way," said Charlie.

"But...?" prompted Daniel, aware that Charlie was having reservations.

"But I can't help thinking there's more to it than that," Charlie admitted. "I can't exactly explain why at the moment but I don't think we're getting the whole picture."

He took another sip of his drink and Daniel waited for him to continue. It was a few minutes before Charlie started to speak again.

"Remember what Martin Greaves said?" he began. "Greaves told us Pemberton was incredibly vain. He wanted all the credit for his discoveries for himself. And now you've just said Emma Nelson thought Pemberton could have been making a deal with Farquharson to publish his notes. If that's true then Pemberton could just have given the notebook to Farquharson himself. There would be no need for Farquharson to kill him to get the information. Even if we found the notebook at Farquharson's home it doesn't actually prove anything; he could have come by it quite innocently. All it would actually show is that Pemberton could have been breaking the Official Secrets Act."

"Are you suggesting Farquharson might be legit?"

"No," Charlie replied quickly. "He would have known the information was top secret and shouldn't be published. Farquharson's probably up to something dodgy as well but that doesn't mean he was involved in Pemberton's murder."

"So what do you think we should do?"

"I think we need to know more about Pemberton," Charlie said. "I'm sure the answer must lie with him. The more we learn about him, the less I'm beginning to think he was just an innocent victim. He was up to something and whatever it was probably got him killed."

Daniel still believed Farquharson was probably involved in Pemberton's death in some way. However, Charlie was right: even if they found Farquharson had the notebook it would not actually prove anything against him. Nonetheless, he was still going to get the warrant to search for it. The Institute needed the notes and, even though he privately agreed with Charlie about the research they were conducting, it was his duty to see if he could retrieve it for them.

"OK," he said, "where do you want to start? It's not going to be easy, we haven't many leads. Pemberton kept pretty much to himself and we've already interviewed everyone at the Institute."

"We still haven't checked all the names we found on his phone. In particular, I think we should start with Yusuf al Shamar. I was going to drop in on him this afternoon if you remember, but then all this happened. Neither of us can think of a good reason for Pemberton to have his number. Now we also know about the people Emma Nelson said Pemberton had met in Brighton. You said she thought that looked suspicious and I tend to agree. I think we should try to find out who they were if we can."

Daniel had been thinking the same thing. The MI6 file on Yusuf al Shamar, or Husam al din as he also called himself, had not yielded much information. He had first come to the attention of MI6 through their discreet monitoring of those attending the Finsbury Park Mosque. Informants had told them of suspicions he was being radicalised when he was a teenager but there had been nothing more positive until he had gone to University and joined a group that MI6 knew had links with Al Qaeda. He had played a small part in demonstrations over the publishing of images of the prophet Mohammed in a foreign newspaper and had then dropped out of circulation until his late twenties. His name had then cropped up again in connection with a planned terrorist attack on an army barracks in Wiltshire. Daniel had played a small pat in the investigation at the time and that was how he had first come across the name. There had been no evidence to prove Yusuf had any involvement apart from the say-so of an unreliable informant. Nonetheless, he had been brought in for questioning but by that time he was working for the Eastern Spice Company and an expensive lawyer had almost immediately secured his release. Since then there had been nothing. He now seemed to be leading a blameless life. MI6 had kept an occasional eye on him over the years but their resources were limited and there were far more significant people occupying their attention. His name, like many others, had remained on the files, but there had been no more reports of illicit activity and he had gradually drifted down their list of priorities until now he was little more than a footnote.

Daniel had never been entirely convinced Yusuf had not played some part in the barracks incident. His lawyer had been too quick on the scene and innocent men usually wanted to co-operate with the security services. Moreover, the Imam at the mosque Yusuf attended had come under suspicion of radicalising some of the young men in his congregation. Nothing had been proved but, putting all those things together, Daniel thought it was suspicious to say the least and had never been happy at letting Yusuf off the hook so easily. That had been several years ago but the name had stuck at the back of his mind and now it had come up again.

"It'll be quicker to get results if we split the work," he said. "Now I'm back in London, I'll take over looking at Yusuf, if that's alright. Do you mind following up the lead Emma gave us?"

"Are you sure you wouldn't prefer that side of things?" Charlie asked. It occurred to him that Daniel might like to have more opportunities to meet with Emma Nelson.

"I know what you're thinking," said Daniel with a shy grin, "but it's more your line of work. Anyway, you're probably going to be better at it then I am."

At that moment, the doorbell rang.

"Supper," Charlie announced hopefully. "About time."

★

Yusuf al Shamar sat in the passenger seat of the jeep as it made its way across the Syrian scrubland in the dark, his mind still going over the various possibilities that might explain what had happened. It was a pointless exercise without more information but he couldn't help himself and what else could he do whilst they drove through the night? Like his companions, he was now dressed in western clothes. He was on his way back to the UK and in order to do that safely he first had to make a clandestine crossing over the border into Turkey. From there he would fly to Amsterdam where he could make a connecting flight to London. It was a long journey but one he had made several times before and it was still the most secure route to get back without the authorities knowing he had spent time in Syria. He was not alone. Habab and Shiraz al-Assad, the Tunisian brothers who had been with him in the hills near the Belen Pass, were in the back. He had always intended Habab should accompany him. The young man had very specific skills he would need, but there was something about Shiraz he thought made him unreliable. He had only agreed Shiraz could join them after Habab had insisted his brother could help and had undertaken to look after him. Yusuf still didn't know for sure what awaited him on his arrival in London but it made sense to be prepared for anything and, if he was still able to go ahead, it was possible Shiraz could prove useful.

The coded message had come as an unexpected blow. The news that Pemberton was dead might not be the complication he had first thought. If the scientist had been able to complete his task before dying, the operation could still go ahead. But the report that the virus might be lost was a different matter. Yusuf badly needed to find out exactly what had happened. Had Pemberton been careless? Is that why he was dead? Had he managed to create the virus and, if so, was it still safe? The questions repeated themselves over and over again, like the tolling of some insistent bell inside his head. But he had no answers. He could do nothing but wait and stared ahead at the darkness as the jeep continued its secret journey through the night.

Chapter Four

Simon Warbeck had slept badly and woke late the following morning with a dry mouth and a headache. Even before he washed and dressed, he took a paracetamol and by the time he was having breakfast he was starting to feel better. It was unusual for him to sleep so badly and he put it down to large amount of whisky he had drunk the night before. Too much had happened too quickly and, although he was normally adept at improvising to changing situations, by any reckoning what had happened the day before had made demands on him that were completely out of the ordinary. However, as he finished his coffee and rinsed his cup under the tap, he reflected that perhaps things were not that bad.

He had taken care of Rick Townsend; he had passed on Pemberton's notes to his own buyer and now all that remained was to get hold of Farquharson's address book containing the names and contact numbers of the clients he wanted. In one way, at least, Farquharson's accident had a good side to it: Simon would now be able to provide the clients with a plausible reason for him taking over without having to go into any explanations which might spook them. He knew the people he was going to be dealing with would be wary of change in a long-established working relationship, but they would understand the necessity once they learnt how Farquharson was now indisposed. They would be grateful that business was able to continue.

His own buyer for Pemberton's notes had been reasonable. The five per cent reduction in his fee had been a good sweetener and, anyway, Simon knew their relationship had to continue; they were both benefitting too much for it to come to an end over what had, after all, been only a slight delay. What his buyer would have said had he known there was more information Simon was keeping back might have changed that, but so far

112

Simon was not telling anyone what else he had found amongst the contents Pemberton had been carrying in his briefcase. In addition to the notebook containing his work on the genetic modification of bacteria, Pemberton had been carrying a number of loose sheets of paper. Simon had read everything. He had not been able to understand all the information in the notebook; he was not a scientist and many of the terms were as bewildering as the equations Pemberton had scrawled in his spidery handwriting across its pages. However, he knew they would mean something to somebody and he knew what they ultimately meant. His client had only asked for the notebook and that was what he had delivered. He had his own ideas about how it was going to be used but that was not his business. He dealt in information not morality and it simply didn't bother him that possibly thousands of people might die as a result of what he had done. That was the way the world operated these days and his philosophy now was to look after number one. That was why he had kept the other papers and not mentioned them to anyone. What had Pemberton been thinking to hold on to them? You didn't have to be a scientist to understand what they implied and, as far as Simon could make out, they promised to be of far greater value than the notebook. There was another deal to be made here but first he needed Farquharson's contacts.

He would have to take a taxi to Chelsea where Farquharson lived. Once there he was not worried about gaining entry to the house. Andrew would undoubtedly have had some sort of security measures installed but Simon had long ago acquired the skills to get past them and was confident that would not be a difficulty. The real problem was going to be in actually finding the book. He was sure that Andrew had not stored the information on his computer. Not only had he specifically mentioned a book, but he, perhaps more than most people, would have been aware just how insecure data stored in computers was. It was going to take time but Simon was ready to spend the whole day if necessary looking for the address book. He arranged for a taxi to pick him up and take him to a street around the corner from where Farquharson lived. He knew it was better to arrive on foot rather than draw up outside the house; taxi journeys could be traced.

It was almost ten o' clock by the time he stood outside the small front garden of Farquharson's house. Fortunately, Andrew had valued his privacy and a tall privet hedge surrounded the property in the front, shielding it from the view of any passers-by on the street. A six foot, wrought-iron gate provided the only entrance and Simon gave it a gentle push. He was not surprised it was unlocked; Andrew would need to leave it open for the postman amongst other things. He walked up the front path. He had been here only once before when he was brought by a mutual friend to a party Andrew was giving. That had been their introduction and was a long time ago. Nonetheless, Simon could still remember the lay-out of the house and, to be on the safe side, decided to gain entry from the back door. He walked across the lawn that ran round the side of the house and saw the wooden gate which gave access to the back garden. It too was unlocked and opened as he gave a push. He walked quickly over to the kitchen door and automatically tried the handle. To his complete surprise the door opened. He slipped inside and closed it silently behind him. Suddenly, a man appeared in the doorway leading to the hall.

"Who are you?" the man demanded, stepping into the kitchen. "What are you doing here?"

Simon thought fast.

"I might ask you the same question," he replied.

"In the kitchen!" the man shouted as he moved behind Simon to prevent him from leaving. "We've got a visitor!"

Almost immediately, two more men appeared in the hallway and quickly entered the small kitchen, making it crowded.

"Who are you?" Simon asked angrily, his heart starting to beat fast.

He already thought he knew but realised an aggressive attitude might help.

"We're the police," said the man who had spoken first. "Now identify yourself."

Simon tried to make himself appear to relax.

"I thought you were burglars," he said. "You scared the hell out of me."

"Who are you?" the man repeated.

"Simon Warbeck, I'm a friend of Andrew Farquharson who lives here. Might I see some identification?"

The man reached into his pocket and pulled out a leather wallet which he flipped open. Simon caught a glimpse of some sort of ID card before the man folded it shut and put it away again.

"What are you doing here?" the man asked curtly.

"Andrew's in hospital," Simon said. "I thought he might need a few things and came round to collect them for him. Why are you here?"

At that moment another man stepped into the door way and Simon saw the others stiffen slightly. This was obviously the man in charge and Simon decided to address his questions to him.

"Can someone please tell me what's going on?" he asked.

Daniel looked at the man standing in front of him. He was neatly dressed in a grey suit, lean and probably in his late thirties. He seemed to be genuinely confused but that was easy to feign. Daniel had already been there with the others for about an hour. Having obtained the search warrant early that morning, he had been carefully sorting through the upstairs rooms looking for Pemberton's notebook when he had heard the shout from the kitchen.

"This is a routine enquiry," he said. "We received a report from a neighbour that someone might be trying to break in. We're just checking it out. Do you have any means of identification?"

"Only a driving licence," said Simon, reaching into his jacket pocket and drawing out his wallet."

He offered it to Daniel who took it and looked at the photograph on the licence, glancing quickly at Simon to check it was him. He gave the wallet back and nodded at the other men.

"Would you mind coming through?" he said to Simon. "I would like to ask a few questions if that's alright."

"Am I in trouble?" Simon asked innocently. "I was just trying to be helpful."

Daniel didn't answer. Instead, he moved back into the hallway and turned left into the front room. Giving the other men a quick look, Simon followed him. He knew he had been lied to. There were no police cars outside, none of the men were in uniform and four plainclothes policemen would not have been sent on a routine enquiry. He was going to have to play along with this charade. As he entered the front room, Daniel was standing by the fireplace and gestured toward a chair.

"Please," he said, "sit down. I won't take up too much of your time."

Simon sat down. He was nervous and knew it showed. He couldn't help it but that would be a natural reaction in someone innocent as well.

"How come you know Mr Farquharson?" Daniel asked.

"We're friends," said Simon. "I've known him for a couple of years now."

"Are you in publishing too?"

"Oh no, nothing like that. I'm a business consultant. I've sometimes helped Andrew out with some of his affairs."

"How did you know Mr Farquharson was in hospital?"

"I was there when he had the accident," said Simon. He knew it was better to tell as much of the truth as he could. "We'd just had lunch and said goodbye when he must have tried to cross the road and was run over. I hung around a bit to find out what was happening and someone told me they were taking him to St George's."

"Did you tell the police you saw what happened?"

"I didn't actually see it. As I said, we'd already said goodbye and I was walking away. I had my back to him."

"So you didn't speak to the police, not even to tell someone you knew who he was?"

"I suppose I should have done but with everything going on, it didn't occur to me. Nobody asked me and, to tell the truth, I think I must have been in a bit of a shock. It was all very sudden, you see. There was a large crowd around him and I wasn't thinking about things like that."

"You said you were going to visit him?"

"Yes, I thought I could fit it in later today."

"I'm afraid Mr Farquharson is not able to receive any visitors at the moment."

"I – I didn't know," Simon said. "Is it very serious then?"

"I'm afraid so. How were you planning to get into the house? Do you have a key?"

"No, but I know Andrew sometimes leaves the back door open. He can be a bit careless like that. I just thought I'd take a chance."

"It was locked when we arrived," said Daniel.

"Then it was lucky you were here when I came. Is it alright if I have a quick look around for some things to take to Andrew when I see him?"

"I think it would be best if we left everything just as it is for the time being," said Daniel.

"Yes, yes, of course," Simon agreed quickly.

He looked at Daniel but couldn't read what the man was thinking behind the bland expression.

"Well, if that's it, can I go now?"

Daniel paused a moment before replying.

"Yes," he said. "How can I get in touch with you again? If you like, I can keep you informed of Mr Farquharson's progress."

"There's no need for you to do that. I can contact the hospital myself."

"I should still like to have your details," Daniel insisted gently, "just in case I need to speak to you again. You did say you were at the scene of the accident."

117

"Yes, of course," Simon said, standing up. He pulled out his wallet and removed a business card which he handed to Daniel. "That's got my mobile number. You can reach me any time on that."

"Thanks," said Daniel, holding the card by the edges before pocketing it.

"Can I go now?"

"Yes. Thanks for your help."

Simon left the room and turned right to go back into the kitchen.

"You can use the front door," Daniel called out. "It's open."

Simon turned and nodded before making his way along the hall. Daniel heard the front door open and close and then went into the kitchen where the three men were still waiting.

"Follow him," said Daniel looking at two of them. "But be careful. He's lying."

★

It had been a long time since Emma Nelson had felt this way and it was a little unsettling. In fact, she wasn't too sure exactly what she was feeling and that was perhaps the most confusing thing of all. The demanding hours and even the very nature of her work had made it difficult to lead a social life outside of the laboratory. Virtually everyone she knew was a scientist and, in order to be accepted and taken seriously in such a male dominated environment, she had found it necessary to try and sublimate almost everything feminine about her. Naturally, some of her colleagues had still made advances but she had rarely taken them seriously. She had modestly believed the men she worked with felt obliged to try and seduce her simply because she was a woman and she was there. She had always interpreted such incidents not only as a way of them trying to assert their masculinity but also as an attempt to put her to the test. She thought they wanted to see whether they could make her succumb to their flattery and prove herself to be less than a committed scientist; to be just another bimbo in a white lab coat trying to seem more clever than she actually was.

She had long ago learnt how to deal with those situations. She had always insisted on being treated as an equal and her frosty rejections of such advances had ultimately succeeded in giving her an intimidating reputation. That, along with her work, her achievements and her dedication had, in due course, earned her the respect she presently enjoyed. People took her seriously now but it had come at a cost. The few relationships she had entered into since leaving university had eventually petered out. They had all, inevitably, been with other scientists and she had been better at her job than they were. Unable, or perhaps unwilling to accept the competition, those men had left when they discovered she was not going to abandon her career for them. The choice had been hers and she had never regretted it. Now she was one of the world's leading authorities on biogenetics and she had felt her life was full. Then she had met Daniel Rankin.

She had not given much attention to him at their first meeting; there had been too many other things to think about when he came to her house and told her Pemberton's notebook was missing. But their second meeting had been different. He had been different. She had thought they were going to be business-like but he had wanted to know more about her as a person. She was not naïve and recognised he was interested in her but, if she were honest, this time she was flattered by the attention. It almost came as a surprise to discover she still liked being treated as a woman rather than a scientist and there was something about Daniel that intrigued her. He was not like the other men she knew or had known. He was obviously successful in his own very different job and, although she sensed a vulnerability in him, he had a confidence she found reassuring. After that initial misunderstanding when she thought he was being patronising, she had begun to feel she had nothing to prove and with that knowledge had come the freedom to relax and trust him. She had talked about herself with a candour she had not enjoyed for many years and she believed he had been equally open about his own background. They had enjoyed their meal together and, at the end when they had to go their separate ways, as they were shaking hands, she had impulsively leant forward and given him a quick peck on the cheek. In the elaborate ritual of modern relationships, a ritual with which she had admittedly now grown unfamiliar, she nonetheless knew it had signalled something between them. Quite what it was she was not entirely sure but she instinctively felt he had thought so too. Now, if she had interpreted things correctly, it was up to him to make the next move. It was with some disappointment, therefore, that when she received a call from London that morning it turned out to be from Charlie Watts.

"I hope I'm not interrupting anything," Charlie began after introducing himself, "is this a convenient time to talk?"

"Yes, I'm in the lab but I'm not busy at the moment."

"Daniel would have liked to speak to you himself but I'm afraid he's got a lot on this morning and asked if I could follow up some of the things you talked about yesterday. He thought it might be important and didn't want to wait."

"How can I help?" Emma asked.

"It's about that meeting you said you saw Pemberton have with those two people."

"Yes?"

"I was hoping you might be able to give us some more details."

"I think I've already told Daniel everything I know," Emma said. "What sort of details do you mean?"

"Anything you can add to their description would be useful."

Emma paused as she tried to remember exactly what she had seen that night.

"It was dark and I couldn't see them properly," she said, "but there was something familiar about the woman. Perhaps she lives in Brighton and I've seen her around somewhere. I don't think Michael had a girlfriend so it can't have been with him but I did get the impression they could have been together that night."

"What makes you think that?"

"Just the way she was standing so close to him. I could be wrong but I thought they might even have been holding hands. I told Daniel this. She had her back to me so I couldn't see her face. I'm sorry, but that's the best I can do."

"What about the other man?"

"He definitely looked foreign, probably in his early thirties with dark hair and a beard. I thought he could have been from the Middle East but I can't be entirely sure. Look, as I said, I've already told Daniel all of this. I'm sorry but I don't think there's much more I can add. Daniel thought the most important thing was the man had a limp. Doesn't that help?"

"Everything helps," said Charlie. "The more information we have the better. Can you remember the exact date this meeting took place?"

"Just a minute," Emma said, "I've got my desk diary with me now and I can look it up."

She put the phone down and picked up her diary which was lying on the bench in front of her. She quickly thumbed back through the pages before picking up the phone again.

"Yes, here it is. September 3rd. I was in town that night with some of the people from the Institute. We'd been to see a film and I was on my way back to the car-park when I saw Michael so that would make it sometime between ten-thirty and eleven I suppose."

Something clicked in Charlie's mind.

"Can you hold on a minute," he said, "I just want to check something."

Emma heard him put the phone down and waited. It was less than a minute before Charlie returned.

"You're sure of the date?" he asked.

"Yes. It was the night we went to the pictures. Is that important?"

"It might be," said Charlie, "as I said, all information is useful."

"Well, I'm sorry, I know it's not much but I think that's about all I can tell you. Was there anything else?"

"Just one more thing," said Charlie. "Did Michael ever mention the name Husam al din?"

"That's an Arab name, isn't it?"

"Yes."

"No, I don't think I've ever heard of him."

"What about Yusuf al Shamar?"

"No, I haven't heard of him either. Is one of them the person you think Michael was meeting?"

"It could be," said Charlie. "If I were to show you a photograph, do you think you might be able to recognise the man you saw that night?"

"Possibly," said Emma. "I'll have a go if you want."

"I'll get something arranged," Charlie said. "Well, I think that's about it for the time being. Thanks, you've been very helpful. Either Daniel or myself will be in touch again soon about the photograph. Bye for now."

"Glad to have been of help," said Emma. "Bye."

Charlie was in Daniel's apartment and, as he ended the call, he pulled toward him the phone records they had got from Robert at the MI6 office and looked down the list again. There it was. Just the one brief call on Pemberton's phone. September 3rd at 3.45 pm and alongside it the phone number belonging to Yusuf al Shamar.

★

As soon as Simon Warbeck left Farquharson's house he knew he was going to be followed. The reason he had given for being there was probably sound enough but his explanation of taking a chance that the back door would be open was not. He would not have believed it himself but what else could he have said? If he had been asked to hand over the key and been unable to produce one, he would probably have been detained on the spot. In fact, he was a little surprised they had let him leave as they did, but what surprised him the most was that whoever it was he had met in the house had got on to Farquharson. He was sure now they must have been Secret Service and, fighting the urge to run and walking as casually down the street as he could, he began to wonder how long they had known about Farquharson. They could have been watching him even before Pemberton's death. That thought sent a shiver down his spine. Just how much did they already know?

His training had prepared him to be ultra-careful and he was sure that until that morning they could not have known about him; the man he had spoken with would have behaved differently if they had, but he knew all that was about to change. Simon was angry. Everything had been falling into place just as he had wanted and then, without any warning, all his plans had suddenly been shot to shreds. He knew he could no longer even think about taking over Farquharson's operation; he even doubted whether it was now safe to run Rick Townsend as his own operative. In fact, the more he thought about it, the more it dawned on him that was going to be too dangerous. Simon had never taken risks with his own safety. His immediate priority must be to make himself secure but he was beginning to realise his options were narrowing and whatever action he was going to take, he would need to do it quickly whilst he still could.

He stopped abruptly outside a newsagent and looked in the window at the personal notices and advertisements which had been stuck to the inside. He wasn't reading them; he was looking at the reflection in the glass of the street behind him. He had been right: on the opposite side of the road, about twenty yards behind, he saw one of the men who had been in the kitchen. The man hesitated but didn't stop and carried on walking. Simon waited until he had passed and was a little way ahead before going into the shop and looking at the racks of sweets in front of the counter. He selected a bag of mints and paid for them. He hung around in the shop a moment, appearing to examine the magazine rack against the wall but in fact looking through the window onto the street. He knew how these things were done and was sure there must be another man further down the road, waiting for him to leave. After a few minutes, he pulled open the door and looked both ways along the pavement before continuing his walk up the street. The first man was now lost to sight and Simon hadn't recognised anyone else amongst the few people he had seen behind him. But he knew they were still there. He saw a taxi coming toward him on the opposite side of the road and stepped off the pavement to hail it. The taxi slowed, allowing a few cars to pass before making a U-turn and drawing up next to Simon. He knew this was not going to be enough to stop the tail, but it would probably give him a brief window of opportunity to do something before it could resume. He instructed the driver to make for Westminster and settled back in his seat.

He realised he needed help. Although he had previously prepared a number of strategies to get out of the country quickly should the need ever arise, he had no arrangements in place that would provide for this particular situation. He had never anticipated having to get the Secret Service off his tail before he could make an escape. He might be able to lose them for a short time but as soon as that happened, he knew within a few minutes they could have the ports and airports covered. This was not something he was going to be able to manage on his own.

As the taxi took him toward Westminster, Simon considered his options. He had always worked alone; there was no personal network he could rely on. He needed someone who would consider his security as important to them as it was to himself. And he could think of only one person. He made a decision. He let the taxi continue its journey for another five minutes and then, as it passed a telephone kiosk, he leant forward and tapped on the glass partition between himself and the driver.

"Could you stop here, please?" he said. "I've changed my mind. This will do, thanks."

The taxi drew up to the pavement and Simon paid the fare and got out. As the taxi pulled away, he made his way back to the kiosk. He had to make a phone call but there was no way he was going to use his own phone now. He lifted the receiver and dialled the number. It only rang a few times before being picked up and Simon heard a familiar voice.

"Yes?"

The voice was deep and cultured with a slight accent. Simon was relieved to hear it.

"Hello, this is Personal Packaging Services," he said. "I'm sorry to trouble you but we've got a slight problem."

"Yes?"

"That last delivery we made, I believe someone else is interested in it."

There was a moment's silence before the man spoke again.

"Who are they?"

"A company like yourself, I think, though based in England. I'm sorry, but I'm sure you'll understand this has put me in a very awkward position. I was hoping we could meet to decide how to handle the situation."

"What makes you think I should help you?"

"I know how much your company values its privacy. I expect these people are going to be very persistent and I'm sure you wouldn't like any publicity if they were to become difficult. I think if you were able to help me out we could settle this matter easily."

There was another silence.

"This is rather urgent," Simon continued, unable to keep the note of desperation from his voice. "I believe they're already chasing me for a response."

"Where are you?" the man asked.

"Somewhere near Eaton Square. I'm using a public telephone."

"Are you alone?"

"Yes, for the moment."

"OK. I'll send a car to pick you up outside the Saatchi Gallery in about half an hour's time. Do you know it?"

"Yes, I'll be there."

The line went dead and Simon wondered whether he had done the right thing.

★

Daniel was thinking that Andrew Farquharson had suddenly become a much more intriguing individual, a person of interest as the official jargon liked to express it. Not that Daniel hadn't thought him interesting before. He and Charlie had both believed Farquharson was up to something and Daniel remained convinced he was somehow implicated in Pemberton's death even if Charlie still had reservations about going so far. Now, with the unexpected arrival of Simon Warbeck on the scene, if that was his real name, there was something doubly suspicious about Farquharson. Daniel was certain Warbeck had come to look for something in the house and, if that were the case, he thought it more than likely to be Pemberton's notes. If he was right, then it clearly pointed to Warbeck being a part of the conspiracy.

As soon as Warbeck had left, Daniel phoned through to his office to ask for a check on the man but unsurprisingly that had turned up nothing. Daniel had then contacted Robert at the MI6 communications office and asked him to check the phone records for the number on the card Warbeck had given him. He didn't expect much to come from that either; Warbeck would never have given him the card so easily had he believed it was not safe to do so. However, in addition to the phone number, the card also had Warbeck's fingerprints on it. Daniel had been careful only to touch it at the edges and it was now on its way to the forensics lab in an evidence bag. They would be able to match any prints against their extensive records and hopefully let him know if Warbeck was in their files, perhaps under a different name. For the moment that was all he could do. For the next stage of his investigation, he had to wait for the men following Warbeck to report back. Meanwhile, feeling more positive than ever now that Pemberton's notes must be somewhere in the house, he thought he needed some more men to help look for them. Several hours later, however, he and his men had not found anything that even looked like the notes and Daniel reluctantly decided to call off the search. They could go no further without causing damage to the property and he was not prepared to do that just yet.

The search had not been entirely fruitless: in Farquharson's study Daniel had found two address books. One had been open on top of the desk but the other he found tucked away at the back of a drawer under various papers. The one on the desk had contained the full names, addresses and telephone numbers of various people who were obviously either friends or people Farquharson had must have had regular business dealings with. But the other was different. It wasn't so much an address book as a notebook. Each of its entries consisted of just two letters, each followed by a series of numbers. Daniel guessed the letters probably stood for the initials of people and the numbers were how to contact them. It wasn't exactly what he had been hoping to find, but Farquharson had obviously taken pains to be a little secretive over what it contained and Daniel wanted to know what information it held. He had sent both books over to Robert at the communications office for examination and said he would drop by later that evening to find out what Robert had discovered.

It was with a sense of hopeful anticipation that Daniel now made his way to the Eastern Spice Company. Although he had Farquharson's address books, he wanted something more to cancel the disappointment he had felt at not recovering Pemberton's notes. He had not made an appointment; he and Charlie had agreed the best way to confront Yusuf al Shamar was to take him by surprise. Charlie had phoned to say that Pemberton had called Yusuf the same day Emma had seen the scientist meeting with someone. Like Charlie, Daniel thought it was too much of a coincidence and, for his part, went some way to confirming that Yusuf was involved in some sort of secret activity with the scientist. Daniel hadn't discussed the idea with Charlie yet, but at the back of his mind he was developing a theory which involved Farquharson and Yusuf working together to get Pemberton's notes and then killing him once they had them. By making it appear like a suicide they would have hoped to prevent any investigation that might raise awkward questions.

To test his theory, he was planning to tell Yusuf that it was now believed Pemberton had died in suspicious circumstances and see how he reacted. If al Shamar denied knowing Pemberton, which was what Daniel expected, that would be proof he was lying; however, if al Shamar offered some explanation as to how they knew each other, Daniel would at least have something new he could follow up.

It was late afternoon by the time he eventually parked his car in the customer courtyard of the premises belonging to the Eastern Spice Company. It was starting to rain and he turned up the collar of his coat as he made his way toward the entrance. He was less than ten yards away when the door opened and a young woman came out. She gave him a quick glance before turning round and locking the door behind her. As Daniel approached, she opened an umbrella and started to walk away.

"Excuse me," Daniel called out, "I was hoping to see Mr al Shamar."

The woman stopped and looked at him.

"We're closed," she said. "Did you have an appointment?"

"No, I was trusting to luck."

"Well, I'm sorry, Mr al Shamar is not here. You should have called to make an appointment."

"Do you know where I could find him?" Daniel asked. "It's rather important."

"He's been out of the country for a while," said the woman, "on business."

"When did he leave?"

"Last Wednesday."

"Do you know when he'll be back?"

The woman shrugged.

"Sorry, I can't help. You could try giving him a call next week."

Daniel felt frustrated. This was not turning out as he would have wished.

"Do you know where he's gone?"

"Amsterdam. We've got a warehouse near Schiphol, but I don't know if he was staying there. I'm sorry, I have to go. Try again next week and make an appointment this time. That's the best thing."

She hurried away toward her car, leaving Daniel standing alone in the centre of the courtyard. He was thinking rapidly. Pemberton had been killed last Friday. If Yusuf al Shamar had been out of the country at the time then it was beginning to look as if he might not be involved in the actual murder. It was possible he had told his office he was going to Amsterdam but had actually remained in England. That would be easy enough to check out but Daniel was already starting to think his theory was falling apart. Nonetheless, he was still sure that Yusuf and Pemberton had been involved in something together, just as he was sure Pemberton had also been working in secret with Farquharson. Perhaps the two things were not connected. Perhaps he was wrong to try looking for links between them. He wanted to get back and talk it over with Charlie. Charlie had a knack for getting to the bottom of problems like this; that was why he had gone to him in the first place.

★

The journey from Turkey had so far been uneventful. Yusuf and the al Assad brothers had travelled separately, even to the extent of Yusuf going business class whilst they were in economy, and they had arrived at Schiphol on time. In his briefcase, Yusuf now carried a number of signed contracts which had been made on his behalf in Amsterdam whilst he was in Syria. They had been passed to him at Amsterdam airport and should anyone wish to examine his luggage, a glance at the documents would confirm he had simply been abroad on a successful business trip to Holland. There was nothing to show where he had actually spent the previous ten days.

As soon as he had reached his friends in Turkey, he had logged on to a computer and read the news reports of

129

Pemberton's death. He didn't believe for a moment that Pemberton had committed suicide. But if he hadn't killed himself then who had finished him off? Yusuf had not liked Pemberton and felt no sorrow over his passing but his death signalled a change in the operation. Yusuf had to consider the possibility that the British authorities had discovered what Pemberton was doing and got rid of him to save a lot of embarrassment down the line. That was one possibility but there were others. He had known Pemberton was unreliable from the start: he was too vain and too greedy and Yusuf thought such men were untrustworthy. Could Pemberton have been working a double-cross? Had he developed the virus as planned and then passed it on to someone else prepared to offer something more? And then had that person finished him off to tie up the loose ends? Was the virus still secure? Most important of all, was Farquharson involved? Not knowing the answers was frustrating. He needed to talk to Angel urgently but knew better than to try and get in touch with her directly. He would have to wait until she was able to contact him and he was sure she would as soon as she knew he was back. He just had to wait but that was the most difficult thing of all. Then that evening he got a telephone call.

It was whilst he was waiting to board the connecting flight from Schiphol that Kylie, the young secretary he worked with at the Eastern Spice Company, contacted him. She had got in touch to report a visit to the office made by a middle-aged man that afternoon just as she was leaving.

"He weren't no customer," she said. "He weren't wearing no uniform but he had police written all over him. I said you wouldn't be back until next week and told him to make an appointment."

"Did he say what it was about?" Yusuf asked.

"No, just that it was important."

Yusuf's brain moved up a gear. He trusted Kylie's perception of events. Despite her youth, she was an experienced and streetwise woman; if she said the man was police then he almost certainly was. There was no reason at this point to believe the

British Secret Service had made a connection between himself and Pemberton. Apart from one small, unavoidable lapse in protocol, he was sure he had taken all the necessary precautions to remain at a distance. It could be something completely unrelated but then, on the other hand, it might not. He needed more information and he needed it fast.

"Hello, are you still there?" Kylie asked, breaking into his thoughts.

"Yes, thanks for letting me know. I think I'll take a few days off, Kylie. I need a break so I won't be coming into work for a while. I'll stay at the flat. Could you do me a favour and get it ready for tonight? I have two friends who will be staying with me. I'd be grateful if you could arrange to have enough food and things like that for us when we arrive so we don't have to go out."

Kylie knew something was wrong but if her boss didn't want to tell her that was OK. She was quite happy to help him without knowing the details.

"Will do," she said. "Is that all?"

"Not quite. Could you let Angel know I'm back tonight and would like to see her as soon as possible? I think that's about it for the time being. Let me know if the man comes back and I'll get in touch if there's anything else I need."

"OK, bye for now, then."

Yusuf switched off his phone and looked around the airport lounge. He still felt reasonably confident the authorities had not made a connection between himself and Pemberton. He had laid down very specific ground rules and kept to them rigidly. It was unfortunate Pemberton was an amateur and hadn't understood just how necessary such rules were. There had been just that one lapse; a brief phone call between the two of them when Pemberton had panicked about a week before Yusuf had left the country. Yusuf had terminated the call immediately after telling Pemberton to make contact through the usual channels; the call had lasted for less than thirty seconds but he knew that could have been enough to show the two men knew each other. Now things had changed, the authorities might be getting curious

131

about Pemberton's background. Yusuf had to consider if that call was going to have any consequences. He quickly came to a decision. There was a very slight risk he might be stopped at Heathrow but even if that happened, he was sure there was no evidence to tie him in with what Pemberton had been doing. It was a risk worth taking; the alternative was to abandon the operation and Yusuf had waited too long to let that happen now.

When they reached Heathrow three hours later, they all cleared the airport with no problems and Yusuf gave Habab and Shiraz al-Assad the address of the flat so they could make their own way separately by taxi. He had not mentioned anything about the phone call from Kylie. He did not want to spook them just as they were reaching the UK, especially Shiraz who, just as he had feared, was proving to be a liability. Anyway, he decided there was no need for them to know. The flat was in the basement of one of the large houses in Westbrook Grove and Yusuf arrived first. It was not Yusuf's own home, the flat was actually in Kylie's name but she had never used it. It was somewhere Yusuf could put up visitors when he needed and would now provide a good hideaway until he was ready to act. He was the first to arrive. The key was under the mat where Kylie had left it and he let himself in. He was pleased to see she had filled the refrigerator and he had already put a family-sized ready-cooked lasagne in the microwave when the brothers arrived.

This was not the first time they had been to the UK but their English was not as good as Yusuf's and when they talked together it was in Arabic. They were all worn out from a long day of travelling and the meal had made them feel even more tired. Habab and Shiraz were about to go to bed when Yusuf's phone rang. It was Kylie again.

"What's up?" Yusuf asked as he put the phone to his ear.

"I've been in touch with Angel and she said she could see you tomorrow at the usual place about eleven o'clock."

"Good," Yusuf said. "Incidentally, thanks for doing the shopping and getting things ready."

"No problem," said Kylie. "Bye for now."

Yusuf switched off the phone and looked across at the brothers. They had waited to see if the call was important.

"I've got to go out tomorrow morning," he said. "I want you to stay here until I get back. I expect there'll be a few things to do."

The brothers nodded and then left the room to go to bed.

Yusuf stayed up for another half an hour. He wanted to think. There were still many questions in his mind but, hopefully, Angel would be able to answer some of them when he saw her the next day. She might not be very bright but she could find out things. Most importantly, he knew he could trust her with his life and, with a grim smile, Yusuf thought that was exactly what he was doing.

It was no chance that they had met. He had contrived their first meeting six months before by seeming to bump into her by accident when she was laden with shopping. Her bags had spilled onto the ground and he had insisted on replacing an extravagantly iced cake which looked as if it had been damaged by the impact. In fact, it had actually been crushed when he discreetly stepped on it, but the offer had led to a coffee where his good looks and natural charm had persuaded her to agree to another meeting when she was next in London. That had followed only a few days later and Yusuf knew then she had come back to London not to shop as she claimed, but to see him again. He had been very attentive and their affair had begun a couple of days after that.

Within a few weeks, she had poured out her frustrations at the routine life she led and the dull, uninspiring companionship her boring husband thought was enough to keep her satisfied. Once she had opened up to him, it had been easy to convince her there was an exciting alternative. By the time she learnt who he really was, or rather the man he wanted her to believe he was, she didn't care. Suddenly, for the first time in her life, she felt valued as a woman. Her life had fresh meaning and, most important of all, she believed in the possibility of a different future to the one she had resigned herself to. Her world had suddenly become exciting. She knew most people would consider what she was

133

doing was wrong but she was now so deeply in love it didn't seem to matter. He had taught her you had to make your own way in this life. Everything came with a price and now, just as he had planned, he knew she sincerely believed this was her only chance left of finding some happiness.

Yusuf stretched and stood up. He didn't want to think any more that night; he needed to go to bed. The following day was likely to be busy and he wanted to be fresh. He looked around the room before turning off the light and making his way along the hall to his room.

★

It was getting late when Charlie and Daniel left his Hammersmith apartment to make their way back to the carpark where Pemberton had died. The vagrant was the only person who had actually seen someone that night and, now they had photographs of some of the people their investigation had turned up, Charlie wanted to see if he recognised any of them. At the moment, the vagrant was their best chance of establishing a link between any of their suspects and Pemberton on the night he died. Robert had called shortly after Daniel had returned home to say his search of the records from Warbeck's phone had turned up nothing out of the ordinary. All the numbers related to respected members of the business community and all the information he had been able to find on the man himself simply tended to confirm what Warbeck had told Daniel that morning. He was an independent business consultant with a number of highly placed contacts. If he was in communication with others involved in some sort of doubtful activity, then it was probably on a different phone.

The tail Daniel had placed on Warbeck had not been any more successful. They had not been able to follow the taxi but they had got the registration. Unfortunately, all they had been able to find out was that Warbeck had been dropped off somewhere near Eaton Square and there the trail went cold.

Warbeck had not returned to either his office or his home, but both were still being watched. He seemed just to have disappeared for the time being. The fingerprint search was still going on but Daniel was starting to believe that would lead to a dead end as well. Simon Warbeck was obviously not what he appeared to be, but he had been very careful and that made Daniel sure he was dealing with a professional.

Getting photographs of Farquharson, Yusuf al Shamar and Warbeck had been straightforward. Daniel's men had photographed Warbeck as he got into the taxi and images of the other two featured on the websites for their businesses. Armed with these, Charlie and Daniel had set off for the carpark. Garage space in London is a luxury and Daniel paid an annual exorbitant fee for a resident's parking spot near his apartment. As he and Charlie walked along the street to his car, they noticed a large Mercedes parked on double yellow lines ahead of them. Charlie was just about to make some remark about how the wealthy seemed to think they were above the law when the driver's door opened and a tall, well-built man got out of the driver's side. He stood in front of them, blocking the way, and they both stopped.

"Mr Rankin?" said the man.

Daniel was taken by surprise at being addressed by his name but said nothing.

"My employer would like to have a quick word if it's convenient," the man continued and leant forward to open the back door. As it swung open, he stood back again, stopping them from getting past.

"Would you mind moving out of the way, please," said Charlie. The driver's sudden appearance had unnerved him and he knew he was no match for the man should he try to force his way through.

"Mr Rankin." The voice from inside the car was deep but did not sound threatening. "Mr Rankin," the man inside the car repeated, "please get in. You are in no danger. I just wish to have a word."

Daniel took a step forward and peered into the car. The man sitting in the back seat was grossly overweight but dressed in an expensive suit that had clearly been hand-tailored. There was a smile on his round face and he was completely bald.

"We have never actually met," said the man, "but I think we probably know a great deal about each other. At least, I know a great deal about you. Perhaps it would help if I introduced myself, I am Ira Goldstein."

Daniel relaxed a little. Now he knew the name he began to identify the face. He had seen a photograph of the man once but that had been a long time ago and the figure in the picture had been much younger, slimmer and with a thick mane of black hair.

"I didn't recognise you without the hair," he said.

The man laughed.

"I lost that many years ago. Thank you for not mentioning the extra weight. That's what happens when you leave the field and sit behind a desk. No doubt you will find out for yourself one day. Please, get in."

Daniel stood up again and turned to look at Charlie.

"It's alright," he said. "I know him."

Ira Goldstein was his counterpart in Mossad, the Israeli Secret Service. Whilst there was always a lot of communication between the Secret Services of Britain and its allies, there was rarely any need for their heads of departments to communicate with each other directly and Daniel and Goldstein had never actually met or spoken together. As Daniel bent down to get in the car, Charlie took a step forward to follow him and was blocked by the driver who put a hand out to stop him.

"Just Mr Rankin," he said.

Charlie looked to Daniel for help and Daniel nodded.

"It's alright," he said. "Just wait here."

Charlie stepped back and, as Daniel got into the back of the car, the driver closed the door behind him and stood in front of it with folded arms.

Now he was sitting next to him, Daniel could see more clearly how the years had not been kind to Ira Goldstein. He looked tired and there were deep lines etched into his face.

"Well, you said you wanted to talk, go ahead."

Goldstein seemed to avoid looking at him and stared abstractedly out of the window. Daniel got the impression this was part of a performance for his benefit.

"It's a rather delicate matter," Goldstein began. "I am here to ask a favour."

"We have the proper channels for that sort of thing," Daniel said. "Why did you come in person?"

"Sometimes the personal touch can succeed more quickly where the proper channels will be full of delays. And this could be important."

"Of course," said Daniel in a matter-of-fact way that showed he understood the real reason why they were meeting like this, "and there is no official record."

"Precisely," said Goldstein, breaking into a smile. "I am glad you have grasped the nature of the situation so quickly. As far as our two countries are concerned, I hope we can continue to say we have never met."

"Agreed," said Daniel. "Now what exactly is this favour you want?"

"You are trying to find Simon Warbeck, aren't you?"

It was a statement, not a question, and all the more surprising for being unexpected. Daniel said nothing.

"I would like you to stop looking for him," Goldstein continued.

"Is he one of yours?" Daniel asked.

"Not exactly."

"Then why are you so interested?"

Goldstein ignored the question and smiled enigmatically.

"I will come to that," he said, "but can you tell me first why you're looking for him?"

Daniel was not sure he wanted to tell Goldstein but his curiosity overcame his reluctance.

"I want to ask him a few questions."

Goldstein looked at him and raised an eyebrow. Daniel knew it was not enough.

"I believe he may be involved in the murder of one of our leading scientists," he added.

"Let's not play games, Mr Rankin," admonished Goldstein. "We should be honest with each other. A man like you does not waste his time in trying to solve a common-place little murder. I think you want him so you can get your hands on Michael Pemberton's notes for the genetic modification of a virus."

If Daniel was surprised at the extent of the man's knowledge he was not going to show it. There was a short silence between them before he replied.

"Actually, it's a bit of both."

"In that case," said Goldstein, "I can perhaps help you with the one but not the other. I am prepared to confirm Simon Warbeck was indeed involved in the murder of Michael Pemberton."

"And the notes?"

"That I cannot help you with. You are not going to get the notes."

Daniel was beginning to get impatient. He knew he was at a disadvantage and didn't like it.

"And just what makes you so damned sure?"

"Because I have them now, or rather, my country is looking after them. Don't worry, they are safe and I don't expect those notes will ever see the light of day again."

It took Daniel a moment to absorb what he had just heard. He believed Goldstein. There was no reason for him to lie and someone had to have the notes; it even made some sort of sense if it was the Israelis. It was the second part of what Goldstein said that he had trouble getting his head around.

"I don't understand," he said uncertainly. "Why go to all that trouble if you're not going to use the information?"

Goldstein waited a moment before answering, as if he was trying to order his thoughts.

"Michael Pemberton was a clever man," he began, "some might say too clever. He made a discovery that would change the very nature of war in the future. I think we are all agreed that biological warfare is a terrible thing. Pemberton was about to set loose the worst of the four horsemen of the apocalypse and, as a Christian, you should know once that happens we are close to bringing about the end of the world. No one in their right mind wants to do that but no one tried to stop him, not even your own government. What Michael Pemberton eventually discovered he kept secret, not because he was scared, as he should have been, but because he knew the value of his discovery. He was going to pass the information on to those who would use it for their own ends.

"Let us be kind and say your government was just being naïve, too trusting, that because he had signed the Official Secrets Act he would never betray them. But although they knew what he was working on, they did nothing to improve their security. They were doing nothing to stop him from passing the information on to someone else. It really was negligence of the highest order. Someone had to intervene."

"You?" said Daniel disparagingly.

"As I said, we have his notes now and they are safe; nobody will ever be able to use them."

"Except you, of course."

"Why should we want to do that?" Goldstein seemed genuinely surprised. "I have just explained we believe they are too dangerous for anyone to use. We may be many things but we are not that foolish. If the atomic age has taught us anything it is that some discoveries are probably best left unexplored. We have already almost destroyed the world once. Someone needs to act as a policeman to stop these things from happening again."

"And that's you, is it? Israel has now become the self-appointed policeman of the world? Need I remind you there are international agreements in place to prevent the use of biological warfare. My government is a fully signed up member. We would never have used it. We would have stopped it."

"But you had your chance and did nothing. You knew what he had discovered and, let's face it, we both know your government was secretly delighted. Do not tell me your armed forces weren't thinking of using the information for themselves. I know all about their arguments. Now they say the use of biological warfare is justified under the terms of those agreements. They explain it would only be used as a defensive measure. They argue its use could save many lives. They said the same thing about Hiroshima. Your generals have become very clever with words, using rhetoric that could eventually destroy the world. We decided in this case action was better than words. Life is too precious for such niceties."

"And what about the life of a brilliant scientist?" Daniel retorted bitterly. He was angry and frustrated now; he knew Goldstein was right but didn't want to admit it. He wanted to accuse his counterpart of being as big a hypocrite as he was asserting the UK government was. "A thousand deaths or one," he continued, "is there any moral difference in the end? Let's be real, Israel couldn't care less about the preciousness of life provided it gets what it wants. You're just as bad; you killed Pemberton because you wanted his notes, not because you want to make him some sort of example."

"Pemberton's death was unfortunate but necessary," Goldstein replied patiently, as if he was speaking to a temperamental child. "And if we had we wanted to make an example of him, we would hardly have gone to the trouble of making his death look like a suicide. No, that was not the reason Pemberton died; you are not thinking properly, my friend. What is the point of our having the notes if he were still around to make another copy? If we wanted to make certain this information is kept from the world for ever, he had to go. Think of it as collateral damage. You may not agree with our actions but I think we have done you a favour. He was about to betray your country. As I said, he was going to pass on the information. Would you rather some of your enemies got hold of it?"

"I can't say as I'm exactly overjoyed that it's in your hands now. Who's to stop you from using it?"

Goldstein laughed. A rich, deep booming laugh that filled the car.

"*Quis custodiet ipsos custodes*? Is that it? Who guards the guardians? I have always thought that was a good question. But the answer is obvious, isn't it? The only guard you can have faith in is the one you trust with your life and, in a situation like this, I trust my country."

"Do you really think that's good enough? Do you honestly believe Israel is not going to use the information for itself?"

"If we cannot trust our own country," said Goldstein, suddenly becoming serious, "then what is either of us doing here?"

It was a good point and Daniel had no answer.

"What about Simon Warbeck?" he asked instead.

"What about him?"

"What's going to happen to him now?"

"To tell you the truth," Goldstein mused, "I haven't quite made up my mind. The answer partly depends on what you intend to do."

"According to you he murdered a UK citizen."

"He was acting on my instructions."

So that was it, Daniel thought. He was being asked to let Warbeck go. It left a bitter taste in his mouth but now he knew that Mossad was involved, even if he continued to look for him, should they not want Warbeck to be found then the chances of ever seeing him again were extremely remote. But was that what they wanted? Goldstein had said what happened now depended on what Daniel was intending to do. That suggested there was something to negotiate.

"You haven't told me everything yet, have you?" he said.

Goldstein relaxed back into the seat. He reached into his coat pocket and drew out a pack of cigarettes and a lighter. Taking one out and putting it in his mouth, he offered the pack to Daniel. Daniel shook his head and Goldstein put the pack away and flicked the lighter, automatically shielding the flame in his cupped hands as he held it to the tip of the cigarette gripped between his lips. He took a long draw and blew the smoke out slowly.

"There has been a long friendship between our two countries," he said. "We may have had our occasional differences in the past but today we find that we have many enemies in common. Rather than fight amongst ourselves, surely it is better to work together and overcome those who are trying to destroy us both?"

Daniel nodded his agreement.

"Simon Warbeck is someone who can help us do that," Goldstein continued. "He has information, contacts, and he is an expert in his field. What do you know about him?"

"Very little at the moment," Daniel admitted. "We crossed paths for the first time today and so far my team has not been able to turn up much."

"You will find nothing," Goldstein said confidently. "As I just told you, Simon Warbeck, or Moshe Leventhal to give him his correct name, is a highly-trained agent. Seven years ago he was one of our best undercover men. He had a knack for getting information others could not. He worked in Pakistan, Afghanistan, many other places and he was good, very good, and then, as sometimes happens, he changed. I expect you have found the same thing. You train someone hard, teach them all the skills they need to survive in a hostile world, ask them to act without question, sometimes to do unspeakable things, push them as far as you can and still expect them to remain a loyal normal human being. Some people can do that, Simon is not one of them."

"What does that mean exactly?"

"He went rogue. He decided to use the skills we had taught him for his own benefit. Five years ago, he dropped off the map quite suddenly and for a long time we believed he had been captured and killed. It was three years before we found him again, quite by chance. He had created a new identity for himself and was operating as an independent business consultant in London.

That was his cover, but in fact he was getting information, important secret information, and selling it on."

"What did you do when you found out?" Daniel asked.

"We had a choice: we could either take him back to Israel where he would stand trial and five years of training and investment would have gone to waste or we could use him. He was now in a position to provide us with some very useful information. What would you have done?"

Daniel said nothing.

"We came to an arrangement. We agreed to let him continue his little business. Everything had to be cleared by us first and we could have first bite of any cherry he came across. I think we must have become one of his best clients over the last two years. The information he's supplied has been extremely good and I have never regretted making that decision. We trained him very well. How do you think we found out about Pemberton in the first place?"

"Why are you telling me all this?" Daniel asked.

"I thought you should know what he is like before you decide anything. When I spoke to him today, he told me something I think you ought to know, but there are conditions. He wants to make a deal."

"What sort of deal?"

"He has made a very comfortable life here for himself. He wants to keep it going just as much as we do but he will only be able to do that if you agree to leave him alone. In exchange, he is prepared to give you certain information which, if it is true, will, I believe, more than make up for the loss of Pemberton's notes."

"What do you mean, if it's true?"

Goldstein gave a smile and took a final draw on his cigarette before opening the window and tossing the glowing butt onto the road.

"Tonight I am only a messenger. He has not told me everything but you wouldn't expect him to, would you? I cannot guarantee if what he has to say is true but in the past I have always found his information to be one hundred per cent reliable. If I were in your shoes, I would make the deal."

"What do I get if I agree?"

"Like I said, information."

"What sort of information?"

"I can only tell you what he has told me. He said that London is about to face the greatest threat in its history since the Black Death, but you can still stop it."

"Is that it?"

"His exact words. Isn't that enough?"

Daniel knew the decision he was being asked to make was going to be important. For a moment he was at a loss what to do but there was something about Goldstein which Daniel felt he could trust. His counterpart obviously believed in this threat and, anyway, what did he stand to lose? If he didn't go along with the deal it was certain now he would never see Warbeck again.

"Very well," he said, "I agree. What happens next?"

"Now I think it is about time you and Simon met again. I will take you to him."

"If I'm going anywhere," said Daniel, "I want Charlie to go with me."

Goldstein hesitated for just a moment before opening the car door and getting out. Charlie and the driver were standing a few feet behind the car. Charlie was looking anxious but stepped forward as soon as he saw him.

"What's happening?" he asked.

"We're going for a drive," said Goldstein briskly, opening the front passenger door of the car. "Please, get in the back. Mr Rankin would like you to join us. He will explain everything."

He got into the front passenger seat and closed the door. The driver started to get in the car and Charlie opened the back door and bent down to look at Daniel.

"It's alright," said Daniel. "Get in. We're going to meet Simon Warbeck."

A look of surprise flickered across Charlie's face but he did as he was told. He closed the door behind him as the driver turned the key in the ignition. The engine purred into life and the car drew away quickly from the pavement before speeding into the silky blackness of the night.

★

Simon Warbeck was standing by the window, peering along the dark street in front of the house. One hand held back a heavy curtain and the other was arched over the glass, trying to stop the reflection of the brightly lit room behind from obscuring his view. He had been standing like that for almost an hour and knew it was a pointless exercise; looking for the car would not make it arrive any sooner. There had been many occasions in the past when he had been forced to wait for long periods and none of those had caused him the anxiety he was feeling now. But this was different; this time he was not the one in control.

The house in which he was staying was a small detached building on the outskirts of London. It had been constructed in the 1950's as part of the small housing boom that followed the post-war years. Like most of the four-bedroomed residences built at the time, the rooms were not large but adequate. For many years, it had belonged to a wealthy Jewish businessman and his family. Once his sons had grown up and left to make their own way in the world, he and his wife had decided to downsize and move to the country where he could enjoy his retirement. That was when the house had been acquired by the Israeli Secret Service. As threats from the Cold War and then the PLF grew more significant, the need for safe-houses where agents and others could stay hidden became more important. Although by the twenty-first century the politics had changed, the necessity for such places had not. Every Secret Service in the world had similar houses in the major cities of every country, each one regularly modified to accommodate the latest advances in security technology.

Simon waited another quarter of hour before letting the curtain fall back into place. Although there were two other people in the house, they were occupied with other things and he was alone in the room. He walked over to the door and opened it. He was about to call out when he changed his mind and, closing the door quietly, went over to sit in one of the armchairs in front of the fireplace. Unlike some of the rooms in the house, this one had been left almost unaltered apart from the furniture. It was the rest-room, a place where the agents who worked there could unwind when they were off-duty. It was a comfortable place to be but Simon was unable to relax. So much of his future depended on what was happening outside of the room and he was unable to influence any part of it.

Another half an hour passed before he heard a car pulling onto the gravel driveway. He resisted the temptation to get up and look through the window again. He wanted to give the impression of being at ease, of being the one in control. If they sensed his anxiety then his position would be weakened. He had to appear calm and knew that was best achieved if they found him looking as if he hadn't a care in the world. He picked up a magazine from the table and started flicking idly through the pages. And waited.

Ira Goldstein was the first into the room, followed by Daniel and then Charlie. Simon looked up from the magazine as if slightly annoyed at the interruption. Daniel wasn't fooled by the performance. He understood perfectly what must have been going on in Simon Warbeck's mind and felt no sympathy for him. Warbeck had been instrumental in the death of Pemberton and, although Goldstein had not said so specifically, Daniel was now sure that Warbeck had been the one to pass over Pemberton's notebook to the Israelis. The idea of negotiating with the man was repugnant and he had only agreed to come this far because he had known there was nothing else he could do in the circumstances. He hadn't liked doing it but this sort of thing came with the job. He needed to keep his personal feelings to himself; this was business.

"Mr Warbeck," he said curtly, "or do you prefer Leventhal?"

Simon was completely unfazed by the use of his correct name. He casually put the magazine aside and stood up.

"Warbeck will do," he said. "I've got used to it now."

"Mr Goldstein said you wanted to see me."

"I'm glad you came, Mr Rankin," Simon said and stretched out his hand.

Daniel made no attempt to take it and, after a moment, Simon let his hand fall back to his side. He should have expected that. First round to Mr Rankin, he thought.

"I have played my part," said Goldstein, turning to Daniel. "I will leave you alone now to discuss your business in private. Call me when you have finished and I will take you back to your apartment."

He gave a slight nod and left, closing the door discreetly behind him. They all knew the room was bugged and privacy was the last thing they could expect but nonetheless, with Goldstein's exit the atmosphere changed slightly.

"Please, make yourselves comfortable," Simon said and sat back down in the armchair, glancing at Charlie. "I was expecting you to come alone."

"Charlie Watts is working with me," said Daniel as he sat opposite. "Anything you have to say you can say in front of him."

"I don't know who Mr Watts is," said Simon.

"If that's going to be a problem, then I can leave now," said Daniel, making as if to get up again.

"No," said Simon quickly. "If you're happy for him to stay then so am I."

Round two to Daniel Rankin.

Charlie sat down on the settee against the wall opposite the fireplace. He knew he was not going to be a part of the discussion. His role was to observe Simon Warbeck. There was a drawn out silence between Daniel and Simon as they weighed each other up; each of them was reluctant to be the first to speak. After a few minutes, Simon's nerves got the better of him and he cleared his throat. Three nil to Mr Rankin.

"Has Goldstein explained what this is about?" he said at last.

"He said you wanted to make a deal."

"That's right. I take it that by coming here tonight you have already accepted my terms."

"I've agreed to listen to what you've got to say," Daniel said grudgingly. "If your information's good we've got a deal, if it isn't then you'd better not show your face again in London."

"I don't think you'll be disappointed," Simon said. "Goldstein's explained what I want in return?"

Daniel said nothing but gave a slight nod. One round to me, thought Simon.

"Just so we're clear," he continued, "I will get complete immunity. You will call off your dogs and I'll be free to continue my business without being watched in the future. I assume Goldstein has told you how I make my living. There will be no interference and anything that happened between me and Pemberton will be forgotten."

"Just so we're clear," said Daniel, deliberately echoing Warbeck's words, "we will leave you alone but your immunity only extends to Pemberton. If I find out you're working against the UK again or murdering any more of its citizens, then I'll hunt you down even if I have to go to the ends of the earth."

"As a matter of fact," said Simon with an ironic smile, "I didn't actually kill Pemberton myself. But what you've said sounds fair. I am not an enemy of the UK. It might interest you to know that some of my clients have been highly-placed members of your own armed forces, I have even had dealings with some of your government ministers. The way things with Pemberton turned out was not of my seeking. His was a very particular case. It's not how I normally conduct my affairs and I don't expect anything similar to happen again."

"So, now we're agreed on my part of the bargain," said Daniel grimly, "what's yours? Let's hear this information you've got."

Simon sat back in the armchair. He was starting to feel he was taking charge. He waited a moment as if thinking what to say next before speaking. He had a story to tell and, if he wanted

Daniel Rankin to think the deal was one worth making, he needed him to appreciate fully the drama behind it.

"When I was eventually able to see exactly what Pemberton was carrying in his briefcase, I discovered it contained more than just the notebook. Pemberton kept all his private notes in that briefcase. It went everywhere with him. He must have thought as long as he never let it out of his sight his secrets would be safe but, although he may have been a brilliant biologist, he had absolutely no idea about security. He had probably heard enough stories to believe computer technology was not reliable and didn't trust them for his private research so -"

"So he wrote everything down by hand," interrupted Daniel abruptly. "I already know all this. Get to the point. What else was in the briefcase?"

"Papers," said Simon calmly, concealing his resentment at not being able to tell the story in his own way. "Papers in his handwriting that showed he was working on something else, this time something the Institute knew nothing about. After reading his notes, it became clear Pemberton had been researching the experiments carried out at Porton Down in less fastidious times. In particular, he had focussed on one test carried out on the London Underground in the sixties. Perhaps you already know of it; the scientists secretly introduced just 30 grams of a bacillus into a Tube train on the London Underground."

"Why should anyone do something that stupid?" Charlie broke in, unable to keep silent at such a shocking revelation.

"It was benign and they wanted to find out exactly how vulnerable London might be in a biological attack," Simon explained, leaning forward. He knew he now had their full attention. "Within four days, they were able to find traces of the germ over a radius of more than ten miles on all the major lines. It proved to the scientists just how rapidly a virus could spread when used in a tactical way. But that's not all. London was very different then and the bacillus they used was harmless. Using that information, Pemberton was extrapolating how rapid the spread would be today using a virulent form of a disease. He reckoned that using just one particular virus London would be completely closed down after just fourteen days."

"Did the notes say what sort of virus?" Daniel asked.

"Ebola."

Both Daniel and Charlie looked at each other in silence.

Simon sat back again, pleased with himself. He had produced the effect he wanted. Another round to me, he thought. This was starting to go well now.

Daniel remained silent, staring ahead and trying to think. He knew no more than the average layman about Ebola but the very name of the virus was enough to raise the hairs on the back of his neck. There had been a number of outbreaks in recent years, all originating in Africa but, in these days of quick and easy travel, all of them had sent the Western world into a panic. He knew the disease was easily passed through body fluids and that the mortality rate was extremely high. There was no known cure. If what Simon was saying proved to be true, Daniel realised he would need to know a lot more about the disease but, even before that, he needed to establish exactly why Pemberton had been conducting research into its effects. There was one possible chilling answer. He looked back at Simon.

"So, Pemberton was working on Ebola," he said in measured tones. "What's so odd about that? He must have been looking at lots of different diseases every day in his work at the Institute. What makes you think I should be interested in this particular one?"

Even though Daniel was trying not to show it, Simon could tell he was unsettled. It was time to deliver the final blow.

"In the notes," he began slowly, "Pemberton claims to have created a particular variant of the Ebola virus, one that he thought was going to change the nature of warfare in the future. In fact, the notes suggest he had already prepared some samples ready for use. He called it 'Husam al din'."

Daniel showed no reaction on hearing the name but inside he felt a heavy weight in the pit of his stomach.

150

"It's Arabic," Simon continued. "It means 'Sword of the Faith'.

"I know what it means," said Daniel curtly. He wasn't going to say it was also the alias used by Yusuf al Shamar.

"It's an odd name for him to choose, isn't it?" Simon mused. "I didn't think Pemberton knew any Arabic but, of course, someone might have suggested it to him. However, it makes me believe Pemberton could have been working for a terrorist organisation and about to unleash this virus on London."

"Just because he used an Arabic name doesn't mean he was working for terrorists," said Daniel, not very convincingly.

"True," Simon agreed, "by itself it might not mean anything, but start to put all we know about Pemberton together and a different picture begins to emerge. First, this information is in his private notes, in his own handwriting and kept in a briefcase he never let out of his sight. That suggests this was not connected with his normal work for the Institute. I don't think they knew anything about it. You can check, of course, but I think you'll find he was keeping it secret from them. Secondly, why should he be researching the effect such a virus would have in London unless he was actually thinking of releasing it there? Finally, not to mince words, we both know now that Pemberton was a traitor. He was going to pass his information on genetic modification to others. I think he was also going to pass on the samples he had prepared."

Daniel said nothing but the look on his face showed Simon that he was thinking the same thing.

"So," Simon said, stretching out his hand, "do we have a deal?"

"We have a deal," Daniel said, reluctantly taking the outstretched hand and giving it a brief shake. "But I want all those notes of Pemberton you haven't already passed on and I want them tonight."

Simon nodded and stood up. Game, set and match to me, he thought.

Chapter Five

After leaving the safe-house, Goldstein had taken all three of them into central London together. They had stopped at Simon's flat where they had collected the remaining papers Pemberton had with him when he died and then Goldstein had taken Daniel and Charlie back to the flat in Hammersmith. It had already been a mentally exhausting evening but Daniel and Charlie still stayed up late going through the notes. They clearly revealed, even to a layman like Daniel, that Pemberton had been working on the experiments conducted by Porton Down in the sixties and using that information to forecast what impact the release of the Ebola virus in London would have today. His results were chilling. Worst of all, Simon Warbeck had been right. There was the suggestion in the notes that Pemberton had actually succeeded in producing samples of a variant of the Ebola virus and christened it Husam al din. That could not have been a coincidence.

It was also very apt. The Ebola virus would strike like a sword into the very heart of the city, silent and deadly, and then, almost inevitably, it would slice its way across the rest of the country and probably many more countries as well. As Goldstein had hinted, such an event would be nothing less than Armageddon; the last battle between good and evil before the Day of Judgement. If IS was truly behind this, then, given their fanatical beliefs, they would be thinking such a strike really was coming from the 'sword of faith'.

Daniel had not gone to bed. As soon as he had finished looking through the notes, he had alerted all the proper authorities. Whilst Charlie slept, he had spent the rest of the night reporting to a number of people, including the Prime Minister, in a hastily convened session of COBRA, the Cabinet Office Briefing Room A, part of the Civil Contingencies

Committee which meets to plan government responses to civil emergencies. Daniel had not entirely agreed with all their decisions but he was not a policy-maker and could understand why they had reached them. At the moment, they just didn't know enough. However, they had all been able to agree on three things: the first was that a biological attack by terrorists using the Ebola virus was imminent; the second was that the target was likely to be one of London's Underground stations. Pemberton had used the Port Down experiment to judge the effect and nothing else would facilitate the spread so well. The third thing on which they had agreed was that for the time being all the information Daniel had shared must remain top secret. The last thing the government wanted was to make public anything that might panic the population. That could be almost as disastrous as a real epidemic. Unfortunately, it would be impossible to close the Underground and there was no way that a watch could be maintained on all the stations. Daniel was told he had to act fast.

He was to continue his investigation until a real threat could be confirmed but, unfortunately, the conditions they imposed meant he was going to be limited in the resources he could use. He was not even allowed to inform members of his own department. Given the nature of the possible danger, the fear was that no one could be relied upon to keep the threat to themselves. People would naturally want to protect their own family members and act accordingly. Inevitably, sooner more likely than later, the results of their precautions would lead to the information seeping out to the press. For the moment, Daniel appreciated the government was hamstrung. He knew they could only act once they knew exactly where it was going to happen, who was going to do it and how. That was what he had to discover. Until then, he was to report back several times a day. Written reports would need to follow but it was faster and more efficient, given the circumstances, to do things by word of mouth for the time being.

Daniel had eventually been told to go home and get a brief rest but he had known he would not sleep and there were still things he could do. Having now read Pemberton's notes for himself, he needed more information. He had called Emma when he thought she would be up and arranged a meeting in her Brighton home for that morning. He and Charlie travelled down together first thing and he had dropped Charlie off at the Institute before going on to Emma's house to ask a few questions.

★

Emma Nelson pointed at one of the six photographs laid out on the table in her kitchen. She had taken her time and studied each of the photographs very carefully before coming to a decision.

"I think that one could be him."

"Are you absolutely certain?" Daniel asked.

"No. That's why I said I only think that could be him. I'm sorry, but it was some time ago now and it was dark. But out of all of these I think that's the one closest to the person I saw with Michael."

Daniel looked at the photograph she was pointing toward. It was Yusuf al Shamar. Just as in any line-up, he had brought with him a number of photographs for Emma to look at. They were all men of Arabic origin who had become westernised and he had done his best to select a group that looked as similar to each other as he could find. It wasn't that he was trying to catch her out, this was just the best way for him to be as sure as he could and he needed to be certain. He swept the photographs into a pile and shuffled them together before putting them back in his briefcase.

"Thanks," he said.

"Is he your suspect?" Emma asked. "Who is he?"

"His name is Yusuf al Shamar," Daniel replied. "I'm afraid I can't tell you any more than that, but this has been very useful. Thanks for your help."

"Another coffee?" asked Emma, getting up from the table and going to the sink. She didn't want Daniel to leave straight away and she was hoping he didn't want to go either.

"Please," said Daniel. He thought another shot of caffeine would help to keep him going and he knew he still had a busy day ahead.

"Is there anything you can tell me?" Emma asked as she filled the kettle. "It's not just idle curiosity, we really do need those notes and, even though I didn't particularly like him, Michael was a colleague; I would like to see his murderer brought to justice if that's what really happened."

So would I, Daniel thought to himself, but that's not going to happen now.

"At least, can you tell me if you are any closer to finding the notes?" Emma continued as she busied herself making the coffee.

"I'm afraid you're not going to get Pemberton's notes back," he said.

She immediately stopped what she was doing and turned to face him.

"What do you mean?" she asked.

Daniel took a deep breath and let it out slowly. He was about to break the Official Secrets Act and go directly against the Prime Minister's specific orders, but he didn't care. He trusted her and holding information back would only cause delay. He thought she was the best equipped person to help him at that moment but she would not be able to do so properly unless he gave her a certain number of facts. She didn't have to have the whole picture but he knew as an intelligent woman she would probably be able to figure out certain things for herself. That couldn't be helped.

"You were right," he said. "Pemberton had written down all the notes for his discovery in that notebook he showed you, but although I know where it is now, it has passed beyond our reach."

"I don't understand," Emma said, coming over to sit opposite him. "If you know where it is why can't you get hold of it?"

"I'm sorry, I can't tell you that," Daniel sighed, "but, if it's any consolation, I genuinely believe the people who have it now are never going to use the information it contains. Incidentally, that's classified. Don't tell anyone."

Emma was flattered by the confidence but still didn't understand. She studied Daniel carefully and realised how weary he was. In her pleasure at seeing him again, she had not noticed it before but now she could tell he was exhausted. He had been hiding it until then but something had changed when he told her about the notebook. Now she was able to see beyond the mask.

"Are you alright, Daniel?" she asked gently. "You look totally done in."

"Just a bit tired," he said. "I had to pull an all-nighter."

"Look, why don't you have a short lie-down? You can use the spare room. You don't have to get back to London straight away. Have a nap for an hour or two."

"Thanks," Daniel was tempted but Charlie would be waiting for him. "That's kind but I've got to collect Charlie from the Institute later and there are still a few more things I was hoping you could help me with."

"Can't it wait?" Emma said. "I can pick Charlie up if you like and a few hours won't make any difference."

"Unfortunately, I'm afraid it might," said Daniel with a grim smile. "I really need to know these things now."

Emma sensed the urgency behind his words. It alarmed her slightly but she instinctively knew better than to show it.

"OK," she said, concealing her concern and becoming business-like. "But have your coffee first, it'll help. I'll make it strong and then we can talk."

She got up and went over to the sink. Daniel relaxed. It was a nice feeling to have a woman fussing over him again. It was one of those things you didn't know you missed until it started up again and it had been a long time since his divorce. Emma brought two mugs of coffee over to the table and sat down opposite him.

"Drink," she said. "I've put some cold water in yours so it's not too hot."

Daniel obediently raised the cup and took a large gulp. He set the mug down and looked at Emma. She smiled and he thought again how beautiful she was. This morning her blue eyes seemed a shade darker, more like sapphires than cornflowers, and she was also wearing a light touch of lipstick. He knew she didn't usually wear make-up and suspected it was only because she had been expecting him. He was flattered she had taken some trouble and wanted to say something that would compliment her in return, something that would convey what he was feeling, but suddenly he felt shy.

"You have a lovely smile," he said instead.

She blushed but he could tell she was pleased.

"You must want my help very badly if you're trying to butter me up," she said. "Now, what do you want to know?"

Daniel sighed. They had shared a brief moment of quiet intimacy and he would have liked it to continue but right now there were more urgent matters demanding his attention.

"It's about the sort of work Pemberton was engaged in," he began. "Everyone I've spoken to seems very impressed by what he was doing, but just how important was this breakthrough? Where was it heading?"

"He was working on developing variant strains of viruses."

"What does that mean exactly? What's involved?"

Emma smiled.

"Just how much science do you know?" she asked.

"Not much, so keep it simple."

"I expect you've heard of GM foods," she said and then paused as she saw the blank expression on Daniel's face. "Genetically modified food," she explained patiently. "Well, it's a bit like that. If you want to change an organism, give it a particular quality it doesn't have in nature, you have to alter its DNA. You start by identifying the gene carrying the desired characteristic you want to transplant. That is found in the genome of a different organism to the one you're working on. You then cut that out from its DNA using restriction enzymes and introduce it into the DNA of the organism you want to modify. To do that, you just use the same method in reverse. You cut open the DNA of the organism you want to change, again with a restriction enzyme, insert the gene bearing the new quality you want it to have and then seal the DNA up again with a ligase enzyme, a bit like using superglue. The modified organism will now share the characteristic of the gene you've introduced. When it reproduces, that characteristic will be passed on."

"That's the simple version?" Daniel asked with a smile.

"Sorry, I know it was still a bit technical but that's it, in a nutshell, and as basic as I think I can make it."

"If they've already been doing that with food, then what was so special about Pemberton's work?"

"Nobody has been able to do it successfully with a virus before. Not in the way Michael did. Michael claimed he had managed to introduce a gene that made it sensitive to particular temperatures, but that's just the start. Mutations happen in nature all the time, in fact, viruses often mutate by themselves, think of the flu virus. New strains are always developing. That's why you have to get a different flu jab each year. But we've never been able to control the specifics. Michael's work opened a door that could enable us to design a particular variant - if we only had his notes."

"So he could have produced a mutant form of a deadly virus capable of doing something the original could not?"

"Exactly."

Daniel finished his coffee in one gulp and set the mug down on the table. Although it confirmed what he already thought, he had been hoping to hear something different.

"Is that it?" Emma asked. She could sense his disappointment.

"Not quite," Daniel began. "In your work you must deal with a wide range of diseases, what can you tell me about Ebola?"

The question took Emma by surprise but she knew there must be a good reason for asking it.

"It's a disease originating in Africa," she said. "It first came to light in 1976 in a village near the Ebola river. That's where it gets its name but there are different types, in fact, five different variants have been identified so far. Was there a particular one you wanted to know about?"

"The most virulent, I suppose."

"They're all pretty virulent, but the one we know most about is the Zaire species. A lot of research was done on that recently because of the latest outbreak. That caused more deaths than all the others combined; well over twenty thousand. It began in Guinea and then spread overland fairly quickly to Sierra Leone, Liberia and Nigeria. There were even cases reported in Senegal, Mali and the States because of infected people using air travel."

"Didn't they realise they were sick?"

"Probably, but the initial symptoms are very close to other illnesses and fairly mild. There would have been nothing bad enough to make them think they had Ebola at the time and, in most cases, they travelled before a proper diagnosis of the outbreak had been identified."

"What are the symptoms?"

"A bit like flu in the beginning: aches and pains, tiredness, fever, loss of appetite, that sort of thing. Then, after a couple of days, it all gets worse: vomiting, diarrhoea and a high temperature. About half the patients will develop a rash after a week and all of them will feel too ill to do anything but lie very still and stay in bed. Most will suffer some form of internal bleeding. That's usually the main cause of death."

"Is it always fatal?"

"No. Death rates vary from 50 to 90%. It really depends on how quickly they're diagnosed and what sort of care they're able to receive. Some work has been done on producing anti-bodies but so far it's not been reliable. Unfortunately, most places in Africa do not have good care facilities. That's why the World Health Organisation steps in to help stop the spread."

Daniel paused to think about what Emma had said. Until that moment he had believed getting Ebola was like getting a death sentence. Although a fifty per cent death rate was horrifying enough, she had given him some sort of hope that things might not be as catastrophic as he had feared at first. But he still needed to know more.

"Let's suppose, for the moment, there was an outbreak in this country," he began, "say in London for example, would we be able to cope? How fast would it spread here?"

"We have a very good standard of care," Emma explained. "As soon as someone was diagnosed they would be isolated and all their contacts traced and placed in quarantine. The disease is spread through contact with bodily fluids so control of an outbreak is best achieved through containment. As long as that is done effectively then the risk of the disease spreading is lessened dramatically."

"What if," said Daniel, "just for the sake of argument, a lot of people were infected at the same time? Would we still be able to cope?"

"What sort of numbers are you talking about?"

"Could be hundreds, could be thousands."

"That simply couldn't happen. Not at the same time."

"Let's suppose it did."

It couldn't unless it was done deliberately."

Emma stopped as she suddenly realised where this was leading. She stared at Daniel and her eyes widened in disbelief.

"You're not talking hypothetically now, are you? You think this *is* going to happen."

"Could we cope?" Daniel asked again.

"We haven't got the resources, not for those sort of numbers, not all at the same time," Emma said slowly. "It would take too long to try and get everything in place even if we could. No we wouldn't cope. The disease would spread like wildfire. My God! What has Michael done!"

★

Yusuf had decided to walk around for a bit after his meeting with Angel. The sky was clear with no chance of rain and there was a light breeze which was a refreshing change after the time he had just spent in the hot Syrian scrubland. He would take a taxi back to the flat when he was ready but for the moment he wanted

160

time to consider what Angel had told him before discussing anything with the al-Assad brothers.

They had met in one of the large rooms of the National Gallery. It was a place where everyone naturally spoke quietly and, if anyone stood too close, they could move on to somewhere else without attracting attention. It would be easy to spot if anyone was observing them. They had met there many times before and their visits had usually finished with them going to a hotel. Fortunately, Yusuf thought, that didn't happen this time. In order to come to London at such short notice, she had used the excuse of having to do some shopping and had to return early after buying some things from Harrods to maintain the fiction for her husband.

Yusuf had always wondered why women in the western world thought they could cheat on their husbands with impunity. Even their own holy book forbade it, not that it made much difference; the West had become godless. Yusuf's own adoptive mother had never left the house without wearing the full burqa and had always covered her face modestly with a niqab even in her own home. He was sure she now had her place in Paradise just as he was sure Angel would be damned. How ironic that she had chosen that particular codename to arrange their secret liaisons; Yusuf could hardly imagine anyone less like a messenger from God. He was glad that soon he would never have to see her again.

It wasn't that he didn't enjoy the sex. Years of being trapped in a dull relationship had made her ripe for any sort of excitement and, if he was imagining some beautiful young woman when they wrapped themselves around each other under the sheets, she was not to know that. She said she was in love with him and he had carefully done everything he could to make her believe he felt the same. It hadn't been difficult: women like her were so eager to believe what they wished to be true. No wonder they were called the weaker sex.

Yusuf crossed Trafalgar Square and paused for a moment to look at the hundreds of tourists gathered around the base of

161

Nelson's Column. They were also going to play an essential part in what he planned. They would know nothing about it, of course, but as they made their journeys home across the countries of the world, many of them would be carrying the virus in their bodies, unwittingly spreading the contagion as they went. Once they were correctly diagnosed, it would not be long for London to be established as the common factor between them. How long after that before London became a no-go area? A few days? More likely a few hours. London was going to grind to a halt. As one of the prime economic centres of the world, the knock-on effect would be devastating. Financial markets would crash; the Western economy would be in chaos. It would take years before any recovery could start, if ever. And long before that, the caliphate would have seized the opportunity to deal the coup de grace to its crippled enemy; the world was about to change. But before it could begin, he still had things to do.

The information Angel had given him that morning had been reassuring. The police and the Ministry of Defence were apparently still treating Pemberton's death as a suicide. Although Yusuf was sure the scientist hadn't killed himself, it meant any investigation they were carrying out was going in the wrong direction and was good news. The most important thing was that Angel believed the virus was still secure in the Institute. All he had to do now was get it and he knew he had to act quickly. There was always the possibility that with Pemberton gone and unable to look after them, someone would dispose of the cans containing the virus, completely unaware of the significance of what they were doing. Although Angel was known at the Institute that actually worked against her trying to fetch them. She didn't have security clearance for the area where they were stored and, if she were spotted, would be recognised. She would not be able to explain what she was doing there or how she had got in. It was too risky for her to make the attempt so he would have to get them himself. The sooner the better. It would have to be done when everyone at the building had left for the day and Angel had now provided the means.

In the inside pocket of his jacket he had photocopies of two different security passes: one would get him into the Institute building and the other would gain him access to the closed off section for government research where Pemberton had worked. Yusuf could hardly believe how lax security was considering the nature of their work. A simple bar-code once swiped would allow him to punch in a digital code that would open each door. All he had had to do was make himself good copies of the security passes, replacing the photograph of the undistinguished man on them with one of himself. Now Angel had given him the numbers for the digital codes, there should be no trouble getting in.

Deciding not to waste any more time, Yusuf hailed a taxi. The al-Assad brothers would be able to make proper copies of the passes and, if they worked quickly, he might even be able to go down to Brighton that evening. Yusuf felt his heart quicken at the prospect. He looked out of the car window as the taxi made its way toward Westbrook Grove. The streets were crowded with tourists and people going about the business of their daily lives. Enjoy yourselves whilst you can, Yusuf thought to himself, you don't have long.

★

Sitting in the Prof's office, Charlie drummed his fingers impatiently on the arm of his chair and hoped Daniel was faring better than himself in finding out information. Whilst Daniel had been talking to Emma, he had been closeted with The Prof, trying to discover if the woman Emma had seen that night of September 3rd could have been one of the workers at the Institute. From what he and Daniel had learnt of Pemberton, it was the most likely possibility. Pemberton had rarely made trips into Brighton itself and if there was some sort of conspiracy involving other people, as now seemed the case, then it made sense if they were working in the same place. No longer sure who could be trusted at the Institute meant Charlie had to treat everyone who worked there as a suspect and that made it extremely difficult to ask questions without revealing just how much he and Daniel had actually discovered. If he were to spook whoever it was, not only might it give them a chance to escape but, more importantly, it could have the effect of bringing forward the date of the operation they had planned. Daniel and Charlie knew they had to tread carefully and that was what Charlie had been doing at the Institute that morning.

His meeting with Professor Ken Robinson had so far achieved mixed results. Of course, apart from Emma, no one at the Institute knew the exact nature of their investigation and The Prof was still under the impression Pemberton had committed suicide. He still seemed more anxious to avoid being blamed for Pemberton's poor record-keeping and the loss of the notes than in helping Charlie get the information he really needed. To avoid alerting anyone to what they had uncovered, Charlie had taken the line that they now believed it possible Pemberton was having a secret relationship with one of the women at the Institute and killed himself when it came to an end. It was a flimsy cover story and Charlie was not happy using it, but it had proved effective and those he had talked to at the Institute so far had accepted the notion without question. Unfortunately, Charlie was disappointed with what they had been able to tell him.

Emma was the only female member on the team of Operation Sundown and she was the only one at the Institute whom Charlie and Daniel had ruled out. There were a few other women biologists working there on some of the non-government projects and a number of female lab assistants, but Pemberton would have had little if any contact with any of them. Trying to establish the identity of the woman with Pemberton when he had met Yusuf was going to be more difficult than Charlie had hoped. Emma's description of the woman would narrow down the field a little and they needed to question those women about their whereabouts on the evening of the meeting. However, Charlie's gut was already telling him none of them was going to be the one they were looking for. He had already thanked The Prof for his time and been about to leave when Daniel arrived in the office to join them.

One look at the grim expression on Daniel's face was enough to tell Charlie that the interview with The Prof was not over. Without being invited to do so, Daniel removed his coat and put it over the back of a chair before sitting down. He crossed his legs and leaned forward, staring intently at The Prof. He was in no mood to be polite: he wanted information and he wanted it quickly. He now knew that to develop a variant, Pemberton must have used an original strain of the Ebola virus to start with. The first thing to discover was if and when he might have had access to such a sample. The next step would be to find out what sort of variant he had introduced. He needed to know exactly what viruses Pemberton had been working with and what characteristics they had. Armed with the information Emma had given him, Daniel wanted to learn how the Institute acquired the active viruses they needed for their practical work. He began by asking The Prof what viruses Pemberton had been working on to modify the DNA to make it temperature specific.

"It was one of the first things I checked when I realised his notes were in such a mess," The Prof said, and Charlie thought he sounded a little embarrassed. "If we knew the exact virus he was working on when he made his discovery, it would help enormously in trying to replicate what he had done."

"What did you find?"

"Nothing," The Prof replied reluctantly and hesitated before continuing. "That was the strange thing. Michael must have been working on at least one active virus at some point to achieve the results he claimed but, well, to be blunt, I can find no records identifying it."

He paused again as if expecting some comment but Daniel just looked at him. There was an awkward silence and then Daniel asked, "What's the procedure for getting a virus?"

"As you probably already know," The Prof continued, "we can order any virus we need through one of the secure labs located in various parts of the country. When someone on the team requires an active sample to work with, they have to clear it with me and, once I've authorised it, the order goes in and it's usually delivered within a day or two. Everything's properly logged."

"And you're sure Pemberton must have been working on one?"

"Yes. Well, I thought he must be if he was able to achieve the results he claimed."

"But you just said you couldn't find any record of it, how come?"

"That's what I don't quite understand," said The Prof with a resigned shrug of his shoulders. "I always make a note of such deliveries on the computer. Details of when the order was placed, what and who it was for and when delivery was made. Once the work has been completed, the virus is usually destroyed and I record how and when that is done. It's not just for security, it's also a standard procedure for safety. But when I checked the computer there was nothing there for Michael for the last two months. It would appear he had not ordered any virus recently and yet I'm sure he asked for some samples not so long ago."

"Can you remember what virus that was? Could it have been Ebola?"

"I'm sorry. You've got to bear in mind I get many requests from my teams all the time. I simply can't remember them all. I rely on the computer to keep those sort of details should I ever need them. That's why I'm careful to log everything. But, as I said, when I checked for Michael there was nothing and yet, at the back of my mind, I'm still sure there had been something. The problem is, without the computer to confirm it, I just can't be completely certain now."

Daniel snorted angrily and The Prof looked slightly helpless as he adjusted his glasses and peered apologetically at Daniel.

"I'm sorry," he said. "That's all I can tell you."

"Is it possible you forgot to enter everything properly on the computer?" Charlie asked. "How certain are you the records are correct?" He wasn't entirely sure why Daniel was following this line of questioning but knew it must be important.

The Prof stiffened at the implication.

"Michael may not have kept all his notes up to date, but I can assure you, I am very meticulous about that sort of thing."

Charlie could easily believe it. The Prof struck him as a pedantic type, a stickler for detail in his own work. He would not have forgotten to do something so basic and routine and he was not the sort of person to make mistakes. However, Charlie was now out of his depth. He had no idea how computers worked but he knew they sometimes broke down and data was lost. He had heard people talk of things like hacking and crashing and he had never thought computers were as reliable or safe as most people believed them to be.

"Could the computer have got it wrong then?" he asked. "Could someone in the Institute have tampered with it?"

"I can't think why anyone here should want to do such a thing," said The Prof, startled at the idea. "Anyway, we have a very secure system. Such things just don't happen to us. That's why I can't understand it. Perhaps, my memory's playing tricks and I'm the one who's wrong. And yet," he hesitated for a moment, "I still can't be entirely sure that Michael didn't put in a request for something."

Daniel remained silent for a few minutes and then stood up abruptly.

"Well, thank you for your time," he said. "We'll let you get back to your work. I expect we'll have to speak to you again soon and I'll get in touch then."

Daniel could see The Prof had found it uncomfortable to admit as much as he had. He was a foolish man, more concerned over his reputation than in getting to the truth, but then, he didn't know what was really going on and Daniel knew there was no point in pressing him further. Besides, the information he had already given was enough to confirm Daniel's worst suspicions.

★

Charlie took over the driving back from Brighton. He thought it would give Daniel a chance to catch up on some sleep so, apart from a brief exchange where Daniel updated him on what Emma had said, neither had talked during the journey. On arriving in London, Charlie parked the car in the Daniels' reserved space and they were walking back to the flat when they saw Ira Goldstein sitting on the low wall outside the building. Judging by the cigarette butts on the pavement at his feet, he had been waiting some time and Daniel immediately wondered what more bad news could have brought him there. As they approached, Goldstein shifted his large bulk from the wall and stood up, hand outstretched to greet them.

"Let's go inside," he said as they shook hands. "I have some news."

Daniel led the way to his flat and they had not even removed their coats before Goldstein began to explain the reason behind his visit. Neither Daniel nor Charlie were surprised to learn he had heard everything that had passed between them and Simon the previous night; they had all known the room was bugged. What did surprise Charlie was the speed with which Goldstein had acted on what he had learnt.

"Yusuf al Shamar," Goldstein announced abruptly. "He's in London right now. He arrived back in Heathrow yesterday evening and now he's gone to ground."

"You've checked his home and workplace?" Charlie asked unnecessarily.

"Of course," said Goldstein. "He's not there. He's hiding up somewhere and I don't like it."

"How do you know?" Charlie asked.

Goldstein gave him a scornful look.

"Unlike your own Secret Service," he said, "we took Yusuf al Shamar a little more seriously. We've kept an eye on him ever since his arrest over that army barracks affair. We weren't happy that you let him go so easily. We still like to know where these people are, when they leave the country, where they go and when they return. It's only basic stuff but it keeps us informed. When I realised last night that he could be involved in what's going on, I ran a check on him and this is what turned up. I thought you should know as soon as possible. I'm sorry it's so little but from this point on it will be easier and quicker for you to follow it up rather than us."

"Were you tailing him?" asked Charlie.

"We don't have to do that nowadays, thank God!" said Goldstein. "Think of the manpower involved if we did. No, today virtually all international travel arrangements are made on computer. Once we've marked someone, their name will come up as soon as they make a booking anywhere in the world. If something starts to look suspicious we might do more, otherwise we just keep a record tracking their movements. It has proved useful in the past to know these things."

Charlie was impressed but Daniel had already guessed something of the sort. "Can we have that record?" he asked.

"You can but I don't think it will be very useful. It's just regular trips to Schiphol and back for this last year. Of course, he may have moved on from there using a different name or travelling by other means. That we don't know. Until last night we had no reason to think he was getting involved in anything serious."

"And you have no idea where he could be now?"

"Sorry."

"No matter," said Charlie. "I'll check the taxis from Heathrow. They might turn up something."

"I was going to suggest it," said Goldstein. "You have the manpower and authority for that sort of thing. You might also like to check whether he was travelling alone. If he is planning to do something then it would make sense to find out if anyone else was with him. That is something I am sure we would all like to know."

Charlie had already thought of that but was not put out by Goldstein making the suggestion. He had noted Goldstein's deliberate use of the word 'we' and realised he was suggesting a shift in the make-up of the investigation. It didn't trouble him; he believed the more heads they had working on this the better, even if they might sometimes overlap. But the decision about such things was not his to make.

"Does this mean we're going to be working together now?" he asked, looking at Daniel for confirmation.

Daniel paused. He did not have the authority to agree to Goldstein's involvement. He could imagine the reaction of some of the members of COBRA if they learned he had invited Mossad to help without consulting them. However, Goldstein was already involved and just that morning in his conversation with Emma, Daniel himself had already broken the Official Secrets Act; did it really matter in the larger scheme of things?

"Unofficially," he said, "I can't see a problem with that. Of course, officially this is still a UK operation and under my direction. I hope that is understood."

He looked at his Mossad counterpart and Goldstein nodded. Israeli politics were different; the relationship between his government and its Secret Service was more flexible, less bureaucratic, but he knew how things worked in other countries. He believed this operation was going to be just as important to Israel as to the UK and was not bothered if Daniel wanted to see himself as leader.

"Keep me in the loop and let me know if I can do anything," he said. "Now I should go. I have other matters that need my attention. I'll leave you to get on with your side of things."

He reached into his pocket and drew out a card and a pen. He scribbled a number on the reverse and handed it to Daniel.

"This number will reach me directly without having to go through any official channels," he said. "I think we are both agreed it is probably better to continue the way we have begun."

He smiled grimly at them both and left, closing the door behind him.

★

Charlie had insisted Daniel get some rest that afternoon. It only needed one of them to go to Heathrow and, whilst Daniel was attending his various meetings the night before, Charlie had been able to get some sleep. He had thought he wouldn't be long at the airport but evening was already approaching before he got back to the flat after talking to the taxi-drivers. He had not foreseen that many of the taxis would either not have come on shift yet or would be away from the airport working. He had been forced to wait a couple of hours for them all to turn up before everyone could be shown a photograph of Yusuf al Shamar but his patience had paid off. One of the drivers thought he recognised the picture and, after checking his records, was able to give Charlie an address in Westbrook Grove. Armed with this information, Charlie had then been able to go through the previous day's records of all the cabs working at Heathrow and eventually discovered another taxi had taken two foreign gentlemen to the same address about half an hour after Yusuf al Shamar.

The fact Yusuf was not alone and that all three men were staying together somewhere other than Yusuf's home was enough to instil a greater sense of urgency. Charlie had immediately called Daniel to let him know and, whilst he travelled back to central London, Daniel had rapidly organised the Westbrook address to be put under twenty-four hour surveillance. It was half-past five before Charlie finally returned to Daniel's flat and, as he walked through the door of the living-room, he recognised Robert, the young communications officer, standing next to the table looking over Daniel's shoulder at some papers spread in front of them. They were deeply engrossed in conversation and Daniel just nodded a greeting as Charlie entered and settled himself in an armchair in front of the gas-fire.

"Can you do it?" Daniel asked, turning back to Robert.

"Yes," the young man replied, "but I'm afraid I can't say how long it will take. We'll have to wait until someone logs on and then hope they either go to e-mail or the net."

"Do what?" Charlie asked.

"You remember Charlie from the other night," Daniel said to Robert who gave a brief smile.

"Hello again," said Charlie.

"I want to get access to their computers," Daniel explained, "find out what's on them. If anyone can do that it's Robert."

"It's quite simple, really," said Robert modestly. "If I'm near enough I can pick up the Wi-Fi signal and then I can get the IP address. Once I've got that –"

"I'm sorry," interrupted Charlie, holding up his hand, "you lost me when you said Wi-Fi, but it doesn't matter. Provided you can do what Daniel wants I'm quite happy to remain ignorant."

Robert looked disappointed at not being able to finish his explanation. He enjoyed sharing his passion for all things technological as much as he relished using the sophisticated equipment provided by the government for his work.

"When can you start?" Daniel asked.

"Straight away. I just have to pick up a few things from the house and get there."

"The sooner the better," said Daniel, standing up to indicate their meeting was at an end. "That's all for the moment. I won't keep you any longer but let me know as soon as you have anything."

"Will do, sir," said Robert, collecting up the papers from the table and putting them into a folder which he tucked under his arm. "Speak to you again soon."

Daniel walked with him to the door, closing it behind Robert as the young man left. He turned back to Charlie.

"Well done on getting the address at Westbrook Grove," he said, trying to stifle a yawn.

Charlie looked at him. Daniel seemed exhausted but that was hardly surprising: he could only have got a couple of hours sleep at most that afternoon. Charlie would have liked to tell Daniel to go back to bed and rest some more but now they knew Yusuf was back in the country they had to work fast. Neither he nor Daniel had been surprised that The Prof thought Pemberton could have ordered a virus within the last few weeks; it was exactly what they might have expected. It was frustrating, however, not to be able to confirm it or know how much of it had been ordered and when it had arrived. Charlie's feeling was that if Pemberton had been able to produce samples of a new variant of the Ebola virus, Yusuf didn't have it yet. He had been out of the country for over a week and, although Daniel had raised the possibility that Yusuf could have obtained it before he left, Charlie just didn't feel that was right.

It would have helped if they could establish the timing of deliveries to the Institute and discover exactly what viruses had been ordered but that presented its own problems. Daniel was sure either Pemberton or his accomplice had accessed the computer and deleted all the details to cover up what they were doing. He knew it might be possible to retrieve the data eventually if it was there, but he was reluctant to get a warrant to search the computer's hard drives for the information. It was unlikely such a move could be managed secretly enough not to send a warning to whoever else might have been working with Pemberton. Until such time as they knew who that was, Daniel felt it better to wait. It was eventually Charlie who came up with a solution after they had talked things through.

"I think we should see Simon Warbeck again," he said.

"Why?" Daniel asked in surprise. "What do you think he can do?"

"I was thinking," Charlie said. "For years, apparently, he's been getting secret information to sell. How does he do that? I mean, I just don't accept we have that many traitors prepared to pass our secrets on to him and I gather that until yesterday nobody really knew the information was being leaked. I'm the first to admit I don't know much about these things but, from what The Prof said, I understand most of what Warbeck was getting would have been stored on computers. Doesn't it make sense that he's somehow tapped into them to get what he wants? That way, nobody would know their secrets were being stolen. If that's what he was doing, it's more than likely he's tapped into the computers at the Institute. After all, he knew about Pemberton's work and, although Pemberton wrote the important stuff down by hand, Warbeck must have known something about it beforehand. How did he find out unless he was able to get into their computers?"

Daniel immediately caught where Charlie was going.

"You're right!" he said, suddenly becoming animated. "I've been so preoccupied with al Shamar that I hadn't really given it much thought, but you're on to something! Simon must have hacked into the Institute's computers and that means he should still be able to look through their files without anyone knowing. Charlie, you're a genius!"

Charlie grinned shyly. However, he thought there might still be a problem.

"There is just one snag," he said. "Professor Robinson wasn't able to find the records and you said they must have been deleted. Does that mean Warbeck won't be able to find them even if he can get into their computers?"

"I'm not sure," said Daniel. "It depends how he hacked into them in the first place, I suppose. Even if the files have been deleted, they should still be somewhere on the hard drive. Whether he can hack into those is something we need to find out urgently. I'm going to call Goldstein right now and ask him to set up a meeting for tonight."

He jumped up from his chair and quickly went over to the table to fetch his phone. Charlie was glad to see Daniel getting some of his vigour back. It was good to be doing something positive again but, in addition to that, Charlie was feeling quietly pleased with himself. It was surprisingly rewarding to have thought of something to do with computers which hadn't occurred to Daniel.

★

About the same time as Daniel was on the phone to Ira, Yusuf arrived on the outskirts of Brighton. He had left London about an hour before Daniel had been able to arrange for the flat in

Westbrook Grove to be put under surveillance. It had been a fast trip down and Yusuf knew he would have to wait around for a while before he could make his way into the Institute but that didn't matter; it was better to be early than late and it meant he would have some time to prepare himself for what lay ahead. Despite Yusuf's reservations about him, Shiraz al-Assad had done a good job on the computer that afternoon and in the pocket of his jacket lying across the passenger seat were two identity cards. They might not perhaps stand up to any prolonged visual scrutiny but Yusuf was confident they would be enough to get him past the electronic security measures at the Institute.

On his way back to Westbrook Grove that morning, he had stopped at a supermarket where there was a booth for taking passport photographs. On returning to the flat, he had shown the photo-strip to the brothers and Shiraz had been able to reduce one of the photographs to the correct size and made two copies. It had been a simple matter to paste them over the pictures of the man on the photocopies Angel had provided, rewrite some of the details and then make a copy of each new pass on the computer before laminating them. Not having the actual cards to work from meant they could not be sure of making perfect replicas but Yusuf wasn't worried; he knew the important part was the barcode which was clearly defined on each card. He was not anticipating any trouble but had armed himself as a precaution. He had never fired a gun in his life before but Ibrahim Khan had given him the weapon at the time of the barracks incident and told him to keep it. The gun would only be used as a last resort; it was unlikely he would be stopped but he had no intention of allowing himself to be detained. It had been a long and convoluted journey to get his revenge and he didn't want anything going wrong now he was so close to achieving it. Parking a few streets away from the Institute, he settled back in his seat and waited.

Pemberton's death had been inconvenient but it was only a minor setback. The scientist had already provided the information Yusuf needed and had also produced a variant of the virus before he died. All he had to do now was get the sample. Although he had never anticipated breaking into the Institute, Yusuf was confident that using the security passes, he would soon have the virus and be able to put the next stage of the plan into operation. There was just one niggling thought that now resurfaced whilst he was waiting: although Angel had told him the authorities were treating Pemberton's death as a suicide, Yusuf still didn't believe for one moment that men like Pemberton would do that sort of thing, especially when they were about to get what they had always wanted and were on the verge of making a new life for themselves. No, someone had killed him and that could only mean they had found out what he was doing. Now the question Yusuf pondered was exactly how much the killer knew and if they had been able to make a link with himself.

Discovering the identity of the killer was key: Yusuf really needed to know who had killed Pemberton and why if he was to make a proper assessment. One possible answer was that the British Secret Service had found out what he was up to and discreetly got rid of him in a way that would avoid an embarrassing public scandal. But Yusuf didn't believe that either. If the Secret Service had found out what Pemberton was doing then they would have managed things differently. They would have wanted to know whether Pemberton was acting alone and questioned him, perhaps keeping in the background and letting things play out until they could be sure of catching everyone involved in their net before things got too serious. But if it wasn't the Secret Service, who was it?

Although he had arranged to have Pemberton watched for almost a year, Yusuf had only actually met him twice. He hadn't needed to see him any more than that; Angel had successfully managed everything else. Yusuf had only been keeping Pemberton under surveillance for a few weeks before discovering he was having an affair with her and thought he could use the fact. He had already found out enough about Pemberton's character to know the scientist could not be bought for money.

But if he wanted Pemberton to help him then he had to be able to offer something other than blackmail. Threatening to reveal the affair with Angel simply wouldn't work. As a single elderly man, Pemberton had nothing to lose by it becoming known he was still sexually active, even if it was with someone else's wife. In fact, Yusuf thought the aging scientist might actually take some sort of ridiculous pride in it. To be sure of getting his co-operation, he needed to discover Pemberton's weak spot and, as he learnt more about the scientist and got to understand his character better, Yusuf had come to the conclusion that the scientist's greatest weakness was his professional vanity and a bitter resentment that his brilliance had never been properly acknowledged.

Yusuf could easily understand why it had never happened. The British like their heroes to be role models and there was nothing about Pemberton which fitted that description. He may have had a brilliant mind but he was arrogant and self-centred. Yusuf quickly discovered it was nigh on impossible for anyone to establish a good working relationship with him. The British accepted eccentricity. In the right circumstances they even thought it was an endearing quality, but Pemberton was just an ill-mannered thug; an ego-centric bully in a lab coat and his colleagues despised him.

Yusuf had decided that if Pemberton's weakness was an overwhelming desire for recognition of his genius, then that was what he would have to be offered. The problem would be keeping any deal secret until he was ready to act. In order to avoid any connection being made between himself and Pemberton, Yusuf had hit upon the idea of starting his own affair with Angel and using her as a go-between to persuade the scientist to do what was needed. He had recognised early on that the middle-aged woman was not in love with Pemberton but just looking for some excitement, and he felt modestly confident that given the choice between an exotic young lover and an ageing scientist, she would choose him. He had been right. Years of pent-up irritation at her husband and her boring existence had made her desperate

177

to share the frustrations of her life and he provided the sympathetic ear that the self-centred Pemberton could not.

Their affair had only been going a few weeks before she told Yusuf all about her relationship with Pemberton and how it had begun. At that point, Yusuf knew he had her; women only talked about their previous lovers when they were looking to escape the memory of them. She had become a different woman now; she was like some love-sick teenager when she was with him and he had played his part well, making her believe he felt the same. It wasn't long before he thought she was ready to do whatever he asked. He began slowly, first complaining that they had to spend so much time apart and then suggesting, if only they had the funds, how good it would be to make a life together. If they had enough money he could return to his homeland and take her with him. There he would set up his own business and look after her as he wanted to. It would be a fresh start for them both. She had lapped up every word, believing it might happen because that was what she wanted to believe. Then, one day, he had told her of a chance that could make it all come true.

He had spoken vaguely at first of being approached by one of his fellow countrymen to do something dangerous and illegal. He needed to test the waters to see how she would react and, without going into details, told Angel he had rejected the proposition out of hand but they were being very persistent. They had offered a substantial amount of money, enough to make their dreams of living together in his own country a reality if he could get her to help him but he told her he had turned them down. He explained he thought what they wanted to do was too risky. If he were to agree he would have to involve her and the last thing he wanted was to do anything that might put her in a dangerous position. Angel had been both intrigued and excited, just as he had known she would be. She wanted to find out more and, over their next few meetings as he allowed her to draw out some details of what might be involved, she had not rejected the notion; instead, she had started to give it some serious thought.

She returned to the subject whenever they met. She wanted to find out exactly what they would be expected to do.

Yusuf initially pretended reluctance to pursue the idea, fully aware that the more he did so the more insistent she would become. Eventually, after she had pressed him many times to reconsider, he allowed her to believe she had persuaded him it was the only thing to do if they wanted the chance to be together. Even when she found out the details of what was required, she had not been deterred by the prospect of what it could mean. She was not a cold, heartless woman by nature but by this time was morally blinded by her love for Yusuf and an overwhelming desire to start a new life with him. This appeared to be a golden opportunity and, to Yusuf's surprise, she found the prospect of being involved in something risky was exciting. She had never felt anything like it before and, if she ever gave a thought about the possible dangers, she just focussed on the idea that she would be starting over again with Yusuf by her side. And now he was proving his love by finally agreeing to join with her in making it possible.

They had discussed various plans and eventually agreed Angel should get back in touch with Pemberton. She was to tell him that the Institute had learnt the Abdullah Medical Research Centre in Saudi Arabia was looking to recruit someone to fill the post as Head of a new Department of Bio-medicine they were planning to open. Because of her position and contacts, Pemberton would believe her and Yusuf knew he would be interested in such a prestigious position. To avoid possible complications with the Institute, she was to say she could arrange a secret meeting with one of the Centre's representatives so that The Prof would remain ignorant. Pemberton had jumped at the chance and told her to go ahead.

The meeting Angel later arranged with Yusuf in London had worked out just as they wanted. Pemberton had been eager to impress and it had not taken much prompting for him to discuss the latest developments in his research on the Ebola virus. Yusuf showed especial interest in his work on aeroionisation and congratulated the scientist on his remarkable breakthrough, just the sort of thing his department was looking for to mark their opening. Yusuf assured him such an exclusive announcement would make international headlines, making Pemberton world famous and putting the new department at the Abdullah Medical Research Centre on the scientific map. Their meeting had concluded with Yusuf offering him the post as Head of the new Department of Bio-medicine on the condition Pemberton brought a viable sample of the airborne virus with him. Because of the significance of the discovery and the publicity it would bring, the Abdullah Research Centre would even be prepared to delay the opening until a sample was ready. However, in order to preserve their arrangement, it was essential that his latest research should remain totally secret. Pemberton agreed.

Until such time as a sample of the virus was ready, Pemberton needed to make sure nobody at the Institute knew what he was working on or planning; if word were to leak out then the offer would be withdrawn. Pemberton had agreed immediately. It was a reasonable request given the circumstances. Fortunately, although the team at the Institute knew of his work on making the virus temperature sensitive, they had remained ignorant of his latest developments. Scientists, like the institutions they worked for, were jealous of their reputations and the last thing he wanted now was to give the Institute any grounds to make some sort of claim that they owned the rights to his research. His defection to Saudi Arabia with the virus was bound to cause the Institute some embarrassment and Pemberton even found some satisfaction in the fact: if they had only shown a proper appreciation of his work before this, they would not find themselves in that position. They only had themselves to blame. Meanwhile, Angel was to act as a go between, keeping Yusuf informed of progress. Everything had been going smoothly and a sample of the virus was almost ready when something had happened to make Pemberton panic.

Ignoring his instructions only to use Angel as a messenger, Pemberton had called Yusuf directly. Yusuf was annoyed. He had stressed the importance of secrecy in their negotiations and refused to discuss anything over the telephone. He told Pemberton to get in touch with Angel and arrange a face to face meeting before ending the call. When all three of them had met in Brighton that same night, Pemberton was still in a pronounced state of anxiety. He told them that Andrew Farquharson, the editor of a science magazine, had contacted him for an interview after somehow managing to find out details of what he was working on. Pemberton was convinced someone at the Institute must have been spying on him and discovered his plans. They must then have leaked the information to the editor, no doubt in an effort to compromise him and spoil the deal, forcing him to remain in England.

It had taken all of Yusuf's patience and charm to persuade him this did not necessarily change anything. If Pemberton had followed the instructions on keeping his notes, then the most Farquharson could have discovered was a rumour that Pemberton had been working on the genetic modification of viruses and wanted some sort of scoop. He suggested Pemberton agree to an interview but confine any comments to generalisations about viral genetic modification. He explained that in some ways this could even be made to work to their advantage. Hinting to the world that a breakthrough in genetic engineering was about to be made would whet the appetite for more information and, when it was finally revealed that the King Abdullah Research Centre in Saudi Arabia had the blue print, it would be a major publicity coup for the new department. Yusuf had finally managed to calm Pemberton down and reassure him that their arrangement was still in place but he nonetheless wondered what sort of game Farquharson was playing and realised he needed to bring his own plans forward. He knew Pemberton had almost completed his work and the aeroionised form of the virus should be ready by the time he returned from his trip abroad. They had parted company with Yusuf feeling satisfied there was nothing for him to worry about. Even if someone else was chasing the discovery, they would be too late. Then Pemberton had been killed.

Who else could have known what Pemberton was up to? How much had they found out? Of course, it was possible, even likely that Pemberton himself had been indiscreet. Knowing the man's vanity, Yusuf would not have been surprised if he hadn't made some sort of veiled reference to what he imagined his future was going to be. Could someone have worked out that he was planning to leave the Institute and take his research with him? Could Pemberton himself possibly have hinted at this latest development in his career? Yusuf considered it was a possibility but, even if that were true, he didn't believe it would have been sufficient reason to get him killed. There had to be another, more viable reason to explain his death.

Yusuf realised his thoughts had brought him back to where he had started and he was still no nearer to finding an answer. Deciding that it was not going to make any difference now anyway, he glanced at his watch and saw it was almost seven o' clock. The cleaners would be finishing soon and he ought to leave. He had to time it just right; late enough for most of the cleaning staff to have left the building, but not so late that it would seem odd for one of them to still be finishing up. He removed the gun from the dashboard compartment and put it in his jacket pocket. Checking he had both security passes, he got out the car and began to make his way toward the Institute.

★

"I was not expecting to see you again," said Simon Warbeck rudely as he opened the door and saw Daniel, Charlie and Goldstein waiting outside. "What do you want?"

"Can we come in?" asked Daniel. "We've got a few questions."

"I thought we had finished with questions," said Simon curtly. "We've already made our deal."

"Yes," Daniel agreed with a grim smile, "we have. I'm not here about that. Think of me this time as more of a client."

He paused and registered the slight surprise on Simon's face.

"You're in the business of selling information," Daniel explained, "I'm here to buy."

Simon hesitated. This was not what he had expected when Goldstein had telephoned to say they were coming round.

"I suppose you'd better come in," he said and held the door open so they could pass through to the wide hallway. He led the way into a large, expensively furnished room.

"Make yourselves comfortable," Simon said, pointing to a large settee whilst he remained standing next to the plain marble fireplace. "If you're here on business then perhaps I should warn you my services don't come cheap."

"I can tell," said Daniel looking around the room as Goldstein and Charlie sat down.

The furniture was modern and stylish; the latest in Italian design. In one corner stood a large glass cabinet, its shelves displaying a collection of antique porcelain, and on the walls were a series of colourful abstract prints and original paintings. It was not to Daniel's taste but he recognised the quality. Simon could see the room had made an impression.

"You said you wanted information?" he prompted.

"In a manner of speaking, yes," Daniel said as he sat down next to Charlie. "It's obvious you get a lot of your information by hacking into computers."

Simon was about to say something and Daniel held up his hand to stop him.

"There's no point denying it," he continued. "It's the only way you could have found out about Pemberton's discovery in the first place. If you've managed to infiltrate the computers at the Institute, we want to look at a few of their other files."

"You're MI6," said Simon, "why don't you just ask them?"

"I'll come to that in a moment," Daniel said. "Can you do it?"

"Yes."

"There is just one difficulty," Daniel continued. "It would appear that the files we're looking for could have been deleted. It means you will have to search the hard drive and it's important that no one at the Institute knows you have done it. Will that be a problem?"

Simon paused. He didn't know what sort of program Rick Townsend was using or how it operated. He knew he could search current files but was uncertain whether Townsend's virus could penetrate the hard drive to find what had been deleted.

"To be honest, I don't know," he admitted. "You're right in thinking most of the information I get is obtained from hacking, but it's not something I do myself. Other people are involved. I'll have to check with them before I can give you an answer."

"How long will that take?"

"How soon do you need to know?"

"This is urgent," said Daniel impatiently. "Can you do it tonight?"

"Probably, but it will cost."

"How much?"

Simon paused to think. Daniel Rankin was obviously not used to these sort of business arrangements. He had already laid all his cards on the table and left himself with nothing to negotiate. The MI6 officer had shown he was desperate for this information and that meant he would probably be prepared to pay a lot for it. Simon had been thinking of a figure whilst Daniel was talking and now decided to double it.

"A hundred thousand."

Daniel and Charlie suddenly sat upright. They had realised Simon would probably expect to be paid for his trouble but were both shocked by the man's greed.

"You do know what we're working on, don't you?" said Daniel angrily. "You realise what's at stake here?"

Simon shrugged his shoulders.

"That's the price," he said calmly.

Daniel sank back into the settee. It was an outrageous amount of money for what he was asking. He didn't have the authority to spend such a sum and, even given the circumstances, he couldn't be sure his superiors would consent to such an amount. There were bound to be delays and the evidence he would have to provide the bureaucrats to convince them was speculative at best. And yet he was sure in his own mind that the information was both urgent and crucial.

Goldstein sat forward and gave a brief cough.

"Perhaps I could step in here," he said with an apologetic look at Daniel for interfering. "I think I might be able to help."

"By all means," said Daniel.

Goldstein turned to face Simon.

"We have known each other a long time, Simon," he began slowly, "so you know what I can do. It's important we have this information and we need it tonight. You know what the consequences might be if we fail so we are not going to pay the sum you just mentioned or anything like it. Instead, I want you to take us to this man who works for you. You will ask him to provide the information we want and then we will leave. You will do this without payment, out of the goodness of your heart, or you will be arrested and deported to Israel where you will stand trial for treason and murder of a British citizen."

"But we had a deal!" Simon protested angrily. "I have immunity, you promised!"

"Me?" said Goldstein feigning surprise. "I promised you nothing. Your deal was with the British."

Simon realised Goldstein was being perfectly serious. He went over to an armchair opposite the settee and sat down. He was thinking furiously but knew he had been out-manoeuvred and had no choice. Anyway, it wasn't as if he was going to be out of pocket; he had no intention of paying Townsend for anything the man might find. He looked up and smiled ruefully. At least he could be gracious in defeat.

"If you want that information tonight," he said, "then we'd better leave now."

★

The Bioprix Institute for Research and Development consists of several squat, concrete buildings on the outskirts of Brighton. Situated in its own grounds at the end of a curving, tarmacked drive, the Institute is surrounded by tall trees and set back from the main road so it cannot be seen. Only a wooden notice-board next to the main entrance identifies it and anyone driving past would not give it a second glance. Originally constructed in the 1980's, it was deliberately designed to look anonymous and there is nothing about its appearance from the outside that would prepare the visitor for what lies within. At the end of the drive are four two-storey buildings, three of which extend underground for another two floors. The smallest of the four, set aside from the others, is the only one to have any sign of individuality. Curtains can be seen at the windows instead of blinds and the double front doors are made of panelled wood rather than glass. This is where some of the important people who worked at the Institute have their own apartments; in fact, Pemberton had been one of them. The remaining rooms are used by their guests and the visiting scientists from abroad who are sometimes invited to lecture or assist in the research being carried on in the other buildings.

As Yusuf walked up the drive, he was looking down at his feet but was still able to catch sight of the occasional CCTV camera hidden in the trees that lined the path. He was wearing a cap pulled down over his forehead and a scarf muffled the lower part of his face. He was not concerned about being watched; even if his face could be properly seen, by the time anyone was able to make any identification it would be too late anyway. The day had been overcast and the sun was setting as he reached the buildings. The top floors were now silhouetted against the darkening sky and the rest merged into the blackness of the woods behind. He was relieved to see only a few lights on at the windows. He had timed it just right: most of the cleaners would have finished their work by now and be preparing to leave if they hadn't already done so. As if to confirm this, he saw a small group of people turn the corner of the building nearest him and begin to make their way down the drive. Two of them were pushing bicycles and, as they passed, one of them gave him a smile before continuing down the path.

Although Yusuf had never been there before, he knew exactly where to go. Angel had described the layout and told him precisely which door he had to use to gain entry to the correct building. He reached into his pocket and pulled out one of the security passes Shiraz al Assad had prepared that afternoon. He passed the first building and approached the one behind which was in darkness. He didn't make for the double glass front door that led into the foyer but instead walked around the side and saw the single wooden door just as Angel had described. He was about ten metres away when it suddenly opened and two people, a man and a woman, came out. They watched Yusuf approaching and the man stopped. Yusuf instinctively put his hand into his coat pocket and felt for the gun. He gripped the butt and hesitated.

"Come on, then," the man called. "Hurry up!"

He was holding the door open and Yusuf relaxed. He quickened his pace and nodded to the man as he reached the door.

"Thanks," he said and passed through into the building.

The door closed behind him with a soft click and Yusuf relaxed. He was in a small, dimly-lit lobby. A concrete staircase was immediately in front of him and to the side was a corridor stretching behind. Yusuf paused but could hear nothing apart from the sound of his own breathing. He walked forward cautiously. There were three doors on his left before the corridor turned a corner at the end and he stopped outside the second one, putting his ear to it as he gripped the handle. He waited a moment but there was no sound from within; the room must be empty. He slowly turned the handle and tentatively opened the door a fraction. The room was dark. He pushed the door open and felt for a light switch on the wall.

He was in a locker room where the cleaners stored their outside clothes before donning overalls and setting off for work. Taking the gun and the security passes from his pocket, Yusuf quickly removed his raincoat, cap and scarf and looked around. There were about twenty lockers set against the walls, most of them closed but a few with their doors ajar. Two benches stretched next to each other along the centre of the room. He laid the gun carefully on one of them before approaching the nearest open locker. Inside was a blue overall and a high-visibility jacket. He removed the overall and hastily pulled it over his own clothes. Picking up the gun, he put it in one of the pockets and slipped the passes into the other. After another quick look around, he turned off the light and slowly opened the door. The hallway was still empty and silent. He left the room, quietly closing the door behind him, and began to walk along the corridor.

Just past the turning at the end was a small landing where there was a lift and a flight of stairs giving access to all levels. He peered over the steps leading to the floor below and saw it was deserted. Sliding his hand along the rail, Yusuf made his way down to the next level. Angel had told him the rest-room for the government scientists working on Operation Sundown was located on this floor. In order to reach it he had to pass through two more security doors and, as he reached the landing below, he saw the first of these ahead of him. Although the stairwell was lit, a quick glance through the glass panel in the door told him the corridor beyond was almost dark. There was just a small amount of ambient light coming from the safety lights set into the ceiling. They only gave off a dim glow but it would be enough for him to find his way. Yusuf was relieved; if the main lights were off then it was likely everyone had now left. He took out the second of the passes.

Thanks to the man who had held the door open for him, he had not needed to use the first security pass and so could still not be certain whether the photocopied barcodes would work. He was about to find out. Alongside the door and set into the wall was a small metal box with a digital number-pad on the front.

There was a narrow slit at the top and Yusuf took the pass and slid it into the box. Nothing happened. He took a deep breath and carefully punched in the seven figure number Angel had given him. There was a soft click and he gave the door a gentle push. It opened. Yusuf paused a moment to make sure no alarm was going off and then passed through into the dim passageway as the door automatically shut behind him.

He now moved quickly, counting the doors as he went, and stopped outside the fifth one along. This should be it, he thought. Unlike the other doors, this one had no glass panel in it. He placed his ear against the wood and listened but could hear nothing from within. There was another digital box on the wall alongside and Yusuf slipped the security card in the slit at the top. He punched in the code and turned the handle. The door opened. The room was in darkness and Yusuf felt for the light switch on the wall. Turning it on, he slipped quietly into the room and closed the door behind him.

★

Rick Townsend sat on the edge of his unmade bed and looked anxiously at the four men crowding his bedsit. There weren't enough chairs to seat everyone, so Daniel and Charlie were sitting on the settee, Goldstein was occupying the single armchair and Simon stood impassively by the window, looking distastefully around the room. When Townsend had opened the door twenty minutes before, he had believed Simon was going to be alone. The presence of three other men behind him, all of whom exuded the imposing self-confidence of authority, had been an unpleasant shock. Townsend's first thought was that Simon had brought the police and they were there to arrest him for Pemberton's murder but that idea was immediately dispelled when Simon told him he had an urgent job that needed doing that night.

Simon had not introduced the others and they had remained silent whilst he explained what information he wanted and asked whether Townsend could find it. Although he was the one doing the talking, from the way Simon kept glancing at them, Townsend thought it was the three men with him who were actually in charge. That was quite a daunting realisation; he had found Simon threatening enough but it was even more intimidating to have others in the room more powerful and therefore, to his mind, probably more ruthless. Whilst Simon talked, Townsend tried to get a feel for who they were and had the impression the obese man sitting in the armchair was probably the most important of the three. He therefore addressed his answer to Goldstein when Simon had finished.

"I think I can probably find what you want," he said nervously. "If something's been deleted it should still be on the hard drive, it's just a matter of looking for it. Do you have the file name?"

"No," said Goldstein.

"That's a pity," said Townsend. "It may take a while then. Can you tell me what sort of information is in the file?"

Goldstein looked at Daniel.

"Is that important?" he asked.

"It could be," Simon replied. "If I had something to start with, some clue as to its content, it might not take me as long."

"Records," Daniel said. "Orders for viruses; when they were made, when they were delivered, things like that. We don't think the whole file was deleted, just part of it. That's the bit we're looking for."

"So the main file is still active?" Townsend asked.

"Yes."

"Well, that makes it a little easier but it really would be helpful if you could tell me more," said Townsend. "There must be hundreds, possibly thousands of different files on their computer. Without more information to narrow it down, I'll probably have to search through all of them before finding what you want. That's going to take a long time."

Daniel realised Townsend was right.

"Try anything to do with administration," he said. "The file we're looking for was worked on by Professor Ken Robinson."

"OK," said Townsend, "that's helpful. It's a start."

"Then get on with it," said Simon. "We're in a hurry."

Townsend looked at them nervously. He got up and fetched his laptop from the table, bringing it back to the bed and switching it on. After a few seconds the screen-saver appeared and he typed in his password. The screen cleared and, pulling the keyboard closer to shield it from view, he began to type in a series of numbers and figures. About thirty seconds later, he looked up at the others.

"OK," he said, "I'm in. You said it was Professor Ken Robinson, that right?"

"Yes," said Daniel.

Townsend hesitated. He looked around at the men who were now watching him carefully.

"If you don't mind," he said timidly, "I need a few minutes alone before I go on."

"We're not going anywhere," said Simon curtly. "Just get on with it."

Townsend sensed the impatience behind Simon's voice and accepted he was not going to get any privacy. He paused to look at them again and then reluctantly leant over and pulled out the drawer from his bedside cabinet. He turned it over and the others could see a plastic envelope containing a slim notebook attached to the underside. Townsend slipped the notebook out of the envelope and thumbed quickly through the pages.

"You do realise, don't you," said Goldstein with an amused smile, "if anyone was searching for that, it would be one of the first places they would look?"

Townsend looked up, startled.

"Just thought you might like to know," said Goldstein, unable to hide his enjoyment at the clumsy attempt to conceal the book. "Don't worry, we won't be doing anything like that."

Townsend was rattled. He laid the book flat on the bed and, after glancing at it, quickly typed in another series of letters and numbers that were on the page in front of him. He waited a moment and then looked up.

"Shouldn't be long now," he said. "I've got Robinson's files and there's one for administration. I'll just have a look around inside it."

The others waited patiently. Despite the fact it had been his idea in the first place, Charlie was still shocked at the ease with which Townsend had been able to access the supposedly secure information stored on the Institute's computer. A few more minutes passed and then Townsend looked across at Daniel.

"Is this what you're looking for?" he asked, turning the screen around so Daniel could see it.

Daniel stood up and went over to the bed to look at the display.

"I think so," he said, "but this looks like the main file. We want to know if anything's been deleted and what it said."

"Now I know I'm in the right place," Townsend explained, "I should be able to find that out soon enough."

He turned the screen back to himself and went to work on the keyboard again whilst Daniel sat down on the bed next to him. Goldstein crossed his arms and began to hum tunelessly to himself. He was used to waiting and was perfectly relaxed but Charlie was starting to get impatient. Time was an important factor; there was still a lot to be done and none of them knew how much of it they had.

"Would you mind not doing that," said Simon, looking at Goldstein who was still humming. "It's starting to get on my nerves."

Goldstein ignored him and Simon was about to say something when the ringtone of Daniel's phone suddenly startled them all. Daniel stood up, reached into his pocket and withdrew the phone.

"It's Robert," he said, glancing quickly at Charlie before speaking into the receiver. "Hello, how's it going?"

He walked across the room away from the others. They could not hear what Robert was saying but the expression on Daniel's face as he turned back to them was triumphant.

"Good, well done," he said and then paused whilst Robert spoke again. "No, I don't know how long I'll be," he continued and gave Townsend an inquiring look.

Townsend shrugged his shoulders.

"OK," Daniel said into the phone, "no, I don't think it should wait either. I'll send Charlie round now." He paused. "You can? OK, then do it. I'll ring off now and wait for you to call back."

He switched the phone off but didn't put it away.

"Robert did it," he said. "He's found something on their files which he thinks is important and is sending a copy over the phone now."

Townsend had stopped working and was looking at them. From what he had heard it was easy to guess they had someone else hacking into another computer and he wondered again who these men were and why they were looking for this information so urgently.

"Don't stop," said Goldstein quietly. "You've been doing so well."

Townsend obediently returned to the keyboard as Daniel's phone rang again. Daniel pressed a few buttons on the keypad and stared intently at the screen.

"Oh God!" he said quietly.

Charlie immediately got up and went over to look at the phone. Daniel passed it to him and displayed on the screen he saw a document that was obviously some sort of security pass. In one corner was a passport type photograph of Yusuf al Shamar and, although the rest of the writing was too small to be clearly legible, the heading at the top was easy enough to read: '*Bioprix Institute for Research and Development*'.

★

Emma was working late. Having already taken the morning off to see Daniel, she had made the practical decision to distract herself with work rather than stay at home and brood over what she had learnt. Her trip abroad the week before meant she was now slightly behind in some of her projects and needed to catch up. However, she had not achieved much since arriving at the Institute that morning. She had tried to concentrate but couldn't completely shut out of her mind what Daniel had told her. The idea that a colleague could have been involved in a plot to deliberately spread the Ebola virus had been shocking, even incredible, but Daniel believed it and she trusted his judgement. Her anger at Pemberton's betrayal was fuelled by her impotence to do anything about it. She couldn't help imagining what a pandemic of Ebola in London would be like and the more she thought about what might happen, the more frightening the prospect became.

It had gone seven and everyone else had already left by the time she decided to give up for the day and go home. Daniel had given her his private number and she wanted to call him. What Daniel had told her was top secret and he was the only person with whom she could share her thoughts and fears. She reasoned that if she was feeling like this then he might be too. When he had left that morning to pick up Charlie, as they stood together on her doorstep he had kissed her. It had not been passionate but she had felt the tenderness in his lips and knew their relationship had moved onto a different plane. He may be doing a tough job and doing it well, he may have other people he could talk things over with, but she remembered the vulnerability she had sensed when they lunched together two days before. It was one of the things she had found attractive in him. Despite his confident exterior, she was sure that although he had come down to Brighton that morning looking for information, he had sought her out in particular because he wanted the same sort of comfort she was needing now.

She looked around her empty lab before turning off the light and making her way down the corridor to the stairs. The dim safety lights in the ceiling gave enough illumination for her to see where she was going and, as she turned the corner, she was surprised to see a light spilling under the door of the rest-room half-way down. She had believed she was the only one there and thought someone had probably left the light on. It wouldn't be the first time. She took out her security card, slipped it into the box and entered a number on the keypad. As she opened the door, she saw a man with his back to her, crouched down by the refrigerator in the small kitchen area they used to make coffee and microwave snacks. The fridge door was open and he was looking around inside. She stopped in surprise.

"What are you doing here?" she demanded.

"I'm the cleaner," the man said, jumping to his feet guiltily.

She hadn't recognised him at first but now, as he turned round to face her, she suddenly knew exactly who he was. She had seen his photograph that morning spread across her table at home amongst the others Daniel had brought down to show her. It was Yusuf al Shamar.

"You!" she gasped in shock, unable to stop herself.

She froze for a moment before quickly turning to leave. But not quickly enough. Her recognition of Yusuf had shown in her face and Yusuf had realised it. The moment she had spent staring at him had given him enough time to stride across the room. He grabbed hold of her arm and pulled her toward him with one hand whilst he used the other to push the door shut. He roughly pushed her into one of the easy-chairs and stood over her.

"Do you know who I am?" he asked menacingly.

Emma stared at him and shook her head. But the slight limp as he walked had confirmed it.

"Don't lie. I can see it in your eyes."

"You're mistaken. Who are you and what are you doing here? You're not one of the cleaners."

"You know who I am. How do you know?"

"I just told you, I don't."

Yusuf paused and took a step back. Now he was unsure. But it was too late to go back to pretending he was a cleaner.

"I- I thought you were a burglar," Emma stuttered, her breath coming in short gasps. "You frightened me."

"That's right, I'm a burglar," Yusuf said. "Now shut up and stay there."

He took another step back, keeping his eyes fixed on her.

"I won't tell anyone I saw you," Emma gulped. "Just let me go and I promise I won't say anything."

"I said shut up!"

Yusuf was uncertain what to do. He was still unsure whether she had recognised him or not. It made no difference now anyway. He couldn't take the risk. He pulled out the gun and pointed it at Emma. She shrank back into the chair.

"What are you going to do?" she gasped.

Yusuf didn't know the answer himself at that moment. He had the containers holding the virus in a plastic carrier-bag which was lying beside the fridge. He needed to leave quickly but now all hope of his visit being unnoticed had disappeared. He didn't know if anyone else was in the building. If he killed the woman here, the sound of the shot might bring others running before he could make his escape. Nor could he risk taking her with him; it was too far to get her quietly to the car. Keeping the gun pointed at her, he stepped back to the fridge and picked up the carrier-bag from the floor.

"Stand up," he barked.

"Please, don't hurt me."

Emma's voice trembled with fear.

"Get up and go to the door," Yusuf ordered as he moved toward her.

Emma stood up warily and, keeping her eyes fixed on Yusuf, backed slowly toward the door.

"Open it!"

Emma turned. There was a sudden explosion of blinding agony and she fell to the floor.

Chapter Six

Emma slowly opened her eyes and immediately became aware of a throbbing ache at the back of her head. She was lying flat on her back and, as she tried to look to the side, there was a sudden sharp stab of pain. She closed her eyes and groaned.

"She's coming round."

Emma didn't recognise the woman's voice but it was comforting nonetheless. She opened her eyes again and realised she was on a bed in a hospital room.

"Don't try and move," said another voice and this time she recognised it was Daniel.

She opened her mouth to say something but her throat and mouth were so dry the only sound to emerge was a rasping croak.

"Don't try to speak," said Daniel, coming close to the bed and bending over her. "Here's some water."

She felt Daniel's hand slip behind her shoulders as he raised her head from the pillow and she saw he was holding a plastic cup with a straw. She took a long sip and let the water swirl around her mouth before swallowing it. It felt good. She took a few more long sips and Daniel gently lowered her head back to the pillow.

"Thanks," she managed to say.

"Don't speak," Daniel said quietly. "You've had a nasty blow to the back of your head but everything's going to be alright. You're probably going to feel groggy for a while and I expect it hurts like hell, but they've done the scans and there's no serious injury to the skull and no internal bleed. Your brain is going to be just as sharp as it ever was."

"I saw him," Emma whispered.

"I know," said Daniel. "Just try and get some rest now."

But Emma didn't want to rest. She wanted to tell Daniel that Yusuf al Shamar had been at the Institute, that he had done this to her. She needed to warn Daniel. She tried to sit up but Daniel gently pushed her back.

"I told you to lie still," he said. "Just do as you're told for a change and let me do the talking."

"OK," Emma whispered and closed her eyes.

"That's better," said Daniel. "I know you saw Yusuf al Shamar in the rest-room. You must have interrupted him and then he attacked you. We don't need to know any more details about that just yet. I want you to rest now and get your strength back. You're perfectly safe here. I've got a guard outside and no one is going to get past him. Try to get some sleep."

But sleep was the last thing Emma wanted to do at that moment. She had too many questions, too many things she urgently needed to explain.

"He was at the fridge," she whispered hoarsely. "He was looking for something. I think it must have been the virus."

"I think you're right," said Daniel, realising she was not going to be quiet until she had had her say. "We're testing everything in the room but if it was the virus then, I'm afraid, it looks like he may have got away with it."

"How – how did you find me?"

"We found a copy of a security pass for the Institute with Shamar's photograph and guessed that was where he must be going. I immediately alerted Professor Robinson and the local police and they made a search of the buildings. Professor Robinson was the one who actually found you."

"Good for The Prof," said Emma quietly.

"Yes. You were unconscious and they brought you here."

"How long?"

"How long have you been out?"

Emma nodded and winced as a sharp pain struck again through the dull ache.

You were found at half-past eight," said Daniel, looking at his watch. "It's now two-thirty in the morning so you've been out for at least six hours. You might have to stay here a while."

"And you?"

"I was already on my way down when I was told they had found you. I dropped Charlie off and came straight here."

"I meant, what are you going to do now?"

"Find Yusuf al Shamar."

Emma gave a weak smile. He made it sound so simple but if anyone could find him she was sure Daniel would.

"What about -"

"I think that's enough questions for the time being," Daniel interrupted. "I want you to rest. I'm going to leave now but I'll be back later this morning. Get some sleep and when you're better I'll answer every question you can think of. Promise."

He smiled gently as he bent forward and kissed her lightly on the forehead. Emma gave a satisfied sigh and closed her eyes. She felt safe now and Daniel was right; she needed to rest.

Daniel nodded to the nurse who was standing behind him and slipped out of the room. After exchanging a few words with the guard he had placed outside the door, he left the hospital. Charlie was still at the Institute and Daniel made a quick phone call to let him know he was on his way before getting into the car and setting off. It was a short journey at that time of the morning. The roads were clear and Daniel drove fast. He had told Emma he was going to find Yusuf al Shamar and was now more determined than ever to do so quickly. It wasn't just the terrible consequences of what al Shamar was planning that compelled him; now it was also personal.

Charlie was waiting outside the building as he drew up and parked.

"What have you found?" Daniel asked as soon as he got out the car.

"I've looked at the CCTV tapes and it was al Shamar," said Charlie. "Believe it or not, one of the cleaners actually let him in the main building."

"Having met Professor Robinson, nothing would surprise me," said Daniel angrily. "The security in this place is a shambles."

"Let's go in," said Charlie. "Robinson's in his office. I told him he couldn't leave until you had spoken to him. He wasn't happy about it or the police presence, but he's been waiting quietly. Martin Greaves is with him now."

"They can wait a little longer. I want to see the restroom first. Have our men finished in there?"

"Yes. It's been dusted for fingerprints and trace finished about half an hour ago."

Charlie led the way. There were a number of uniformed policemen stationed along the corridors and the stairwell. One of them actually gave a half-hearted salute as Daniel passed which he ignored. When they reached the room, the door was open and another policeman was standing outside. Daniel flashed his ID card and the policeman stood aside. There was a pool of congealing blood just inside the door and Daniel felt his anger rise again as he carefully stepped over it into the room. He looked around slowly, carefully scanning everything to see if anything was out of place.

"Very tidy, isn't it?" he muttered. "Doesn't look as if anything's been disturbed."

"This is exactly how it was when we arrived," said Charlie. "If al Shamar was looking for something then he must have known exactly where to find it," said Charlie.

Daniel walked over to the fridge and opened it. He crouched down to peer inside but it was now completely empty.

"Emma told me he was looking in the fridge when she interrupted him," he said.

"Everything in there was taken away for testing," said Charlie. "Nothing suspicious, just the usual sort of contents: a few sandwiches, ready meals, dairy products, mainly."

"Do we know if he took anything?"

"No. We've not spoken to everyone yet, but so far nobody seems to remember exactly what was in there. It seems the people who used it each had their own little corner to store stuff apart from a few things like milk and butter which they shared. I'm working on the idea that Pemberton must have had his space as

200

well and that's where he stored the virus, but no one's been able to remember if he had left anything in there before he died. If he did, no one's admitted to clearing it out."

"I think you're probably right," Daniel said, standing up again. "It makes sense. People get very annoyed if someone interferes with their food and if Pemberton was storing stuff here he could be reasonably certain no one else would touch it. He was not the sort of man anyone wanted to cross. When you think about it, it's the ideal place; hidden in open sight and yet perfectly secure."

Neither of them spoke; each lost in his own thoughts.

"So it looks as if al Shamar may have got away with the virus," said Charlie, breaking the brief silence.

Daniel said nothing but just nodded.

"Where do you want to go from here?" Charlie asked.

"Well, it should be a lot simpler to find him now," said Daniel. "We're not ham-strung by having to keep everything so secret to avoid panic. Al Shamar has broken into a government building and attacked one of its staff. We can put out an alert to the public to be on the look-out. We say he's armed and dangerous and to let the authorities know immediately if anyone spots him."

"I'll get onto the press right away," said Charlie. "We've got his picture and we can go nationwide with it."

"Good. While you're doing that, I'm going to speak with Professor Robinson. He's got a lot to explain."

★

It was still the early hours of the morning by the time Yusuf reached the outskirts of London. He had stopped at the first motorway café he passed to call the al Assad brothers from a public phone and told them to move to a hotel immediately. He said they should leave their new address with Kylie when they got there and not leave the room until he contacted them later. He had then left the motorway and found a lay-by on one of the

201

country-roads where he could stop and rest up for a while. He wanted time to plan what he should do next. Although he now had the virus in his possession, very little else had gone as planned at the Institute and he realised he would have to change his timetable. He didn't know how badly injured the woman was; he had hit her hard with the butt of the gun as she turned to open the door and he had seen a lot of blood, but he had no idea how soon it would be before she was found and made sufficient recovery to tell her story.

He didn't regret not killing her; it would have served no purpose. Whether she had recognised him or not, and he now felt certain she had, he was sure it would not take long before the police knew who he was. The man who had held the door for him would be able to provide some description and, even if the CCTV cameras had not picked up his face, he could not conceal his limp as he had walked up the drive. In addition to that, and more significantly, his fingerprints were in the restroom. He had counted on no one realising there had been a break-in, but now he knew the room would be forensically examined. He knew his prints must be on file from when he had previously been arrested and it would not take long before a match was made.

The real puzzle was how the woman had known who he was. There was only one explanation he could think of: somehow the authorities must have learnt he was planning to go to the Institute. They had circulated his photograph to the people there and told them to be on the look-out for him. And yet, if that was the case, how come Angel had not warned him? She would have known if anything like that had happened and he simply could not believe she was double-crossing him; she would never have helped him to break in if that were true. Moreover, he would never have been allowed to get that far if the authorities knew exactly what he intended to do. He went over all the possibilities, but whatever line of reasoning he tried to follow, he couldn't come up with an explanation that fitted all the facts.

It was an academic problem, anyway. Having had time to think about it, he decided it wasn't that important now; really more of an inconvenience than a disaster. However, it meant he couldn't risk returning to the Westbrook Grove flat. If the police knew his identity, all his friends and associates would be carefully looked at and the flat in Kylie's name would eventually be discovered - if it hadn't already. It didn't matter; there were enough hotels in London that didn't ask questions of their guests and he could stay in one of those until he was ready to make his move. That would now have to be sooner rather than later.

He decided to try and get some sleep in the lay-by before continuing his journey and didn't set off again until it had passed midnight. He then drove into central London and found a carpark where he intended to abandon the car. He would not be able to use it again and removed from it anything he thought might be useful, putting everything in a plastic supermarket bag. Once back on the street, he hailed a taxi and gave the name of a hotel where he thought he could hold up. The manager was an Iraqi and they had known each other for a number of years, ever since Yusuf had begun supplying the hotel with the spices it needed for its specialist cuisine. The manager would not be suspicious when he arrived with no luggage and Yusuf was confident that if anyone came around asking questions, the manager would not say anything to give him away.

When he arrived at the hotel, the lobby was deserted. It was still very early in the morning but a receptionist appeared from a side office as soon as Yusuf rang the bell on the desk. He asked to see the manager and, after fifteen minutes, the manager arrived, having obviously just got out of bed. He was surprised but pleased to see his friend. Yusuf told him he had had a violent row with his girl-friend who had called the police. She had thrown him out of the house they shared and he needed somewhere to stay for a few days whilst things cooled off. The manager understood perfectly. After initially refusing to accept any payment, he finally took the wad of notes pressed on him and personally showed Yusuf to a room.

Yusuf stored the carrier bag with the cans containing the virus in the mini-fridge and the other things he had removed from the car he put in the wardrobe. He then left the hotel. He wanted to find a public telephone to call Kylie. She had been expecting to hear from him and, despite the early hour, answered almost immediately. She had no idea what he was planning but she knew the police wanted to speak to her boss and that he didn't want to speak to them. That was enough. She knew where her loyalties lay and was determined to do whatever she could to help him. She told him the al Assad brothers had found a hotel and booked in under the name of Aswat. She gave Yusuf the address and telephone number. After promising to get in touch again soon, Yusuf rang off and dialled the number she had given him. The receptionist at their hotel put him through immediately to the brothers' room but, after giving a greeting, before Yusuf could say anything further Habab's voice at the other end interrupted and told him not to speak.

"My brother thinks we were followed," Habab continued. "This line may not be safe. If you need to contact us, use your friend."

"I understand," said Yusuf.

The line went dead and he replaced the receiver, his mind in a turmoil. If the brothers had been followed to their hotel, then someone must have been watching the Westbrook Grove flat before he had called them with orders to move. There was no way anyone could have known about the flat in the short time between the woman being found and his call to the brothers almost immediately after he had left the Institute. If they were now being shadowed, and Yusuf had sufficient confidence in the brothers' experience to believe them, then the authorities must have found out about the flat before they left. He was sure that he had not been followed to Brighton himself; he was well-trained in spy-craft and, like the brothers, would have realised if anyone was tailing him. That meant the authorities could only have learnt about the flat sometime between his leaving London and his telephone call to the brothers. Someone must be giving them information. As he made his way slowly back to the hotel room, he realised that he was now in a race. If the operation was to succeed then he would need to start putting it into place whilst he was still ahead of the game. And his first priority had to be keeping the al Assad brothers safe.

★

Robert House was feeling rather pleased with himself. He didn't often get to work in the field and had jumped at the opportunity when Daniel asked him to watch the Westbrook Grove flat. Although he had been taken on as an expert in communication technology, at heart that was not the sort of work he had really wanted to do when he joined the SIS. This was a chance for advancement. If he was able to impress Daniel Rankin sufficiently now, other opportunities might open up in the future. So far he thought he had done well. Using the latest Wi-Fi technology developed by MI6, he had been able to access the computer the men inside the flat were using when they opened their e-mail. Now he was able to look through their documents, it didn't take long to find the security passes they had been working on earlier in the day and send the pictures to Daniel. He knew Daniel had thought that was an important discovery. When the two men had unexpectedly left the flat later that night with their suitcases, there had been no time to call in what was happening before the men had set off and so Robert had used his initiative.

He had followed them in his van to a hotel but, unfortunately, his skill-set lay elsewhere so he had not realised the men in the taxi he was tailing had been aware he was behind them almost from the start of their journey. He had parked further down the road from the hotel where they had been dropped off and waited for back-up. It was not long in coming.

Richard Spiller was an experienced agent. Now approaching retirement, he had been with the SIS for twenty-seven years after leaving the teaching profession in his early thirties. He was a bear of a man; tall, well-built with sharp features and piercing dark eyes. Something of the schoolmaster still hung about him and when he climbed into the van and asked for an update, Robert felt like a student about to make his report in front of the class. He quickly explained what had happened and that he had followed the two men who were now in the hotel and had not seen them leave since arriving.

"Pity about that," said Richard shaking his head, and Robert couldn't help feeling he had somehow made a mistake.

"What's wrong?" he asked.

"Your area is communications, right?"

"Yes."

"You've received no training in the field, have you? No one's explained how you should tail someone."

"No," Robert admitted, "but I was very careful."

"Possibly not careful enough," said Richard. "These are trained agents. They might have spotted you from the start."

"I didn't think I should let them out of my sight," Robert said a little defensively.

Richard sighed.

"London has more CCTV cameras per square mile than any other capital city in Europe," he explained. "If you had just taken the taxi number, we could have known exactly where they went without even having to leave the base. As it is, if they have any wit at all, they've probably realised by now they were being followed."

Robert felt embarrassed. That was something he should have known. He had reacted instinctively and was now mortified at the thought he might have blown the operation.

"I'm sorry," he said, thankful that the night prevented Spiller from seeing him blush a deep red, "I didn't think of that. What do we do now?"

"First thing," said Richard, "we move this van. If they haven't already clocked you then we don't want them seeing it again the moment they leave the hotel - that is if they do. Second thing, we try to access their communications. That's where you could make yourself useful. If they're going to make contact with anyone, we need to find out what they're saying, though, if they already know we're on to them, I doubt they will use their phone."

"I can access their e-mail," said Robert eagerly. He wanted to redeem himself.

"If they're not going to use their phones then I doubt they will risk using a computer. They probably suspect by now that's compromised too. What are their alternatives?"

He paused and Robert realised he was waiting for him to come up with an answer. It really was like being back at school.

"They will either have to use a public landline," he said, "or an intermediary."

"Now you're beginning to think properly," said Richard, sounding just like the teacher he had once been and he smiled. He understood how the young man must be feeling and wanted to give encouragement rather than apportion blame. "If you were in their shoes, which would you choose?"

"An intermediary," replied Robert at once. "It may carry its own risks but it's still safer for them and makes it more difficult for us to know what's happening."

"Difficult, but not impossible."

"So," Robert hesitated, despite his blunder he did not want to be taken off the operation, "what do you want me to do now?"

"We can't completely rule out them using telephones or their computer yet. You should get on with that now and I'll sort out how to deal with an intermediary if there is one. Right now, I think you should move the van."

Robert smiled as he turned the ignition and switched on the lights. He was already starting to feel better.

★

Daniel finished speaking and an uncomfortable silence filled the room. Professor Ken Robinson sat behind his desk and glanced at Martin Greaves who was standing by the closed blinds of the window opposite. The Prof had called his assistant director to meet him at the Institute as soon as he had received the call

207

from Daniel eight hours before. He had grown impatient at having to wait for so long but now he was reeling a little from the information Daniel had just revealed. He turned back to stare at the man he had now discovered was an MI6 officer and shifted awkwardly in his chair, taking off his glasses to rub the bridge of his nose between finger and thumb. He wasn't sure what to think and stuttered in his confusion as he picked up on the least significant thing Daniel had told him.

"You – you said you were from the Ministry of Defence."

"I didn't," said Daniel. "You just assumed it and I never corrected you."

"Did you know anything about this?" The Prof asked accusingly, turning to Martin.

Martin shook his head.

The Prof replaced his glasses and leant forward to confront Daniel.

"Why didn't you tell me the truth from the start?" he demanded.

"You didn't need to know," said Daniel.

"I am the director of this Institute," said The Prof a little pompously. "I have been in charge of Operation Sundown since it began and I think that should have entitled me to know what's been going on. There are things I might have been able to do."

Daniel realised the man had a point but he was still annoyed enough not to make things easy. At their first meeting he had formed the impression The Prof was one of those bureaucrats who was more interested in covering his back than in trying to help. He had met the type before and recognised The Prof was already laying down the groundwork to put the blame for what had gone wrong onto someone else.

"To be perfectly honest," he said, "we weren't too sure what was going on ourselves to begin with. Once we found out, however, it was clear Pemberton wasn't acting alone and we didn't know who could be trusted. We believed someone here was helping him."

"Are you suggesting I was a suspect?"

"Everyone here was," said Daniel, ignoring the fact that the previous day he had told Emma what was going on.

"But I have the highest security clearance," The Prof protested.

"So did Pemberton."

The Prof sat back and glared angrily at Daniel.

"If you don't mind me saying so," he bristled, "that was your department's responsibility. I can't be blamed for their mistakes."

Daniel had been expecting some sort of comment like that and leaned back in his chair, keeping his eyes fixed on The Prof.

"The man who attacked Emma was actually let into the building by one of your cleaners," he said calmly. "Not that it was necessary since someone here had already given him a security pass which he copied. We have also learnt some of the information stored on your computers has already been sold on to others as well as your own personal files tampered with. You remember those records you couldn't find yesterday? Well, I was looking at them only a few hours ago. Someone got into your computer and deleted them. The security in this place is a joke and, as the director, that's your responsibility. I don't think you're in any position to start questioning the competence of my department."

The two men stared at each other in silence for a moment.

"My computer has been hacked?" The Prof asked hesitantly, picking up on the one new piece of information that directly concerned himself.

Martin quickly stepped forward and stood beside the desk.

"There's nothing to be gained by arguing who's responsible for what," he said. "I think we're all agreed this is a mess and from what you've just told us, it sounds like everyone's made some mistakes. Shouldn't we be trying to sort it out?"

Daniel knew he was right and was annoyed with himself for having let The Prof get under his skin.

"That's why I'm here," he said. "The most important thing I need from you at the moment is information. If we're right in thinking this man now has the virus, I need to know as much about it as possible. All I know so far is that Pemberton had developed a technique to make a virus sensitive to temperature. What else can you tell me?"

The Prof was still flushed with indignation and looked at Martin.

"You probably know more about that than I do," he said brusquely. "You were the one actually talking to Michael on a daily basis."

Daniel turned his attention to Martin.

"Well?" he asked.

"I'm sorry," Martin said with a shrug of his shoulders, "there's not much I can say that you don't already know. I told you before that Michael was secretive about his work. He didn't talk about it much and, in fact, you were the one who told me he was writing things up in a private notebook. I never even saw it."

Daniel realised he needed to be more specific.

"It seems Pemberton could have been storing the virus in a fridge in your restroom," he said. "Could that be important? Does it have to be kept cold?"

"Not necessarily," Martin explained. "Like any living organism, a virus will react to its environment. Certain conditions will be beneficial and others may be more hostile. Temperature was just one factor among several that Michael was working on. Most fridges operate at somewhere between four and five degrees centigrade. That's cold enough to slow it down perhaps but not enough to harm it."

"You said Michael was working on other things than temperature."

"That's right," Martin continued. "As you know, Operation Sundown was initially set up to detect and identify the presence of a virus. We were looking at all sorts of ways to do that. When Michael made his discovery and the Ministry began to show an interest in actually using it for military purposes, he started investigating other areas he thought might be useful to them."

"Like what?"

"Other ways of restricting its spread, primarily. Temperature is actually not the best means of doing that; it's too unreliable. I know he did some experiments on the effect of ultra-violet light but nothing came of it."

"Is that it?" Daniel was becoming impatient.

"We did once talk about possible delivery systems but all that was hypothetical and quite some time ago. I don't know if he did any work on it but I remember Michael asking my opinion on the aeroionisation of the virus. He thought it would be the most effective method of dispersal but I disagreed."

"Aeroionisation?" queried Daniel. "What's that?"

"You know, an aerosol, like a deodorant spray," Martin explained. "The problem is finding an agent that will hold the virus without harming it whilst keeping the pressure needed to atomize it for delivery. It's not as easy as it sounds. I didn't think it could be done, at least, not with Ebola. The virus is transmitted through the exchange of bodily fluids; an airborne delivery is nigh on impossible for military purposes. For a start, the virus needs a host. It simply cannot exist for long once it's exposed to the atmosphere."

"Was Pemberton researching anything like that? Could he have developed an aerosol delivery system that worked?"

Martin paused a moment before answering.

"If you had asked me that yesterday I would have said no but, after what you've just told us, now I can't be absolutely sure about anything. As I said, I remember we had a brief conversation about it as an idea. For all I know that's as far as it went."

Daniel sat back in the chair and pulled thoughtfully at his lower lip. Until that moment he had only been occupied with the effect of the virus and how long it could be kept active until ready for use; he had not even considered how it might actually be delivered. Now he realised he had been wrong not to think about this crucial element.

"Could Pemberton have made something like an aerosol can?" he asked. "Would he have known how?"

"Of course," The Prof butted in, starting to get alarmed now he realised where Daniel was leading the discussion. "The engineering's not that difficult. A schoolboy could do it given the right equipment but, as Martin just said, it wouldn't work unless he could find some way of keeping the virus alive in the atmosphere. There would be no point."

"But if he could do that?" Daniel persisted.

"He couldn't."

"Actually," said Martin slowly, "we can't be completely sure of that."

The Prof turned angrily to face him but before he could say anything Daniel held up his hand.

"Explain," he demanded.

"Well, we already know Michael had successfully conducted experiments with the DNA of the virus to make it sensitive to temperature, it's possible he could have employed the same technique using the genome of an airborne virus to create a new strain of Ebola, one that could exist in the atmosphere without a host. He never claimed to have done so but it's the next logical step if he was thinking of a delivery system. The idea isn't new, it's just that no one's been able to do it yet. But then, until Michael no one had been able to engineer the DNA of the virus to meet specific conditions of any sort. I just don't think we should rule it out, that's all."

Daniel looked at The Prof.

"So it is possible?"

"Well," said The Prof, almost scornfully, "theoretically yes, I suppose so. Theoretically anything is possible but it's one thing to modify the reaction to temperature in an existing organism, quite another to create a new variant that can live in a totally alien environment. The two things are very different."

Daniel had stopped listening. Even though he must realise the seriousness of the situation, The Prof was still determined to be unhelpful; he was too concerned with trying to limit the damage he believed would be visited on the Institute and his own reputation. Daniel abruptly turned back to Martin.

"But you still think he might have done it?"

"I said I thought we couldn't rule it out," Martin corrected him.

"Assuming he had, is this aerosol thing the best way to spread the virus amongst a large group of people?"

"Probably," Martin replied, "but there are drawbacks. Assuming Michael had been able to create an airborne variant of the virus, once it was released into the atmosphere there would be no way of stopping it or controlling where it went. That makes it useless for most military purposes."

"What about this temperature specific strain he had developed, wouldn't that be enough to limit it?" Daniel asked.

"I suppose it could to a certain extent," Martin admitted, "but as I just said, the temperature range is too unreliable for military use at the moment. That's why Michael was looking at other ways for restricting its active life-span. The actual importance of his discovery was in establishing it could be done and finding a method of altering the DNA to achieve it. That was the real breakthrough."

"And that's the point," The Prof broke in, "so let's just stop there for a moment and think about it. Don't you think you're starting to get a little ahead of yourselves? I'm not going to underestimate what Michael achieved or what he was capable of, but he had only just opened the door. Months of research still lie ahead; experimenting, testing on different strains, all these things take time involving dedicated teams. Michael only made his initial breakthrough a comparatively short while ago. There's still a great deal of work to be done, possibly years of testing before it can be properly developed for any military use."

Daniel was silent. What The Prof had said was probably true but it didn't make any difference. If Pemberton had actually managed to create an airborne strain of the Ebola virus then none of the rest mattered. It wasn't the military intending to use it.

★

Yusuf slept late into the morning. After returning to his room at the hotel, he had spent the next few hours thinking about what to do. One thing was certain: he had to bring the operation forward. He couldn't be sure exactly how much the British authorities had discovered but now they were in pursuit of him and the brothers he knew he was in a race. If he was to keep ahead then there were two things he had to do urgently. The first was the more difficult; he had to get Habab and Shiraz out of their hotel room without the British knowing. The second was to find somewhere safe where they could stay until ready to act. That would be easier and he already had someone in mind he thought would put them up for the short time necessary: Andrew Farquharson. Although they hadn't seen each other in months, it seemed fitting that he should be involved at the end when everything had begun with him in the first place. And he was in no position to refuse.

It was through Farquharson that Yusuf had learned of Pemberton's research in the first place. He didn't know exactly how the man had got hold of the scientist's discovery; he never did find that out but it didn't matter. When Farquharson had first contacted the Imam at Yusuf's mosque, he was taken seriously. His position as editor of a leading science journal had given his offer a credibility that was worth pursuing and Ibrahim Khan had approached his favourite radicalised follower to start negotiations. Yusuf's first meeting with Farquharson had been enough for him to see the possibilities of what was on offer. He had reported back to the IS in Syria but, after showing some initial interest, they had decided not to take it any further. It wasn't just that they didn't have the resources to develop the material to a point where it could be used effectively, there was a sense of fear perhaps that, despite the claims, once such a weapon was unleashed it could get out of their control and wreak havoc amongst their own men. They were not going to take the risk of using this untried and dangerous technique. But Yusuf had other ideas.

He saw, at last, an opportunity to get his revenge on a scale he felt was deserved. It didn't matter to him that this weapon was untested and could develop a will of its own. In fact, the more out of control it became, the more it would suit his purpose. Those who had killed his family and left him with a permanent limp would now feel the same suffering he had endured only a hundred times worse. He told Farquharson that IS was interested in the offer and wanted more details before committing to a deal. With the additional information Farquharson provided and using his own contacts, it wasn't long before Yusuf had been able to identify Michael Pemberton as the man behind the discovery. Once he knew this, he was able to dispense with Farquharson entirely. After telling him that IS had decided they were no longer going to pursue the project, there were no more meetings. He believed Farquharson must have found another buyer because all contact between the two of them stopped but, by then Yusuf was already fully occupied with his own agenda. Now it was time for them to meet again.

Once Yusuf had decided where they were going to hide out, he turned his mind to planning how to get Habab and Shiraz away safely. They had told him to make contact through his friend, by whom he knew they had meant Kylie, and, although he had no way of knowing whether she had been compromised yet, he realised there was no alternative but to use his loyal employee. It did not take him long to formulate a plan. It was risky but was the best he could come up with at such short notice. There was no time to waste and, despite the late hour, had called Kylie again to give some very specific instructions. She had been surprised at his directions but agreed to do what he asked and they made an arrangement to meet that afternoon at three o' clock. Now he could do nothing but wait. If the British were watching her then he would soon find out.

Now he had committed himself to a plan he couldn't help but think of the many pitfalls in it and sleep eluded him for a long time. However, although he went over many alternatives in his mind, none seemed better and he eventually slipped into a restless slumber. It was almost ten o' clock before he finally got out of bed and had a shower. He had planned on staying in his room until it was time to leave but was too anxious to sit around doing nothing for that long. He waited until lunchtime and then went down to the small restaurant at the front of the hotel overlooking the street. There was a smattering of guests already seated, most of them from the Arab Emirates, and Yusuf was pleased to see they were almost all dressed in their traditional robes. Even as he looked around the tables, two women glided in behind him, moving silently across the carpet in their black, full-length abayas, their faces framed by the hijabs which fell to their shoulders. He selected a table close to the kitchen entrance, facing the arched double doorway to the restaurant before sitting down. A waiter immediately went over to him.

"Are you here for lunch, sir? May I get you a menu?"

"No thanks," said Yusuf. Although he had not had a meal since the evening before, he was feeling too anxious to eat. "I'll just have a coffee, Americano please."

"Certainly, sir," said the waiter and deftly began to clear away the place-setting in front of Yusuf.

"Do you have a newspaper?" Yusuf asked.

"Yes, sir. Is there a particular one you want?"

"No. Any afternoon edition will do, thanks."

The waiter moved away and Yusuf sat back and surveyed the room. He was not surprised to see that most of the guests were women. Their husbands would have brought them over to entertain themselves with shopping whilst the men conducted their business affairs. London had now become a major centre for trade and commerce with the Middle East and quickly discovered there was a lucrative side-line to be had in providing businessmen's families with things to occupy themselves whilst they waited for their menfolk to complete their deals. At one time it would have been rare to see people walking the streets in full traditional Arab dress but now, in this cosmopolitan city, it was a common sight and nobody gave them a second glance.

The waiter returned with the Americano on a platter and a newspaper tucked under his arm. He placed the cup and a jug of milk on the table and placed the folded paper next to it.

"Will that be all, sir?"

"Thank you."

The waiter returned to his station and Yusuf picked up the paper and began to turn the pages. He was not interested in the news; he just wanted something to occupy his mind whilst he waited until it was time for him to leave for his meeting with Kylie. But then an article at the bottom of a page suddenly caught his eye. It wasn't so much the article but the photograph alongside that had grabbed his attention. Staring back at him from the newspaper under the headline '*Have you seen this man?*' was a picture of himself taken from the website of The Eastern Spice Company.

★

Kylie looked around nervously as she reversed the white van out of its parking space in the courtyard of the Eastern Spice Company. She shifted into first gear and slowly edged forward until the nose of the van was just poking through the open double-gates leading onto the road. On arriving at the offices an hour before, she had carefully scrutinised the cars parked on the street outside and looked carefully to see if any pedestrians were loitering around. She wasn't entirely sure what she expected to see but Yusuf had told her to take these precautions in case the building was being watched. Satisfied that nothing looked out of the ordinary, she pulled onto the road and drove off, checking her mirror frequently to ensure she wasn't being followed.

She was now sure that whatever trouble Yusuf was in, it was pretty damn serious and she was worried on his behalf. Although she had few academic qualifications, her mind was sharp and her education on the streets of Brixton had proved far more valuable than anything she had learnt at school. The arrival of a plain-clothes policeman a few days before and Yusuf's decision to stay in the flat with his friends had been enough to convince her he was engaged in some form of criminal activity. That didn't bother her. Most of the people she knew were involved in crime of some sort; it was a way of life where she had grown up. She didn't expect her boss to tell her what was going on and she wasn't going to ask. He had been good to her in the past and, if he wanted her to help him now, she would do what he needed without question. Loyalty was the most important thing in her world.

Despite the temptation to put her foot down and get away quickly, she drove carefully, keeping well within the speed limit; the last thing she wanted was to attract any attention by going too fast. She had given herself plenty of time to cross London and knew she would probably be early, but that was better than arriving late for her meeting with Yusuf. Anyway, before then she had to collect his friends and didn't know how long that might take. She had got up early that morning to make sure she could find the things Yusuf had asked for. She had anticipated some difficulty but, in fact, it had been quite easy. For some reason there had been an increased demand for what was needed and she had found exactly what she wanted at the first supplier she tried. The shopkeeper had not shown the slightest surprise at her request and the box containing the goods was now stashed in the back of the van.

She made good time and within half an hour was parking the van outside the back entrance of the hotel where the al Assad brothers were staying. She got out and looked around, slinging her bag over her shoulder. She was sure she had not been followed but was not going to take any risks. Once satisfied that no one was paying her any attention, she opened the back doors of the van and removed the box. It was quite light and, although bulky, just fitted under her arm. She had not been to this particular establishment before but most hotels were the same and operated in a similar way; managers did not want tradespeople using the main entrance at the front so deliveries of all sorts were made at the rear. That suited her purpose. The back door to the kitchen was open and two men in white aprons were standing just outside, chatting idly whilst they grabbed the opportunity for a smoke now the lunchtime service was over.

218

Kylie put on a cheerful smile and went over to them, carrying the box.

"I've got a delivery here for one of your guests," she said. "What do you want me to do with it?"

"Manny's inside," said one of the men, jerking his head at the open door. "You'd better speak to him."

"Thanks."

Kylie pushed her way past the two men and went inside. Everyone there seemed to be occupied and no one gave her a second glance. She looked around and on the other side of the kitchen saw a man in a grey suit with a red tie talking to one of the chefs next to a double swing door. She went over to them.

"Manny?" she asked.

"That's me," said the man in the suit. "How can I help you, love?"

"I've got a delivery for one of your guests."

"Just leave it here and I'll see they get it."

"I'd rather give it to him personally if that's alright. I've got a couple of things to explain and need to speak with him myself. I should have been here over an hour ago and he's probably going to be a little mad at us for the delay."

Manny glanced quickly at his watch and then gave her an appraising look. She was dressed in a neat bottle-green skirt, black tights and a white blouse. He had a lot of things to do and was already running late. She didn't look trade and he decided she would pass muster to enter the reception area.

"Through the diner," he said, pushing one of the swing doors and holding it open, "George is at the desk. He'll help you out."

Kylie gave him a thankful smile and crossed through the diner to the lobby where she saw a young man standing behind the reception desk. She made her way over and smiled again at him.

"Hi," she said, "Are you George?"

The man nodded.

"I've got a parcel for one of your guests but I don't know the room number. It's for Mr Aswat. It should have been here an hour ago."

"You can leave it with me," said George. "I'll see he gets it,"

"If you don't mind," she said, still clutching the box under her arm, "I would prefer to deliver it myself so I can explain why it's late. He's waiting for it now and I don't want to get into any more trouble."

George hesitated. It was against the rules to allow anyone other than guests onto the floors above and he was not supposed to leave the desk unattended.

"Manny said I could take it up," Kylie added, flashing him another radiant smile.

At the mention of Manny's name, George relented and looked down at the register.

"Number thirty-two," he said. "Third floor. You can use the lift."

"Thanks."

Kylie went over to the lifts and pressed the button for up. Within a few seconds, the doors slid open and she stepped in. As she did so, she noticed a man sitting in one of the chairs on the far side of the lobby, holding a newspaper in front of him. He was a large man in his late fifties and had slumped down in the armchair so his shoulders rested comfortably along the mahogany frame at the back. She couldn't see an outside coat and decided he must be one of the guests. It looked as if he was about to doze off but, as the lift doors closed, Richard Spiller spread the open newspaper across his lap and reached into a pocket for his phone.

Kylie got out at the third floor and walked along the corridor. Room number thirty-two was on the right and she paused outside to shift the box under her arm before gently knocking on the door. She heard movement from the other side and then a voice called out.

"Yes, who's there?"

"Kylie."

A moment later she heard a click as the door was unlocked and opened a few inches, revealing the sliver of a face.

"Are you alone?"

"Yes," Kylie said and patted the parcel she was carrying under one arm. "Yusuf has been in touch and told me to bring you this."

The door opened and Habab al Assad stepped aside to let Kylie come in. He was nervous and looked past her into the empty corridor as she entered the room. Kylie tried to give him a reassuring smile.

"It's alright," she said. "I made sure I wasn't followed."

Habab closed the door and Kylie walked across to lay the parcel on one of the twin beds. Shiraz al Assad was standing next to one of the windows, looking anxiously through the net curtains to the street below, and Kylie gave him a brief nod before turning back to Habab.

"Yusuf wants to see you," she said. "I'm to take you to him."

Habab quickly glanced across at his brother.

"Didn't he tell you we think we're being watched?" he said.

"Yes, but we've got that covered."

"Just how do you think we're going to leave the hotel without being seen?" asked Shiraz.

Kylie smiled.

"It's alright, I've got it sorted," she said, tapping the parcel. "I've arranged to meet him at three o' clock so we'd better get a move on."

★

Daniel's phone gave a loud buzz, rather like an angry wasp trapped in a bottle, and he pulled it quickly from his pocket. He should have been tired; he had only managed a few hours' sleep in the past two days but adrenalin was keeping his mind sharp and he barked his name into the phone. It was Richard Spiller. They spoke briefly and then Daniel ended the call and looked across the room at Charlie with a satisfied smile.

"It's the girl," he said. "She's turned up at the hotel. I think they're going to make a move."

"Shall we go?" Charlie asked.

Daniel glanced at the papers strewn over his desk.

"No," he decided. "Richard's got it covered. Let's wait and see what happens. I think we're better occupied here for the moment, making sense of this lot."

They were sitting in Daniel's office at MI6 headquarters. It was a sparsely furnished room. Unlike some officers of his rank, Daniel preferred a practical working environment and eschewed the luxurious touches most of his colleagues used to mark their seniority. The single concession to comfort was the expensive chair he used behind his desk and that was only because he suffered from a bad back. He was normally obsessively neat and liked to keep a clear workspace in front of him but that was not the case today. Papers and photographs were heaped in apparently random piles on the desk but the untidy chaos was deceptive; Daniel knew exactly what was there and could place his hand on any document he wanted within a few seconds. He stifled a yawn and turned back to the files Ira Goldstein had sent over.

After snatching a few hours' sleep on returning from Brighton, he and Charlie had arrived at MI6 headquarters that morning to find photographs of Habab and Shiraz al Assad were already waiting for them. They had been taken from one of the CCTV cameras installed in the hotel lobby. Although the brothers had kept their heads down when they signed in at the desk, they had neglected to do so as they came through the main doors and Richard Spiller had managed to find a couple of hazy images from which they could just be identified. Daniel had sent copies to Ira and within two hours he was holding all the information Mossad had collected on the two men. Unfortunately, there was not much and none of it current. The brothers were not high in the ranks of ISIS; their role appeared to have been primarily a part of the support network for some of the more active members and had not merited much attention from the Israeli Secret Service. Their presence in England with Yusuf al Shamar clearly heralded a recent advance in their careers as terrorists.

"The question that's bothering me," said Charlie, holding up one of the photographs, "is why Yusuf al Shamar brought these two men here in the first place."

"He needs their help."

"Yes, but help to do what, exactly?" asked Charlie. "I mean, let's assume you're right in thinking al Shamar is going to use an aerosol to spread the virus; it hardly takes three of them to press a nozzle."

"What are you thinking?"

"There must be a reason for them being here. We know al Shamar acted alone to break into the Institute so it obviously wasn't anything to do with that."

"Well, we know they helped to make the security passes for him," said Daniel. "The documents were on their computer but you're right, there are lots of people in London who could have done that."

"In which case, they're here to do something else and, whatever it is, it's important and still has to be done. If it weren't, why should al Shamar risk getting himself caught by sending the girl round and keeping in contact? If he didn't still need them he could just abandon them."

The same thought had already occurred to Daniel.

"The most likely explanation," Charlie continued, "is that they possess some sort of skill-set al Shamar needs but doesn't have himself. Unfortunately, we don't know enough about them yet to work out what that might be."

"Goldstein might be able to help," said Daniel. "I'm sure he's already sent over all he has but I'll give him a call and let him know what we're thinking. He has more contacts in the area than we do and might be able to dig a little deeper."

"Then you don't think we should pull them in now?" Charlie suggested hesitantly. "If they're that important, it might just put a stop to whatever al Shamar is planning or, at least, throw a spanner in the works, give us more time."

"It's tempting," Daniel replied, "but now we know al Shamar is still in touch with them, I think they're going to be our best chance of finding him and he's the one holding the virus. Getting that back has to be our priority. He's got some sort of timetable and, although I know there's a risk in keeping them loose, taking the brothers out now might just panic al Shamar into acting early and going it alone. That's a bigger risk. Now we know where they are, we can pick them up anytime and so far they're our only lead to al Shamar."

"There's still his contact at the Institute," Charlie reminded him.

"That's if we knew who it was," said Daniel bitterly, "but we're still no further in finding that out than when we started. All we know for sure is that it's a woman."

His tiredness and the lack of progress was starting to make him frustrated and irritable.

"That's not quite true," Charlie pointed out reasonably. "Emma's given us some sort of description. It may not be much but I've already been able to eliminate a number of people. Now, thanks to Robert, we also know that whoever it is must have provided al Shamar with an original security pass to copy. Since nobody's reported having lost one, it must mean either it was her own or she has access to one. That should narrow the field down even more. Once I've gone through the lists and done some more checking, I should be able to come up with a couple of names we can look at in more detail."

"You're right," said Daniel, realising he might have sounded critical of Charlie's efforts. "I'm sorry. I know you're going as fast as you can and it is a good lead. Why don't you get on with that whilst I get in touch with Ira, see if he can help us find out why al Shamar still needs the al Assad brothers."

He picked up his phone and began to make the call. Charlie pulled a file toward him and opened it thoughtfully. He knew Daniel was right to concentrate on the al Assad brothers at that moment but something was telling him that the woman was going to prove more important in what lay ahead. She also had a part to play and he wanted to find out what it was.

★

Kylie was the first out the door. She looked up and down the hotel corridor before turning back to Habab and nodded.

"All clear," she whispered unnecessarily. "Come on."

She started down the corridor to the stairs and the brothers followed her out of the room. They were wearing abayas, the black, full-length garment worn by devout Muslim women to preserve their modesty, and their faces were almost completely concealed by niqabs. Only their eyes were visible through the narrow horizontal slits and Kylie had even applied some eyeliner to try and make them appear more feminine. She had obtained the outfits from a fancy-dress supplier in Brixton but, although the brothers were now unrecognisable, as soon as they started walking they looked like men in drag. Given more time and some practice they might have been able to disguise their masculine gait but, striding behind Kylie, there was something completely incongruous about the way they moved. She realised immediately they were going to attract attention as they walked through the lobby and when they reached the top of the staircase she stopped for a moment to give them new instructions before starting down.

The stairs turned a corner just before reaching the ground floor and the brothers waited there whilst Kylie continued down to the lobby. She looked around and saw George still at his post behind the desk. There were three people now sitting in the small reception area to the side: the middle-aged man was still sprawled in his chair, reading the newspaper, and an old couple were engaged in conversation, seated on a settee in front of the coffee table. Deciding it was probably not going to get quieter than this, Kylie went over to George and placed her open shoulder-bag on the desk.

"Hello, George," she said, giving him one of her best smiles, "can you spare a minute?"

"Sure," said George. "Did you deliver your parcel alright?"

"Yeah, no problems, but now I need to get to Kensington and I'm not sure of the best way to go."

George thought for a moment and then reached down to a shelf under the desk and produced a street map of London which he placed in front of him and turned round so it was facing Kylie. She leant forward over the desk and, as she did so, picked up her open bag by the bottom corner as if to move it out of the way. Half the contents spilt over the counter and onto the floor at George's feet.

"Oh, sorry!" she said. "Can you get those for me, please?"

George bent down behind the desk and started to gather up the items that had fallen from the bag. As he did so, Kylie turned round to look at the stairs and saw the two brothers come down. They quickly made their way across the lobby to the main door and had left before George stood up again. Kylie glanced at the others seated in the reception and was relieved to see none of them had paid any attention to the two figures hurrying past. However, now the brothers were out of the hotel, she knew she had to act fast. She had told them to turn left on reaching the street and to walk slowly until they reached the corner of the road that led behind the hotel where she had parked the van. They were to wait there until she picked them up.

George took his time explaining how to get to Kensington and Kylie had to work hard to conceal her impatience. He would have liked her to stay chatting a little longer but she told him she was in a hurry and, after another grateful smile, walked quickly through the diner and out of the kitchen at the back to where the van was parked. She could see the brothers already waiting at the corner and drove quickly over before stopping to let them clamber into the back and moving off. As she drove down the main road, the two men pulled off their disguises in the back and wiped the make-up from their eyes using spit and the black robes they had worn.

"Look in the mirror!" Shiraz hissed urgently. "Are we being followed?"

Kylie had already been checking her wing-mirror.

"No," she said. "Relax. I've got this covered."

But neither Habab nor Shiraz could relax. They had not met Kylie before but recognised she was new to this sort of thing. It wasn't that they didn't trust her but she was an amateur. The robes she had brought them had obviously not been the real thing. The synthetic material was wrong and the style was a clumsy attempt at imitation. They were clearly fancy-dress and the brothers had felt nervous, thinking someone would probably stop them as they left the hotel. The fact they had got away and were now in the van didn't reassure them; they had been lucky so far but there was still a long way to go before they could feel secure.

Kylie glanced at her watch. She had arranged to pick Yusuf up outside the Victoria Monument in front of Buckingham Palace at three o' clock and was now unsure whether she would be on time. Traffic was the main problem: London's streets had become increasingly clogged over the years and none of the measures adopted by successive mayors had helped to ease the flow. Although she thought she had allowed enough time, she had misjudged how long it would take to get the brothers out of the hotel and now she was cutting it fine. She checked the mirror again and pressed her foot down on the accelerator.

★

Yusuf was waiting under one of the trees that lined The Mall on the lead up to Buckingham Palace. He had chosen his position carefully. From here he would be able to look up the wide road and see the van approaching from a distance. He could watch it pass on the opposite side of the road before it turned into Constitution Hill and look at the cars behind. Once Kylie reached Hyde Park Corner, she would double back through Green Park and he would be able to check whether she was being followed. If all was well, he would change places with Kylie and go back up The Mall. Events were changing fast and he needed to be cautious if he was to remain one step ahead. He ran his hand slowly over his smooth chin. It felt strange not to have a beard after so many years and he regretted having to lose it. As soon as he had seen his photograph in the paper, he had returned to his room and shaved before leaving the hotel. It had been an impulsive decision, more of a panicked reaction than a considered judgement, but, when he had studied himself in the mirror afterwards, he was satisfied his appearance had now changed sufficiently for most people not to recognise him from the published picture.

He was reluctantly impressed by how quickly the British had acted. It had been less than twenty-four hours since he had left Brighton and already the al Assad brothers were probably under surveillance and the public had been notified he himself was a wanted man. But Yusuf didn't believe it was just down to skill and top of the range resources. Nobody was that fast whatever their equipment: someone must have informed against him. And he now believed there was only one person who could have talked.

Yusuf had gone through the facts, placing them in sequence. Pemberton had died on the Friday of the previous week and Kylie had contacted him at Schiphol airport six days later to say the police had visited the Company offices looking for him. Kylie knew nothing of his plans so she couldn't have betrayed him. Besides, she was the one who had warned him and was still helping him. Yusuf was in no doubt he could continue to rely on her. He was also now certain the woman in the Institute had recognised him. Clearly, the British Secret Service had established a link between himself and Pemberton and had been expecting him to go to Brighton. They must have warned the staff there to be on the look-out and he realised it was only by chance that he had got away.

His first thought had been that Pemberton himself must have talked. He had got cold feet once before and Yusuf had been

228

obliged to make the trip down to Brighton to see him. Perhaps he had not reassured Pemberton enough and the scientist had got scared and told the Secret Service what he was planning to do. On the other hand, perhaps he hadn't done anything deliberately to betray Yusuf. He could just have been careless. Yusuf thought that was perfectly in keeping with what he knew of the man. His vanity and sense of self-importance had been the very weaknesses Yusuf himself had exploited. It wouldn't have taken much: a veiled boastful remark, perhaps, or an oblique reference to moving abroad for a better job would have been more than sufficient. Pemberton was just the type of man to have enjoyed dropping mysterious hints: it would have fed his sense of superiority. Once he had said something, word that he was behaving suspiciously would have quickly reached the security services and a covert investigation set in place. How long then before Pemberton's affair with Angel was discovered? And, once that was known, MI6 could have found out her secret liaisons with himself. A quick search of his background would have been sufficient to ring alarm bells and set up an operation to uncover precisely what was going on. But Yusuf no longer believed Pemberton was responsible. It explained some things but not all of them. If the al Assad brothers were right in believing they were being followed, MI6 must have known they were staying at Westbrook Grove. There was just one person who had known he was going to fetch the virus and also knew about the flat. Angel.

It was the only possible explanation. He and Angel had once used the flat for one of their early liaisons when she had been able to spend the night in London. He realised now it had been a foolish mistake on his part but she had insisted on cooking for him and had not wanted a hotel. There was no way he was going to take her back to his own house and she must have given the Westbrook address to MI6 when she betrayed him. But why had she done it?

One obvious reason sprang to mind: Pemberton's death must have scared her. She would not have believed the suicide story and perhaps realised she was now involved in something far more dangerous than she had originally assumed. She would have been frightened and probably believed her only way out was to abandon the operation and go to the British for protection. It was strange that after all her declarations of love she would betray him but who could tell how the mind of such a woman worked? She might even have thought he was at risk and gone to the British in an attempt to save him from whoever had killed Pemberton. Whatever the reason, she must have panicked and passed on the information he had given her and which she believed to be true.

With Pemberton unable to pass the virus over, the British would have realised he would now try to get it himself and must have worked with Angel, persuading her to set him up by providing the security passes so he could be caught red-handed with the virus after breaking in. That would also explain how the woman in the restroom had recognised him. MI6 must have warned them to be on the look-out and were probably preparing to set a trap. But he had moved too fast. They probably had not had sufficient time to set their plans in place and they had underestimated his own resources. Luck had been with him that night but he couldn't rely on it again. The more he thought about it, the more convinced he became that the source of all his present troubles had to be Angel and Yusuf decided he would make her pay for it once he had finished. But, now he believed she had turned informer, he needed to think carefully about what he was going to do next.

Angel had never known anything about the real operation. The security services might have believed the story he had given her about passing the virus on to someone else but none of that mattered now he had it in his possession. Whether or not they knew his true intentions, he knew they were going to be ruthless in their pursuit of him. Yusuf would not have been surprised if it was the British who had killed Pemberton. In fact, that made a lot more sense than suicide. However talented the scientist might have been, he had shown he was a loose cannon and going to be a security risk as long as he lived. Yusuf had enough knowledge of security services to know they believed some risks were just not worth taking.

He checked his watch. It was five minutes past three and Kylie was late. Although he knew the traffic in central London was bad, he couldn't help but feel a stab of panic. There were so many things that could have gone wrong. If he hadn't needed the brothers he would have abandoned them, but they knew how to do things he couldn't. He didn't have a back-up plan and to organise something now would take time, time and resources he didn't have now he was a fugitive. He looked up The Mall and suddenly saw the van in the distance. The traffic was moving slowly and he resisted the urge to step out so he could be seen. He had to wait for the van to return up Constitution Hill before he revealed himself. He needed to be sure it was not being followed. He moved back behind the tree and watched the van slowly approach.

As it drew level with him on the other side of the road, he could see Kylie behind the wheel. There was no sign of the brothers but he knew they were in the back. The driver's sunshield was down and that was the signal that so far everything had gone according to plan. Yusuf felt some relief but didn't relax. It was still possible they were being followed and Kylie hadn't picked up on it. She was a bright girl but this was unfamiliar territory for her and she wouldn't necessarily know what to look for. Yusuf watched the van approach the Monument and signal right as it reached the lights.

Kylie was driving slowly; the volume of traffic gave her no option and Yusuf was glad he had chosen this place as the pick-up point. He was no longer looking at the van but scanned the cars behind. As the van turned right at the imposing Queen Victoria Monument, Yusuf carefully looked at the people in the cars that followed it. So far, nothing looked suspicious but he would have to wait until the van returned to be sure. Once it was out of sight, he walked across to Constitution Hill and waited. It took longer than he thought to come back but then he saw it and carefully looked at the cars behind. None of them were the same as those that had followed Kylie down The Mall. Now satisfied she wasn't being followed, Yusuf stepped forward to the curb where he could be seen. For a moment he thought the van wasn't going to stop. He raised his hand and waved and the van pulled in. Immediately, the cars behind began to sound their horns and a taxi tried to pull out to pass. Yusuf quickly walked in front of the van and pulled the driver's door back.

"I almost didn't recognise you," said Kylie. "You've shaved your beard off!"

She slid off the seat onto the road and stood aside to let Yusuf clamber into the van. He looked at her as he took hold of the wheel and smiled.

"A small sacrifice," he said. "Thanks for everything. Don't try and contact me. I'll be in touch."

He smiled again and put the van into gear as Kylie slid the door shut. He pulled away from the curb and joined the stream of traffic. Glancing briefly in the wing mirror, he took a last look at Kylie standing by the side of the road. He knew he would not see her again.

★

Ira Goldstein settled himself with some difficulty on the small seat at the back of the café in one of the many side streets near the river and waited. Since getting Daniel's call that afternoon, he had been hard at work and now had some information that could prove crucial. He looked around with distaste at his surroundings. The walls were covered with stained and peeling travel posters of Venice. The café had probably once been clean and fresh but Ira thought that must have been many years ago. This was not a place of his choosing. He had been in many worse but even so, although he had ordered an espresso, having seen the machine behind the counter he had no intention of drinking it. How Daniel Rankin had come to know of the place he could only guess but it served their present needs: it was within short walking distance of MI6 headquarters and the few tables past the counter were well-spaced. Not that it mattered; Ira was the only customer and the background music of some Italian tenor was so uncomfortably loud that Ira thought if anyone wanted to overhear their conversation they would have had to sit at the table with them.

He did not have to wait long. Five minutes after the espresso arrived, Daniel came through the door with Charlie a few steps behind. Daniel nodded at the man behind the counter and went straight over to join Ira at the table. The café owner returned the nod and walked across to lock the door. He turned round the sign hanging from a sucker on the glass to say the café was now closed and then went through a door behind the counter, leaving the three men alone. Suddenly, the Italian tenor was cut off mid-note and Ira breathed a sigh of relief.

"I was wondering why you wanted to meet here," he said. "Now I understand."

"It's convenient," said Daniel.

"Is the coffee drinkable?"

"Not if it came from the machine," Daniel replied with a smile. "Eduardo keeps a separate brew for us and our friends; the machine is for customers. They don't often come back but we prefer it that way."

Ira looked at the coffee in front of him, hesitated and then pushed it to one side as he leant across the table.

"I've got the information you asked for on the Assad brothers," he said. "We think they might be engineers."

"What sort of engineers?"

"I haven't been able to find out their exact qualifications yet, we're still looking into that, but up until three months ago they were employed by a firm in Turkey that installs and services air-conditioning units."

"Air-conditioning?" Charlie repeated in surprise.

"Hotels, offices, places like that," said Ira. "They need quite complicated systems. The brothers seem to have been good at their job; the manager of the firm was very annoyed to lose them at the start of their busiest time of year."

"Why did they leave?"

"They told him their mother was ill and needed them back in Tunisia.""Never mind their mother," said Daniel impatiently. "What have they actually been doing for the last three months?"

"We don't know for sure," Ira replied with a shrug of his shoulders. "It seems they just disappeared off the map for that time. Nobody seems to know where they were until they resurfaced in London a few days ago. They certainly didn't go back to Tunisia; I suspect they might have made a foray into Syria, there's something brewing in the hills on the border. I can't say exactly what that is yet, but I can say I'm certain it has nothing to do with what's going on here. In fact, our sources have said nobody there seems to know anything about an operation planned for London. The only odd thing I've been able to find out, and I don't know if it's connected with this, was a message sent to IS headquarters in Aleppo. It was sent last Tuesday, just two days before Yusuf al Shamar set off for London, and we haven't been able to link it to anything else."

"What was the message?" asked Daniel.

"The peacock is dead and the eggs are missing," said Ira. "That's it."

"Who sent it?"

"It came from London but that's all I can tell you."

"All you know or all you can tell us?" asked Charlie. He was becoming familiar with the way these agents worked.

"All I can tell you," Ira repeated with a faint smile.

"What are you thinking?" Daniel asked after a moment.

"It could be referring to Pemberton. 'Peacock' sums him up and the virus could be 'the eggs'. The timing fits."

"Except the virus isn't lost."

"Perhaps the sender didn't know that or perhaps 'the eggs' wasn't referring to the virus at all."

Daniel sat back in the chair and drummed his fingers on the table. All these little bits of information were like the separate pieces of a jigsaw puzzle. Some of the pieces were beginning to fit together now and a picture was beginning to emerge. For a moment all three of them sat in silence, occupied with their own thoughts. It was Charlie who spoke first.

"If, as you say, IS doesn't know of an operation planned for London, could that message really have been for al Shamar? In fact, can we be sure they are the ones behind it?" he asked.

"I only said our sources haven't been able to confirm it," said Ira. "That doesn't mean it isn't an IS operation. For what it's worth, I believe that message was intended for al Shamar. We know he is an IS operative and such an operation would be known to only a few, an elite few at the very top of the organisation. There is nothing strange in that and would explain why we hadn't heard about it. Of course, he could also be on a frolic of his own; there have been precedents."

"I was only thinking," said Charlie as he gave Ira a meaningful glance, "if that message really was intended for him, then there's someone else here in London who is helping him. Perhaps we should be looking for them."

"And we will," said Daniel before turning to look at Ira. "More importantly, I think after what you've just told us, we now know how al Shamar is intending to spread the virus. Pemberton had been researching that experiment carried out by Porton Down. All the underground stations and almost all the trains carry air-conditioning now. If the Assad brothers have the know-how to introduce the virus into the system then ..."

His voice tailed off and they looked at each other grimly as they contemplated what would happen. Suddenly, Daniel's phone gave an insistent buzz and he reached into his pocket to pull it out.

★

There were only five screens in front of Richard Spiller and the Major but that was enough. There were many more in the large rooms on the floor above, each receiving a picture sent by the hundreds of CCTV cameras spread across the streets of London. A technician in one of the larger rooms was selecting which pictures to send from an enormous array in front of him and was making a good job of it. His knowledge of the view and range of each camera was greater than either Richard's or the Major's sitting next to him but they were in communication so could direct the technician if they wanted. Two of the screens Richard was viewing were tracking the progress of the white van carrying Yusuf and the two brothers and the other three were focussed on streets surrounding the route it was taking. From this small room the Major had watched the van make its way across London from the moment it left the hotel and Richard had joined him shortly after.

Major John Harding was a tall, slim man in his early forties though he looked older. He had joined the anti-terrorist squad ten years before and his skill in handling complex operations had quickly given him a reputation for getting results. Daniel had asked for him specifically when they knew the Assad brothers were at the hotel and the Major was now in charge of tracking the van. Although he and Richard had never met, the MI6 officer knew of his reputation and was happy to take a back-seat. They had seen the van stop in The Mall and Yusuf get into the driving seat. The Major had observed Kylie walking away and ordered her to be picked up but now came the difficult part: It was time for Yusuf and the brothers to be brought in. Richard had seen the brothers leaving the hotel in their disguise and it was impossible to determine if they had been concealing weapons under their burqas as they hurried through the lobby. There could have been more weapons stashed in the van and they had to assume Yusuf himself was armed. If they tried to stop the van in the crowded streets then a gunfight was highly likely and the possibility of civilian casualties was high. There could even be a hostage situation or the van might be rigged with a bomb. Richard was glad the next important decisions were not his to make.

He had contacted Daniel again as soon as he had arrived at the centre and been told to keep track of the van. Now it was on the move, even Daniel would have to step aside and let more experienced officers in the field take over. This is what they had been trained for but Richard realised no amount of training could take into account all the variables they were going to face.

From The Mall, the van had driven past Charing Cross Station and was now making its way up The Strand. Through his headset the Major was in direct communication with four separate mobile units converging on their target as he kept them updated on its position. He didn't need a map; his knowledge of London's roads and back streets was the equal if not better than any taxi-driver.

"Now entering Fleet Street," he said into the headset. "Still heading east."

Richard was surprised at the calmness of the Major's voice. He could feel his own heart beating fast as they watched the van on the screens in front of them and his hands were so tightly clenched the knuckles were white. He was watching the middle screen which showed the view west down Fleet Street and he could see the van making its way toward the CCTV camera. Suddenly he felt the Major stiffen beside him.

"Unit two!" Major Harding said urgently into the headset. "Hold your position! You're in front of the target!"

Richard saw the large van carrying the anti-terrorist officers suddenly appear on one of the screens as it came into sight at the corner with Chancery Lane. Like all the vans used by the squad, it was clearly marked. Despite the fact there was a gap for it to merge with the traffic on Fleet Street, it stopped abruptly and waited for Yusuf's van to pass before joining the stream of traffic about a hundred yards behind.

"Unit two break off!" ordered the Major.

Driving down Fleet Street, as soon as Yusuf saw the van stop at the corner of Chancery Lane he was immediately alert. He recognised the markings, like any Londoner would, and was suspicious at once. The van had stopped despite a gap in the stream of traffic and had not come out until he had passed and was already some way down Fleet Street. That was not normal but, although there could have been an innocent explanation, he wasn't going to chance it. He took the next turning left into

237

Fetter Lane and slowed down slightly, checking the wing mirror to see if the van was going to follow him. It didn't. He relaxed a little and tried to work out the best way to get back on route.

"Shit!" the Major muttered to himself.

As long as the units were converging on their target from different directions and without knowing exactly where the van was heading, there had always been a possibility that the van might eventually meet one of them by accident. It was a risk they had been forced to take. The Major's job had been to try and keep the units just far enough away so they wouldn't be seen, yet close enough to spring into action as soon as the opportunity for interception presented itself. It was a difficult juggling act and luck had not been with him. The traffic had been light at that particular moment and Unit two had been travelling faster than he had anticipated.

"Do you think he saw us?" Richard asked quietly.

Major Harding said nothing. He was concentrating hard on the screens in front of him.

"Target now turning left into Fetter Lane heading north," he said. "Repeat, Fetter Lane. Unit two continue along Fleet Street and make a left at Farringdon Road. Do not follow yet. Repeat, do not follow."

If only we knew where the van was making for, thought Richard, this would be so much easier.

"Unit three," said the Major, "target heading your way. Pull in where you can and wait." He pulled the microphone in front of him closer and spoke directly to the technician in the room above. "Hatton Garden, please, looking down to Holborn Circus."

Within a few seconds, one of the screens in front of them changed to show the view down Hatton Garden from the north and Richard saw the van which he presumed was Unit three pull into the kerb and park on double yellow lines.

"Forget Fleet Street now," the Major said to the technician. "Give me Holborn Circus."

The two men watched the screen change and waited. A few minutes later they saw the van coming towards the lights at the end of Fetter Lane. The lights changed to red and the van came to a stop.

"Now," said Major Harding quietly to himself, "which way are you bastards going?"

Richard found he was clenching his fists again and made a conscious effort to try and relax. The lights changed and the van started to move off.

"Shit!" the Major whispered under his breath. "Target crossing into Hatton Garden going north. Unit three, hold your position and wait."

Yusuf saw the second van ahead as soon as he turned into Hatton Garden. It was parked on double yellow lines on the other side of the road and the driver was still at the wheel. He was in uniform. One van might be explained but two was a coincidence Yusuf was not prepared to risk.

Richard watched the van approach the Unit and held his breath as it gathered speed and passed by on the other side of the road.

"Are we blown?" he asked.

The Major said nothing. He was still staring intently at the screen.

Yusuf made a rapid decision. He turned to speak to the Assad brothers sitting in the back.

"Change of plan," he said quickly. "You're going to have to make your own way to the house."

The brothers looked at each other, first confused and then, with a sense of panic, Shiraz protested, "We don't know the way!"

"Take a taxi," said Yusuf as he suddenly pulled at the steering wheel and turned right without indicating.

In the small room, Richard and the Major both sat up.

"Target turning right into Cross Street," the Major suddenly barked.

Richard had seen the van suddenly make the turn without signalling and realised something was wrong.

"I need Farringdon Road by the underground station," Major Harding spoke urgently into the microphone on the desk. "Now!"

As he straightened the wheel, Yusuf checked the wing mirror. He was clear behind but now he had decided on a course of action he was not going to change it.

"You have the address and money," he said to Habab. "I'm going to drop you off at a station. Take the first tube anywhere then get off after two stops and get back on the streets. You'll find a taxi easily enough but keep in the crowds as much as you can."

"What's happened?" Habab asked.

"I think we might have a tail. I can't be sure but I'm not going to risk it."

"What about - ," Shiraz began but Yusuf cut him off abruptly.

"Just do it!" he snapped.

He had now reached the junction with Farringdon Road and had to stop. The traffic was heavy and he could not see any gaps. The road sign indicated no right turn but Yusuf ignored it as he edged the van slowly forward, indicating right and forcing the cars on the main road to stop.

In the small room, Richard and the Major watched the van emerge from the side street opposite the camera and begin to push its way into the stream of traffic. "He's doubling back," said the Major grimly. "Shit! He's spooked."

In the van, Yusuf was thinking fast. He ignored the questions from the brothers and focussed on driving as he inched slowly across the main road. The cars to his right were sounding their horns angrily as he blocked the entire lane but he ignored them and looked left. The approaching cars were slowing down as they saw what he was attempting and Yusuf slowly crawled his way into the opposite lane and gave a wave at the driver who eventually stopped to let him in. In the back of the van the brothers were still demanding answers.

"There's a station at the next corner," Yusuf said, ignoring their questions as he changed gear. "I'm going to stop there. Get ready to jump out the back and go straight down to the platforms."

"But - ," Shiraz began to protest.

"Shut up, both of you!" Yusuf ordered and Shiraz immediately fell silent. "Take the first train. Split up when you can and meet outside the house. I'll be with you as soon as I can."

"What if you don't come?" Shiraz asked nervously.

"Then you're on your own!" Yusuf shouted impatiently and then paused. He didn't want to panic the brothers. "Give me until seven o' clock and then you can leave, but I'll be there. It's going to be alright." He turned round, trying to give them a reassuring smile. "Take the bag with you," he added as an afterthought. "If I don't make it, you know what to do. I wouldn't like to think this has all been for nothing."

"But you said -"

"We're here," interrupted Yusuf as he abruptly stopped the car in the middle of the road on the corner outside Farringdon station. "Now get out quickly!"

Habab jerked the handle down and pushed the back door open. Shiraz grabbed the bag from the floor and jumped out of the van. Habab immediately followed him and pushed the door closed as he started running. Through the passenger window, Yusuf saw them entering the station entrance as he pulled away and made a quick left turn, pushing his foot down on the accelerator.

★

"Shit!"

Major John Harding banged his fist on the desk. This was exactly what he had been trying to avoid. It didn't matter that it wasn't his fault; he still felt responsible.

"All undercover moves off! Units Two and Three to Farringdon Station double time. Two targets are in the station right now. Get them! Units One and Four to Smithfield asap!

241

One target still in the van heading east along Cowcross Street. Stop and apprehend. Repeat. Covert operation is off!"

As the van moved out of range from the camera, the Major leant forward to the microphone.

"Get me Cowcross Street, quick!" he barked.

"Sorry, no can do," The voice of the technician in the room above came from the loudspeaker on the desk. "Best is Smithfield."

"Do that, looking west. Everything you've got."

The screens in front of them went blank for a moment and then three of them flickered back into life.

"Come on, you bastard," said the Major impatiently as he scanned the screens, looking for the van to appear on one of them. "Where are you?"

★

Yusuf knew he didn't have long. He wasn't sure exactly how they had found him. But how didn't matter at that moment; he still needed to get away. By splitting up he had already divided their resources. If he left the van that would divide them further but was that the best thing to do? The question was what would give him the best chance of escape?

The traffic ahead of him began to slow down as it entered Charterhouse Street and Yusuf became more anxious. He began to beat his hands on the steering wheel in frustration and leant forward so he could look up at the sky through the windscreen. It had suddenly occurred to him that there might be a helicopter spying on the van from above. He decided he needed to get off the streets himself. The van had now reached Smithfield on his right and the cars ahead had almost crawled to a stop. There was no time to waste; Yusuf knew the moment had come. Charterhouse Square came up on his left and he turned into it. He drove along to the end and stopped in the middle of the road. Leaving the engine running, he slid the door back and jumped out. He knew this area well and began to run. He could now hear sirens and quickened his pace. He quickly reached Carthusian Street and kept running until he reached Aldersgate. Here he had to stop a moment to let the traffic pass but then, holding up his hand, he stepped recklessly into the road and quickly ran across as the cars screeched to a halt.

Barbican tube station was now immediately ahead of him and he ran through the entrance into the ticket-hall where he was able to mingle with the crowds and slow down to a walking pace. He was breathing heavily with the exertion of running and could still hear sirens in the distance but, for the moment, he felt safe as he joined the throng making its way down to the platforms. He was still ahead of the game.

Chapter Seven

"Nothing at all?" Daniel asked, barely able to conceal his frustration.

"I'm sorry, sir," said Richard Spiller. "We found the clothes they used to leave the hotel but, apart from some documents to do with the spice business, that's about it for the van so far. No containers or anything like that. Forensics are still going over it and might get something more."

"And the girl? What's her name?"

"Kylie Johnson, sir."

"Is she talking?"

"We haven't finished with her yet but, for what it's worth, I honestly don't believe she had any active part in this. I think she was just trying to help her boss. She thought the police were after him for some business fraud or other. I got the impression she was a bit soft on him. There could even have been something between them once but, if so, he's moved on since. She's scared, but now she's beginning to realise exactly what she's got mixed up in she is being co-operative."

They were in Daniel's office in MI6 headquarters. He and Charlie had gone there directly from their meeting with Ira. Richard had called to say that Yusuf had taken over the van at The Mall and Daniel had immediately contacted the Commander of the Anti-terrorist Squad. Now they just had to wait. There was nothing else they could do; oversight of the next stage of the operation had passed to someone else for the moment but Daniel was ready to resume command again as soon as Yusuf and the brothers were apprehended. The news they had escaped had been a demoralising blow.

"Keep her locked up anyway," said Daniel, "and keep the interrogation going. Since the squad messed up, she's all we've got."

"Major Harding did his best, sir," Richard said defensively. He thought Daniel was being a bit harsh. "I was with him. It was just a bit of bad luck. There was nothing else he could have done, not without putting the public at risk."

Daniel thought the public were now at much greater risk but he said nothing. He knew he had been unfair: only a few people, those who needed to know, were aware of the true facts and he was under strict orders not to divulge them. He appreciated the need for secrecy but it meant he felt his hands were tied. Not only Yusuf but the al Assad brothers had managed to get away. And they had the virus with them. Now they were somewhere planning their next move, a move that Daniel knew could cost the lives of thousands and bring London to a grinding halt. Would the Major have acted differently if he had known all this? Daniel admitted to himself he probably would have done.

"There's still the lady friend in Brighton," said Charlie, trying to bring an optimistic note to the proceedings. "I've been able to make some progress there."

"You already know about her?" Richard asked in surprise. "The Johnson girl said his latest flame was someone in Brighton."

"Why didn't you say so before?" Daniel demanded angrily.

"I'm sorry. I was about to. I thought you'd want to know the other things first."

Richard had only just begun his report. From his perspective, establishing the results of searching the van and the girl's role, if any, had taken priority. Daniel realised he was being unfair again; lack of sleep was making him uncharacteristically irritable.

"Carry on, then," he said a little more calmly.

"Angel. The girl said her name was Angel. Could be Angela."

Daniel looked quizzically at Charlie.

"No one of that name on my list."

"The girl says she sometimes passed messages between them. She thought the woman was probably married."

"So the girl has a contact number, an address?" Daniel asked hopefully at this sign of a fresh lead.

"Yes, a number. It was on her phone. I've got it here somewhere."

Richard started sifting through the thin sheaf of documents in the file he was carrying. The notes were still handwritten. There hadn't been time to get them typed up before he thought he should make his initial report. He put the file down on the desk and extracted a sheet of paper which he handed to Daniel.

"Excellent!" Daniel quickly scanned the paper and then handed it to Charlie. "Give this to Robert and ask him to work on it, will you. If she's been helping him, there's a chance he'll still try to get in touch."

Charlie took the paper and left the office.

"Now," said Daniel, turning back to Richard and smiling for the first time since he had returned to the office, "let's hear the rest of your report."

★

Yusuf was confident he had shaken off the British. He had taken the first tube from The Barbican and travelled two stops to Liverpool Street Station before getting out and taking the Central Line to Oxford Circus. There he had walked through the tunnels and ridden the escalators for over an hour, doubling back on himself several times and keeping amongst the crowds, constantly checking to see if anyone was tailing him. Eventually satisfied he wasn't being followed, he had taken the Bakerloo Line to Edgware Road and emerged onto the streets just as it was getting dark.

He had told the brothers to wait until seven and knew he couldn't afford to delay any longer before making his own way there. Taking a taxi to within twenty minutes' walking distance of the house, he had paid the fare and set off slowly. He wanted to have a look around before approaching the house itself. Although he had found out the address long ago, he had never actually been there before. He thought it extremely unlikely the house was being watched but he needed to be sure.

As he approached the main road where Farquharson lived, Yusuf saw Shiraz first. The brother was walking slowly along the street ahead of him, silhouetted against a street light and, to Yusuf's relief, still carrying the bag he had taken on leaving the van. They had had the sense to follow his instructions and split up so he knew Habab would not be far away. He quickened his pace and soon caught up with Shiraz.

"Any problems?" he asked casually as he fell into step alongside him.

"What went wrong?" Shiraz demanded nervously. "Why did you make us leave the van?"

"Just a precaution," Yusuf replied calmly. He didn't want to make Shiraz any more jittery than he obviously was. Telling him of the two anti-terrorist squad vans he had spotted would only make him nervous about the rest of the operation. "I thought it would probably be safer if we split up."

"You said something about being followed."

"I said I couldn't be sure. It was just a precaution, a spur of the moment thing, just in case. Anyway, I thought it made more sense to make our way here separately. I was only being extra careful, that's all."

"I don't like sudden changes in plans," said Shiraz angrily. "You scared us. We should stick to what we agreed."

"It doesn't matter, does it? We're all here now. And we're safe. Where's Habab?"

"We split up like you said. We arranged to meet near the house just before seven."

Yusuf glanced at his watch.

"Then we'd better get going."

They walked quickly to the end of the street and turned the corner onto the road where Farquharson lived. About three hundred metres ahead, they saw Habab walking slowly toward them. Apart from him, the road was deserted. As soon as he caught sight of them, he stopped and lit a cigarette, taking his time as he did so. Yusuf and Shiraz had to walk past

Farquharson's house as they made their way toward him and they could see there were no lights on.

"You made it then," Habab said unnecessarily as they reached him. "What was all that business in the van about?"

"He said he was just being careful," Shiraz muttered, still annoyed. "Never mind what he put us through."

"Stop complaining," Yusuf said sharply. "You got here safely and that's what counts."

"I've already passed the house once and it looks empty," Habab said. "What do you want to do?"

"I want to get off the streets," Yusuf replied.

"You said he wouldn't be expecting us," said Shiraz. "I don't think anyone's there. Perhaps we should try somewhere else."

"No. This is the best place. If necessary we can break in."

"What if it's alarmed?"

"You know how to deal with that, don't you?" said Yusuf impatiently.

"Habab does, but -"

"Then let's go," Yusuf said curtly. Shiraz's negative attitude was getting on his nerves.

There was no reply when Yusuf rang the front doorbell. Peering through the letterbox he saw no lights on inside and, after waiting a few minutes, they went round to the back of the house. Farquharson was a man who valued his privacy and the tall shrubs and trees against the back garden walls guaranteed they could not be seen by the neighbours. It was then a simple matter to pick the lock on the back door and gain entry. Shiraz had been right: the house was alarmed. As soon as they entered, the beeps from the alarm switch led Habab directly to it in the cupboard under the stairs and, although he was unfamiliar with this particular make, the principles were the same for most house alarms and he quickly managed to turn it off before the alarm cut in. The lights from the movement sensors high up on the walls still flashed red but that was all.

They had not switched on any lights and Yusuf made his way quietly up the stairs in the dark, leaving Shiraz and Habab in the hall below.

"The house is empty," he shouted down after a few minutes. "He's out somewhere or gone away."

"What do we do?" Shiraz shouted back.

Yusuf came back down to join them.

"We make ourselves comfortable," he said, clapping Shiraz on the shoulder, "and we wait until morning."

★

"Don't you think it's a bit soon to be out of hospital?" Anne Greaves smiled sympathetically as she began to lay the tray for coffee. "I mean, Martin said you were quite badly hurt."

"Not that bad," said Emma, returning the smile. "I was lucky. The scans showed there was nothing serious and a few stitches saw to the rest. Anyway, I don't like hospitals and there's nothing more they can do that I can't do for myself. I'd much rather get back home and sleep in my own bed."

"I still think you'd be better off in hospital. You've got to be careful with head injuries."

The two women were in the kitchen of Martin Greaves' house where Daniel had stopped off as he was taking Emma home. He was now in the front room giving Martin an update on the progress they had made whilst Emma and Anne were using the time the men were talking privately to make some coffee.

"I'm sure I'll be alright," said Emma. "Daniel said he'd look in on me to check up. He – he's been very kind."

"Is there something going on between you and Mr Rankin?" Anne asked coyly.

"What do you mean?"

"Well, if you don't mind me saying so, you seem to be getting rather special treatment," Anne said with a discreet smile. "Not everyone gets such personal attention from the men at the Ministry and I saw the way he was looking at you."

Emma gave an embarrassed laugh.

"Do I detect a little romance in the air?" Anne persisted.

"As a matter of fact," Emma admitted shyly, "we have been seeing each other. We first met when he came down to follow up that business with Michael and we've been out a couple of times since then."

"So it's getting serious?"

"Could be," Emma mused. "But we're very different people. My life is so routine stuck in a lab but he's dashing off all over the place. He's not actually Ministry of Defence, you know, he's MI6," she added confidentially.

"Yes, I know. Martin told me," Anne said and began to arrange the cups on the tray. "Sounds exciting."

"It is in a way," Emma agreed, "but it can also be a little disturbing. He actually knows the man who attacked me. His name is Yusuf al Shamar."

Anne paused and then turned round to face Emma.

"That sounds foreign."

"Yes, it's Arabic. Daniel said he was after something in the Institute and I just happened to get in the way."

"So they know exactly who it was?"

"Oh yes. Daniel said not to worry about anything. They're onto him now and know exactly where he is. He won't get away."

"You're starting to make Mr Rankin sound like a knight in shining armour," Anne said with a laugh. "All this chasing after the villains and racing to your rescue."

"Well, when you put it like that, I suppose he is a bit," said Emma, returning the laugh. "At any rate, he knows where this man is hiding out and they're closing in. Daniel said they were expecting to make an arrest any time soon. Could even be tonight."

"Well it's good to know someone's looking after you. I can't imagine Martin doing anything like that."

Emma smiled.

"I think that's everything," said Anne, standing back and surveying the tray. "I expect the men have had enough time to finish their business by now. Let's go and join them."

She picked up the tray and Emma held the kitchen door open before following her into the front room.

★

"Well?"

Daniel was impatient to find out if his plan had worked and Emma had barely got back into the car before he asked. She pulled the door shut and drew down the seat-belt, clicking it into place before she spoke.

"Please, don't ever ask me to do anything like that again." She gave an involuntary shudder. "I thought my heart was going to burst it was beating so fast. I don't know how you manage to do this for a living."

"Did you manage to give her the information?" Daniel asked. "Did she try to find out how much you knew?"

"As soon as she thought you and I were an item she didn't exactly ask me questions but sort of encouraged me to talk. You know, prompting me on. I only told her exactly what you told me to."

"Did she believe you?"

"I'm fairly sure she did. She's a cool one, though. She didn't react at all, just carried on making the coffee. Are you sure she's the one?"

"She has to be," said Daniel firmly. "We'll know for certain if she tries to get in touch with al Shamar to warn him."

"What if she doesn't?"

"It's her phone that's being used and she could easily have made copies of her husband's security passes to send on to Yusuf. I doubt very much if Martin's actively involved but, just in case he is, I gave him the same story. One of them, I'm sure, will try to make contact and then we'll have them."

"I hope it's just her and not Martin," Emma said.

251

"She fits the description you gave us. What do you think now you've seen her again? Was she the woman you saw?"

Emma paused a long time before speaking.

"I still can't be sure," she said at last. "It could be. I told you I didn't see her properly that night. I thought there was something familiar about the woman I saw with Michael but I couldn't place it then. I've only met Anne Greaves a couple of times; I last saw her over a year ago. She's lost a bit of weight since then and changed her hair. There are similarities but it could still have been someone else. I'm sorry. This is just too important to make a mistake and I don't want to confirm anything unless I'm absolutely sure."

"That's alright," said Daniel, starting the engine. "You've been brilliant. Now I think I should get you back to the hospital. You look about done in."

"No," Emma said abruptly. "I don't want to go back."

"You want to go home?" Daniel asked doubtfully.

"Not really. Look, I just don't want to be anywhere in Brighton right now." She paused and looked away before continuing. "Would you mind, I mean, would it be too much trouble …"

Her voice trailed away and she appeared embarrassed.

"What?"

"I know it's a bit much to ask, but could I stay with you for a few days?" she said quickly, turning to face him. "Just until this is over. I won't get in the way, I promise. I won't need any looking after."

Daniel was surprised but unexpectedly pleased.

"Are you sure?" he asked hesitantly. "I'm not going to be around much. It's going to get busy and I'll probably even have to pull some more all-nighters. We won't be able to see a lot of each other."

"I – I didn't mean …"

She left the sentence unfinished and blushed as she suddenly realised what he might have been thinking.

252

"It's alright, I know exactly what you mean. I'm just not sure you should be left on your own at the moment. If you hadn't been the only one I could trust to help, I wouldn't have taken you out of hospital in the first place."

"I told you, I don't need any looking after. I just can't face staying here. I don't want to see anyone from the Institute, not knowing what I do now about Martin and his wife. I need to get away. Somewhere I can feel safe."

"Well, if that's what you really want, of course," Daniel said slowly. He was still uncertain but could understand how she felt. "We can stop off and pick up a few things from your house on the way back." He paused. "You're sure you wouldn't rather stay with a friend?"

"Yes, quite sure." She sounded definite. "Anyway, all my friends are in Brighton apart from you. I can make myself useful if you like. I'll do the cooking."

Daniel smiled.

"I don't think I'll have much time to eat at home over the next few days."

"Your loss, then," said Emma, returning his smile. "I'm a very good cook."

★

Daniel was still driving Emma back to London when the call came through to Kylie's phone. She was sitting at a table in one of the small interview rooms at MI6 headquarters. Charlie was sat opposite her, writing up some notes, and her phone was attached to a machine that would not only record the call but also enable everyone in the room to hear what was being said. As soon as the phone buzzed, Kylie jumped and looked across at Charlie.

"Give it a moment before answering," he said. "Don't want to make them think we've been waiting for a call."

Kylie picked up the phone and, after a few moments, Charlie nodded and she pressed the call button.

"Hello, Kylie here."

"It's Angel."

Kylie looked scared.

"Yes," she said, "what's up?"

"I need to speak to Yusuf. It's urgent. I've tried phoning him direct but he's not picking up."

Anne Greaves' voice sounded impatient.

"I know," Kylie said. "I tried to get through myself a while ago. I think he's probably switched it off for the moment. Why don't you leave it an hour or so and try again?"

"I need to speak to him now. Like I said, this is urgent. I don't suppose you know where he is?"

"Sorry. Don't you?"

Kylie and Charlie had spent an hour scripting a rough scenario in case a call was made. She was still having to improvise but knew exactly what information she had to get and what to say. There was a long pause at the other end before Anne Greaves spoke again.

"Have you seen him today?" she asked.

"Yes. He wanted the company van and I dropped it off for him."

"Was he alright?"

"Yes, but I think he's in trouble. The police were round the office this morning asking questions. I didn't tell them anything but I'm worried. What's happening?"

"I'm sure there's nothing for you to worry about, but I do need to speak to him. Did he say where he was going?"

"No, just that he wanted to take a couple of days off. He said you would know where he was."

"Me?" Anne sounded surprised.

"Yes. Didn't he say where you could reach him?"

Kylie looked anxiously at Charlie who nodded his approval.

"No." Anne was beginning to sound frustrated.

"Well," Kylie continued, "that's what he told me. Do you know of any friends he could have gone to?"

There was a long silence as Anne tried to think.

"Is that all he said?" she asked at last.

"Yes. We didn't speak much, he was in a hurry, but when I asked what to say if you should call he just said you would know where to find him."

There was another long pause and, as the silence grew longer, Kylie looked nervously at Charlie again. For a moment she thought she had made a mess of things and Angel had hung up.

"Hello?" she said tentatively.

"I'm still here," said Anne. "Look, if he should call, can you ask him to get in touch with me urgently. It's important." She hesitated before quickly adding, "Tell him I think the police know where he is."

"Can't you tell me what's going on?" Kylie asked. "Perhaps I could help."

"No, that's alright. You've done enough already. Just give him that message and I'll keep trying to get through. That's all. Bye."

The call ended and Kylie breathed a sigh of relief.

★

Anne Greaves was not the sort of woman who used bad language. She had always believed it was the sign of a poor education and looked down on those whose every other word was a vulgarism. But she swore now. A torrent of the crudest words she knew fell from her lips and when she had used them all up, she started over again. It didn't help. She stared out of her bedroom window in frustration and wondered what she could do next. She could have slapped Emma Nelson for sounding so smug when she said the police knew where Yusuf was and were closing in on him. Anne knew she had to warn him but didn't know how. If only he had told Kylie exactly where he was going. He had obviously believed the message he left would be enough to let her know but, sitting on the bed and gripping the duvet in both hands, she had no idea. She realised she needed to calm down; she would achieve nothing in her present state of mind. She took a few deep breaths and tried to think rationally.

Yusuf obviously knew the police and Secret Service were after him. He was on the run. He needed somewhere to hide out so where would he have gone? The police would soon know about the flat in Westbrook Grove if they didn't already, so it couldn't be there. His regular circle of friends were out of the question; they would be the first ones to be watched. Yusuf would realise that. So who else was there? Suddenly her mind became clear. There was only one person she knew who could offer Yusuf the sanctuary he needed: Andrew Farquharson.

She had never met the man but that night when Pemberton told them he had been approached by Farquharson, she had realised Yusuf also knew him. She had seen how he had reacted on hearing the name and realised he must know more about the man than he was letting on. When they saw each other in London a few days after that meeting in Brighton, she had pressed Yusuf for an explanation. Although reluctant to talk about it at first, when she persisted he had eventually admitted that Farquharson was the man who had approached him about the virus in the first place. They agreed that he must have got impatient to have contacted Pemberton directly and Yusuf had said he would sort things out. A week later when they met again, shortly before Yusuf had to go abroad on business, he said he had seen Farquharson and the matter had been resolved. She had not thought about it since but now realised Yusuf must have gone to Farquharson for help! Farquharson knew everything and he was the one person who could not betray Yusuf without involving himself.

Now she considered it, she realised Yusuf must have known she would work it out eventually. He couldn't tell Kylie where he was going. She knew nothing about what was really happening and, anyway, she was bound to be questioned eventually; if he had told her his location she might have said something to the police. Anne was the only one who knew about his connection with Farquharson; the only one he could trust completely. Yusuf had to be there. She got off the bed and went downstairs.

She knew very little about Andrew Farquharson apart from the fact he was the editor of an important science journal. But Martin had close contact with the press, it was part of his job as assistant director of the Institute and he had got to know many of the people involved socially as well as professionally. It was more than likely he would know how to get in touch with the man. All she had to do was get him to tell her. As she reached the hall, she could hear Martin making himself a cup of tea in the kitchen and changed her mind. She didn't want to ask him about Farquharson unless there was no other way. She went into the study and looked through Martin's address book. There it was: underneath Farquharson's business details was his home address. She turned over the page but there was no home telephone number. Almost crying with frustration, she copied the address quickly onto a post-it and put the book back. She went into the hall and was putting on her coat when Martin emerged from the kitchen holding a mug of tea.

"Going out?" he asked.

"I thought I would nip round and see Margaret," Anne replied, giving the first excuse she could think of as she slipped a silk scarf around her neck. "She's not been well and I said I would drop by to see how she is."

"Give her my regards," said Martin.

"Will do. Don't wait up, I expect I'll be late."

"Not too late, I hope. You know how irritable you get when you're tired."

Anne gritted her teeth. One of the things she had grown to hate about Martin was how he always looked for ways to criticise her.

"Stop fussing," she said irritably. "Just leave it alone, will you. If I want to stay out late then I will."

"I was only -" he began when Anne cut him off. She was now desperate to be on her way.

"You're always trying to run my life these days. Stop interfering with everything I do. I'll be back when I'm back!"

She gave him an angry look and slammed the door as she left.

Martin shrugged. He had got used to these sudden bad mood swings of his wife. He went into the front room and turned on the television.

★

Yusuf stared at the two aerosol cans in front of him. So small and yet so lethal. Disguised as containers holding instant whipped cream, they looked completely innocent; the sort of innocuous things you might find in any fridge. But just one of them was sufficient to unleash immeasurable harm and panic on an unsuspecting world. As he admired them and thought of what they could do, Yusuf felt overwhelmed by the sense of power now at his disposal. It almost sublimated the thirst for revenge he had nurtured for so many years and even eclipsed any ambitions he had held for establishing the caliphate. It occurred to him that this was what being a god must feel like. He picked up one of the cans and ran his fingers over the smooth metal surface, enjoying the cold touch against his skin. I am holding the means to change the world, he thought. He placed the can carefully back on the table and sat back in his chair. It was a strange feeling to have control over the life and death of thousands. This really was the power of God. Then the full horror of what he was about to do suddenly hit him. Until that moment the consequences of his plan had been an abstract notion, a means to an end. Now he had a vision of a city stalked by plague and it made him pause. It wasn't conscience so much as uncertainty. For the first time since he had embarked on this plan he felt the shadow of a doubt. God is merciful, he thought. Can this really be his will?

It was not a question he had previously considered. He had been encouraged from the start by his Imam. His friends and companions in the IS had never asked themselves if what they were doing was right: they knew they were acting for the glory of God. They knew their jihad was blessed and were certain they would be rewarded with a place in Paradise. But he knew deep in his heart that it was not the glory of God that had led him to this point: all he had ever really wanted was revenge for his family's death. He suddenly remembered a line from a play he had read many years before when he was at school. '*The last temptation is the greatest treason, to do the right deed for the wrong reason*'.

Had God read his heart and would he be judged for it? Yusuf felt uneasy as the uninvited thought filled his mind. He stood up and went into the kitchen to get himself a glass of water. He was alone downstairs. Habab and Shiraz had gone up to one of the bedrooms to get some sleep and he could hear them snoring gently as he padded down the hall in his socks. He had to turn the light on in the kitchen to find a glass and carefully lowered the blinds before doing so. He didn't think the neighbours could see the back of the house but, if they knew Farquharson was out, there was still a risk in showing a light. He took a sip of water and tried to dismiss the thoughts that had now started to run through his head.

He went back into the front room and sat down again in front of the two cans on the table. It was no good. He had to work this out. The question was simple: would he be blessed or damned? And it was not something that could be put off: he was about to gamble with his soul. He forced himself to try and think objectively. Was revenge really such a bad thing? After all, God was not only merciful, He was just; and wasn't that what this was all about? As a servant of that same God, wasn't he simply carrying out a sort of justice on His behalf? Yusuf began to feel a little comforted by the thought. After all, it was God who had made it possible for him to get the virus in the first place. If there was something wrong about what he was intending to do, then surely God would have stopped him instead of finding ways to help. And God had assuredly helped him. There had been all manner of obstacles put in his way: Pemberton's death, the woman at the Institute stumbling upon him by accident, Angel's betrayal and almost getting caught by the British in the van could each have put an end to everything. But all these problems had been overcome. He had supposed at the time it was luck but now, the more he thought about it, the more convinced he became that he would never have got this far without God's help and that could only mean it was part of His plan. God wanted him to do this. Feeling somewhat reassured, Yusuf took a large gulp of water and was about to set the glass back down on the table when the front doorbell rang.

★

Anne Greaves had driven as fast as she dared and arrived in London earlier than she had hoped. The satnav directed her to Farquharson's address and she drove past it, taking the next turning along before she parked. Now she was here, she was uncertain what to do next. During the drive up, she had worked out a cover story in case something happened. She would admit to her affair with Pemberton and say that before he died, he had told her Farquharson had been trying to get in touch with him. She would tell them it had suddenly occurred to her that Farquharson might have some information on Michael's death and she had come up to London to confront him. There was sufficient truth in the story, perhaps, to cause anyone to have doubts about whether she had a connection with Yusuf. It might explain why she had gone to the house but would it be enough to allay suspicion? She was sure Yusuf would try to protect her. He would deny having any connection with her but who would believe him given all the circumstances?

She turned off the ignition but instead of getting out she remained sitting in the car. Emma Nelson had said they knew where Yusuf was; did that mean the house was already under surveillance? She hadn't seen any signs when she had driven past but that signified nothing. If they were watching and saw her go to the front door, she knew that would be enough to implicate her in some way. She felt sick with fright at what might happen but her priority now was to warn Yusuf. That was the most important thing. At the very least she had to give him a chance to get away and, as he wasn't picking up his phone, that meant she had to go the house. The longer she delayed, the greater he was at risk.

Deciding she had no better alternative, she opened the car door and got out, locking it behind her. She walked along the side-street and turned the corner onto the main road, a hundred metres from Farquharson's house. She paused to look around but saw nothing out of the ordinary. A woman and young man were on the opposite side of the road making their way toward her but, apart from them, the pavements were deserted. A few cars were parked in the driveways and, as she began to walk along the road, she looked at them carefully and saw they were all empty. She quickened her step. Perhaps they hadn't got anything in place yet. Perhaps Emma Nelson had got it wrong and MI6 were acting on incorrect information, watching some other place in another part of London. It made no difference now; she had committed herself. She reached the iron gate outside Farquharson's house and pushed it open. Taking a deep breath, she walked up to the front door and pressed the bell.

Nothing happened. She waited a full minute and then rang again. She bent down and pushed the letterbox flap open to peer through. The hall was dark but at the end she could see a light coming from the kitchen at the back. So someone must be in.

"Mr Farquharson," she called softly through the flap.

Nothing.

"Mr Farquharson," she repeated, this time a little more loudly.

Still nothing.

She stood up and walked over to the window. The curtains were drawn. She hesitated a moment and then tapped gently against the glass. She had not anticipated this and was unsure what to do. She went back to the door and called again through the letterbox.

"Yusuf!"

Upstairs in the back bedroom Shiraz and Habab were awake. At the sound of the first doorbell they had both sat up in alarm. They had been lying fully-dressed on the double divan and now jumped up and went quickly to the bedroom door. Shiraz eased it open and peered out cautiously. The landing was dark but some light from the kitchen spilt through into the hall below. Moving like a cat in the shadows, Habab pushed past his brother and stepped quietly onto the landing to look over the banister. Shiraz followed him. He was scared.

"What's happening?" he whispered.

Outside the front door Anne was beginning to feel desperate. She pressed the bell for a third time and bent down to call through the letterbox again, this time more loudly.

"Yusuf! It's me, Angel!"

Yusuf was still in the front room. He had recognised Anne's voice the first time she called and had felt a surge of panic. He had been convinced she was now working with the British Secret Service and wondered how they had managed to track him to the house. But if she was there, surely the British must be outside too.

"Open the door, Yusuf! I've come to warn you! You've got to leave!"

Anne's voice sounded fraught and urgent. Yusuf was uncertain what to do. He still had the gun the Imam had given him. It was in the pocket of his coat hanging in the hall, but he knew it would have little effect if the services were waiting to burst into the house. And he had no intention of going out in some sort of blaze of glory.

"Yusuf! Please! Let me in!"

Yusuf hesitated. He realised she was not going to go away. If Angel was not genuine then she was putting on a very convincing act. He made up his mind. He opened the door to the front room and, keeping behind it, called out.

"Why have you come? What do you want?"

Anne could have cried with relief.

"It's me!" she called through the letterbox. "Let me in! I think the police know you're here. They're probably on their way right now!"

"Are you alone?"

262

"Yes! Yes, of course. Please, let me in."

Yusuf understood there was nothing else he could do now. He stepped into the hall and cautiously turned the lock of the front door. Anne pushed it open and stumbled through, throwing her arms around him and holding him tightly as he kicked the door shut behind her.

★

Daniel was still travelling back to London in the car with Emma and had just reached the outskirts of the city when he got the call from Charlie. They had stopped off at Emma's house for almost an hour to collect some things and have a quick coffee before leaving. That had given Anne Greaves a long head start and Charlie had been calling him regularly to let him know what was happening. This time he had sounded very excited over the speakerphone.

"Where did you say?" Daniel asked incredulously as Charlie finished giving him the latest update.

"Farquharson's house," Charlie repeated. "What do you want to do?"

Daniel paused. He should have thought of Farquharson's house before. He had known of the connection between him and Simon Warbeck but there had been nothing to link him with al Shamar. Now a picture of conspiracy was starting to emerge.

"How long before you can get in position?" he asked.

"We're still on our way, could be about ten minutes, but the surveillance team that followed her are there now and keeping an eye on the place."

"OK."

Daniel paused. He desperately wanted to be in on the action when the operation went down but he was still about half an hour away.

"Is she still inside?" he asked.

"Yes," Charlie's voice crackled over the speakerphone.

"Any sign of activity?"

"Doesn't seem to be."

"Let me know as soon as the squad's in place and then wait. I want to be there if I can. I'm on my way right now. I'll be less than half an hour."

"Right. What if they try and make a break for it?"

"If everyone's in position then you'll have to go in, if not then just keep them under surveillance. Don't let them out of your sight but don't try anything until the armed unit is there. We know he has a weapon and I don't think he'll hesitate to use it this time. I don't want anyone getting hurt unnecessarily."

"Will do," Charlie said. "Is that all?"

"For the moment. Let me know immediately of any change."

"Right."

Daniel paused. "We've got him Charlie! It's over!"

He couldn't keep the note of satisfaction from his voice. Everything was starting to fall into place at last.

"Not until the fat lady sings," Charlie cautioned, "but I think it's safe to say the music's started. See you soon."

Daniel chuckled quietly to himself as the call ended and turned to Emma.

"Sorry about this," he said, "but you heard what the man said. We're making a short detour. I've got a date with the fat lady."

★

As soon as Yusuf had kicked the door shut, Habab and Shiraz ran down the stairs and Anne quickly jumped back in surprise. She had not known anyone else was in the house and looked anxiously at Yusuf.

"It's alright," he said. "These are my friends. They're helping me. Why have you come?" He paused before adding, "How did you know I was here?"

"There's no time to explain," Anne said urgently. "You've got to leave now. The police know you're here."

"How do they know?" He paused a fraction of a second before snarling, "Did you say something?"

Despite the urgency of the moment, Anne was suddenly taken aback and gasped at the accusation and the harshness in Yusuf's voice. He had never spoken to her like that before. For a few seconds she was at a loss for words. The thought that Yusuf could suspect her of betraying him, even by accident, stung like nothing else could. She took a step forward and grabbed him by each arm, staring wildly into his eyes.

"How – how could you think that?" she demanded.

Yusuf was silent. He looked at her intently and wondered if she could be feigning her reaction. He was a master of deception himself but knew even he would find it difficult to pretend the pain and desperation that he saw in her eyes. Could she really be that good?

"Then how did they find out?" he said at last.

"I don't know. But you've got to believe me. They're probably on their way now!"

Anne let him go. She took a step back and tried to calm herself. The most important thing at that moment was to get Yusuf out of the house and to do that she had to make him believe he was in danger if he stayed. There wasn't time to go into long explanations about Emma Nelson but she needed to say something that would convince him.

"Martin told me," she continued hastily. "He said the police knew who you were and expected to make an arrest tonight. He didn't say how they found out but it must mean they know you're here! We've got to get away before they come. Don't you understand, they could be here any minute! We've got to leave now! We can use my car."

Yusuf turned aside. He was used to thinking fast. He could tell she had not given him the real story but did she really did believe they were in immediate danger? If there was any grain of truth in what she had said, then to remain in the house was the last thing he should do. Once the British forces were in place, he would be trapped with no possibility of escape. But what if this was already a trap? What if men were even now waiting for him outside and she had been sent to lure him into the open? He turned back to look at her again. After all his recent suspicions, he still couldn't be entirely sure if she was genuine. He was beginning to think she might be but could he take the risk? Right or wrong, he realised he had no choice.

"Are they outside now?" he asked. "Did you see anyone?"

"No. At least, I don't think so," Anne replied. "I'm sorry. It looked deserted but I can't be sure. I didn't see anyone."

Yusuf turned to the brothers. He had made up his mind.

"We're going now," he said abruptly. "Get the cans and leave everything else."

Shiraz was about to say something but Habab quickly cut him off.

"Do as he says!"

Shiraz looked doubtful but obediently went into the front room to collect the aerosol cans.

"Where are you parked?" Yusuf asked, turning back to Anne.

"In a side street, just along the road. It's not far." Her relief that Yusuf believed her and was leaving showed in her face and she tried to smile reassuringly at him. "I'll go first and make sure it's all clear."

"No," said Yusuf. "We're going to split up."

Shiraz came out of the front room clutching a plastic bag which held the two cans. Yusuf looked at the brothers.

"Give one of them to Habab," he said. "You both know what has to be done. We'll do it tonight."

"How can we?" Shiraz protested as he passed one of the cans over to his brother. "We haven't even got the right jackets yet."

"That won't matter. Just act as if you own the place and no one's going to stop you. If anyone asks, say you were off-duty and called in late because it's urgent. Pretend you don't speak good English. I don't know, make something up. You can do it. Just keep calm and keep your wits about you. It's up to you now. Go through the back garden and over the wall. Split up and meet at the station by Victory Arch. If one of you is caught, the other can still go ahead. Go now. There's no time to waste!"

"What about you?" Habab asked.

"Don't worry about me. You can manage perfectly well by yourselves." Yusuf smiled grimly. "If anyone's outside then I'll provide a diversion. I can probably hold them up long enough for you to get away. If it's all clear," he glanced briefly at Anne and then at his watch, "I'll meet you at ten o' clock under the Arch. You've got money?"

"Yes," said Habab, patting his pocket to make sure his wallet was there.

"Then go now," said Yusuf and stepped forward to embrace each of the brothers. "God be with you."

Habab and Shiraz went quickly down the hall and into the kitchen. Habab switched off the light and turned to give Yusuf one final look before closing the door behind him. Yusuf went over and placed his ear against it, keeping perfectly still until he had heard the back door open and close. He remained there a few minutes longer and then walked back to Anne who was waiting at the other end of the hall.

"I didn't hear anything," he said. "It sounds as if they got away."

"What now?" Anne asked.

"Now it's our turn," he said, pulling his outside coat off the hook in the hallway and slipping his arms through the sleeves. "You lead the way and I'll be a few paces behind. If anything happens don't turn round, just make a run for the car."

Anne reached up her hand to pull his face toward her and kissed him long and hard.

"If anything happens," she said quietly, looking into his eyes, "I just want you to know it's been worth it."

He smiled at her and she turned away to open the door. As it swung open, he reached into his coat pocket and pulled out the gun he had kept there. Keeping it low and aimed directly at the small of Anne's back, he followed her into the front garden.

★

267

"Something's happening! A man and a woman are coming out!"

The two men who had followed Anne from Brighton were now on the main road outside Farquharson's house. Having left their car in the same side street where Anne had parked, they had split up and were now left and right of the house, a couple of hundred metres apart on each side of the road. As soon as he had seen Anne and Yusuf reach the pavement and start toward him, the man who had just spoken turned his back on them and took a packet of cigarettes from his coat pocket. He removed one and lit it before walking away in the direction he was facing. He was no longer able to see them now but his partner on the other side of the road could still keep them under observation.

Lighting the cigarette had been a ploy to explain why he might have stopped for a moment; it was enough to fool Anne who was inexperienced in such matters but not Yusuf. As soon as he had emerged from the gate, he had immediately seen the two men and guessed who they were. He let Anne get a few paces in front of him and raised the gun, still keeping it pointed at her back. He knew it could now be seen but that was what he wanted. Completely unaware of what was going on behind her, Anne continued walking quickly toward her car.

"He's armed!" said the other man. Although he spoke quietly, the small microphone attached to his collar picked up the urgency in his voice and transmitted it to his companion's earpiece. Others were also listening in, but they were still several minutes away in the van speeding toward the house.

"I think the woman is a hostage," the man added quickly. "His gun is pointed at her!"

Major John Harding cursed under his breath. They were just that little bit too late! He and his armed squad were in two vans and another team of unarmed men, including Charlie, was in a third van, all now speeding toward their target. They had set off as soon as the report came in that Anne was on the outskirts of London. Constant updates had kept them informed of her progress and, along with three other civilian cars carrying agents from MI6, they had been able to maintain a position that kept each of them within a half-mile radius of where she was. As soon as she had parked, they had all begun to converge on the spot but were still not going to make it in time.

"Stand down!" the Major said into his microphone. The orders he had been given were clear but it was going to make things more difficult. It would have been a lot better had they been able to surround the house whilst everyone was still inside.

"Any sign of the other two?" he asked.

"Negative" came the reply.

"They could be round the back," said John. "Can you confirm?"

"Not at the moment," said the man who was still some way behind Yusuf. "I can't see. I'll have to go round myself to do that and I'm about twenty yards away."

"Don't," said John. "Keep the targets you have in sight but drop back."

"Targets now turning into Brecknock Street," said the man.

It was infuriating to be working blind. The Major needed to be on the spot to be effective. He had no clear idea of the layout of the area, how the houses were arranged or the distances involved. And there were no CCTV cameras in the immediate vicinity. It was a quiet residential district and any moment innocent bystanders could emerge from one of the houses. One thing was now obvious, however: the targets were making for the woman's car and must be planning to leave. After Yusuf had managed to elude them that afternoon, Daniel realised the Major needed to be told exactly what was at stake if he were to make the right decisions. However, even though he was now better informed, told that there must be no casualties, all he could do was keep the targets under observation and this time he mustn't lose them.

"Tiger, Lion, Cheetah," he said, addressing the three civilian cars by their codenames, "you heard all that. Move in but keep out of sight. B team go with them and be ready to provide back-up if necessary. I'll deal with the house."

He knew there were two more targets and had to make sure whether they were still there. It meant dividing his forces but that was why they had two vans.

"Targets now getting into her car," came the voice of the man who was following Yusuf and Anne. He had now reached the corner of the street where she had parked and could see Yusuf closing the passenger door.

"Did they check for the tracker?"

"No."

Before the two men had taken up their positions on the street, they had attached a small magnetic tracking device to the bottom of Anne's car and smeared it with grease. This would let them know the car's position to within two metres wherever it went.

"Follow them but keep well back," Major Harding said. "Support should be with you in a couple of minutes."

As Anne's car pulled away from the curb, the van carrying the Major and his team turned the corner onto the road two hundred metres down from where Farquharson's house now lay silent, dark and empty.

★

"Where are we going?" Anne asked quickly as she shifted up a gear.

"Just keep driving for the moment," said Yusuf.

"You'll have to direct me. I don't know where I am. I used the satnav to get here."

Yusuf twisted round in his seat to look behind. The road was clear but he kept watching for several minutes before turning back to focus ahead.

"Are we being followed?" Anne asked anxiously.

"No."

"Then we've done it!"

Yusuf wasn't so sure but at least he had a breathing space. He had returned the gun to his pocket as he got in the car. Anne had not seen it and, for the moment, anyway, he wanted to keep it like that. He was sure those two men had been agents and that meant the British must have followed her to the house. That was the only way they could have found out where he was but now he was starting to think she might not have realised it. She had simply been used by the British. There was one way to make sure.

"You can tell me now," he said. "How did you really know where to find me?"

Anne quickly explained that Emma Nelson had told her the police knew his whereabouts and that she had tried to warn him through Kylie who had passed on the message that she would know where he was.

"Kylie said that?" Yusuf interrupted.

"Yes. It didn't take me long then to realise you had to be with Farquharson but you were taking a big risk. What if I hadn't been able to work it out?"

"But you did," said Yusuf grimly.

He was thinking fast. She sounded too relieved, too pleased with herself to be lying. He had left no such message with Kylie so, if Angel was telling the truth, it meant the girl must now be co-operating with the British. That would explain how they had been able to track him when she had dropped off the van. That, more than anything else, confirmed to him now that Angel must have been an innocent dupe and Yusuf wondered just how long Kylie had been working against him. Fortunately, he had never told her anything about his plans but the British clearly knew a lot more than he had given them credit for. They had known he would go to the Institute to get the virus and Kylie must have told them about Anne. Just how much more did they know? For a moment he considered abandoning the brothers to make his own escape. Even if they all managed to get to the station, and there was no certainty in that, what practical use could he be? He didn't have the knowledge to fit the cans into the air-conditioning units. The brothers could do that without him but he was reluctant to leave them now they were so close to completing the operation.

More importantly, he realised that unless he was actually there in person to direct and lead them, there was a real possibility they might not go ahead.

Shiraz was the weak link; he always had been. Yusuf was sure he could have trusted Habab to act alone. In fact, his original plan had been to use just the one brother but Habab had insisted on his younger sibling coming with them. Yusuf had never completely trusted Shiraz. He had thought the man was vain and manipulative; someone who wanted the admiration of others but was not prepared to make the sacrifices and risks that might involve. However, Habab was devoted to his brother and had seen the operation as an opportunity for the young man to prove himself. Yusuf had reluctantly agreed he could join them, but Shiraz had proved a problem from the start. He had always been nervous about what they were going to do, finding difficulties where none existed and constantly looking for excuses to abandon the scheme. The truth was Yusuf believed the young man was actually a coward at heart, though he would never have dared express that opinion in so many words to Habab who indulged his brother in everything. Yusuf thought if he were to leave them now, the operation would depend for its success entirely on the two brothers and one of them couldn't be trusted to see it through. If he wasn't there to make sure they did the job and Shiraz tried to back out, could Habab persuade him to go ahead, especially now they all knew for sure the British were onto them, or would he try to protect his brother, abandon the operation and help Shiraz make a break for it?

"Yusuf!" Anne's voice suddenly cut across his thoughts. She sounded panicky. "I said where do I go?"

Yusuf jumped. He had been so preoccupied he hadn't heard her the first time. They were now rapidly approaching a roundabout and had to make a turn. One road would take them back into central London, the other led to Hammersmith, the M4 and the possibility of escape. He twisted round in his seat again to look behind and then turned back. He had made his decision.

"Make for central London. We're going to Waterloo Station."

Chapter Eight

Habab and Shiraz did not split up as Yusuf had directed. Going over the back garden wall of Farquharson's house, they had found themselves in another back garden. From there, climbing over a series of walls, they had worked their way along the houses that ran parallel to the road behind the main street on which Farquharson lived. When they came to the last house, they moved silently down the path that ran alongside and into the front garden. Once there, they paused for a few minutes, crouching behind the hedge that bordered the street. Habab wanted to check the way was clear before going onto the pavement. From the moment of Anne's arrival, everything had happened so fast there had been no time to think. Yusuf had taken control and they had simply followed his instructions. Now they were on their own and had the chance to consider their situation and what to do next.

"We'll separate here," said Habab. "Find a taxi and take it to the station. Wait outside and I'll meet you there."

He was about to pull out his wallet and give his brother some money when Shiraz grabbed him by the arm to stop him.

"No," Shiraz hissed quietly. "I think we should stick together."

"Yusuf said we should split up."

"Yusuf said!" Shiraz whispered scornfully. "Yusuf's not here. It's over. We have to look after ourselves now."

"What do you mean?" Habab thought he knew what Shiraz was implying but he wanted to make sure.

"The operation's blown," said Shiraz. "The British know all about it. You heard what the woman told him."

Habab said nothing but the same thought had been eating away at the back of his mind whilst they had made their escape.

"There's no point in trying to go on," Shiraz continued. "They'll just be waiting for us. We should leave now whilst we've got the chance. I've been saying so since we were followed from the flat."

Habab remained silent. He couldn't disagree with his brother but felt reluctant to call it a day. Yusuf had still believed they could complete the operation. Perhaps they should make one final effort to see it through.

"Why don't we go to the station and just check it out?" he said at last. "Yusuf said he would meet us there. If he doesn't turn up we can think again."

"You go to the station if you like," said Shiraz. "That's exactly what they'll be expecting. We'll be walking straight into a trap. Is that what you want?"

"So what do you suggest?"

"We've still got the virus," said Shiraz, trying to sound reasonable. He could tell his brother was wavering and just needed a little more persuasion. "We don't have to do anything tonight, in fact, it would be foolish to try. We should wait for a better time."

"What about Yusuf?" objected Habab. "He'll be waiting for us."

"That's if he's there. You heard him. He didn't know if he could make it. He even told us to go ahead without him. I think he's looking after himself now, that's if he hasn't already been caught. We should do the same whilst we've got the chance. What about it?"

Habab realised there was some logic in what Shiraz was saying but his loyalty to Yusuf and his leadership was still strong so he hesitated.

"You have that address Yusuf gave you?" Shiraz asked, sensing Habab was undecided. "We should go there. If Yusuf has got away, he'll know that's where we've gone and join us."

"He told me to use it only in an emergency, as a last resort," said Habab.

"What do you call this?" Shiraz sounded impatient. "It's our best chance of being able to complete the operation if that's what you still want. But we need somewhere to go right now." He looked at his brother to see the effect of his words before adding, "We can wait there until the time is right."

Habab was persuaded. Shiraz hadn't mentioned it but they both knew their passports had been left behind in the rush to leave the house. Even if they went ahead with the operation that night and were successful, they would not be able to leave the country without documents. They would eventually have to go to the address Yusuf had made him memorise if they were to stand any chance of returning to Tunisia. If Yusuf had managed to get away, he would realise that. He was a good planner and this was exactly the sort of emergency he might have anticipated and prepared for.

"Very well," Habab said at last.

Shiraz breathed a sigh of relief. Yusuf had not trusted him with the address and he needed his brother to lead the way. Once there they should be safe for a time at least. Time enough, at any rate, to get new passports and time enough for him to persuade Habab that the operation should be called off completely. He was sure he could do that. They had done their best but no one could blame them for the way things had turned out.

"Let's make a start then," he said. "But we stick together."

Habab nodded and stood up. He peered out onto the road. It was empty. He took a step onto the pavement and gestured for Shiraz to follow him.

★

It didn't take long for Major Harding and his team to establish the house was empty and, by the time Daniel and Emma arrived, all the rooms had been searched. They had looked at the bed where Habab and Shiraz had been sleeping and knew that two people had used it. If further confirmation was needed that Habab and Shiraz al Assad had been there, by the side of the bed was a plastic bag containing two passports. They were made out in different names but the photographs showed they had been used by the two brothers. It was now clear they must also have been in the house when Anne Greaves arrived and had managed to get away. What Daniel didn't know was who was carrying the virus and precisely where it was at that moment.

"That must be our priority," he said. "We have to get it back and make sure it's safe."

"My men are following al Shamar and the woman," said the Major. "We've got a tracker on their car and I can pull them over any time you want."

Daniel was tempted but thought he didn't have enough information to decide if that was the best thing. He now believed Yusuf couldn't carry out the operation by himself. The al Assad brothers were the ones who knew how to install the aerosols into the air-conditioning systems so it was more than likely they were the ones who now had the virus. But he couldn't be sure.

"No," he decided. "That's too much of a risk. We've been in this situation once before. If we're to stand any chance of getting hold of the virus, we need to know where all three of them are before we do anything. If al Shamar doesn't have it then the others do. We must just hope he will lead us to them. Keep him and the woman under surveillance but don't let them know we're watching. Do you think he recognised your men when he left?"

"Sorry, I can't be sure," admitted the Major. "I told them to drop back when the couple left the house but there's no telling if the targets realised who they were."

Daniel was thinking quickly. Yusuf had eluded them once already when they were on his tail. What if he tried the same trick again and ditched the car, making for one of the many underground stations?

"Keep your men back. I want him to believe he's got away. As long as he thinks he's in the clear, he'll probably keep to the car. He could be on his way to meet the others but, if he realises we're onto him, he might just try to make a run for it. If only we could tell what's going through his mind."

"You said you thought the operation was going down somewhere in London?" said the Major.

"Yes."

"Then if he tries to leave the city now, that might mean he's going on the run."

Daniel considered the idea for a moment. There was no guarantee the Major was right but it was a good suggestion.

"How long before you can tell?"

"Not long. He's on the outskirts as we speak. If he makes for the M4 then he could be trying to escape; if not …"

The Major left the sentence unfinished.

★

Charlie was still sitting uncomfortably in the back of the van carrying the B team. He was squashed between two of the eight armed and armoured men who made up the complement and was wishing he had been able to travel in one of the civilian cars instead. There hadn't been time to discuss seating arrangements once word came through that Anne Greaves was approaching the outskirts of London and Charlie knew he should be grateful that he had been included at all. Because he had been working with Daniel, Major Harding had assumed he was part of MI6 and Charlie hadn't corrected him. He had wanted to be there when Yusuf al Shamar was caught and, since he had been closely involved with the operation from the start, felt that he deserved a place.

When news came through that Yusuf had left the house with Anne Greaves and the other two had escaped, the feeling of frustration amongst the team had been almost tangible but it had set Charlie thinking. Like Daniel, he knew they needed to have all three men in custody if they were to be sure of securing the virus. Daniel was hoping al Shamar would lead them to the brothers but, if the terrorist had decided to abandon them and was making a run for it, that plan would fall apart.

During his years as a police officer, Charlie had learnt to stand in a fugitive's shoes and over the last week he had started to get a feel for the way Yusuf al Shamar thought. Even though the terrorists now knew they were being pursued, nobody thought for one minute that their operation had been cancelled. In fact, both Charlie and Daniel firmly believed the events of that night would only have served to bring the operation forward and the al Assad brothers were on their way to the target at that moment. Charlie was sure Yusuf was not the sort of man who gave up easily but now even he must realise he could play no useful part in it himself; he didn't have the skill set to put the aerosols in place and was probably going to make his escape whilst the other two went ahead without him. If they were to stop the operation from going ahead, Charlie realised they needed to find out more about the specifics of the terrorists' plan and began to review what they already knew.

The brothers were not the masterminds behind this operation; they were just following Yusuf al Shamar's orders and had only been brought in because of their engineering background. Everyone was agreed that one of the Underground stations was going to be the target but there were hundreds of them. He was sure Yusuf had a particular target in mind and, if only he could work it out, Charlie believed they might still be able to get there before the brothers and wait for them to turn up. If they were arrested before they could do anything, then al Shamar could be picked up later wherever he was. Discovering what the target was had to be the key.

However fiendishly clever his plan had been, Yusuf did not have an original mind. He was an opportunist. He may have been the one who decided to use the virus against London but, apart from understanding the effect it could have, he would have known nothing more about it. Pemberton's research had given him the idea and the full potential of Yusuf's operation, in fact, everything about it could be traced back to the scientist. That idea set Charlie thinking along a different track. Instead of trying to work out what was going on in Yusuf's mind, it dawned on

Charlie that the answer to his problem could lie with Pemberton. He tried to recall all he had learnt about the scientist and his research. And then suddenly it struck him. He reached into his pocket and pulled out his phone.

It took less than fifteen seconds for Daniel to answer.

"What's up, Charlie?" he asked.

"I think I know what their target is!" Charlie said, unable to suppress his excitement. "It's Waterloo Station!"

Daniel paused before saying anything. They had all believed the target was going to be one of the underground stations, the problem had been trying to identify which one amongst the hundreds running under the busy metropolis.

"Interesting," he said. "What makes you think that's the one?"

"Don't you remember?" said Charlie. "That night when Simon Warbeck told us about the virus in the first place, he said Pemberton had been following up research into a previous experiment made years ago by the people at Porton Down."

"Yes, what of it?"

"They tried it out at Waterloo Station! I was so shocked at what they had done I actually checked it out. Al Shamar is going to do the same thing! I just know he is, I can feel it in my gut!"

Daniel paused again. Like the others on COBRA, he had thought Pemberton was just making use of previous research to determine the effect of the virus if it was released on the underground today. His notes had not specified which station had been used then and there had been nothing in them to suggest Waterloo Station would be the actual target now. However, even though their friendship had been comparatively short, Daniel had learnt to respect Charlie's instinct and this did make sense. Waterloo Station was the busiest one in London. If Yusuf wanted to infect the greatest number of people possible then Waterloo Station fitted his purpose perfectly.

"It makes sense," Charlie insisted eagerly. "Don't you see, Yusuf couldn't have worked out the best place to use the virus by himself; he wouldn't know how, he would have relied on Pemberton to do it. That's what Pemberton had been looking

279

into for the military, what he based his figures on. It has to be Waterloo Station!"

"They're heading back into central London," interrupted Major Harding. "What do you want me to do?"

"Keep tracking them and start to close in," said Daniel. "We need visual contact now in case they try and ditch the car but don't intercept until I give the word." He turned back to speak again into the phone. "Charlie, I've got to go but I think you could be right. Anyway, it's a chance worth taking and we'll find out for sure soon enough. Yusuf al Shamar is heading back into London. I'll get a team in place at Waterloo in case he turns up and I'll meet you there. I can direct operations from the station just as easily as anywhere else. See you soon."

He gave a low chuckle.

"What's up?" Charlie asked.

"Nothing," said Daniel, "I was just thinking. If you're right, Yusuf is about to meet his own Waterloo."

He was still chuckling to himself as he ended the call.

★

Ibrahim Khan was working late. His desk was spread with various papers and several books were piled up untidily behind the open laptop. An angle-poise lamp cast a pool of concentrated light over the computer and he was hunched over the keyboard, lost in thought as he tried to work out exactly what he wanted to write. It was unusual for him to have an evening alone. As an Imam at one of the many mosques that had now sprung up on the outskirts of London, his nights were more often than not spent in meetings with groups and individuals who sought his advice and guidance. Some of those individuals were especially important to him and many evenings had been occupied in talking to them, inspiring them to devote their lives to the word of Allah as he had come to understand it. He now had many followers, some of whom had left London to fight for their faith in countries abroad.

He leaned back in his chair and rubbed his eyes. He had been staring at the screen for a long time and decided to take a break. He reached across the desk to straighten the photograph of his wife. She had died in childbirth seventeen years before and the child had been stillborn. Despite the urgings of friends and relatives to marry again, he had remained single. He had found another purpose and direction in life and he felt no need to complicate it with a family. He did what he did as much in memory of his former wife as for his own beliefs and had never wavered in his conviction that she would have approved. He pushed the chair back and stood up, stretching his arms and yawning. The room was stuffy; the gas fire had been on all evening and the heat had made him tired. He wanted to finish what he was writing before going to bed and thought a glass of water would help to refresh him.

He was in his late forties and a large man. He had a healthy appetite and no inclination or time for exercise; his girth had increased with middle-age and his belly now strained at the white taub which reached to his feet. He walked slowly down the hall to the kitchen and was just reaching for a glass when the front doorbell rang. He glanced at his watch and wondered who could be calling at that time of night. It was too late for a social visit and he had not been expecting anyone. He went back down the hall and put his eye to the spy-hole in the door. Two men were standing outside, both in western clothes despite obviously being Arab. He didn't recognise either of them and paused a moment before opening the door.

"Yes?" he said.

The two men were clearly very nervous and looked at each other before one of them stepped forward.

"We are friends of Yusuf al Shamar," said Habab hesitantly.

Ibrahim concealed his surprise. He and Yusuf had long ago agreed that no one should be aware they still knew each other. Instead, he gave a puzzled smile before he spoke.

"I'm sorry, I don't know anyone of that name."

"He gave us this address."

"As I said, I'm afraid I don't know the man. You must have made a mistake."

Ibrahim was about to close the door when Habab put out a hand to stop him. He looked desperate and Ibrahim wavered.

"Husam al din," said Habab quickly. "He sometimes calls himself Husam al din. He's in trouble. He told us to come here."

Ibrahim paused. Only a select few knew Yusuf by his chosen name. He took a step toward the two men and they backed away nervously. Ibrahim looked around quickly. The street seemed deserted.

"Where did you hear that name?" he demanded.

"Like I said, we're his friends," Habab replied. "He told us to come here if we needed help."

Ibrahim looked at the two men in front of him. His instinct told him not to trust them. They were obviously very jumpy but if they knew Yusuf's warrior name they could be genuine. He knew Yusuf had been planning to get the virus and if these two men were involved and something had gone wrong there was a risk in talking to them. But if Yusuf had sent them, he felt obliged at the very least to hear what they had to say.

"You'd better come in," he said at last.

Habab and Shiraz followed him into the house and Ibrahim closed the door behind them.

"Why are you here?" he asked. "What's happened?"

Now they were inside, Habab and Shiraz relaxed a little. Whoever this man was, it looked as if he was going to help them.

"We need somewhere to stay for a while," said Habab. "Yusuf told me to come here in an emergency."

"You can't stay here," said Ibrahim curtly.

"But Yusuf said -"

"Never mind what Yusuf said," Ibrahim interrupted impatiently. "Where is he? What's happened? What emergency are you talking about?"

They were still in the hallway and Habab was confused. After being let in, he was hoping for, if not expecting some sort of refuge but now this man had suddenly turned unhelpful and the barrage of questions sounded hostile.

"Do you know what Yusuf is doing?" he asked. "We are helping him."

"He never told me he wanted any help."

"There are some things he can't do by himself. He needed us." Habab paused before announcing, "We're the engineers."

Now it was Ibrahim's turn to be confused. When Farquharson had first approached him, it had been his idea to get hold of the virus and smuggle it to the IS in Syria. He knew he couldn't do it by himself and had set up the meeting between Yusuf and Farquharson. Then he had read in the newspapers that Pemberton had died and sent the news in a coded message to Yusuf via the IS. When he hadn't heard back straight away, he had assumed the operation must have been cancelled and was waiting for Yusuf to contact him. Did the arrival of these two men mean he had already gone ahead? But, if that was the case, why should he need engineers? None of it was making sense.

"I don't understand," he said. "Where is Yusuf? Is he safe?"

The brothers looked at each other, reluctant to answer.

"We don't know," Habab replied at last. "I think he is. We were warned the British were coming and Yusuf told us to go. He asked us to take these."

He reached into his pocket and pulled out one of the aerosol cans containing the virus. Shiraz did the same. A look of fear crossed Ibrahim's face.

"Is that ...?"

"This is the virus," Habab confirmed with a nod.

Ibrahim instinctively took a step back.

"It's safe," Habab said quickly.

But Ibrahim was not reassured and backed further away.

"You can't stay here!" he croaked. His mouth had gone suddenly dry and he was starting to panic. "Take those things with you and leave now!"

Shiraz stepped forward menacingly.

"We need documents," he said. "We had to leave our passports behind. We're not going anywhere unless you can provide us with new ones."

Ibrahim put his hand over his mouth and took another step back. The evening was starting to turn into a nightmare.

"Can you do that?" Habab demanded.

Ibrahim hesitated. He couldn't physically force the two men to leave and now he was really frightened. The two cans holding the virus were his immediate concern. As far as he was aware, they contained certain death and he wanted them out of his house. He quickly realised he had no choice but to do what these men wanted and slowly nodded.

"Y-Yes," he stuttered, "but it may take a while."

"Good," said Habab and waved the can in front of Ibrahim. He understood exactly why the man was so frightened.

"Can you take those things outside?" Ibrahim asked anxiously.

Although Habab knew the cans were completely secure, he thought it better to let the man believe they could still pose a danger.

"Have you a fridge?" he asked. "The seal will make sure they can't do any harm - for the time being."

Ibrahim nodded and led the way into the kitchen, still holding his hand over his mouth. Standing well back by the door, he pointed to the fridge. Habab opened it and, taking the other can from Shiraz, placed both on the top shelf and closed the door.

"They'll be alright there for a while," he said. "Now what about those passports?"

"I-I'll need to make a phone call," Ibrahim stammered nervously.

"We'll come with you," said Shiraz.

Ibrahim turned and led the way back to his study. The laptop was still open on his desk and he closed it before reaching for the phone. Habab and Shiraz made themselves comfortable in the two chairs either side of the gas fire and watched as Ibrahim punched in some numbers. The call was answered almost immediately and Ibrahim turned to face the brothers as he spoke.

"This is Ibrahim," he said. "I know it's late but can you come round now? Something very urgent has cropped up and I need your help right away." He paused to listen a moment before continuing, "Yes, your usual service. Bring everything you need here, it has to be done tonight."

★

Located on the South Bank in the London Borough of Lambeth, opposite the Houses of Parliament and close to Westminster Bridge, Waterloo Station first opened in the middle of the nineteenth century. Since then it has developed and grown both in size and importance. Now, with more platforms and a greater floor area than any other station in the United Kingdom, it has an annual turnover of almost one hundred million passenger entries and exits and has become one of the busiest railway stations in Europe, certainly the busiest in London. The main entrance is known as Victory Arch and is situated slightly further down the road from where Daniel had arranged for the so-called 'Neighbourhood Hub Team' of police based at Waterloo to meet his own armed squad.

By the time he and Emma arrived at a quarter to ten, the two teams had already met up and photographs of both Yusuf and Anne Greaves passed around along with the rather indistinct images of the brothers Richard Spiller had obtained from the hotel's CCTV camera. Emma was at Daniel's side as he and Major Harding talked to the senior officer at the scene and, whilst glad to be out in the fresh air after the long drive from Brighton, she was starting to think she should have stayed in the car. When he had gone into Farquharson's house, Daniel had told her not to get out for her own safety but he could hardly use that same argument here where so many members of the public were milling around. He had insisted she now remain close to him at all times but, although she had liked the fact he was being so protective, she was also slightly disturbed at the way he had become ruthlessly efficient as he went about his job. She had not suspected there was this side to him and couldn't help feeling she had become an unnecessary burden by being there.

Daniel had asked for the other entrances to the station to be closed so anyone wanting to go in or out would have to use Victory Arch. It meant, inevitably, that the entrance was much more crowded but, if Yusuf was going to be there, he would now have to pass the plainclothes officers positioned at both the top and bottom of the steps leading to the concourse. Daniel was feeling hopeful; the more he thought about what Charlie had said, the more convinced he had become his friend was correct. If Yusuf was planning a mass infection, then Waterloo Station was the ideal place.

"They're just approaching Westminster Bridge," said Major Harding, "probably about ten minutes away. What do you want to do?"

An earpiece was keeping him in direct communication with the B team as they followed Anne's car. His men in A team and the other armed police were still in their vans parked further down the road. He and Daniel had agreed they should stay there until sure Yusuf was making for the station but now it was time to make a decision.

"Deploy the rest of your men," said Daniel, "but nobody is to do anything until I give the word. To be sure of getting the virus back, we've got to wait for the brothers to appear and remember, he's probably armed."

"It's a go!" said the Major into the microphone attached to his sleeve. "Everyone in position and wait for my say-so before closing in. Repeat. No one is to act until I give the order."

The back doors of the vans opened and the armed men clambered out. Despite being in a public place, they merited hardly more than an occasional glance of curiosity from the passers-by. Londoners have grown accustomed to the sight of armed police, especially at centres of public transport. Although some people showed an interest, nobody was alarmed. Under orders to be as inconspicuous as possible, the squad made a deliberate effort to appear casual, as if they were performing a routine task; there was nothing about them to suggest a small force about to go into action. Most of the crowd were anyway intent on completing their journeys. Moreover, despite the fact each member of the team was armed and wearing a protective vest, some of them were in plainclothes. Not being in uniform, this group was able to mingle quickly and anonymously with the other pedestrians in front of the station. Although there had been little time and there were many unknowns, the Major had nonetheless formulated a general plan and his men knew exactly what to do and where they had to go. As they took up their positions, Daniel, Emma and the Major moved back against a wall next to the large arch that framed the steps leading into the station. And waited.

★

Apart from giving directions, Yusuf had hardly spoken during their journey into central London. Anne had not really noticed; she was concentrating on driving. Having always used the train for her trips, she had seldom used a car in the city and was nervous about getting into the correct lane and not missing a turning. Yusuf frequently looked behind to check whether they were being followed but in the dark and with so many cars on the road, it was impossible to be sure. Besides, he was committed now and there were other things to occupy his mind. He was almost certain the brothers had managed to escape from the house and would be at the station. But what if they weren't? They had the virus and he had no back-up plan. He had said he would meet them at ten o' clock. They should have been able to make that easily. If they weren't already waiting, he decided he would give them twenty minutes and then leave. He would go to his Imam, report what had happened and get help to leave the country. But, as long as there was a chance of success, however small, he felt he had to be there. Having planned it for so long, he did not want to give up being a part of the operation and he wanted to be sure Shiraz would see it through.

"We'll soon be at the station," he said, turning to Anne. "I want you to drop me off and we can meet up later."

"No," said Anne, glancing at him quickly. "I'm going with you. I don't think we should separate now."

The last thing Yusuf wanted was to have Anne with him but he still needed to pretend he cared for her. If she were to suspect he was about to abandon her, there was no telling what she might do; she could just go straight to the police and betray him out of spite. She had to believe he loved her for at least another half an hour. That should be enough time for him to meet the brothers and carry out the operation. Once it was done, then he would never have to see her again.

"It's too risky," he said softly. "I don't want anything to happen to you."

"No," Anne insisted again. "I'm not leaving you now. If anything's going to happen then we're going to face it together."

They were already driving across Westminster Bridge and Yusuf realised he was running out of time. As he looked at Anne and saw the grim determination in her face, he knew he was not going to be able to persuade her before they arrived. He would have to deal with her sooner or later but for the moment he accepted she would have to go with him.

"Very well," he said, "you'll need to find somewhere to park. It doesn't matter where. We should ditch the car anyway. It'll be safer."

"How will we get away?"

"The tube."

"But -"

"We're here," said Yusuf abruptly. "Turn left and look for a space to leave the car."

As Anne did as she was told, they saw a taxi rank just ahead of them. She slowed down and at the end of the line of cabs was an empty space reserved for disabled drivers.

"Over there," said Yusuf, pointing.

Anne drew in quickly and parked. She switched off the ignition and removed the keys. Yusuf took a deep breath and turned to look at her. He would give it one more try.

"Well done," he said gently. "I could never have done this without you, my darling. I know I shouldn't ask for anything more, but now I want you to wait here. I won't be long. Fifteen minutes at the most."

"No," said Anne as she pulled the handle to open her car door. She couldn't explain it but she had the strangest feeling that if she let Yusuf out of her sight now, she would never see him again.

She got out and reached onto the back seat to retrieve her shoulder-bag. Yusuf waited a moment before getting out himself and Anne walked quickly round the car to join him. She slung the bag strap over her shoulder and reached down to grab his hand, giving him a brief smile before they began to walk together along the pavement toward Victory Arch around the corner.

★

Standing close to the wall about fifty metres from the station entrance, Daniel glanced quickly at his watch and then turned to speak quietly to the Major. Emma realised now it had been a mistake for her to insist on going with him. Now he was working, he had become different to the man she thought she knew and her feelings were confused. She could sense the tension in Daniel's body as he stood beside her and knew she didn't belong there. He needed to give his full attention to the task in hand. He already had enough on his mind and she was just something else for him to worry about.

"I'm going back to the car," she announced, coming to a sudden decision. "I'm only in the way here."

She began to walk off and Daniel reached out an arm to hold her back.

"You stay and do your job," she said. "I'm perfectly alright."

She gave Daniel a brief smile and he let her go.

This was a new and totally unfamiliar world to Emma. Having glimpsed into a part of it, she was starting to wonder if she could have a relationship with someone who did this sort of thing for a living. Daniel was the first man in a long time who had made her feel special but she was beginning to realise that he came with a lot of baggage. There was undoubtedly a strong mutual attraction but possibly everything was happening too fast. Perhaps she should take some time to sit back and think whether she wanted this sort of complication in her life.

She reached the curb and looked right then left along the road and waited until a car had passed before starting to cross. Wrapped up in her thoughts, she had not noticed the couple turning the corner. But Anne had seen her.

"Emma Nelson!" she gasped and tightened her grip on Yusuf's hand, pulling him to a halt.

Yusuf did not know the name but followed where Anne was looking and saw the back of a woman hurrying across the road.

"She was with that man from MI6," Anne said quickly, trying to turn back. "She shouldn't be here. We've got to get away! It's a trap!"

Yusuf looked around swiftly. They were now about twenty metres from the entrance. It was busy but he could see nothing out of the ordinary. People were making their way in and out of the station, going about their business just as normal. There was no sign of Habab or Shiraz, though it was possible they were waiting just inside the entrance and out of view. Nothing about the scene gave him any reason to feel suspicious; there was nothing to suggest anyone was lying in wait. Perhaps Angel had been mistaken; he could tell she was in a high state of nervousness and might just be panicking unnecessarily.

"Are you sure it's her?" he asked.

"Of course I am! She's the one who told me they knew where you were. But I left her in Brighton. We must go back!"

She was still tugging at his arm but Yusuf resisted. He could see she was really convinced they were in immediate danger but he was so close. If this was a trap and the brothers were caught, the British would retrieve the virus. He knew he couldn't let that happen; not now. It wasn't loyalty to Habab and Shiraz so much as a fervent desire to make sure the operation could still go ahead that made him decide what he had to do.

"I'm going to check if my friends are there," he said. "You wait here."

"Don't go!" Anne pleaded. "Leave them!"

Yusuf ignored her and pulled his arm free from her grasp. He had only one thought now: if the British were waiting, he was not going to let them get the virus back. He had to warn the brothers if he could, give them a chance to escape with the cans. As long as they were free, the operation would still be able to go ahead, perhaps not that night but someday soon. He had no plan in mind, just an idea that if the British really were there, he could somehow force them into revealing themselves by creating some sort of diversion. That would let Habab and Shiraz know this was a trap and give them time to get away with the virus. He tried to walk quickly but the limp in his right leg was slowing him down. Anne stood still for a moment, watching his back in dismay as he moved toward the entrance, and then hurried after him. As she caught up, she slipped her arm through his and he turned to look at her.

"We're in this together," she said. "What are you going to do?"

"I don't know yet."

For a fleeting moment he felt a surge of comradeship toward Anne. It was the closest thing to affection he had ever felt for her. She didn't have to be there; she could have left him and saved herself.

"Slow down," she warned. "We don't want to draw attention."

But that was exactly what Yusuf was planning to do. They were almost in front of the entrance and Yusuf could now see inside the giant archway and up the steps. He looked around desperately, searching for the brothers. They weren't there! He checked his watch and as he did so heard the chimes of Big Ben booming ten o' clock from across the other side of the river.

★

"How much longer is this going to take?" Shiraz demanded.

The impatience behind his voice was unmistakeable and Ibrahim was unsure how to calm him down. The thought of the two cans containing the virus in his fridge was still very much uppermost in his mind.

"Not long, not long," he said. "My friend has to collect his things but he is not far away. Once he has your photographs he can work quickly."

"Tonight?" Shiraz asked. "Can he get it all done by tonight?"

"Yes, I expect so."

But Ibrahim was far from certain. On previous occasions when he had needed this service there had always been more time to get things arranged. He didn't know if his friend would have the right type of documents with him, if he needed to get particular stamps or even whether he needed someone else to help him. None of those matters had ever been his concern before.

"It's alright, Shiraz," said Habab. "We can afford to wait now. We're safe here, aren't we?"

This last was directed at Ibrahim. The Imam was sitting at his desk and looked uncertainly from one brother to the other.

"For the moment, yes," he replied. "But you can't stay long. I have my work and people will be coming here tomorrow. You should leave as soon as possible - and take those things with you."

"I'm sure you'll be able to find an explanation for our being here if it becomes necessary," said Habab, "but let's hope it won't come to that. Meanwhile, perhaps we can impose on you a little further. Neither my brother nor myself have eaten since this morning."

"There is food in the kitchen," Ibrahim said, pointing at the door. He had no intention of going there himself as long as those cans were still in his fridge. "You can help yourselves to anything you find."

"Thank you," Habab said, standing up. "Coming, Shiraz?"

"No. You get me something and bring it back."

Shiraz didn't trust Ibrahim to remain alone in the study with his phone. Despite Yusuf's belief that the man would help, it was obvious now he didn't want them there and his reluctance to co-operate had made Shiraz suspicious. Habab nodded and left the room. Although he didn't think the Imam would betray them, he understood exactly what his brother was thinking. He went into the kitchen and switched on the light. The small room was neat and clean. The work surfaces had been wiped down and, apart from a small bowl of fruit on the table, all food had been stored away in the wall cupboards along one side by the door leading to the garden. Habab went to the fridge and bent down to look inside. As he did so, he heard the front door bell ring.

In the study, Shiraz sat upright in alarm at the sound and glanced quickly at Ibrahim.

"It's alright," said the Imam. "That must be Hassan. He's earlier than I thought."

He stood up, relieved that he was not going to have to remain alone with the two brothers, and went into the hallway. Shiraz got up and followed him to the study door, concealing himself behind it. He heard the front door open and then a cry of surprise.

In the kitchen Habab was crouched down, looking in the fridge when Ibrahim opened the front door. He was about to remove a plate of cold chicken when he heard the Imam cry out. Something was not right. He stood up with the plate still in his hand and looked around in sudden panic. His first thought was that the British must have followed them to the house and he had to get out. He was about to rush to the back door when he hesitated. What about Shiraz? At that moment, the back door suddenly smashed open and two men burst into the kitchen. Taken by surprise, Habab froze for a moment. He started to turn away but before he could do so, one of the men rushed forward and punched him hard in the diaphragm, pushing all the air out his lungs. The plate of chicken dropped to the tiled floor and splintered into fragments. Knocked off-balance, in pain and unable to cry out, Habab fell backward to the floor. The man swiftly knelt astride him, rolling him over and clasping a hand over Habab's mouth as he did so. With his other hand the man quickly pulled Habab's right arm behind his back whilst his companion hurried forward and tugged Habab's left arm round before securing both wrists together with a plastic tie. Habab squirmed helplessly on the floor as he tried to gasp for air through the hand that was still held firmly over his mouth. Neither of the men had said a word.

Meanwhile, Ibrahim was backing slowly down the hallway with his arms raised. Expecting Hassan to be on the doorstep, he had not checked the spyhole and opened the door to find himself looking down the barrel of a gun in the hands of a stranger. He had cried out once in surprise but the man had quickly put a warning finger to his lips before waving the gun to show Ibrahim should lead the way into the house. At that moment, Ibrahim had heard the back door crashing open and spun round in fear. As he did so, Shiraz entered the hall and saw what was happening. Realising the immediate danger, he instinctively stepped back into the study and tried to slam the door shut but the man with the gun had quickly moved forward and already had his shoulder to it. He was large and heavily built; Shiraz was no match for him and the door gave way, pushing Shiraz back into the room.

"Don't shoot!" he cried out in fear, holding his arms in front of him.

"Silence!" the man said in Arabic. "Keep quiet or you die!"

He was still standing in the doorway, the gun now pointed at Shiraz who was retreating toward the fireplace. The man took a step back and turned the gun onto Ibrahim again.

"Get in!" he ordered, waving the weapon toward the study.

Ibrahim kept his hands above his head and slowly edged past the man to enter the room. He went over to stand next to Shiraz and the man followed, keeping the gun directed at them both.

Suddenly there was the sound of more men in the hall and Habab appeared in the doorway, his arms secured behind him and supported on either side by the two men who had overpowered him in the kitchen. They dragged him into the room and pushed him roughly into one of the chairs.

"Turn around," ordered the man with the gun, waving it at Shiraz and Ibrahim, "and put your arms behind you."

They both did as they were told and one of the other men secured their arms with plastic ties.

"Now sit down," said the man with the gun and waited until they were both sitting before he continued. "Where is the virus?"

Habab and Shiraz looked at each other but before either could say anything Ibrahim spoke first.

"It's in the fridge," he said quickly.

The man with the gun nodded at one of his companions who left the room. He returned a minute later with the cans and Ibrahim's eyes widened in renewed fear. The sight of the cans holding the deadly virus was somehow more terrifying than the presence of the men.

"W-What are you going to do?" he asked nervously.

The man smiled grimly.

"We're going to leave you here," he said unexpectedly.

For the first time, both Habab and Shiraz realised these men couldn't be the British agents they had thought. Both brothers were confused but at the same time understood there was now some hope they might survive this.

"Who are you?" Habab asked.

The man ignored the question and instead continued in the same calm voice as before. "Before we go we have to make sure you can't warn any of your friends what's happened." He paused for a few seconds as he saw a flicker of fear cross each face in front of him. "Don't worry, we're just going to put you to sleep. By the time you wake up it will be too late for you to do anything. We will be far away. My friend is going to inject you with a heavy sedative. It works very quickly and you will feel nothing."

"You're – you're not going to kill us?" Ibrahim asked hesitantly.

"Why should we?" said the man and he sounded surprised. "It would only cause a lot of complications with the police. You're not going to tell them anything and we have the virus now. That's all we came for. Just sit still while my friend gets to work."

He nodded at one of his companions who removed a slim oblong box from one of his pockets. The man opened it and extracted a syringe.

"No!" exclaimed Ibrahim. He hadn't believed the man's explanation and tried to stand up.

"Shut up!" said the man impatiently and pushed him back into the chair.

He held the Imam down whilst the man with the syringe stepped forward and pushed the needle through Ibrahim's sleeve into his arm. Ibrahim struggled wildly for a few seconds and then the panic in his eyes melted away and his lids slowly closed. The man still held him for a moment as he felt the body relax and then released his grip. Ibrahim's head rolled to one side and he started breathing heavily as he slumped back in the chair.

"See," the man said, looking at Habab and Shiraz, "there's nothing to be afraid of. You will sleep for a few hours and that's all. Now, are you going to co-operate or do I have to hold you down as well?"

The brothers looked at each other. Ibrahim was breathing deeply in the chair. He was completely unconscious but he was still alive. They both knew if they tried to resist there was nothing they could do. Habab nodded.

"Go ahead," he said.

The other man had now removed a second syringe from the box and advanced toward him. Habab watched as the man injected him in the arm and then turned to look at his brother. Shiraz was staring at him with a horrified expression.

"It's nothing little brother," said Habab and tried to smile reassuringly. His head suddenly felt heavy and he let it fall forward as he closed his eyes and slipped into unconsciousness.

"No!" Shiraz shrieked. "Don't do it to me! I swear I won't call for help. You can go. Just let me stay here. I swear I won't tell!"

He started to writhe in his chair as the man with the gun stepped forward and pushed him back with one hand, holding him down. Shiraz continued to struggle and protest as the other man came forward with a fresh syringe and plunged it into his arm. Shiraz looked around the room in wild-eyed panic for a few seconds before his lids closed and his body relaxed.

The two men stood back and looked at him in disgust.

"Right," said the man with the gun as he put the weapon away in his shoulder holster. "We haven't much time before their friend arrives. You know what to do. Get on with it."

The other two left him in the study and went into the kitchen whilst he pulled each of the sleeping figures upright and cut the ties which had secured their arms behind them. He arranged each of the drugged men in their chairs so it appeared as if they had been engaged in conversation. Once satisfied that everything looked normal, he turned off the gas fire and then turned the gas on again to full before picking up the cans containing the virus and slipping them into his backpack. He surveyed the room a final time and then joined his two companions in the kitchen. They had already finished their job and were waiting for him.

"We've got two minutes," one of them said.

The senior man quickly checked what they had done and nodded in silent approval before leading the way out of the back door, closing it softly behind them.

The whole operation had lasted less than eight minutes.

★

Yusuf was uncertain what to do next. He had been expecting the brothers to be just inside the arch and was surprised not to see them there. He looked around again but saw no sign of either man amongst the crowd. His first panicked thought was they must have been picked up on leaving the house, but a moment's reflection was enough for him to decide that was unlikely. He was sure the brothers had got away. They would have made some sort of disturbance, at the very least called out to warn him if anyone had tried to stop them, and he had heard nothing like that. The only agents he had seen were the two men at the front of Farquharson's house and he had given them the slip easily enough. In fact, it suddenly dawned on him, perhaps a little too easily. He felt the hair on the back of his neck begin to rise. Something wasn't right. The British weren't that incompetent. Anne may have led them to Farquharson's house but nobody apart from himself and the brothers knew about his plan for Waterloo Station so what were the British doing here before him? And how come he and Anne were still free? What were the British waiting for? And then he realised what must be happening. There was only one possible explanation: Habab and Shiraz had managed to get away and the British didn't know where they were. They had allowed him to arrive at that very spot with no interference as bait to lure the brothers into a trap!

"They're not here," said Anne, breaking into his thoughts as she tugged urgently at his arm. "Let's go. There's still time to get away!"

But Yusuf was not so sure and stood his ground whilst he quickly tried to think what to do. Habab and Shiraz should have been able to get to the station by now but anything, something quite innocent, could have happened to delay them. He was running out of time. The brothers could arrive at any moment and he had to warn them this was a trap. They had to remain free if there was to be any chance of seeing the operation through to the end. They had the virus and the skill to install it in the air-conditioning system. Yusuf was immediately reminded of just how surplus he himself had become to requirements and, with that realisation, suddenly knew what he had to do. If he wanted the operation to still go ahead, he must warn the brothers. He had to get the British to reveal themselves, create an incident that would let the brothers know what was happening and give them a chance to escape. Without warning, he suddenly grabbed Anne by the arm and started to make a run back to the car, pulling her behind him.

"Shit!" said Major Harding abruptly. "Something's spooked him! He's making a break for it!"

Daniel clenched both fists in frustration. He had gambled and lost. He knew he had no alternative now: Yusuf could not be allowed to escape again.

"Close in," he said. "Let's take him!"

"Go!" the Major barked into his microphone. "It's a go!"

Taken by surprise, Anne stumbled after Yusuf and tried to keep up as he dragged her by the arm. Suddenly she tripped and fell heavily to the ground, clutching at Yusuf as she did so. Caught off balance just as he was about to put weight on his bad leg, Yusuf tumbled and sprawled beside her. He was up in an instant but it was too late. He spun round and saw three men racing toward him. It was clear they were not rushing to his aid. He stretched down to pull Anne to her feet and looked for a way out. He could see one of the men had already drawn a gun and was holding it down by his side as he ran. His ruse had worked: this had been a trap! Yusuf knew there was only one thing to do. He reached into the pocket of his coat and drew out his own weapon. There was no time to think and he pointed it into the air and pulled the trigger.

As the shot reverberated against the stone walls surrounding the station entrance, there were sudden brief screams of surprise and fear from amongst the people gathered under the tall arch. Each of the men running toward Yusuf had drawn their weapons and now had him in their sights. They had stopped running as soon as Yusuf had fired and were standing, legs astride and perfectly balanced in a circle about fifteen metres around him. For a moment everything appeared to stop; there were a few seconds of shocked silence and then panic broke out in the crowd. Some people started running, several fell to the ground and covered their heads whilst others were frozen to the spot, staring in disbelief at the scene unfolding before them. There were more terrified cries; amid the pandemonium Yusuf heard a man shouting to his girlfriend to take cover and a mother yelling for her child. Somewhere, someone had started screaming hysterically.

Yusuf suddenly pulled Anne toward him and held her close with his left arm tightly circling her neck. Looking around wildly, he quickly pushed the gun barrel against her head; his finger was still on the trigger.

"Keep back!" he shouted. "Keep back or I'll shoot!"

None of the men pointing their guns at him moved.

"Yusuf!" Anne cried out in fear. "What are you doing? It's over!"

"Not yet," Yusuf muttered into her ear and he started to back away, holding Anne in front of him as a shield whilst he moved toward the station entrance.

Daniel and Major Harding had run forward as soon as he had given the order to move in. They had seen everything and were now standing just outside the circle of men pointing their weapons at Yusuf. A clear space had opened up around them. Most of the crowd had run off in different directions but people were still coming out of the station and on reaching the open, realised something dramatic was unfolding before them. Some young men had even gathered at the bottom of the steps, taking out their phones and excitedly videoing the events.

"Let her go, Yusuf!" shouted Daniel. "We can sort this out! Nobody needs to get hurt!""

"Tell your men to put their weapons on the ground and back off!" Yusuf shouted back. "I'll kill her if anyone gets close!"

"Do as he says," Daniel said quietly to the Major. "He's not going to get away. There's nowhere for him to go."

Major Harding gave the order and the men surrounding Yusuf lowered their weapons. Kneeling down slowly, they laid their guns on the pavement and carefully backed away, their arms in the air and their eyes fixed on him as they retreated. Daniel walked cautiously toward Yusuf and Anne, stopping about five metres away and raised his arms to show he was not armed.

"Yusuf," he called, just loudly enough to be heard, "let Anne go. You don't want to hurt her."

Yusuf looked around wildly, the adrenalin pumping through his body. There were still too many people there. He saw the group of young men filming him on their phones and felt a surge of anger.

"I told you to back off!" Yusuf shouted. "Clear the station!"

"You know I can't do that," Daniel was trying to sound reasonable. "Anyway, it will take too long. Let's just talk for a moment."

"Do it!" Yusuf shouted savagely.

He suddenly turned his gun onto the group of young men with their phones and fired twice at random in their direction. One of the men screamed and folded over as he dropped to the ground. Immediately there was renewed panic and people started to run in different directions, falling over each other in their desperation to get away.

"OK! OK!" Daniel shouted urgently. "Don't shoot! I'll do whatever you want!" He turned his head to look over his shoulder. "Clear the station!" he called out so Yusuf could hear. "Do exactly as he says!"

Yusuf saw men begin to move with their arms outstretched, herding everyone who was in the immediate area further down the road. Some men were already in the archway forcing people back up the steps and, for the first time, Yusuf realised just how many police and plainclothes officers were at the scene. There was only one way out now. He began to edge his way slowly toward the station entrance, still gripping Anne firmly around the neck.

"Keep everyone back!" he shouted.

"What are you going to do?" Daniel called back, slowly following Yusuf as close as he dared. "There's nowhere to go! Why can't we just talk this through?"

"Do as I say," Yusuf yelled and pressed the gun brutally against Anne's head. "I'm going into the station so keep away or I'll kill her!"

Major Harding had acted quickly. His men were holding people back along the pavement and had already cleared the entrance around the archway and the steps. In the distance the sound of approaching sirens could be heard as the civilian police made their way to the scene. The Major realised their presence was going to lead to confusion of command unless he acted immediately and he began shouting instructions into his microphone. He had understood what Yusuf was planning and didn't want the police getting in the way of his trained men.

Yusuf had already reached the bottom of the steps and turned round quickly to check they were clear before shouting once more at Daniel who was still following him at a distance.

"Stay there!"

Daniel stopped. He could see Anne's shocked face as she was pulled back against Yusuf's body.

"Let her go," he called out. "Take me instead!"

With his eyes still fixed on Daniel, Yusuf bent his head down to whisper in Anne's ear, "It's going to be alright. I'm taking you with me. We're going to get away."

He lessened his grip around Anne's neck and felt her relax.

"Do you trust me?" Yusuf continued quietly as he kept his head close to hers.

"Yes," she said without hesitation.

"Then don't struggle. I'm not going to shoot. Just do as I say."

Yusuf still had a firm hold on Anne and kept the gun pressed against her head as he cautiously backed up the steps to the top, leaving Daniel looking on helplessly from the pavement below.

As soon as Yusuf had said he was going into the station, Major Harding had run along the road, turned the corner and raced toward the Waterloo East entrance. Although Daniel had ordered all the entrances apart from Victory Arch to be closed, the escalators here were still working and, as the Major reached the bottom, he leapt onto the moving staircase, taking giant strides until he reached the top. Once inside the station he quickly reached the mezzanine level from where he could look down onto the concourse below. He had men inside the station but he needed to see what was happening before he could decide how to use them. He leaned over the edge and looked to his right where he expected Yusuf and the woman to appear.

By now a large crowd had gathered on the concourse below. With only the Victory Arch exit to the station open and that now being closed off, people had come to a halt along the platforms and were milling about impatiently, pressing forward as their numbers increased by the minute. Most of the people in the station were completely unaware of the drama taking place outside. Some near the Victory Arch exit were starting to hear accounts of gunshots and rumours of a possible terrorist attack, but the vast majority remained oblivious and were simply getting angry at the hold-up. Major Harding couldn't see his targets and he cursed loudly in frustration as he scanned the crowd looking for them. Despite going as fast as he could, he knew he was too late. They weren't there and he realised Yusuf and the woman must already be making their way down to the underground.

He was right. On reaching the top of the steps, Yusuf had lowered his gun and, still holding it firmly, pushed his hand into his pocket so it was out of sight. With so many people and the confusion around the top of the arch, it had not been difficult to pull Anne inside and force his way into the throng. Anyone in the crowd who saw them just thought they were another couple trying to escape from whatever was happening outside. But one of Harding's men had spotted them. He was in plain clothes, helping to stop people from making their way out of the exit but, by the time he had fought his way through the crowd toward them, Yusuf and Anne had already reached the escalators.

"I've got them!" he said urgently into his microphone. "They're making for the underground!"

"Keep them in sight!" Major Harding barked. "Where are you?"

Sergeant Colin Needham knew what he was doing. He had been a member of Harding's armed team for seven years and this was not the first time he had taken part in a hostage situation. But this looked different. The woman was not making any attempt to escape; she was actually following the man as they hurried down the tunnel leading to the platforms. He kept well back, giving a continuous update on his position whilst he followed the couple as inconspicuously as he could.

Yusuf was beginning to think they could make it. The mass of people seething around the Victory Arch had helped to conceal them and, although they had initially slowed him down, he could move faster now he was away from the exit and going in the opposite direction. He knew there were cameras that could track him but that didn't matter. By the time they found out where he was heading he would be gone. Once he was on a platform he could board the first tube that came along. Within minutes he would have left his pursuers behind and within an hour he could be at Ibrahim Khan's house. Most important of all, Habab and Shiraz would still be free! The chaos outside the station was enough to alert them something was wrong and they could escape. They might even decide to make their own way to the Imam's house. He had given Habab the address to use in an emergency and he could imagine their surprise when they saw him arrive. The only problem was Anne. He would have to keep her with him for the moment, just in case he needed her as a hostage again, but once he was back on the streets of London she would have served her purpose and be of no further use. He could dispose of her then.

Outside the station, Charlie had arrived with the rest of Harding's B team. Parking some way from the entrance, by the time they reached Victory Arch on foot, Yusuf had already gone in and Daniel was still standing outside in radio contact with the Major. He held a hand up as Charlie approached and spoke quickly into his microphone before turning back to Charlie.

"They're making for the underground," he explained. "Harding's got a man following them and back-up is on its way."

"What are you going to do?" Charlie asked.

"It's in Harding's hands now," Daniel said, "but I want to be there when he closes in."

Now the situation had changed and the street was safe once again, people were being allowed to leave the station. All the entrances were being reopened and a steady trickle of passengers was coming down one side of the steps under the control of the police. The body of the young man Yusuf had shot was still lying on the pavement, surrounded by two paramedics and cordoned off by several police officers. As the exiting passengers reached street level they gave it a wide berth. Daniel started to run up the other side of the steps and Charlie followed him. He wanted to be there at the close too.

★

Sergeant Needham had kept well back. As the number of passengers in the tunnels thinned, he had allowed himself to drop further behind and was still confident he had not been spotted. He had been careful not to look at the couple directly, keeping them on the edge of his peripheral vision and holding his head down. Although the man had turned to look back several times, they had not changed pace but now, as they approached one of the platforms, they began to slow down and Needham used his microphone to ask for further instructions.

"Just keep them under surveillance for the moment," came Major Harding's voice in his earpiece. "We're on our way. But on no account must they be allowed to board a train. If that looks like happening, they must be stopped."

Needham checked in mid-stride. He needed clarification to be absolutely certain he had understood what the Major meant.

"Does that mean I'm go for fire?" he asked quietly.

There was a moment's pause before Harding's voice came again.

"Yes, but only as a last resort."

Sergeant Needham felt a pulse of adrenalin as permission to use his weapon was given. He was an excellent marksman, as were all of the Major's men, but unlike some of them he had never used his gun in an operation before.

"How long before back-up arrives?" he asked.

"We're probably about two or three minutes away," said Harding. "Until then you're on your own. Be careful but on no account let them escape."

Needham had now reached the platform and could see the couple standing only five metres away. The woman was clinging onto the man's arm and the sergeant now knew for sure she was not a hostage but an accomplice. That simplified matters. He turned in the opposite direction and walked further away, taking up a position about fifteen metres from them. There were only about twenty other passengers on the platform: it was still a little too early for most people to be making their way home. That was another good thing though he would have preferred even fewer civilians on the scene. He glanced at his watch. The Major and back-up would be there any moment now. And then he heard the sound of a train approaching.

Yusuf took a few steps toward the edge of the platform and glanced down the tunnel. Anne was still holding onto his arm and he turned back to her.

"Almost there, now," he said and looked along the platform again.

Needham knew there was no time left and he had to be ready. Casually unzipping his jacket, he reached inside to take hold of the weapon nestling against his ribs in its shoulder-holster. He gripped the pistol firmly and slid a finger around the trigger but didn't take it out. It was still too soon for that. He turned his back on the sound of the approaching train to look at his target and took a step toward him. Out of the corner of his eye, Yusuf saw the man move and was immediately alert. He recognised the man. He had seen him behind them as they were walking quickly through the tunnels. Was it possible they had been followed? He automatically reached into his pocket and

306

wrapped his fingers around the butt of his own gun. And then he saw the man look directly at him. Their eyes met and Yusuf immediately knew what was about to happen. He began to pull the gun out of his pocket.

Sergeant Needham was quicker. His gun was out of the holster and pointing directly at Yusuf before either man could blink.

"Drop it!" Needham shouted and several of the passengers on the platform turned in alarm to see what was happening.

Yusuf was hampered by Anne who was still holding onto one arm but he managed to drag his gun clear and pointed it in the direction of the sergeant, pulling the trigger as he did so. The bullet missed but the sound was magnified by the hard surfaces around the platform, deafening the other passengers. There were cries of fear. Some people instinctively started to run back to the safety of the tunnel, blocking the sergeant's way for a moment as he walked forward with arms now outstretched, his gun clasped firmly in both hands and pointed in Yusuf's direction.

"Everyone keep down!" Needham yelled loudly and several people in front of him dropped to the floor with their hands covering their heads. He now had a clear line of fire.

"Drop it!" he shouted as Yusuf kept his gun aimed at him.

But Yusuf pulled the trigger. Anne screamed at the same moment as Needham returned fire. The bullet took Yusuf in the shoulder and the gun flew out of his hand as he spun round with a cry of pain. Anne screamed again. Had there been more time to think, she might have reacted differently. As it was, she was momentarily paralysed with terror. Anne could see at once the shot had not been fatal but Yusuf was badly injured. There was going to be no escape now. She grabbed at Yusuf to support him, folding both arms around his body as he leant into her, gasping with pain.

"Yusuf!" she cried out in anguish.

In that fleeting moment she knew everything was over. She had a sudden vision of herself and Yusuf in different prisons, separated for ever. That was inevitable now. She had no idea what was going through Yusuf's mind but she had no regrets about what she had done: her love for Yusuf had been the most liberating and fulfilling experience she had ever known. Life without him would be unbearable. Their love should have had a better ending.

All these thoughts flashed through her mind in the short time it took for the train to emerge from the black mouth of the tunnel and begin to slow down with a hiss of its brakes. Suddenly, Anne clutched her lover hard against her body. Almost as if she had rehearsed the moment, she wrapped her arms tightly around Yusuf and swiftly dragged him the few steps to the edge of the platform. She glanced briefly at the sergeant and Needham thought he saw her give a triumphant smile as she slowly leant back and fell in front of the train, pulling Yusuf with her as it ground to a halt. Yusuf's scream as he toppled over the edge was abruptly cut off and there was a sudden silence.

Sergeant Needham, lowered his gun and quickly ran over to where they had fallen under the train's wheels. He looked down at the track where they had landed and turned away quickly. From the moment he had fired, the whole thing had only taken a matter of seconds. There was nothing he could have done to stop it. He replaced his gun in its holster as Major Harding and his men emerged onto the platform. They had heard the shooting as they approached and one look around was enough to tell them it was all over. The exact details of what had happened could be dealt with later; the Major knew his first priority was to look for the virus.

★

It took Daniel and Charlie over ten minutes to get to the scene after Major Harding had arrived. He had already informed them of events so they knew what to expect but they had been delayed by the cordons set up to stop people from coming down the tunnel to the platform. As soon as they were there, Charlie hung back whilst Daniel went over to look at the bodies still lying on the tracks. The train had now been reversed so Yusuf and Anne, or rather what was left of them, were clearly visible. Some of Harding's men were already standing around the rails, trying to decide on where to start clearing up.

"Not the way we would have liked it end," said the Major as he came over to stand next to Daniel.

"Did you find anything on them?" Daniel asked.

"If you mean the virus," replied Harding, "we've turned up nothing yet. Neither of them had it on them. Of course, we've only been able to conduct a preliminary examination of the scene so far. I'll organise a team to look further along the tracks and search their route to the platform just in case, but my guess is they didn't have it."

Daniel nodded. He had thought all along that the al Assad brothers must have taken the virus when they left Farquharson's house. His one hope of getting it back had been if Yusuf was going to meet them. That hope had ended on the tracks and now he wasn't sure what he could do next. He walked back despondently to where Charlie was standing.

"They didn't find it," he said. "We're back to square one."

There was nothing Charlie could say that might help and both men remained silent for a moment, wrapped in their own thoughts.

"Why do you think she was helping him?" Charlie asked at last.

Daniel shrugged.

"It doesn't matter now," he said. "We'll never know for sure but she didn't strike me as a political idealist."

"I think she was in love with him," Charlie continued with his usual insight. "That would explain everything. Who's going to tell her husband?"

"I'll see to that," Daniel said. "Which version do you think he would prefer, lover or terrorist?"

"I think he should decide that," Charlie replied quietly. "Just give him the facts and let him work it out. He's the one who's going to have to live with it."

Daniel nodded. Either way, Martin Greaves' career at the Institute was going to be over. Daniel knew he should tell him soon but, at that particular moment, he had to focus on the operation in hand.

"I'll circulate pictures of the brothers to the Met and put out an alert at bus stations, airports and so on," he said. "That's all we can do for now."

For the next half an hour, Daniel was on his phone organising the manhunt for the brothers whilst Charlie sat in on the debriefing of Sergeant Needham taking place further along the platform. The Major had already given them an outline of the events and nothing the sergeant had to say added anything that might prove useful in finding the brothers. Daniel had just finished his last call and was walking down to join Charlie when his phone rang. It was Ira Goldstein.

"I've been trying to reach you," Ira said impatiently without any greeting.

"I've been using my phone," said Daniel. "What's up?"

"We need to meet," said Ira. "The sooner the better."

"I can't, not right away. Yusuf al Shamar has just been killed by an underground train."

"So I've already heard, but this can't wait," Ira insisted.

Daniel thought fast. He hadn't quite given up hope of finding some information at the station which could help give a lead to the brothers, but Yusuf was dead and other people could finish off what remained to be done there. Ira would not have called unless it was urgent.

"What's happened?"

"I have information on the brothers."

"Where are they?" Daniel demanded briskly. Ira now had his full attention.

"Not over the phone," said Ira. "We should meet as soon as possible."

Daniel paused. Ira understood the urgency of the situation and it was not like him to hold information back without a good reason. Whatever it was, it must be important.

"Where?" he asked.

"It's not a good idea for us to be seen together at your office. How about that awful café we met last time?" Ira suggested.

"OK. But it'll take me about twenty minutes to get there, that alright with you?"

"Yes. See you soon."

The call ended and Daniel quickly turned to Charlie.

"Come on," he said. "We're meeting Ira Goldstein. Let's hope he's got some good news."

★

It had gone past eleven o' clock by the time Daniel and Charlie arrived outside the café. The sign on the glass door said 'closed' but the light was still on and inside they could see Ira sitting at a table toward the back. There was a cup of coffee in front of him and he looked tired, slumped down in the chair with his arms folded on the table, staring at the cup. Daniel pushed the door open and they went in. Apart from them, the café was empty and silent. As Daniel and Charlie approached the table, Ira looked up.

"The al Assad brothers are dead," he announced solemnly.

Daniel felt a sudden weight removed from his shoulders. He didn't doubt Ira's information was one hundred per cent correct.

"How?" he asked, pulling out a chair and sitting at the table.

Charlie sat down opposite whilst Ira took a sip of his coffee before continuing.

"Tomorrow you will read in the papers that earlier tonight there was a massive explosion at a house in Finsbury Park. The building was completely destroyed and all the people in it killed. I expect the papers will call it a tragic accident and demand some sort of public inquiry. Your people will be able to sort out the details, of course, but once it has been set up and sifted through all the evidence, I'm expecting it to conclude there must have been a gas leak in the kitchen. It will be the only possible explanation that fits all the known facts."

"Tell me about the people inside."

"There are three bodies," Ira began, "and, before you ask, I can assure you the autopsies will reveal nothing suspicious about the way they died. The owner of the house was a local Imam, Ibrahim Khan, and with him were two young men. The inquests will not be able to identify them and eventually the authorities will conclude they must have been illegal immigrants visiting at the time. You and I, of course, know those young men are Habab and Shiraz al Assad but I don't think either of us will want that information getting out."

"And the Imam?" Daniel asked. "Who was he?"

"He was the one who sent that message to Yusuf about the peacock being dead, wasn't he?" Charlie asked, though he knew he was right. The realisation had come as the last piece of the puzzle had slid into place.

"Yes," said Ira. "He has been radicalising young men for some time. I'm sorry, perhaps I could have been more upfront when I mentioned it before but you guessed right then: we knew exactly who he was. We've kept him under close observation ever since we learned the Al Assad brothers and Yusuf al Shamar were back in London. His house has also been bugged for the last three days. I thought, no, I was hoping Yusuf and the others might try and contact him or even go there together. I was half right. The brothers turned up tonight and we dealt with them."

Daniel and Charlie were silent; each of them absorbing the news. Daniel didn't blame Ira for not telling them about the Imam before; he understood why and thought if he were in Ira's shoes, he would probably have done the same.

"Was it really necessary to kill them?" Charlie asked at last.

"It was the most expedient thing to do in the circumstances," Ira replied simply. "They were terrorists and now there are no loose ends, no trials or public inquiries to prolong the affair, no publicity, nothing to embarrass your government. I'm sure Daniel appreciates the way things have turned out."

Charlie looked at his friend. He now knew this sort of thing happened in that world but it still made him angry. He had been a policeman too long to appreciate there could be other forms of justice.

"And the virus?" asked Daniel.

"What about it?" said Ira sitting back in his chair.

"Yusuf didn't have it, nor the woman. The brothers must have taken it with them when they left Farquharson's house."

"Then it must have perished in the blast," Ira said with another of his shrugs. "Vaporised completely I expect. Not a trace left behind. I'm sure your superiors will be very relieved to hear it when you tell them."

Daniel didn't believe for a moment that the virus had been destroyed but he knew Ira was right. It was exactly what the Prime Minister would want to hear. With no evidence that the virus had survived and the terrorists involved now dead, this operation would be closed down and the politicians could breathe again. It would be back to business as normal.

"What are you going to do with it?" he asked.

Ira smiled enigmatically and bent forward, folding his arms on the table. He liked playing these sort of games and they were always more enjoyable when he knew he already held the winning hand.

"Just supposing I had been able to get my hands on the virus," he said carefully, looking straight into Daniel's eyes, "if that were the case, I would make sure it was never used. I've already told you that has been my objective from the start."

Daniel returned the innocent stare.

"You do realise, don't you," he said, "this programme isn't going to stop just because of what's happened? It's still going to carry on."

"I hope not," said Ira, leaning back again. "Anyway, Pemberton is dead. Without his notes and samples, it will take a long time, perhaps many years before you're in the same position again."

"But it will happen. If not us then someone else will do it."

"Possibly, and if so I'll just have to be there to stop them."

"You can't be everywhere and Israel is acting alone," said Daniel.

Ira paused and smiled. He looked tired but not like a man who had been defeated. He spread his hands on the table and gave another slight shrug before speaking.

"Perhaps we stand alone for the present but, and you understand I say this without being the least bit judgemental, it's possible your government just might have learned something from what's happened. Now they have been given an opportunity to think again, let us hope they will take it. Sometime in the future, when they have been able to reflect on recent events, perhaps your government will decide they were wrong to pursue this sort of research. If that happens, they also might want to convince others that such experiments are too dangerous to be allowed. If so, they will discover they already have a friend. It would be a beginning and who can tell where it might lead? I believe it's possible something good can still come from this."

Daniel smiled ruefully. He wished it were true.

Chapter Nine

It was past one o' clock in the morning when Daniel and Charlie finally got into his car to drive back to the flat. After leaving Ira, they had returned to Daniel's office where they had worked together on compiling an immediate report for the Prime Minister. More detailed information would no doubt be required later but Daniel had given the essential facts and now the operation would be closed down. As far as the government was concerned, the emergency was over and there would be no more COBRA meetings. Daniel was not just tired, he felt exhausted and thought he could sleep for days once his head hit the pillow of his comfortable bed but that would have to wait. The cover-up was even now underway: the newspapers had been given the story of how an armed robber had been cornered outside Waterloo Station in a shoot-out and regrettably taken his own life along with that of an innocent passenger as police tried to apprehend him. At that very moment, Major Harding was probably already briefing reporters. Sergeant Needham would no doubt be hailed as the hero of the hour but he would have to remain anonymous for reasons of security. In fact, there were going to be lots of unanswered questions, much to the frustration of the press. But the public would understand; they always did nowadays when security was mentioned. Only a few people were ever going to know the real story.

"So that's it then," Charlie said, clicking the seat-belt into place. "It's all over."

"Effectively," Daniel replied.

He started the engine and thought of what remained to be done. Martin Greaves was already on his way to London in a police car and Daniel would have to see him later that morning. The scientist knew his wife had been killed but still didn't know the real circumstances. Daniel knew he would have to tell him in person. That was going to be a difficult interview. He didn't know what would happen to Kylie and, at that moment, cared even less. She would probably be freed in return for her silence but that decision was thankfully not his to make. All the loose ends, as Ira had called them, were being tidied up. No one was going to know the truth: how close London had come to being the centre of a devastating attack.

"Just as a matter of interest," Charlie asked, "why didn't you put in the report that Ira still has the virus?"

"No point," Daniel replied, keeping his eyes on the road ahead. "He's denied it and we've got no proof. Anyway, there's nothing we can do about it. Let's just be glad it's all over."

"I suppose so," Charlie grunted. But he didn't share Daniel's satisfaction at the way things had turned out. As far as he was concerned, not everything had been resolved in the way he would have liked. There were still known villains out there and he had a natural distaste for cover-ups.

Daniel sensed Charlie was unhappy but wrongly attributed it to the fact they hadn't managed to retrieve the virus.

"Perhaps Ira is right," he said in an attempt to lighten the mood. "If the government think Pemberton's work has gone forever, perhaps they will take the chance to think again."

Charlie was silent for a moment.

"You don't really believe that, do you?" he said at last.

Daniel didn't reply at once. He was tired and didn't want an argument but Charlie was his friend and deserved a truthful answer.

"No," he sighed eventually.

"Then why do you do it?" Charlie asked. "I mean, what's it all been for unless you actually believe some good is going to come out of it? At least when I was in the police we went after the criminals, all of them, and it didn't matter who they were. We wanted to do the right thing. I know it's an old-fashioned idea in your world but we believed that justice should not only be done but seen to be done. Much of the last few days has been spent in making a series of dirty deals behind closed doors and no one is allowed to know what really happened. You know, the more I think about it, the more I think your whole operation stinks to high heaven."

"We saved London," Daniel said quietly, "and ..."

"And let Pemberton's killer go free," Charlie interrupted quickly, "and agreed to let Warbeck continue his spying and Goldstein to get hold of the virus and keep it. You've helped to cover up the murder of at least four people and those are just the things I know about. There's probably a lot of other stuff I can't even guess at."

Charlie paused. Now he had been able to give vent to his feelings, the anger and frustration that had been building up over the last few days had abruptly burnt itself out and he felt calmer, if slightly embarrassed at showing his bitterness at the way things had been resolved.

"You don't think it was worth it considering what might have happened?" Daniel asked in the same quiet voice as before.

"Yes, yes I suppose it is when you put it like that," Charlie admitted grudgingly. "That's not what I mean. I'm sorry, it's just that I think I know the sort of man you are. You're basically good and honest. You don't just believe in your country, you believe in doing the right thing and I simply don't understand how you can go along with all this and still manage to get up the next day and start doing it all over again."

A silence filled the car as Daniel finally understood the real reasons behind his friend's resentment and disappointment.

"It's difficult to explain," he said after a while. "I suppose you could say it comes down to whether you believe the end justifies the means."

"You don't believe that."

"I don't want to, perhaps, but you've got to be realistic. There are times when you can't afford a moral agenda. Like when my family is involved, for instance."

Daniel looked sideways at Charlie to make sure he had understood before continuing.

"Some things are just too important, too big for us to think about counting the cost in the way you would like. You see, just like you, I want to see justice done and, in my own way, I'm trying to achieve it. But at the moment the world is still a dirty place and it's getting worse. If that means I sometimes have to get my own hands a little dirty then so be it. I wish it wasn't like that, of course I do, but I'm not going to let some set of idealistic scruples get in the way of doing what I know is the best thing".

He looked across at his friend again.

"This is not a perfect world, Charlie. You have to fight to make it the best one you can and sometimes that means you have to compromise. In the end, it comes down to what you feel is most important. This isn't about ideals and morality; if I'm honest, perhaps more than anything else it's about something more personal. You see, I'm part of the world too, a small part admittedly, and I'm only human. I suppose I'm always hoping I can achieve a better future for myself and those I love. I want the world to become a better place for them. That's why I'm prepared to compromise to keep that hope alive. It may be difficult at times but I'm not going to give up just because things don't always work out the way I want them to."

Daniel paused. He realised he had spoken more forcefully than he had meant and felt a little self-conscious. He had not intended to open himself up like that. It was probably because he was so tired and his natural defences were down. He gave an embarrassed laugh.

"Sorry," he said. "I expect that must have sounded a bit much. I didn't mean to preach."

"Not at all," said Charlie. He had been impressed by the passion of Daniel's conviction. "You meant it, every word, and it does help me to understand. Really. In fact, I think part of me agrees with you. It's just that it still seems so ..."

He left the sentence unfinished as he tried to think of the right word.

"Unjust?" prompted Daniel.

"Yes, I suppose that's what I mean."

"It is," said Daniel, "but I'm afraid life is full of compromises. Either you accept that or you walk alone in your virtuous wilderness."

They had reached the parking space outside his apartment and Daniel neatly reversed into it. As he got out of the car, he remembered there was some food in the flat and decided to have a quick bite before stretching out on his bed. He still had the interview with Martin Greaves to go through when he got up and later that day he would have to see the Prime Minister for a full debriefing. He knew he needed a few hours' sleep before he could face either of them. He had arranged for Emma to be taken to his flat from Waterloo Station and was careful to be quiet as he opened the front door. She had said she would wait up for him to get back but, following his meeting with Ira, everything had taken longer than he thought and he was fully expecting her to be asleep. He didn't want to disturb her and put a finger to his lips to let Charlie know not to make any noise.

There were no lights on in the apartment when they went in but the curtains were still open in the lounge and there was just enough glow from the street-lamps outside to show them it was empty. Emma must have gone into one of the bedrooms. Daniel switched on the light and Charlie sat down in one of the chairs. He was looking forward to getting into his bed and sleeping late into the morning. Daniel went down the hall to check which bedroom Emma was using but quickly returned looking confused.

"She's not here," he said.

Charlie looked up in surprise.

"Her suitcase has gone as well," Daniel said.

He walked over to the desk and, lying in a clear space on the red leather top, he saw a folded sheet of paper with his name on the front. He picked it up quickly and began to read what Emma had written. Charlie stayed sitting in the chair. Daniel's face remained expressionless as he read but Charlie could guess the contents of the note.

"Where is she?" he asked as Daniel came to the end and folded the sheet of paper again, running his fingers along the crease.

Daniel said nothing but walked over and passed the letter to Charlie who unfolded it and began to read.

Dearest Daniel,

I've gone back to Brighton. I'm sorry, but I'm sure it's for the best. We may have only known each other a short time but already I think you are the most caring and wonderful man I've met. I know you were wanting something more and I thought I wanted that too, but it's not going to work. I realised that tonight outside the station when I saw what your life is really like. I think part of me will always be in love with you but I can't ask you to change and I don't think I can share the sort of world you live in. It's better for me to leave now before either of us gets hurt. I am going back to the Institute. I hope you can find it in your heart to understand. I will always wonder what might have happened if only things could have been different.

Love, Emma

"I'm sorry," Charlie said quietly as he finished reading and handed the note back.

Daniel said nothing. He glanced once more at the sheet of paper before folding it again and carefully replacing it on the desk. Charlie was unsure what else to say. He was thinking of what Daniel had told him in the car about hope and fighting for those you love to get what you want in the world. But he hadn't said anything about what you do when they wanted something different. Then he saw the expression on Daniel's face change.

"What are you going to do?" he asked.

"I'm going to suggest we could reach a compromise," said Daniel. And grinned.

Author Biography

Born in Bristol, Barry was educated at the Cathedral School and then read English at St Peter's College, Oxford. After graduating, he worked in the Civil Service before teaching at a Bristol Secondary School. Thinking he would like a change of career, he later qualified in Law at the University of West of England, but decided to remain in education. He expanded his teaching to include Law as well as English and Drama.

Barry is a keen amateur artist and has illustrated a number of texts for others as well as providing paintings for websites. He has also worked on set design for local drama groups and written several plays, including one musical.

A few years ago he took early retirement to concentrate on writing. Following a trilogy of books for young adults, he started to write action thrillers and 'Bad Blood' is the third story featuring DCI Charlie Watts and the MI6 agent, Daniel Rankin.

Barry still lives in Bristol where he enjoys spending time with friends, visiting the theatre, gardening and water-colour painting.